'McDonagh skilfully weaves a web of intrigue. This
perfectly paced slice of rural noir is extremely addictive'
Business Post

'This novel is smart, compelling, and
nothing if not topical and timely'
Sunday Independent

'I flew through it. A page turner with a scenario
at its core which feels terrifyingly possible'
Andrea Carter

'A compelling page-turner with well-drawn characters who
have secrets to keep. It will keep you guessing till the end'
Sheila O'Flanagan

'Cleverly plotted and unpredictable with
a fantastic cast of characters'
Rachael English

'A rural *Succession* ... a superbly crafted mystery,
an original tale highlighting the volatility of family
relationships and the invisible ties that hold them together'
Swirl and Thread

'Pacy and highly enjoyable. Think
Glenroe with a very sharp edge'
Woman's Way

Michelle McDonagh is an Irish journalist with over twenty-five years' experience, including twelve years as a staff reporter at the *Connacht Tribune* in her native city, Galway. She now works freelance, writing features and health pieces for various publications, including *The Irish Times*.

She is married with three children and lives in Cork. *There's Something I Have to Tell You* is her first novel.

There's Something I Have to Tell You

MICHELLE MCDONAGH

HACHETTE
BOOKS
IRELAND

First published in Ireland in 2023 by
HACHETTE BOOKS IRELAND
First published in paperback in 2024

1

Cataloguing in Publication Data is available from the British Library.

Paperback ISBN 978 1 39971 643 7
Ebook ISBN 978 1 39971 642 0
Audiobook ISBN 978 1 39972 053 3

Typeset in Cambria by Bookends Publishing Services, Dublin
Printed and bound in Great Britain by Clays Ltd, Elcograf, S.p.A.

Hachette Books Ireland policy is to use papers that are natural,
renewable and recyclable products and made from wood
grown in sustainable forests. The logging and manufacturing
processes are expected to conform to the environmental
regulations of the country of origin.

Hachette Books Ireland
8 Castlecourt Centre
Castleknock
Dublin 15, Ireland

A division of Hachette UK Ltd
Carmelite House, 50 Victoria Embankment, EC4Y 0DZ

www.hachettebooksireland.ie

To my lovely mother, Lucy –
a Mammy through and through

Prologue

Tuesday, 9 January 2018 – Glenbeg, County Galway

It was the dog who raised the alarm first. Or tried to at least. His frenzied yelping and whimpering were ignored for hours, but afterwards, people would recall that they had registered the sound somewhere in the background of their minds. Too preoccupied with their own business to pay heed to the unremarkable circumstance of a dog yapping in a farmyard, it wasn't until early afternoon that anybody began to wonder where Jimmy had got to.

To Ursula's displeasure, her husband still insisted on eating his dinner in the middle of the day – unusually, he had not given in to her on this one. Sometimes, he joined the lads who came to The Creamery at Glenbeg Farm Park every day for their midday meal: a rag-tag gaggle of ripely scented widowed and bachelor farmers who set the world to rights over their daily repast before heading back out to the land. More and more lately, though, Jimmy had taken to eating alone at the kitchen table in the farmhouse.

When there was no sign of him by one o'clock, Kate sent one of the girls from the kitchen over to the house with a cling-filmed plate bearing four slender slices of lean beef, two creamy hillocks of mash and a small mound of carrots and peas, a steaming ramekin of onion gravy on the side and a strong pot of tea to wash the lot down.

It was Kate who had figured out that her father-in-law had forgotten how to make tea when she picked up the pot one day and realised it was stone cold. He had remembered to put in the tea-leaves but forgotten to boil the water. This once simple task now involved a step too many for his withering brain to grasp. The same man could still drive from Glenbeg to the centre of Dublin city without getting lost, or calve a cow with his eyes closed, but the boiling-water step of the tea-making process seemed to have dropped right out of his head.

The girl went straight in through the back door, singing out 'Special delivery', lest, God forbid, she disturb her boss's husband wandering around starkers. Not that it had ever happened – yet, anyway – but she had heard that people with the same thing Jimmy had wrong with him were taken to stripping off whenever the mood came over them, so she wasn't taking any chances.

There was no naked Jimmy, though – no sign of any Jimmy at all, in fact, which was unusual given that he was a man who adhered to a strict daily routine. Up at six, no matter if his head hadn't hit the pillow until four with the calving. Breakfast at half seven, dinner at half twelve, a mug of tea and a couple of buttered Rich Tea biscuits around half three. And his tea to run concurrent with the six o'clock news.

It wasn't until around two-ish that Rob, hopeful of a cuppa on his return from his appointment in town, popped into the farmhouse to find the uneaten beef dinner congealing on the counter and realised his father was on the missing list.

There was no sign of his mother around either, but there was nothing strange in that. He assumed she was in her office: Mission Control. He had barely seen her since the previous Wednesday night, hadn't wanted to see her. He didn't feel good about it, the harsh words spoken, but he wouldn't take a single one back. He had never been comfortable with confrontation but, if anything, his failing had been in not speaking up sooner.

There was no point in asking Christina if she knew where their father was. She was going through one of her bad patches and was in her room with her curtains drawn.

The breakfast dishes were still lying on the draining board. A mug proclaiming Best Grandad, a Belleek china cup with a pretty floral design. One cereal bowl. Two plates. Two knives and a clutch of teaspoons.

He didn't notice his mother's precious Mulberry handbag sitting on the table, or her mobile phone beside it.

Having confirmed that his father wasn't in the house, Rob started to search outside. His mother's new-model Range Rover Velar was parked out the front alongside his sister's Mini Cooper. His father's battered Land Rover was in its usual spot in the yard. It was as he headed towards the milking parlour that Rob finally connected the near-distant sound – that his brain had dismissed as being of no importance – with its source.

Samson. His master's scruffy shadow. Rob took off in the direction of the barking, his Fitbit recording a spike in his heart rate as he realised where he was being led.

1

Kate

Kate ignored her phone the first time it rang. The café had been mental for lunch today, a blessing in disguise, as it kept her distracted. They were short-staffed as usual in The Creamery and she was helping to clear tables.

When her phone rang again straight away, she took a deep breath and answered it. 'Hi, love—'

'Kate … it's my father! I think he's in the pit the dog was barking his phone is on the side with his cap Jesus Christ his dinner's sitting on the counter … I can't find him anywhere!'

'Slow down, Rob, I can't understand you.' Her heart was beating like a bodhrán. She could feel the heat rising up her neck, flushing her face as if somebody had just turned her thermostat up full blast.

'GET MOTHER, YOU NEED TO GET MOTHER!'

'OK, just calm down a minute, love. Where are—?'

'Jesus Christ, Kate, will you just get Mother? Please, just get her!'

She could hear the dog whimpering in the background, as if he was in pain. Then she realised that it wasn't the dog at all, it was her husband. Her gut clenched like a fist ready to punch. Rob was the solid, unflappable one in their relationship, the low-strung antidote to her chronic catastrophising. He wasn't given to histrionics.

'OK, love, I'm going to get her now. Where are you exactly?'

'Oh God, oh God, oh Jesus! I can't find him anywhere, the dog was barking like a lunatic outside the shed, the agitator was on and the door was closed—'

'The agitator? What's the agitator doing on?' Although a born-and-bred city girl herself, Kate had been living on the farm, just outside the east Galway market town of Glenbeg, long enough to know that slurry spreading was banned at this time of year. It was an EU directive. Something to do with protecting drinking water.

I don't know what the hell he was at but I can't find him anywhere ...' Rob's voice quavered, pitched too high. 'The slats have been lifted inside ... I think he might be in there, Kate ...'

'You're not in the shed now, are you?'

Kate was all too aware of the dangers of the slurry pit, particularly in the first half an hour after mixing started, when the gases were at their most lethal. Jimmy was a stickler about it since his grandkids had come along; it had been very different in his own children's day. Every now and then, there was

6

another news story about another tragic slurry-pit accident. And every time Kate had the same thought: *What an awful way to go.* Her own kids were banned from going anywhere near the sheds that housed the farm's two pits.

When Rob had brought her on a tour of the eighty-hectare Kennedy farm during her first visit, about three months into their relationship, she had been astounded at the size of the underground tanks. There were two slatted sheds, one for the dairy herd closer to the farmhouse and one further back for the beef cattle. The tanks – each about twelve feet wide – ran underground the full length of the galvanised cattle sheds either side of a central feeding passage. That day had been the first and, sadly, one of only a handful of times she had met Rob's older brother, Mark, who had chuckled when she squidged her nose at the ripe stench of decomposing cow shit and explained that the cows 'piss and crap where they stand' down through the slats in the floor into the pit below. Poor Mark. As if this family hadn't been through enough already.

'No, I'm outside,' Rob said. 'I turned the agitator off. And I called 999. There's an ambulance on the way, but if he's in there ...'

He didn't need to spell it out. If her father-in-law was in that tank, it was far too late for an ambulance.

She couldn't believe it was happening.

Kate took the stairs to Ursula's office on the first floor of the main farm-park building two at a time and barged in without

Michelle McDonagh

knocking, something she would never normally have done. Her mother-in-law was not at her desk. Her computer screen was black and there was no sign of her bag or coat.

She tried calling Ursula's number from her own phone as she ran back through the café, asking as she went if anybody had seen her around. There was no answer from her phone and nobody could recall seeing her that day at all. She hadn't appeared in the restaurant for lunch earlier, but there was nothing too unusual in that. People would assume that Ursula was on another one of her health kicks, had knocked back a wheatgrass shot or a green protein power smoothie at her desk. The elegant blonde, who looked at least a decade younger than her sixty-four years, certainly didn't fit the stereotype of the typical farmer's wife; she did own a pair of wellies, but they were spotless Hunters that rarely ever set foot in the farmyard.

Kate stopped briefly to let Nellie, her right-hand woman in the café, who was on the till, know what was going on.

'Have you seen Ursula around, Nellie?'

'No, love, not today. Is everything all right?'

'Rob just rang me in an awful state. He can't find Jimmy anywhere but somebody's been mixing slurry down the back shed and he thinks he might have fallen in ...'

'Lord God Almighty. I'll ring Brendan straight away and get him over. Jimmy told him not to come in today, he said he'd manage away without him.' Nellie had been part of the Kennedy family even longer than Kate, since Rob and his siblings were children. Her husband, Brendan, worked with Jimmy and Rob as a part-time farmhand. She wiped her skinny hands on her apron now and called one of the girls to take over from her.

'I'll run out and check the farmers' market,' Nellie said,

8

heading in the direction of the car park where local food producers plied their wares every Tuesday and Saturday. Ursula was a big fan of the spinach hummus and stuffed olives from the Popeye and Olive stall.

'Thanks, Nellie. Tell her to ring Rob straight away if you find her,' Kate said.

Then she hared over to the farmhouse where her in-laws lived, making the two-minute walk in less than one.

As she stepped into Ursula's kitchen she heard her mother-in-law's phone ringing. The distinctive old-style telephone *brinng brinng*. The gold iPhone, a recent upgrade, vibrated frantically on the sleek walnut table, beside Ursula's mushroom leather handbag.

Kate's hands shook as she clumsily swiped the screen.

'Mother ... it's Daddy ...'

'Rob, love,' she cut in quickly. 'It's me. Her phone was on the kitchen table. I can't find her anywhere.'

2

Kate

It felt as if she had fallen asleep watching the six o'clock news and woken up on the wrong side of the screen. Or in a Netflix true-crime documentary. *CRIME SCENE NO ENTRY*, the blue and white garda tape repeated over and over along the cordon that encircled the cattle shed. The thin plastic tape as effective as a reinforced steel barrier in keeping out all but those working the scene.

A young garda, fresh from the oven at Templemore and tightly packed into a fluorescent yellow jacket, manned the entrance to the cordon, painstakingly entering the particulars of everybody who went in and out of the shed in his regulation beige notebook. The door at the front of the shed was wide open now, but Rob told her it had been closed down when he had got there earlier, the poor dog almost collapsing in relief when he saw him. Thank God, thought Kate, the children had been collected from school as usual by their childminder, Jenny, and brought to her house, so they wouldn't be arriving home to this spectacle.

A desultory dusk had fallen and it was spitting down drizzle, the stealthy kind that soaks through clothes without even seeming that wet. The yard was lit up by powerful floodlights which beamed onto a large metal poster screwed to the side of the galvanised shed, highlighting a black and white skull and crossbones. *Always obey safe agitation guidelines*, the sign cautioned. *ONE LUNGFUL OF SLURRY CAN KILL.*

The place was crawling with emergency personnel, scurrying in and out between their vehicles and the large shed, immersed in their various roles. A red and yellow fire engine was parked parallel to the open door, blocking sight of what was happening inside. A plump hose snaked its way from the Scania truck inside the building, into which fire fighters in fluorescent gear, wearing breathing apparatus, had disappeared.

There were three squad cars parked in the yard, as well as an unmarked garda car and a white crime scene investigation unit van a few feet away from where Kate and Rob stood just outside the cordon under a striped golf umbrella, with Jimmy's brother Kieran, his brother-in-law Jarlath and Nellie's husband, Brendan. There was also a neon yellow HSE ambulance, a familiar sight and sound on the road heading for Our Lady's Hospital on the edge of town, lights flashing, sirens wailing and yelping. Kate automatically blessed herself every time she passed one and prayed there was nobody belonging to anyone she knew in the back of it.

She kept her mother's old brown scapulars in her glove box, tangled up amid the accumulated crap that had been stuffed in there. It wasn't as if the two small pieces of woven cloth joined by string, an outward sign of her mother's devotion to Our Lady, had done the woman much good, but the little tattered pile somehow made Kate feel safer on the road.

She felt an inappropriate urge to burst out laughing bubble up inside her now as they stood watching the crime scene investigators gearing up. The same urge that came over her at funerals. As the team pulled their prospecting paraphernalia from the vehicle, Kate was reminded of Mr Fox's van from *Peppa Pig*. Lily had lived and breathed that bloody pink pig for about five years. There was nothing that Freddy Fox's dad didn't have in the back of his little blue van: grandfather clocks, bicycle bells, a live chicken, even a cement mixer. She half expected him to pull out a dildo some day or a box of gimp suits. The garda CSIU van was a bit the same, only it was boiler suits and masks and booties and goggles and tape measures and rulers and swabs and cameras and God only knew what else.

Rob stood silently beside her, watching the investigators – two men and one woman – zip their white boiler suits up the middle. They looked like giant toddlers zipped into flimsy plastic sleep suits. Two suits each, double bagged. They pulled thick industrial booties over their wellies, securing them with tape around their knees. Hoods up, goggles on, masks fastened around their heads. Six pairs of blue latex gloves snapped on to three pairs of hands. All that was visible when they were finished were three pairs of eyes topped with foreheads. As if there had been an Ebola outbreak on the farm.

Rob had finally stopped clutching at straws as to his mother's possible whereabouts. The entire Glenbeg Farm Park property and grounds and the adjacent working farm had been searched to no avail. She wasn't in her own house, nor, unsurprisingly, was she in Kate and Rob's cottage at the far side of the yard. There was no sign of her in the main building that housed the café and offices, or the new barn conversion at the edge of the property. At Rob's insistence, Kate went through the farce of ringing Halo, the hair salon on Main Street where Ursula went for the twice-weekly blow-dries that kept her blonde bob so sleek, even though it was inconceivable that she would have left her handbag, phone and jeep at home.

They had given the gardaí the numbers of Ursula's friends in case somebody had collected her and maybe taken her off somewhere, out of the norm. Nobody had seen or heard from her all day. Then Rob had another brainwave: maybe she had a doctor's appointment. His mother was a private woman; she might have kept this to herself. A call to the surgery put paid to that notion.

'It just doesn't make any sense, none of this makes any sense.' Rob kept saying the same thing over and over, trying in vain to knit some sense from the ball of knotted yarn in his brain. His lovely brown eyes were filled with confusion.

'He must have got mixed up, love. Maybe he was worse than we thought – he could have been hiding it from us,' Kate said.

'No matter how confused he was, he would never have gone agitating at this time of year. And to leave it wide open like that? I can't get my head around any of this.'

'I know, love, I know. Maybe he had another mini-stroke without anybody knowing and that affected his thinking.'

When Ursula had finally managed to drag Jimmy in for tests eight months ago because of his memory issues, a scan of his brain showed that he had suffered a mini-stroke at some point in the previous year. A couple of weeks later, he had received the devastating blow of a diagnosis of vascular dementia.

'But what about Mother? Why the hell would she come down here? There's no way she'd have gone near that tank while the agitating was going on, not a snowball's chance in hell. Unless Daddy got into trouble and she heard him calling ...'

There was nothing Kate could say. Guilt curdled into bile in her stomach and rose up her throat. She swallowed it back down, wincing at the bitter taste. The sour, vomity stench of the slurry that hung in the air wasn't helping either.

She laid her head against her husband's chest, wrapped her arms around his broad shoulders and held him tight to her, watching the surreal scene unfold before them. Despite being above average height for an Irish woman, she always felt petite beside her tall, broad-backed husband.

The rain was coming down heavier now, tap-tapping off the roof of the galvanised shed and dripping off the edge of the umbrella, filling the air with its earthy scent, and the sky had darkened to a dirty grey. A plaintive chorus of mooing came from the shed where the dairy herd were housed for the winter. As if they sensed the tension in the air.

A memory played in Kate's mind. Of Jimmy answering one of Lily's endless random questions in that gentle, patient way of his. Too gentle and too patient, it had been his downfall.

'How can you tell if one of your cows is sad, Grandad?'

'Oh, they're well able to let you know if they're not happy, Lily peteen. They start mooing like mad, a high-pitched kind of a sound, and they might tuck their tail between their legs. They could give you a kick or a butt too if they're really vexed with you.'

Kate couldn't fathom that she was never going to see her father-in-law again. She swallowed the thought back down. She couldn't allow herself to go there, not now. She had to stay strong. For Rob and the kids. And Christina, who was fragile at the best of times.

A uniformed garda with rosacea-stained cheeks and a head of unnaturally black hair ducked under the plastic cordon and made his way over to them. Des Tuohy, a detective sergeant from Glenbeg station, who was some class of a cousin of Rob's a few times removed.

Kate felt her husband tense beside her.

'Look, lads, given the situation inside,' the guard nodded back towards the shed, 'and the fact there's still no sign of either of them, we have to assume there's a strong possibility they could be in the tank. So we need to get it drained asap. I've been onto Josie Clarke and he's on the way now with the tanker.'

Josie Clarke was a local contractor the Kennedys regularly hired to pump slurry from the pits.

'Jesus, Des, you can't just leave them in the tank. Can you not send somebody down to check …?'

The sergeant shook his head.

'I'm sorry, Rob. I know this is desperately upsetting for you and the family but we can't go near that tank ourselves. It's a health and safety issue. The slurry will have to be pumped out first. If we do find either, or both, of your parents in there, the lads from the fire brigade will have to get them out.'

'What's the story with the cordon, Snitcheen, and all the lads in the white suits?' Jimmy's brother Kieran asked, nodding his head towards the crime-scene tape. Des Tuohy had never managed to shake off the nickname he had earned in school due to his proclivity for tattling on his fellow pupils.

'It's standard procedure in this type of situation,' the sergeant assured him before turning to Rob. 'I was wondering do you have CCTV here? I'm assuming you probably do with all the break-ins around the place lately.'

'Jesus, the CCTV. I never even thought about that with everything … We have, of course. I only put a new system in last summer after Johnny Buckley's place was done. I have the app here on my phone. My father's always giving out about it, says it's far too complicated, but it's actually very simple. Hang on there a minute while I get it up.'

As Rob typed in his code to bring up the app, Kate just managed to stop herself from hurling the meagre contents of her stomach all over her boots.

3

Rob had barely said two words aloud since he logged into the FarmSecure app and discovered that the farm's CCTV had been turned off. Around midnight last night. The last footage was of his father leaving the farmhouse shortly before midnight and walking towards the main open-farm building, where he disappeared into an area not covered by the cameras, before the screen went blank.

Rob looked utterly confused. Kate knew him so well though, she could imagine clearly what he was thinking.

Where the hell was he going at that time of night?

Why was the CCTV turned off?

Who turned it off?

Why was he mixing at this time of year?

What the fuck is going on here?

She had sensed the mood in the yard change at that point. Had watched the expression on the sergeant's face change as Rob informed him that the CCTV wasn't going to be any help to them. That somebody, for some unknown reason, had turned it off. Which was strange, as Jimmy was a complete technophobe who left 'all that side of things' up to his son. Rob had downloaded the app onto his father's phone but Jimmy never used it, preferring to view the monitor on the wall inside the back door of the farmhouse to see the video footage being transmitted from the cameras located around the yard.

The sergeant walked back to one of the unmarked cars where he spoke urgently to one of his plain-clothed colleagues, who glanced over at the huddle of Kennedy family members standing outside the cordon. He nodded his head and lifted his radio handset to his mouth. Less than fifteen minutes later, another unmarked car pulled into the yard, and a big bald man unfolded himself from the front passenger seat.

'That's the super,' Kieran said. 'Mick Power. They've called in the big guns now.'

The large man conferred briefly with his subordinates before approaching Rob and Kate and introducing himself.

'We're going to need to take witness statements from you both,' he told them, 'as well as your sister, who I believe lives in the house with your parents.'

'We've already told Des and the lads everything we know, superintendent,' Rob explained.

'I'm aware of that, Robert, but we'll still need to take statements. It's—'

'Don't tell me: standard procedure. My parents are probably

lying inside in that tank while you're out here fluthering around with bloody statements!'

'I can assure you, Robert, that if we thought for a second there was a chance there was anybody alive in that tank, we'd have a search and rescue operation underway, but that's not the situation here. As you're well aware yourself, we're dealing with a hazardous scene. There's no way we can send anybody down into that pit until the slurry has been pumped out of it.'

Kate caught Rob's hand, squeezed it. Tried to communicate some bit of comfort to him. Her husband rarely raised his voice in anger. To raise it to a senior garda was a sign of the intensity of his distress.

The super made all the right sounds. He understood how upset they must be, didn't want to add to their trauma. But they would have to give those witness statements.

The superintendent left after less than an hour – back to the heated comfort of his office, probably, or maybe home for his tea. Before he went, he introduced them to the man he was leaving in charge: Detective Inspector Noel McGuire. Built like a pencil, apart from the prominent bridge on his nose, the detective inspector sported a pair of bushy eyebrows a schnauzer would have been proud of. A man of few words, after a cursory hello and formal handshake, the detective got straight to work, taking Rob to one side and making him go through everything he had already told both the first garda on the scene and Snitcheen Tuohy.

Kate could feel the frustration vibrating off her husband when he returned.

'How many more times are they going to make me repeat myself, for Christ's sake? It's like being in feckin' A&E, being asked the same questions over and over by loads of different people.'

'I know, love, it's very frustrating,' she agreed.

Rob made a sudden grab for her arm. 'Where's the dog?'

'He's in the house, asleep in front of the range. He's worn out, poor thing.'

'Jesus, Mother will have a conniption—' He stopped short.

Samson slept in a kennel outside the farmhouse where Ursula and Jimmy lived. It had been a source of immense frustration to Ursula that she was the only one who called the house by its proper name, Hazeldene, while everybody else insisted on referring to it as 'the farmhouse', after she had knocked the original house where her husband's grandparents had lived and had a replica of a regal Georgian mansion erected in its place when she first moved to Glenbeg as a new bride. The cramped cottage across the yard, where Jimmy had been reared and where Kate and Rob now lived with the kids, was a hole in comparison.

Ursula didn't do indoor pets, especially scruffy aul' collies with a dash of Jack Russell and God only knew what else thrown in for luck. Apart from her beloved Cleo, of course – a stunning Siamese who stared disdainfully at the humans she was forced to share her living space with. Grey of body, her limbs and face looked as if they had been dipped in black paint, two stunning blue buttons stitched in for eyes. Her beauty fur deep; Kate couldn't stand that cat. Still, if it wasn't for her ...

'He was in an awful state earlier, poor aul' Sam. He must have been barking for hours,' Rob said, breaking into her thoughts.

It was so typical of Rob, worrying about the dog when it was looking increasingly likely that he was after losing not just one but both of his parents.

Jenny had popped into the cottage to collect the overnight bag that Kate had packed for the kids: pyjamas, a change of clothes, the new Beanie Boo Santa had brought Lily, a book each for bedtime and their iPads. Oblivious to the fate of their grandparents and the drama unfolding in the farmyard, Lily and Luke had been delighted at this unexpected change to the mundane mid-week routine.

'I'll go in to see how Sammy's doing, get us both a cup of tea to heat us up a bit,' Kate said. 'I'll check on Christina again while I'm in there.'

They had been standing outside for hours and she was frozen to the marrow. A cloud of frizz had risen like mist from her thick blonde hair.

The French doors to the farmhouse kitchen stood wide open, despite the miserable evening, releasing most of the heat the four-oven Aga was busy pumping out. The pungent sweetness of burning turf drifted out to greet her. Inside, mucky wellie prints tracked across Ursula's precious Italian porcelain tiles. The dog was curled up on the rug in front of the range, out for the count. The cat, whose emerald velvet throne – chosen by Ursula and her interior designer to tie in with the colour theme of the kitchen – had been moved from its usual spot to make room for Samson, was shooting death stares at her sleeping usurper. She switched her vituperative gaze to Kate when she stepped into the room, tracking her movement across the kitchen.

Nellie was manning the teapot.

She took Kate's icy hands in hers and tried to rub some warmth into them.

'Kate, loveen, you're half-perished. There's hot tea in the pot, and I lit the range when I came over in case ye were in and out.' Nellie was just the kind of person you wanted around in a crisis. Practical, unflappable and innately maternal despite never having been blessed with children of her own.

'Will Rob not come in for a while to heat up a bit? He'll end up with pneumonia.'

'He won't, Nellie. Josie Clarke is on his way over with the tanker to drain the pit.'

'Lord help us and save us,' Nellie muttered, blessing herself discreetly while she poured tea into two of Ursula's Denby mugs. The spaghetti junction of skinny blue veins that traversed Nellie's thin, work-worn hands complemented the distinctively veined Statuario marble countertop that ran the length of the solid-wood cabinetry.

'I'd say you should fire a drop of somethin' stronger into that for himself.' Having taken his own advice, Brendan, Nellie's husband, sat nursing a steaming glass of whiskey at Ursula's hand-crafted kitchen island. The smooth curve of the walnut breakfast bar had buried itself deep in the doughy layers of visceral fat he wore around his abdomen like a lagging jacket. Here so was the source of the dirty footprints. Ursula would have had a fit if she caught him in his filthy work clothes plonked up on top of her good velvet bar stool. She had spent a small fortune on her latest renovation job only last year.

'Make sure and throw plenty of sugar in on top of it for the fright,' he prescribed.

'Thanks, Brendan, I think we might just manage ...' Nellie rolled her eyes heavenward, a position they were well accustomed to after over forty years of marriage to Brendan. 'Kate, I locked up above. The keys are on the counter there. The guards sent everybody away off home after taking their numbers.'

'Thanks, Nellie, I don't know what we'd do without you.'

Locking the main building of the farm park had been the last thing on Kate's mind in the middle of everything else that was going on. She'd be lost without Nellie and counted her blessings on a daily basis that she had stayed on working for the Kennedys after the kids had grown up. The older woman's hearty traditional home-style roast dinners were a big hit with their regular customers, and her baked goods a magnet for the sweet-toothed from miles around. But far more than that, her steady-as-a-rock presence was sometimes all that kept Kate from tipping over the edge that she teetered so precariously on every day.

'They asked us all when we last saw Jimmy and Ursula,' said Brendan. 'I told them I saw Jimmy last evening. I didn't come over today cos he said he didn't need me. And that's the feckin' worst of it cos I'd have talked sense into him—' He broke off.

The tears that dampened the old man's eyes were genuine, Kate knew. There had been few cross words between himself and Jimmy over the years. Few cross words between Jimmy and anybody, truth be told. Nausea roiled in her stomach as the realisation that she would never see her father-in-law alive again walloped her.

'Sit down, love, you're white as a sheet. Here, take a sip,' Nellie said, lifting the mug to her lips as if she was a child.

The queasiness ebbed after a few mouthfuls of the hot sugary tea.

'Thanks, Nellie, I'm fine again. I just want to see Christina before I go back out.'

'She's inside in the sitting room.'

Bookended by Jimmy's sister, Rita, on one side and her cousin Julie on the other, Christina sat on a blush velvet love seat, a slender volume of verse wedged in between two thick tomes. Her dainty face, ashen at the best of times, was the colour of chalk, a mop of dark waves accentuating her pallor, her big brown eyes wide and round as a skittish colt. Even in misery, Rob's sister was a beauty.

Christina reached out for Kate's hand, the bones of her own as fine and light as a baby bird's. A girl wearing a woman's skin. She smelled of Comfort and Lancôme's La Vie Est Belle. Floral and sweet.

'Have they found them?'

'There's no news yet, Chrissie.'

'Do they think …?'

'It's not looking good, no.'

Kate laid her other hand gently on her sister-in-law's head. Christina should have been born marked 'fragile, handle with care'. Like the delicate Dresden figurines Kate used to admire as a child in The Treasure Chest on Shop Street in Galway, their elaborately flounced crinoline skirts made from real lace dipped into liquid porcelain.

'Oh, dear sweet Jesus and all the saints in heaven. Has this family not suffered enough already?' Rita wailed. A star on the local amateur dramatic scene, Jimmy's sister sometimes had to be reminded she was off stage.

'I'll send Rob in to let ye know as soon as we hear anything,' Kate said. 'Just try not to worry.'

Try not to worry – what a stupid *bloody thing to say*, Kate chided herself as she left the room. *As if it was in any way possible not to worry under the circumstances.* She sometimes forgot that Christina was a grown-up, a thirty-three-year-old woman. That she was only three years younger than herself.

The kitchen was empty when she passed back through. She stopped to pull up her hood before heading out, a steaming mug of sweet tea in each hand, Rob's liberally laced with his father's Jameson.

Two people stood a few feet from the open French doors, smoking in the dark, oblivious to the rain and the volume of their voices.

Snippets of their conversation floated in.

'Every family ... crosses to bear, Brendan ... awful heavy load altogether ... never the same man again after ... pure cruel ...'

She recognised the voice of Francis Tierney, an elderly farmer who lived a couple of miles back the road, one of their lunchtime regulars. He must have heard the sirens and cut across the fields to see what all the commotion was about.

'Desperate altogether, Fransheen ... good man ... ne'er a bad word spoke ... years I worked for him ... couldn't say the same for ... still wouldn't have wished that on her ...'

Kate hovered inside the door, keen to return to Rob before his drink went cold, but not wanting the two men to know they had been overheard speaking ill of the woman before her body had even been recovered, never mind pronounced dead.

'Fast, though, Brendan ... known what hit them ...'

She moved closer to the door.

'What in the name of God was he doing with the agitator out at this time of year, though, Fransheen? And not a pick of wind out today.'

'Shure didn't he have the dementia. He could have woken up this morning and thought 'twas the spring. His aul fella went the same way, a gentleman he was too in his day, but he went pure *seafóid* at the end.'

'Ah, Jimmy wasn't that bad at all. He was havin' a bit of trouble remembering things and that was botherin' him, but shure, we'll never know what was goin' through his poor aul' head now anyway.'

A spark arced through the dark. The voices moved away.

Kate sucked down a deep lungful of air. How the hell was Rob going to cope with this? And Christina? She had barely been holding it together as it was.

She walked back towards the floodlit cordon. Past the cubicle shed where Jimmy's hundred-strong herd of Holstein Friesians were snorting and swishing their tails agitatedly. Past the hay shed with its neatly stacked bales of plastic-wrapped silage. Past the state-of-the-art milking parlour and through the holding yard outside and on to the cordoned-off dry cow house, which up until last Friday – when Jimmy sold off the last of them – had housed a beef herd of fifty well-fattened Friesian Hereford and Angus crosses. Past the unmarked car inside which Detective Inspector McGuire sat, his phone pressed to his right ear.

Back towards her husband who stood in the same place she had left him, hunched now with exhaustion, cold and horror. Still waiting to find out if the bodies of his parents were in that tank.

4

Kate

The fire engine had been shifted back to make room for the vacuum tanker, which at this moment was gorging itself on the slimy, viscous contents of the slurry pit – a mixture of fermented cow manure and water that smelt like the shite it was. In the normal course of events, the tank wouldn't be emptied until February or March when the slurry was spread on the fields to fertilise the grass for the cows. But this was far from normal.

Kate glanced at her watch. Just gone six. Jimmy should be inside having his tea in front of the RTÉ news right now. Instead of being the news. She had been taken aback when she heard Sergeant Tuohy tell the super he had put a guard on the main gate down at the entrance to the property to keep the press back. That there were cameras there already. It had never occurred to her that word about the incident on the farm would spread so fast or that it would be such a big news story, but of course, it was. The matriarch of one of the most prominent business families in the county and her husband missing and more than likely dead in yet another slurry pit tragedy. Of course the press would be all over it.

The tea and whiskey had revived Rob a bit and he was back to trying to make sense of it all.

'When did you see Daddy last, Kieran?' Jimmy had always been close to his Irish twin – both born in the same year, Kieran in March 1954 and Jimmy prematurely in December of that year. Their older siblings, two brothers, had left Glenbeg for greener pastures many years before in England and the States respectively. Kate didn't know how they had lived in that poky cottage all on top of each other, but times were different back then, and the two eldest had left home by the time Rita, the youngest, was born.

'It was the day before yesterday, I think,' Kieran said. 'Yeah, it was. Sunday evening. He called in for a pint after his tea, around sevenish.'

'How was he? Did you notice anything different about him?'

'I can't say I did, Rob. He had his two pints as usual and left.'

'And he didn't say anything to you?'

'Well,' Kieran looked uncomfortable, 'he might have mentioned there was a bit of friction going on at home, but he didn't go into detail. You know your father, he's not a big talker.'

It was Rob's turn to look uncomfortable. He turned back towards the activity outside the shed. The rain, jiggling in the spotlights, looked like it was down for the night. Not a hint of a breeze, though; it had been a still day. A bad day for mixing slurry. A hose connected to the tanker had been dropped down through the opening of the pit, a large rectangular hole in the ground outside the shed to the right of the door. The heavy metal three-slatted lid that covered the opening had been lifted back when Rob arrived at the shed earlier, and the agitator, which was attached to the front of Jimmy's tractor, had still been in the tank mixing the sludge. The first thing Rob had done before running inside was to turn off the tractor.

Like Ursula and Christina, Kate rarely ventured into the farmyard, the muckier end of the Kennedy family business, although by far the most lucrative. As MD of Kennedy Holdings Ltd, Ursula ran the open farm and looked after the business end of the dairy farm that Jimmy and Rob worked full-time, as well as managing a portfolio of property and investments.

Kate's own job spec as general manager of Glenbeg Farm Park covered everything from supervising the operation of the open farm and café to donning an apron and serving behind the counter at busy times or taking tour groups out when they were down a guide. Her 'package' was farcical.

Before she had her babies, it was manageable. Even enjoyable.

'The joys of working for a family business,' she had laughed back then.

It wasn't manageable any more, though. And it certainly wasn't enjoyable. Far from it. Especially when Rob worked all the hours God sent on the farm with Jimmy, so not only did she rarely get to see her husband, he wasn't there to give her the support she needed with the kids.

As the hose greedily slurped up the thick stinking liquid, she thought back to her first visit to the farm all those years ago. Mark, so handsome, even in his mucky work clothes, with his dark eyes and clear, sallow skin. Cheekbones she would have killed for herself. A GQ model in wellies. It was no wonder he had girls falling all over him, although, according to Rob, he seemed to have no interest. There was no sign that day – only months before he took his own life – of the pain that must have been hiding behind those smiling eyes.

'Is Rob showing off the slurry pit? Jaysus, he really knows how to impress a woman.'

'I wasn't expecting it to be so big,' she had said.

'That's what they all say, isn't it, Rob?' Mark had winked, dodging a puck in the arm from his brother.

'Watch it, you cheeky pup,' Rob warned.

'I'm only messin', Kate – me little bro is obviously smitten. He's pullin' out all the stops today, givin' you the full tour. Slurry, the ultimate aphrodisiac!'

'Would you ever piss off out of here, you feckin eegit?' Rob said, through his laughter. 'Have you no work to be doing?'

Mark had stayed, though, and patiently explained to Kate how the thick crust on top of the slurry in the tanks was holding some very toxic gases in, and that the most dangerous time for anybody to go near the tank was during the half an hour or so after the mixing started, as the crust broke up and the gases were released.

'It's mad to think that gas from cow shit could be so dangerous,' Kate said.

'It's the hydrogen sulphide that's the killer. Smells like rotten eggs at low levels, but there's no smell at all at higher levels. Just one breath of this stuff can kill you instantly, it's no joke.'

Rob had joined in then. 'More people actually die from drowning in slurry after they've been knocked out by the gas and fallen in than from gas poisoning itself. That's why there's so many regulations around it. Tell her about Bandit, Mark.'

'God yeah, poor aul' Bandit. He was a collie we used to have when we were kids. One day he came tearin' up to the house, barkin' like a lunatic. When I went out, he started runnin' around me in rings, pullin' at my sleeve. I called Dad and we followed the dog. He led us straight down to the tank. The cover was wide open. Jesus, when you think of it now! There were feck-all regulations that time, and us kids runnin' wild around the place. Anyway, when we looked inside the tank, there was Patches, our other dog, clingin' to a big lump of shit. We managed to get him out safely anyway, thanks to Bandit.'

'They're both long gone now,' Rob had said.

Nellie and Brendan joined them at the cordon, bringing hot flasks of tea and coffee and sandwiches wrapped in tin foil. Kate tried to force a plain ham sandwich down, but the bread and cold meat formed a ball of paste that stuck to the roof of her dry mouth and nearly choked her going down her gullet.

'How long does it usually take to drain a tank?' she asked Rob, thinking it must surely be nearly empty.

'It depends really ... hang on, I think there's something happening now ...'

He was right.

Something was happening.

The detective inspector's head jerked towards the shed when a shout went out.

'Inspector, you need to get in here!'

5

Six days earlier
Kate

Sitting in the Aldi car park, Kate felt like banging her head off the steering wheel to try and loosen the tight grasp the stress had on her – as if it had hands and was squeezing her brain. She had read somewhere that the Boston Marathon terrorists had used pressure cookers to create their homemade bombs – TNT, nails and ball bearings their ingredients, instead of bacon and cabbage. Her head felt like an unexploded pressure bomb. Some days, she feared her skull would burst wide open, the fused bones on either side cleaving apart to expel a grey fermented cloud of adrenaline, cortisol and norepinephrine into the atmosphere. Some days, she wished it would happen.

She would have broken down in tears if she had the energy

or time. But she didn't. She was already running late to collect the kids from the childminder.

It was the relentlessness of it all that was the worst part. The fact that no matter how much she got done in a day, she would have to do as much, if not more, the following day and the day after and the day after that. On and on. No end in sight.

When the payment hadn't gone through on the joint-account card, she thought she might cry. Right there in front of the checkout girl and the woman behind her in the queue who coughed politely and pretended to look intently at the sugar-free sweets stacked at the checkout as she excreted impatience into the air around her.

She found it stressful shopping here at the best of times, never mind adding the strain of a drained joint account ten days before pay day. It always felt like a bit of an endurance event trying to hurl her weekly groceries into the trolley before the next customer's shopping came whizzing up the conveyor belt and hurtled into the packing area on top of hers. As if they were all contestants in an endless series of *Supermarket Sweep*.

She had dug her own personal AIB card out of the bowels of her wallet. A chain of tiny sweat beads popped up above her upper lip as she keyed in the number and prayed there was enough left on her overdraft to cover the cost of the shopping. Miraculously there was. At the car, she flung everything willy-nilly into her bags for life: ice cream in on top of toilet bleach; cooked meat in with raw; raspberries squashed under a two-litre carton of milk. Then she slammed the boot shut, before getting into the front seat and slamming her own door for good measure.

She was so tired now that she could easily have closed her

eyes and nodded off as the ice cream melted into a puddle in the boot, but she had to collect the kids and feed everybody and clean up the breakfast mess as well as sort out dinner and put the kids to bed and do a load of laundry and mop the kitchen floor. There was a pile of ironing to be done, the bathrooms needed a good scrubbing, and the beds had to be changed, but they would have to be added to tomorrow's to-do list. Not for the first time, she wished she could plug herself into a fast charger to give her depleted battery a quick blast of energy, just enough to keep her going until bedtime.

The daily drudgery might have been easier to endure if she didn't have the constant worry about money gnawing away at her.

The barn conversion would be the bale that broke this camel's back.

She shut her eyes and let out a deep, worn-out sigh.

She couldn't keep living like this.

She had had enough.

'Fucking ENOUGH!' She punched the steering wheel, which let out a feeble beep.

They should have known they couldn't trust her. Hadn't she promised to do up Rob's grandfather's cottage for them when they first moved to Glenbeg to help out after Mark died? And she had been all talk about extending the cottage after Lily was born so the kids wouldn't have to keep sharing a room and they could have a decent-sized bathroom. Yet apart from the new roof, dry lining and a lick of paint, not another thing had been done. And they hadn't a hope of saving enough to do the work themselves. Instead, Ursula had come up with the idea of the barn conversion. She had shown them online photos of stunning conversion projects in the UK, was bubbling over with ideas for what they could do with the old stone barn on the edge of the property.

'It could be a fabulous home. Just think of all that space. I'll have an architect design it to bring as much light in as possible. It's much more suitable than trying to modernise that old place,' she'd stated.

So that was that. Decision made. The barn would be converted and they would move in there. That had been five years ago. Ursula's early enthusiasm for the project fuelled the hiring of an architect and the drawing up of designs, but things stalled after that, when she became distracted by the development of a new role-play village for the open farm. And then she was off travelling around the UK trying to source alpacas. One excuse after the other.

Then one day out of the blue about eighteen months ago, in typical Ursula fashion, she announced that planning had been approved for a change of use from agricultural to residential, and works would be starting on the barn in six weeks' time. Kate and Rob and the children had watched with feverish anticipation as the barn transformed before their eyes from a roofless ruin choked by ivy and weeds to the modern, spacious home of their dreams.

Even though she would have loved to have had some input into the design of what was to be their new home, and had to nod along and agree when Ursula went on about 'allowing the original features to sing' and the need to 'maintain the agricultural aesthetic' (terms she had stolen from the architect), Kate had to give her mother-in-law credit where it was due. The barn conversion was like something you'd see in *Ideal Home* magazine, with its vaulted ceilings, vast open-plan kitchen and living area, and the double-height living room bookended by a glazed wall that looked out onto wide-open countryside.

The original stonework had been painstakingly repointed and a new slate roof with a raft of Velux roof lights installed. The barn was flooded with natural light that bounced off the milky whitewashed walls and onto the gleaming porcelain floors. A contemporary bifurcated stairway with a glass balustrade led to the mezzanine area that housed the children's bedrooms, a shared shower room and a tiny study. The master bedroom on the ground floor had a wet room and a walk-in wardrobe.

Kate had it all decorated in her head, from the coordinating bed linen and curtains in the bedrooms to the gorgeous mustard sofa that would sit in front of the glass wall in the living room. She knew where every last plant and candle and painting would be positioned. Her favourite feature was the floor-to-ceiling bookcase that formed the back wall of the living area that you needed a ladder to reach the top of. She couldn't wait to start filling those shelves. There was no room for her books in the cramped cottage. She had given a lot away, stored the ones she couldn't bear to part with in her father's attic and made do with downloading books on her Kindle. Not that she ever had much time to read these days anyway.

She had saved every spare cent she could and kept a close eye on the sales. The beautiful cotton bed linen and towels she had bought half-price in Ryan's in Galway were being stored in her friend Ruth's spare room. Her father was insisting on buying the sofa for them after she brought him to see it the last time she went to visit him in Galway, but she couldn't order it until they got a moving-in date from Ursula. And therein lay the rub.

As the costs for the project began to spiral, Ursula's initial excitement started to wane and she spent a lot of time arguing with the architect and builder. First, the whole structure had to be underpinned, then there was the cost of disposing of asbestos she hadn't realised was there. She completely blew her lid when she found out how much the stone repointing was going to set her back.

As Ursula became increasingly vague about when the building works would be finished and they could finally move into their new home, Kate became increasingly nervous. She watched as the new timber sash windows were installed and the electricians and plumbers and other tradespeople came and went in their vans. When the painters turned up, she asked Rob to call over to his mother to find out what the bloody hell was going on. She needed to order beds and the sofa and a new table and chairs. Why could Ursula not just give them a date for when they could start having their furniture delivered? He had come home without an answer. His mother had said she'd 'get back to him on it in a couple of days', as she was 'tied up with something else at the moment'.

The painters were finished downstairs now, though, and most of the other tradespeople were gone. And they still had no moving-in date.

Kate had had to race back to the cottage that morning after dropping the kids to school because Luke had forgotten his hurley and helmet for Gaelic practice. Again. That child would lose his head if it wasn't screwed onto him. The big van with Carey's Catering Equipment emblazoned on the side had turned off the road in front of her onto the long treelined drive leading up to the farm park. She didn't know what made her follow it up around the track. God knew she was running late as it was, but they weren't expecting any new equipment in the café, and she had a niggle in her gut.

She had got out of the car and stood watching in confusion as two men unloaded a gigantic box from the back of the truck and wheeled it with some difficulty into the barn. She followed them into the kitchen. There was no sign of her mother-in-law.

'Hi. Ursula? I just need to get you to sign here for this,' one of the men said, approaching her with a handheld device.

'No, I'm not Ursula. She's probably down at the main building. In her office. What's in the box?' she asked, explaining, 'I'm her daughter-in-law.'

'It's an oven, love, as far as I know. We're just delivering it.' He checked the side of the box. 'Yeah, a Lincat six-burner gas range. A beast of a yoke. Are ye opening a restaurant here?'

'Who knows? Who knows what the hell she's up to,' Kate said as she turned on her heel and left.

By the time she'd dropped off Luke's sports gear and got back to the farm, she was over twenty minutes late for work. She twigged the blinds at Ursula's office window twitching as she walked past. She'd love to have fucked a rock at it. Her mother-in-law's eyrie on the first floor with its wide interior window afforded her a full view of the ground floor of the main building, with its rustic, high-ceilinged café, brightly painted party zone and souvenir shop.

Galling as it was going to be, she would have to get on with her job today and act as if everything was normal. She would make Rob call to his mother that evening and demand to know once and for all what the hell was going on. Her husband, like his father, was a man who didn't like confrontation, but things had gone beyond a joke now.

Nellie had taken a rare week off for a minor gynae procedure so Kate was under even more pressure than usual. She had planned to spend the morning getting on top of the towering pile of admin work in her tiny windowless office tucked away behind the kitchen, but one of the café girls had called in sick so she would have to cover for her until after the lunch rush. It was no wonder they had such a high rate of absenteeism, they were so short-staffed. Kate was blue in the face trying to get Ursula to understand this, but all that woman cared about were her feckin' margins.

The winter was their quiet season for tours of the open farm, but they were still busy with bookings every week for birthday parties and they were just over Winter Wonderland 2017, which had to be dismantled and put into storage again for another year. The annual 'seasonal spectacular' was a major income generator for the business. And a major headache for Kate in terms of organisation.

The open farm had reopened the day after St Stephen's Day, after only closing for three days, as Ursula was keen to capitalise on all the families around over the holiday period. Kate had taken an extra two days off to spend with her own children this year, which she knew hadn't gone down well at all with her mother-in-law, but she hated having to work when they were off school.

She had been run off her feet all afternoon with birthday parties and was late finishing as usual, as she had to go out to check on a sick animal before she left to do the Aldi shop.

She slid back the cover of the mirror on her sun visor now. Her skin looked dull under the remnants of the foundation she had hastily applied that morning, and dark half-circles hung beneath her eyes like baggy grey underpants. Her eyes, once the colour of her favourite Levi 501s and always her best feature, had faded to a stonewashed denim. The strain was woven into the fabric of her face, puckering around her eyes and mouth, rippling across her forehead like sand waves.

Ironically, for somebody who had always battled with an extra stone or so before she had kids, her clothes now draped loose and shapeless on her slight frame. There was a fine line between thin and haggard, though, and she was very close to crossing it.

Ursula often extolled the benefits of microdermabrasion, attributing her own remarkably good skin to regular treatment at an aesthetic clinic in Galway. That and the genes she had been blessed with. Kate didn't know who she thought she was fooling. It was quite obvious she was a fully paid-up member of the Botox brigade, her frozen Barbie doll forehead a dead giveaway. As Kate's friend Ruth, brutally honest as always, liked to point out: 'There's no amount of exfoliation – medical grade crystals or not – that could achieve skin as smooth as that at her age. She looks fresher now than she did in her forties.'

Kate had to bite her tongue when Ursula suggested that

she should 'pop in' to 'her clinic' for a consultation the next time she was in Galway, or make an appointment with the ferociously expensive salon where she got her colour and cut done, as she aimed a pointed nod of her expensively highlighted head in the direction of Kate's dark roots. If she had that kind of cash to spare, Kate would use it to replace her banjaxed old dishwasher or buy a decent mattress for their bed.

It wasn't as if Ursula was mean, far from it. She wasn't afraid to spend money and was fierce *flaithiúlach* altogether when it came to her cronies in the golf club, sending big rounds of drinks to the tables of people celebrating special occasions. *Put that on my tab there, Stephen.* She had offered to pay for Rob and Kate's wedding, but Kate's father wouldn't hear of it. He had money left from the sale of her childhood home and said he'd prefer her to reap the benefit of his legacy while he was still alive to see her enjoy it.

A few months back, Ursula had presented them with an expensive new Miele washing machine, after Kate's ancient Hotpoint had finally packed in. She did things like this from time to time unexpectedly.

'No need to thank me, you needed a decent washing machine,' she'd said, as she stood on their peeling kitchen lino in her LK Bennett pumps, admiring her donation and awaiting their gratitude.

'There was no need, Mother, this is far too much,' Rob had said.

'Not at all, myself and your father are glad to be able to help out.'

'Thanks so much, Ursula, we really appreciate it.' Kate had

squeezed the words out like the last squirt of toothpaste from an empty tube.

'That was very generous of her, wasn't it?' Rob had said after she left. Kate had felt like punching him.

It hadn't always been like this. The first few years after Kate moved to Rob's home place had been good ones, despite the circumstances that brought them there. Her new in-laws couldn't have been more welcoming, comforted by the presence of their son and his fiancée in the midst of their grief. Glad of their help.

Mark's death had come totally out of the blue. He had given no sign of what he was planning. On this, his family and friends agreed. If anything, he had seemed more settled in the weeks leading up to it, the most contented he had been in the previous couple of years. They had learned afterwards that this was not uncommon in people like Mark, once they had made peace with their decision.

The previous year, the Kennedys had invested heavily in the country's first open-farm park, an ambitious venture that had been Ursula's brainchild. They were just getting the business off the ground when Mark, the eldest child, who worked the farm with his father and was set to take it over some day, was found hanging from a beam in the milking parlour.

Kate had flown back to New York to finish out her internship after the funeral, while Rob had stayed on to help his parents run the business. She had felt bad leaving him behind – he was as passionate about the work they were involved in at the Cardozo School of Law Innocence Project as she was, maybe even more so, but he had convinced her to go. She had missed him so much over those months, absence and distance firmly cementing her feelings for him. He had met her at Shannon Airport on her return, standing at the front of the crowd waiting at arrivals, waving a large sign bearing the words: 'Welcome back, Katie McCarthy. Will you marry me?'

6

Kate

'A restaurant? What are you on about, Kate? How could she put a restaurant in there? We're going to be moving in in a few weeks, sure.'

'Are we, Rob? Really? You must know something I don't, then, because it's impossible to get a straight answer out of your mother. She's been acting cagey for months now.'

'There's no way she'd ... Maybe she thought we'd be doing a lot of entertaining with all the new space ... Sure, she couldn't ...'

'It's a six-burner commercial cooker, Rob, for fuck's sake! She's up to something, I'm telling you. If she's changed her mind, if she's going back on her promise to us, I'm telling you now, that's the final straw for me. I'm done.'

'What are you on about, Katie?' He sat up straighter in his

seat – not an easy feat, given the busted springs – and rubbed his eyes with the backs of his knuckles. He had been slouched on the sofa, his eyelids battling gravity as he struggled to watch the TV when she went in to talk to him after the kids were asleep. He hadn't lost his looks despite the long hours of hard work on the farm that left him flattened by the time he got home in the evening. At thirty-six, only a few months older than her, you'd have to look closely to spot the few strands of grey threaded through his thick dark head of hair. There was a time when she hadn't been able to keep her hands off him. Her handsome brown-eyed boy. Nor he off her. Now she couldn't even remember the last time they'd had sex. Even their libidos were chronically fatigued.

'What I'm on about, Rob, is that I'm not prepared to live like this any more. All we do is work and sleep and worry about money. And, please,' she raised her hand to stop him from interrupting, 'do not tell me we just need to be patient for another while. I'm sick to death of it. The only reason we put up with it this long is because we thought we'd be moving into our dream home, and now it looks like that was just another false carrot to keep us dangling like fools.' She tried to keep her voice calm, despite her heart cantering away inside her chest.

'Of course it will happen – my mother's not going to go back on her promise. Look, love, I agree things aren't easy at the moment, but it's not always going to be like this. The farm will be ours some day ...'

She snorted. 'Christ, Rob, your mother has been fobbing us off with that line for years and nothing has changed. Actually, things *have* changed. They've got worse since the kids came along. We're both so busy and so tired all the time, and it's not fair, Rob. It's not fair on them, it's not fair on any of us!'

'You know I've tried talking to her about our salary reviews, on more than one occasion, but I may as well be banging my head off a brick wall. She just keeps saying—'

'Oh yeah, I can just imagine how those conversations went. You tiptoeing around her, afraid to upset her. "Yes, Mother, no, Mother, how high, Mother?" You're just like your father. You're both scared shitless of that woman—'

Kate stopped. She was aware she was losing her cool. She hadn't planned to say any of that, but the time for worrying about going too far was over. She was only speaking the truth and she had to make him see that.

'Please don't talk about my parents like that, Kate,' Rob said, his jaw tensing. 'They've been very good to us over the years. Mother bought us the new washing machine, and she got the kids the iPads for Christmas and—'

'Those bloody iPads, we'll never hear the end of them. Can't you see that's all for show so she can brag to her golf buddies about what an amazing grandmother she is? She wouldn't be half as quick to offer to mind them for a few hours and give us a break.'

Of course the kids had been thrilled with the iPads, especially Lily, who Kate felt was far too young to have one. In a petty act of retaliation, she had allowed the child to buy a tacky plastic World's Greatest Grandma trophy from Dealz to present to Ursula as a thank you, gleefully envisaging the battle between ego and revulsion this would cause her mother-in-law.

'If she really cared about our kids, she'd pay us properly so we're not constantly worried about money. She wouldn't have had us living like this.' Kate gestured around the room, with its ugly red-brick fireplace, sagging three-piece suite and cheap nylon carpet. No amount of pretty soft furnishings or scented candles could brighten up these cramped, dreary rooms. 'We've been years talking about doing the place up, but there was never any money for it.'

They had so many plans when they first moved in, had been so full of enthusiasm and excitement, but the house needed major renovation which they couldn't afford.

'It wasn't supposed to be like this,' she said, softening her tone. 'Our kids deserve better. We deserve better than this, Rob.'

He opened his mouth to speak.

She cut in again. 'Surely you can see that I'm not being unreasonable here? Your parents have the rents from the commercial properties coming in every month, on top of the farm.'

Kate was so sick of people assuming she was loaded since she'd married into the Kennedys, when she had never in her life been so worried about money. Her own family hadn't exactly been rolling in it, but her father had never left them short.

'Of course I'd love to have a nicer place for us all to live,' said Rob, 'but we're lucky to have had a roof over our heads with no mortgage for so long, and we'll be moving into—'

'Are you actually for real? No mortgage? Sure, we don't even own the place. Your mother could throw us out on our arses any time it took her fancy.'

'You're being ridiculous now, Kate. Why would she do

that? You're making her out to be a right thunderin' bitch altogether.'

She stared at her husband. Could he really be so blind? So thick?

Somewhere outside a dog barked, and a reply came from further away. In the kitchen, the fridge seemed to hold its breath before settling back into a contented hum. A football match was frozen in action on the TV screen.

Kate felt the fight drain out of her, down through the seat of the armchair, through the cheap cushions she had stuffed in underneath to bolster the sagging springs, down, down through the manky carpet into the ground.

The thought of moving back in with her father filled her with dread, even though he had moved away from the house where her mother had died and back into the house in the heart of Galway city where he himself had been reared, a place she loved. And the thought of breaking up her children's family, taking them away from everything that was familiar to them, was unimaginable, but she was going to have to find the strength to do it. She could no longer live like this. She needed to start being a proper mother to her children, instead of the short-tempered, shouty version she had become. The unrelenting stress was changing her, and not for the better.

She had lost it with Lily earlier when she'd started her usual antics at bedtime. It had kicked off in the bathroom when she declared herself too tired to brush her teeth.

If Rob had been there, she could have called him to take

over. That would have been enough to make the little monkey behave herself. But Rob wasn't there, as usual; he was working late helping to dismantle the Winter Wonderland. She hadn't seen him all day.

And she hadn't as much as a proton of patience left.

'I actually couldn't give a shit whether you brush your teeth or not, just go to the toilet and get into bed.'

Her daughter's big blue eyes widened gleefully. 'You said a bad word.' Lily smirked.

'Just do as you're told or you'll be putting yourself to bed. I'm too tired for this messing tonight, miss, I'm serious!'

Not for the first time, Kate thought how much she would love to open the front door and walk out, walk into the dark night and just keep going. No destination in mind.

It wasn't until she had dragged as long as possible out of doing her wee, washing her hands and getting into bed, that Lily realised she had left her favourite Beanie Boo in the sitting room. She had about a gazillion of the cuddly toys and her favourite changed with the wind, but she now vehemently declared that there was no way 'in the wide, wide world' that she could possibly get to sleep without Kiki the cat.

'That's it, I've had enough. GET INTO YOUR BLOODY BED BEFORE I THROW YOU IN!' Kate caught her daughter by her skinny arm and dragged her over to her bed.

'Oww, Mom, you're hurting me. Stop, Mom, please, OWW …'

The pain in her child's voice stopped Kate in her tracks. As soon as she dropped her arm, Lily cradled it into her. She had hurt her child, squeezed her little arm too tightly. She felt like a big playground bully.

Lily jumped into bed and turned to the wall. Her little back shuddered inside her fleece unicorn onesie as she sobbed noiselessly. The bonfire of stress that had consumed Kate sizzled into a smouldering heap of regret. The unicorns all around her, on the curtains, the wallpaper, even the lampshade, seemed to stare at her reproachfully.

She was so sick of feeling guilty all the time; it ate into her soul like battery acid. Guilty for not being a good enough mother, a good enough daughter, a good enough anything.

'I'm sorry, pet, I'm so sorry if I hurt you. I shouldn't have done that and I shouldn't have shouted at you. I'm really, really sorry, I'm just ... very tired tonight.' She felt like curling into a ball too and bursting into loud snuffly tears. She put her hand on her daughter's shoulder, tried to turn her around to face her, but she refused to budge.

'I'll get Kiki for you, pet. I'm sorry. Please turn over and talk to me.'

'Mama ... you ...' Too upset to get the words out, as she gulped between sobs, Lily reverted to baby talk. Her first word. Kate could remember so clearly the first time Lily had said it. *Mama*. She had started talking early, had barely paused for air since. Kate had been gutted when her little girl graduated to *Mom* after she started school, one of many Americanisms the kids picked up from YouTube and the rest of the crap they watched instead of TV these days.

'Lily, pet, please don't cry. Mama loves you so much. I'm just so tired. I'm really, really sorry.' She patted her child's back gently, feeling just about as rotten as it was possible for her to feel.

After a few more pats, Lily sat up and grabbed her in a fleecy hug. 'It's OK, Mama.' Her breath hitched in her throat.

Kate felt even worse then. The child as quick to forgive as a kicked puppy. It would have been better if she had started screeching again. She held her daughter in her arms and rocked her back and forth, trying to comfort herself as much as Lily.

After the making up had been made and the story read and the back rub administered, Kate gave her daughter one last lingering cuddle before she left the room.

As she reached the door, a little voice called.

'Mama?'

'Yes, pet.'

'You make me sad when you shout at me.'

Luke had been six months old when Kate went back to work, poor Lily only twelve weeks. It had broken her heart to hand her little babies over to someone else to care for, but she had allowed herself to be pressurised into going back early, against her own instinct. It was a matter of great pride to Ursula that she had returned to work – back in the days when she used to run her own boutique in town – three months after giving birth to Mark and a mere six weeks after Rob and Christina. Unheard of in those days. It hadn't done her kids one bit of harm, she often said.

No, not a bit, thought Kate. One child buried at the age of twenty-one, another only half-living. And her remaining child's marriage falling apart.

A memory floated up to the present. A mind clipping of a different time, a different way of life, when the clocks ticked slower and mothers popped in and out of each other's houses borrowing cups of sugar and jugs of milk and the kids dipped unwashed stalks of raw rhubarb into the sugar bowl when nobody was watching and her mother smiled and chatted as she sat on a kitchen chair in the garden and watched Kate play with her Sindy dolls. A time when the sweet smell of baking filled the house as her mother's apple tarts and queen cakes cooled on a wire tray in the kitchen. A time before the lost babies, each clump of tissue and clots draining a bit more of her mother out with it.

She knew it would devastate Rob to be separated from his children – it was why she had put up with things the way they were for so long – but if he was too weak to stand up to his mother, maybe he deserved it.

'Look, Kate, I'll talk to her again and I'll ask her to give us a firm date to move into the barn,' he said, breaking into her thoughts.

'I can't do this any more, Rob. I mean it,' she said as she got to her feet. 'Either you grow a set of balls and do something about this situation or we're out of here. Me and the kids.'

She turned her back on his gobsmacked face and left the room.

7

Ursula knew it was inevitable, given his diagnosis, that her husband would become mentally incapacitated at some point. It was a matter of when, not if. Of the many imperatives on her mind at that moment, the most pressing was, without a doubt, getting James to sign enduring power of attorney over to her while he was still of sound enough mind to legally be able to do so.

She had instructed their family solicitor to set everything out in black and white for him, but to her utter frustration, James was still humming and hawing over the bloody thing. She had tried to stress to him the urgency of getting his affairs in order, but she could hardly come straight out and say 'before you lose whatever few marbles you have left'.

Signing the document meant that when the time came that James no longer had the capacity to manage his own affairs, she would be in full control of Kennedy Holdings Ltd.

She speed-read the email from her solicitor confirming that he had received the required statement from her husband's geriatrician verifying that, in his opinion, her husband currently had the mental capacity to understand the effect of creating the power of attorney. She would have to quite literally sit James down with a pen in his hand and make him sign it in front of her.

From her lofty perch in her dual-aspect office, Ursula enjoyed a bird's eye view of a large expanse of her fiefdom. Her front window looked out over the car park, her quick brain capable of making a pretty accurate tally of a day's takings by the number of cars and buses parked there. There was little that gave her as much joy as a full car park and a long queue of paying punters at the ticket kiosk.

She had adjusted the blinds on the interior window that looked out over the restaurant and party area on the ground floor so that nobody could see her, but she could see everything below.

Peering through the wooden slats now, she frowned. 'Oh for God's sake, how many times?'

She picked up her phone and tapped on a name saved in her favourites.

She watched her daughter-in-law wipe her hands on her Creamery apron and move towards the phone.

'Kate, can you get somebody to clear the tables at the big window? That mother and baby group left the place in a state as usual, a right mess all over the floor. Far more trouble than they're worth, that lot, for the pittance they spend.'

Ursula rolled her eyes as Kate launched into some longwinded excuse about how 'run off her feet' she was. *Yada yada*. She cut in before Kate got up on her short-staffed soapbox.

'Thanks, Kate, that's great.'

Through the blinds, she watched her daughter-in-law sigh heavily, pick up a cloth and head for the dirty tables. If Kate wanted to be a martyr, let her off. She should have called one of the kitchen girls out if she was short on the floor.

Ursula had explained the situation to her son and his wife in no uncertain terms. She couldn't afford to take on any more staff for the foreseeable future. With insurance premiums rising year on year, business had never been so challenging. It was only by cutting costs to the bone and ensuring that all of the existing staff 'put their shoulders to the wheel' (she loved the image this term conjured in her mind) that the business would continue to remain profitable. They weren't going to be happy about the barn either; she had been putting that conversation off but would have to sit down with them over the next week or two and let them know her plans.

These were never going to be popular decisions, but as owner and boss, she couldn't afford to worry about being popular. She needed to keep her focus on the bottom line, and she certainly didn't have time for Kate's touchy-feely concerns about staff morale and stress levels. Ursula was well aware she wasn't the most sensitive person in the world, but she had erected that shell of toughness around herself out of necessity.

Otherwise she'd never even have survived primary school. Her daughter-in-law was nearly as bad as Christina – far too soft, the pair of them. As she kept telling them, they had to learn to separate their personal feelings from business decisions. Especially in a family business.

As she pulled up the following week's staff rosters on her screen, Ursula's eye was drawn to the garish plastic trophy beside her computer. 'World's Greatest Grandma' it proclaimed. Those words were all that stood between the vulgar gold knick-knack and the bin. Her lips curled slightly as she thought about her adorable granddaughter, Lily. Such a sweet, pretty child, who bore a striking resemblance to Ursula at that age. It was nice to be appreciated by somebody. God knows it didn't happen often. They were all so quick to whinge and gripe. Family and staff alike.

Glenbeg had little enough going for it when she had first seen the potential for a new visitor attraction there. It had been a town on its knees, more people leaving for work in places like Galway city or Athlone on a daily basis than coming in. The closure of the area's three largest employers – a shoe factory, a rubber manufacturer and a computer company – had hit it badly during the eighties and nineties. Its main street was pockmarked by shuttered shopfronts; the pubs and the bookies the only businesses still thriving.

Ursula had first witnessed the open-farm concept in operation in Surrey during a visit to the UK. She had seen the opportunity straight away. There was nothing like it in Ireland at the time – an all-weather amenity that combined education and fun.

It had taken a whole heap of perseverance, and her not

insubstantial skills of persuasion, to talk first their bank manager and then her husband into coming on board with her vision for Glenbeg Farm Park. The business had hit the ground running, attracting families and school tours from all over the country.

There was plenty of competition in the agri-tourism market these days, but Ursula viewed that as a positive. Competition drove her on, encouraged her to constantly improve her offering. Her giant indoor play barn was one of the largest in Europe, and people came from far and wide to visit Santa at the farm's Winter Wonderland every Christmas. One of the newest developments was her role-play village, beautifully crafted from wood and featuring a mini-supermarket, post office and American-style diner.

The ten-acre farm-park site had a pets corner – where kids got to hold bunnies, guinea pigs and other fluffies – a scenic farm trail and a barrel ride. There was an outdoor playground and sandpit, picnic areas and an indoor soft-play zone.

As part of her research, Ursula had visited farms in the UK and Europe and hand-picked her favourite elements from each. The farm was home to pot-bellied pigs, miniature ponies and pygmy goats; sheep, cattle and donkeys; geese, hens and ducks. And of course the alpacas, Alfie and Alice, who were a huge hit with the kids and who she was planning to breed.

Ursula had worked her backside off to get the business up and running, and her efforts had paid off. The place was booked solid every weekend for birthday parties, communions and confirmations. The business had grown steadily over its early years, before Ireland's compo culture began to show its greedy face. Her already ridiculously high insurance premiums had increased 300 per cent over the previous year after a six-year-old tumbled out of the barrel ride and split his eyebrow open, necessitating three stitches. His parents had sued and been richly rewarded for their efforts. It made Ursula sick. Especially when the same parents had allowed their son to clamber around the ride unrestrained, even after he had been asked to sit still a number of times.

She would ride it out, though; she had come through worse. Had survived the recession. Her brain was as sharp as it had ever been, and she was in great physical shape, thanks in part to her strict adherence to a healthy eating and exercise routine, but her work was the life force that sustained her. The business awards – regional and national – that hung on the walls of her office were testament to her success. Through her position as chairperson of Glenbeg Chamber of Commerce, she was heavily involved in lobbying government for reform of the Irish insurance industry. And she was constantly planning ahead. A farm in Cork had recently opened their own ice cream and chocolate factory, which she intended to visit in the coming months. Artisan ice cream was huge all year round now, and she had visions of expanding her range globally, trading on Ireland's reputation for high-quality dairy products.

The idea for the cookery school had been a real lightbulb moment. Deirdre Clarke, the chamber treasurer, had made an off-the-cuff remark at a social event about it being a wonder Ursula hadn't ever thought of opening a Ballymaloe at Glenbeg Farm, pointing out that it would be the perfect venue. She was right. It *was* the perfect venue, and she had the perfect home for it.

You'd never have guessed in a million years that Ursula came from an end-of-terrace council house, a lane that stank of piss and rotting rubbish running alongside it. Even James didn't know. She'd made bloody well sure of that. By the time she met him, her parents were long gone and she and Peter were living in a much better area, but only slightly more genteel squalor, with Aunt Catherine and Uncle Arthur. As it turned out, they might have been better off if they had been left where they were with her father's dosser family.

James knew things hadn't been good for her as a child, knew she didn't like to talk about it, so he had never pushed her. He had no idea about life, really, how people existed from one day to the next in places like St Joseph's Park. Where the weeds poked up through busted sofas in the front gardens and twined around rusting prams, where you had to squeeze a pillow around your head in bed at night to try to block out the sound of the woman next door getting the shit kicked out of her. Where the kids ran wild on the streets and in fields that hadn't yet been swallowed up by concrete, in and out between the horses and dogs and even the odd goat.

There were plenty of decent families living in the estate, of course, people who held down low-paying jobs and put every spare penny into keeping their homes smart. There were even some who managed, against all the odds, to get their kids as far as the Leaving Cert. Not down in the terraces, though, where Ursula's family lived, where some of the houses were boarded up and graffitied, the gardens used as landfill. Ursula had always been frightened of the boarded-up houses, especially at night in the inky darkness, all but one of the street lights smashed. The rumour was that a young girl had been murdered in the second house from the other end of her row. She always ran extra fast past that one.

Her mother had tried her best, God love her, and when she was in good form, she put hours of feverish activity into the house, scrubbing and painting and sanding, but cheap paint and pots of pretty pansies and petunias couldn't block out the wasteland around them. Nothing short of a house transplant could have.

Her mobile rang. Again.

Her daughter's name flashed up on the screen. Again.

She had ignored Christina's last two calls. This was all Ursula needed right now. Christina spent her life building molehills into mountains. She looked after the farm park's social media, hardly a high-pressured position, but she still managed to get her knickers in a twist over minor issues on a regular basis.

'Yes, Christina?'

Her daughter's tension, converted into electrical signals, was emitted via radio waves down the line, wittering on about a negative review somebody had posted on Tripadvisor. Ursula really didn't have the time to indulge her daughter's anxiety-fuelled nonsense this morning, had far more important things on her mind.

She cut across her: 'I've told you to stop taking this stuff so personally, Christina. People can say what they like on the internet – there's nothing we can do about it.'

Her daughter continued to babble into her ear.

'Oh for God's sake, you know his comments aren't true. You could eat your dinner off the floor in those toilets. Why can't you just look at all the positive comments about us, for a change, instead of getting yourself worked up over one post from a cranky pensioner with too much time on his hands?'

Christina was so over-sensitive, she made Kate look like Margaret Thatcher. Ursula knew she would brood over that one bad review for days, turning it over and over in her mind, obsessing about it as if some idiot in Tipperary had personally insulted her. She was so negative all the time, it was draining.

To Ursula's chagrin, she had to concede – though she would never voice the thought aloud – that her daughter had likely inherited her weakness of character from her side of the family. From Ursula's father, to be specific, a man well dead and buried before the possibility of Christina was even conceived. It was a matter Ursula had long mulled over in her own mind. Was there some flawed gene passed on from one generation to the next that had lain dormant in Ursula, just like red hair or a cleft chin, but slithered through the umbilical cord and turned itself on full blast in Christina? She had been whiny and pettish even as an infant, prone to long, torturous bouts of colic. Ursula had dreaded coming home from work in the evenings, the sound of her daughter's cries sawing through her brain like a rusty angle grinder. Mark and Robert had been dream babies in comparison. She had been forced to hire a night nurse after a week of Christina's screaming just to get a decent night's sleep.

Christina hadn't left the house in days. She worked from the desk in her bedroom, where she insisted on keeping the blinds down all day, refusing to even open the window to let in a breath of fresh air. She complained of feeling cold all the time. She was always like this during her bad patches. Christina would have been lost without her cousin and best friend, Julie, who had stuck by her over the years when other friends fell by the wayside. The fact that there was no love lost between Ursula and Julie's busybody of a mother, Rita – Jimmy's sister – had never affected the close friendship between the two girls.

Her phone beeped.

'Sorry, Christina, I've another call coming through. I have to take this, it's my solicitor.'

She tapped 'end and accept', cutting through her daughter's distress, leaving it to drift in the electromagnetic ether.

'Stephen, I got your email about the power of attorney. I'm on top of it, I just need to sit that man down and stand over him until he signs it.'

'That would be great, Ursula. Look, I'm not actually on about that. I've just come off the phone with Jack Forde. He's representing Maura Lally.'

'What?' Her brow furrowed.

'He said his client has brought a claim for constructive dismissal to the Workplace Relations Commission. It's her contention that you made the situation at work so intolerable for her that she was forced to leave her job. She's claiming she was bullied by you over a number of years until she couldn't take any more so she went out on stress leave before handing in her notice.'

Ursula felt the heat rising, up her chest and her neck, to her face, flooding her cheeks. *How dare that common cow with her brood of bastard brats, all with different surnames, threaten her?* Maura Lally should have counted her blessings that Ursula had given her a job in the first place.

'This is completely ridiculous, Stephen. It's far too easy to bandy the "bully" word around these days when people don't want to do the job they're being paid to do. The absolute cheek of the woman.'

His silence unnerved her slightly. The marked absence of his usual breezy reassurance.

He cleared his throat. 'Well, Ursula, unfortunately, as this is not the first time an accusation of this kind has been made against you, it's likely that the WRC will take the matter seriously. She kept detailed notes of the alleged incidents, as well as emails and text messages from you. If this goes to hearing, there's a good chance it will be covered by the local media.' He paused. 'I don't need to tell you how damaging this kind of publicity could be to a business like yours.'

She thought for a few moments, tapping her pen off the desk, her anger swiftly making way for pragmatism. 'How much will it cost us to make this go away?'

She had just sat down to watch *Corrie*, a badly needed glass of Cab Sav in her hand, when the living-room door opened with such force it banged off the wall. Robert clomped into the room in his mud-caked wellies.

This was all she bloody needed after the day she had just put down.

'What on earth, Robert? What are you doing in here with those filthy boots?'

She rooted around her for the remote control, pressed 'pause' with a sigh, the opening theme tune to her favourite soap stopped in its tracks.

'I need to talk to you, Mother.' He stood in front of the gas fire, blocking the heat.

She insisted that her son and daughter call her Ursula at work, so much more professional than addressing their boss as Mother. She wished they would just call her by her proper name all the time – there was nothing so ageing as being called Mother by a grown man with children of his own – but she knew it would probably be taken the wrong way if she suggested it.

'Can't this wait? I've had a really rotten day, and I'm exhausted.'

'No, I'm sorry, it can't. Look, Mother, you're going to have to let us know when we can move into the barn. We need an exact date. Kate has to order beds and other stuff and, to be honest, she's getting worried that it might never happen at this rate.'

'Actually, I was planning to sit down and talk to the two of you about that.' She took a deep sip from her glass. Her easy-going eldest son had obviously been wound up. 'How about we set something up for early next week?'

'Why can't you just tell me now? There's no need for us to have a meeting about it. We just need to know will it be this month, next month? The painters must be nearly finished by now so surely it can't be much longer. Kate and the kids are all excited.'

'Well, it won't be this month or next month, I'm afraid. That's why I want to sit down with you both to explain things. There's been a change of plan—'

He cut across her rudely: 'Change of—? What are you talking about?'

'As I was saying before you interrupted me, there's been a change of plan ...'

'You mean you've changed the plan. Please tell me you're not thinking of putting a restaurant in there. Kate saw the oven going in earlier, but I told her there's no way you'd do that to us, to your grandkids. There's no way you'd go back on your promise. You always said that barn would be ours and we're years waiting for it to happen.'

'Not a restaurant, no.'

'Not a—? Oh my God! She was right. You've changed your mind. No! You cannot do this, Mother!'

He was pacing up and down now in front of her.

'Stop over-reacting, Rob, for God's sake. I haven't changed my mind. The barn will be yours. Just not right away. That's what I want to sit down and—'

'What the fuck are you talking about? Not right away?'

She was shocked. Who was this angry, red-faced man in front of her, shouting at her, using such foul language? Robert had never so much as raised his voice to her before.

'It's not a restaurant, it's a cookery school, and it's only for a few years until I recoup the renovation costs.'

'I don't fucking believe this! A fucking cookery school? Does

Dad know about this? I don't understand. How could you even contemplate doing such a thing? It's not as if you need the fucking money, that's for sure.' He kept pacing. And ranting.

Her brain finally kicked into gear. Sent a tardy message to her central nervous system instructing her body to act. Straight into fifth.

'How. Dare. You. Raise. Your. Voice. To. Me. In my own house.' She pulled herself to her feet, knocking her half-full glass off the arm of the sofa. She wiped the spittle off her lips with the side of her hand. 'After everything I've done for you and your family, the absolute cheek of you. You should be down on your knees thanking me. I've put a roof over your heads, given you and your wife jobs—'

'Given us jobs? Are you for real?' Her son threw her a look of pure repugnance. It was like he was wearing somebody else's face. 'We gave up everything to move down here and help you and Daddy out after Mark. We had our own plans, but we packed the whole lot in because you needed us. Thank *you*? My marriage is falling apart, myself and Kate have never been so miserable, and we barely get to see our kids. *Thanks a fucking lot, Mother!*'

She strode to the living-room door and flung it wide. 'There's nobody forcing you to stay here, Robert. If you're not happy, you and your wife are more than welcome to leave. Off you go now and follow your hifalutin dreams, see how long you last out in the real world ...'

He stood his ground. 'We're going nowhere, Mother. I haven't a notion of leaving Daddy in the lurch the way things are with him. We've worked our arses off for you for years at well below the going rate and we did it with a heart and a half because we wanted to help grow the business, but you've gone too far this time.'

'Oh, you've worked your arses off, have you?' she spat. 'I've built this business from the ground up. I've put my blood, sweat and tears into it. I was willing to let you and your family live in that barn rent-free down the line, but I can tell you, I'll be having a serious think about that now. This is what happens when you do too much for people ...'

'Jesus Christ, Kate was right.' He stared at her, shaking his head slowly, as if he was seeing her for the first time. 'You're an absolute control freak, Mother. You have us all dangling off strings like stupid bloody puppets—'

'GET OUT OF MY HOUSE RIGHT NOW.' Her hands were visibly shaking.

He walked through the door, shouting back from the hallway as he left. 'Don't worry, I'm going, but you're not going to get away with this. I'll be making an appointment to see Paul Sheehan. We have rights too, you know.'

'Get out of this house before I call the guards,' she screeched, slamming the living-room door behind him.

She slid to the floor, her back against the door. Dropped her head into her hands. The Waterford crystal glass lay intact beside her, its haemoglobin-red contents pooled on the polished walnut floorboards and sprayed in a fine mist up the side of her sumptuous green velvet sofa like gunshot spatter.

He was wrong, all wrong. It had never been control that drove her. It was fear.

8

Christina

Christina had woken that morning with a bad feeling. Nothing new there. Sometimes it felt like bad was all she could feel. Today was different, though. Worse. Dread squatted on her chest like a kettlebell.

The curse of the highly sensitive. Her whiskers constantly twitching, picking up the subtlest of vibrations in her environment, detecting danger everywhere. Tuning in to the frequencies of people around her, to their sadness and their pain. As if she didn't have more than enough of her own.

It seemed as though she had always been this way, but as Helen, her therapist, liked to remind her, it was just her brain playing tricks. There had been a time in her life when she wasn't afraid all the time. It was her illness that caused her to view life through a warped mental filter. The way she picked out a single negative detail and dwelt on it exclusively until her vision of reality darkened, like a drop of ink that stains an entire glass of water.

The medication dulled her senses, muzzled the soul-destroyers on her tail. It sedated her spirit too, but that was a small price to pay. Better to feel numb than terrified. Most importantly, the meds stopped the dreams, pressed 'pause' on the horror movies that had plagued her nights. The metal ladder lying on the cow-dung-caked floor of the milking shed. The size thirteen Reeboks dangling bizarrely mid-air. They had slagged him so much over the size of his feet. Like diving flippers. And each time, he smiled and winked and said, 'You know what they say about men with big feet ...'

Her initial instinct that day was to smell a rat. Mark was an awful messer. Always jumping out from behind doors, playing pranks on people, 'just pulling the piss'. But then she had looked up. And realised that life would never be the same again.

He could never have foreseen that she would be the one to find him.

In the weeks and months afterwards, she had been tormented by the images. His horrified, bulging eyeballs. His grotesquely swollen tongue. Night after night. In the horrors of her unconscious, she arrived while he was still alive, fingers frantically clawing at the rope, legs flailing in the air. She tried desperately to hold his weight on her shoulders, but her knees kept buckling beneath her while her brother writhed above her, suffocating. His grasping fingers turning to bone that snapped as he tried futilely to loosen the rope, his runners with his feet still inside them coming away in her hands. Her throat hoarse from screaming even though no sound came out.

She had figured out over the years since that the smaller her world was, the fewer people in it, the safer she was. She had never expected to be still living at home at her age, still single, but it was safer this way.

It had been just after midday when she saw it: the notification from Tripadvisor alerting her that Glenbeg Farm Park had a new review, with a link to the post. Fortunately, the comments on the farm's social media and on review sites like Tripadvisor were mainly positive, requiring only a standard thank-you response.

As soon as she clicked on this link, though, she saw that it was different. Instead of the usual rating of excellent or very good, David M, a grandfather from Tipperary who had visited the farm with his daughter and her children, had rated it 'terrible'.

The nasty words sneered out of the screen at her. *Over-priced. Filthy toilet facilities. Money for old rope.*

Her heart plunged through the soles of her fluffy slippers. A horribly familiar sensation. Like the plummet down a vertical shaft at an amusement-park drop tower. No matter how much she shrank her world, the outside could still get at her.

What would Helen advise her to do right now? Think, think. She pictured her therapist sitting on her funky patchwork armchair across from her, the book-lined wall of her consultation room behind her. Firstly, Helen would tell her to take a few deep breaths. In through her nose, right down into her belly and out through her mouth. Then she would get

Christina to question the veracity of her thoughts, to see that online comments made by strangers were not a personal attack on her. That these people didn't even know of her existence. They spewed venom from their fingertips for the fun of it. Knowing all of this made no difference, though. She was unable to control the alert system in her brain that told her she was under attack, like a faulty house alarm that had hijacked its own settings and was driving the homeowner insane with its incessant shrieking.

She picked up her phone, went into 'Recent' and dialled the last number she had called.

No answer.

She stood up from her desk and started pacing from one side of the room to the other. She dialled again. Still no answer. She moved the phone to her left hand, started picking at the skin around her right thumbnail.

She needed to speak to her mother. To get the agitation out of her brain, across the bridge of her tongue and out her mouth.

She tried her mother's office land-line.

No answer.

She kept pacing.

Dug her nail deeper. Worked it back and forth until she broke the skin. Waited exactly sixty seconds. Tried her mother's mobile again. Peeled back a sliver of newly healed skin. Upstarts, her father called them. It upset him to see the state of her poor fingers. She sucked on the beads of blood that bubbled to the surface of her exposed pink flesh. Salty sweet. Self-soothing.

Finally, Ursula answered. Christina spoke urgently.

Her mother cut through her concern. A Sabatier through

soft cheese. Told her to stop taking this stuff so personally. As if that was possible. Ursula didn't understand. Never had. Asking Christina to focus on the positive comments instead of 'getting worked up over one cranky post' was like asking her to walk on water.

'No, Mother, wait ... please.'

It was no good. Ursula was gone. Someone more important on the other line.

Christina stopped pacing, out of steam.

She closed down the screen of her laptop to protect herself physically, at least, from the vitriol of David M.

She slid her feet out of her slippers and pulled back the bed covers.

She climbed in, turned onto her right side, curled her knees up into her chest. A faint trace of L'Occitane Cocon de Sérénité pillow mist lingered on the crisp cotton pillow case. Bottled serenity. Lavender, sweet orange and geranium. Kate had brought it back to her after a weekend in Dublin; she was so thoughtful that way.

Christina pulled her quilt up over her head. A Laura Ashley vintage print of plump pink cabbage roses on a delicate trellis of green foliage. The weight of the feathers comforted her. She closed her eyes. Blacked out the world. Picked unconsciously at the tattered skin of her thumb. She felt so tired all the time, one of the downsides of the meds, no matter how much she slept. Yet sleep was her only respite.

She drifted deeply for hours, a dead weight on the seabed of consciousness. The bang of a door somewhere in the house broke through, dragging her to the surface. The clock on her bedside locker, wearing twin alarm bells like a set of headphones, told her it was tea-time. She would be awake all night now, but she had to catch up on the afternoon's work anyway. It was a vicious circle; she would be exhausted tomorrow and tempted to sleep during the day again. It was vital that she try to stick to a regular routine of sleep. And a regular meal plan. She had missed lunch today. She didn't feel hungry, never did really, but she had to eat. She didn't want to end up back in hospital.

She could hear her father clattering around downstairs in the kitchen. She was aware that he had come in at some point as she'd sweated under the duvet. Knocked gently on the door. She had sensed him padding to the side of the bed, lifting the duvet from over her head, tucking it in under her chin. Just like he did when she was a little girl.

She would join him for his evening meal in the kitchen as she usually did, make the tea in the teapot with loose leaves, poured through a little metal strainer, the way he liked it. She enjoyed that time in the evenings on their own together. Her father wasn't a man of many words, but their silences were pleasant.

Her mother was usually out and about, going straight from the office to the golf club or a chamber meeting. When she was home, she usually ate her evening meal on a tray in the living room while she caught up on her soaps. Jimmy adjourned to the den to watch the news at six every day, preferring the smaller, cosier space to the more formal good room. Christina preferred it too, the fire spitting and crackling in the open hearth, the sweet earthy aroma of burning turf. In the living room, the flames were trapped behind glass, the logs and heat fake.

After emptying her bladder and splashing cold water on her face, Christina went down to join her father. The savorous smell of frying bacon met her in the hall. Her father was pushing the slender slices of sizzling pig around the pan with a metal spatula, the hot oil spitting all over the place. She would have to scrub down the tiled backsplash when he was finished to hide the greasy evidence.

'Hey, Pops.'

'Hello, pet. What's the news?'

'You'll be murdered if she catches you with the frying pan out again, you know.'

'Ah well, what she doesn't know won't hurt her, will it?' He winked at her, before triumphantly depositing the streaky rashers onto a plate beside three plump sausages, two runny fried eggs and a slick cluster of mushrooms.

'The grill would be much healthier, though, Daddy, with your cholesterol.'

'Ara, I might use the grill tomorrow so, Chrissie pet.'

'You will in your backside,' she said as she opened the huge American fridge and starting pulling out the makings of a chicken salad.

On a medium-sized plate, she laid a grilled chicken breast (she cooked a batch every few days) for protein. She washed and sliced a tomato, some cucumber and a spring onion, and filled out the rest of her plate with leafy greens. She poured them each a glass of chilled water from the fridge dispenser.

She sat at the table where her father had set two places opposite each other, using the cow table mats. Huge pink speckled nostrils nudged up out of the mat, close enough to lick her. The matching teapot, sugar bowl and milk jug huddled together in the middle of the table.

She sliced a small piece of chicken from the breast and chewed it slowly. Her father attacked his fry-up with gusto. He slathered two slices of multigrain bread with soft butter, laid two glistening sausages on one slice, spread a layer of Ballymaloe relish on the other and slapped it down on top of the first one. Took a large bite. Scowled.

'Feckit, it's like eating cardboard. Sure, you can't have a proper sausage sandwich without white loaf.' He munched sombrely.

Ursula wouldn't allow as much as a crumb of white bread inside the front door.

'She's only looking out for you. There's no goodness in that sliced white bread – you need the multigrain for fibre.'

'Jesus, don't you start on about fibre as well, Chrissie. Your mother is obsessed enough with me bowels. Next thing she'll be asking me to fill out a report sheet every time I go to the toilet.'

Christina smiled. 'Come on, now, Daddy. It's not like you're that hard done by. Kate has you well taken care of.'

Like a visitor smuggling contraband into Mountjoy, Kate regularly snuck him over slices of white bread from the café, along with decadent wodges of Nellie's Toblerone cheesecake and thick slabs of her famous rhubarb tart smothered in custard. There wasn't a pick on him, though – he worked every fat-laden calorie off out on the farm.

'Shhh … keep that to yourself.' He winked, reminding her of Mark.

He picked up a sheaf of papers from the table and started to leaf through them. He put them down. Sighed. Picked up his knife and fork again.

'What's that, Daddy?'

'Ah, nothing, love, just something I need to sort out for your mother.'

Her eyes scanned the top page. She strained to read upside down. *Instrument creating enduring power of attorney. Powers of Attorney Act 1996.* One line snagged her attention. *In the event of you becoming mentally incapable of doing so.*

Her father dropped his cutlery onto the plate, leaving two rashers and an egg uneaten. A rare event for a man who usually cleared his plate, mopping the last traces of yolk and grease with a folded slice of bread. He poured a second cup of tea from the pot. Dropped in two heaped teaspoons of sugar and a drizzle of milk from the cow jug.

'Will you have a cup, love? It's still hot?'

'I will, thanks.'

'Let's bring it inside. It's nearly time for the news.'

She sat on the sofa in the den, watching her father watch the news from his armchair in front of the TV.

He tutted away to himself as a report on the trolley crisis panned to a scene in a Dublin A&E department, where a woman was complaining that her ninety-one-year-old mother had spent two days lying on a trolley in a corridor.

'Shocking how nobody seems to be able to sort out that mess – it's going on for donkey's years,' he said, shaking his head.

Despite being a bit weather-beaten from years of working

outside, her father looked well for his age. Naturally olive-skinned, like his sons, he had a healthy complexion all year round that ripened to a deep tan in the summer months. A fine thick head of dark grey hair. No outward sign of the damage being wrought inside his skull.

It had started with losing simple words and the names of people he had known for years, but those moments of confusion, when he looked as if he was lost inside in himself, were becoming more frequent. He still watched the news every day and retained a keen interest in current affairs and sport, although he had stopped reading the *Irish Independent* from cover to cover, merely skimming the pages now.

Christina dreaded the day when they would lose him entirely. The thought that he wasn't going to get any better, only worse, filled her with dismay. He might be doing fine one day, but overnight, he could slip down to the next stage of his illness. The consultant had explained that, unlike the slow, steady steps-on-a-stairs descent of Alzheimer's, the progression of vascular dementia was more like sliding down a slope. They all knew that, including her father.

He had definitely been quieter in himself since the diagnosis. Having seen his own father wither away from it, he knew what lay ahead for him. He had watched the disease peck away mercilessly at James Senior's brain. Sucking up his words first, then his memory, before eventually gobbling up the last remaining fragments of his personality. By the end stage of his illness, there was not a morsel left of the devoted husband and father he had been in that frail husk of a man staring vacantly into nothing.

Christina had visited her grandfather at the home a few

times with her father. He was in the last stage of his illness by then, attached to reality by a flimsy wisp. The strong antiseptic whiff of Dettol had failed to mask the tart underlying note of stale geriatric urine or the dreary top note of boiled vegetables that seemed to seep from the walls of the place. It was beyond depressing. Sitting by the bedside of a man who had no idea who they were or why they were there. Who had no idea who he was himself or where the hell he was.

The old man's brain may no longer have been able to choreograph the complex dance of muscles needed to create speech, but his pale rheumy eyes had whimpered his despair. And now it had come for her father. Grandad must have been terrified at the beginning too, just like her father must be now. Shackled to an incurably broken brain slowly shrinking inside his skull. Billions of tiny nerves misfiring, causing problems all along the assembly lines. Failing to make the synaptic leap. Leaving patches of wasteland where everyday words and the ability to make tea had once resided.

It was over an hour later when they heard the kitchen door bang. Her father was watching a rerun of *Only Fools and Horses*, the episode where a youthful Del Boy and Rodney get into the chandelier-cleaning business with predictably disastrous results. Even though her father must have watched it a dozen times, he still chuckled aloud each time the chandelier fell.

Christina leafed through the latest issue of *Image* magazine, trying to distract her mind from David M's hurtful comments. Ursula had adjourned to the living room to catch up on her soaps. She had popped her head in the door to say hello when she came in. Told them she was after having a tough day and was going to pour herself a large glass of wine and put her feet up in front of the TV. She didn't mention the Tripadvisor review.

Christina didn't know where her mother got her energy from. Ursula worked such long hours every day, often continuing late into the night and weekends, tapping away at her laptop in the living room or in her home office. She thrived on being busy: overseeing the operation of the business, doing the books, hiring and firing, managing the rental properties. She had been like this for as long as Christina could remember, even before the open farm, back in the days of the boutique.

Christina certainly hadn't inherited her mother's business brain. She couldn't figure out where she had come from. Maybe she had a bit of her Granny Kennedy in her. She had been very creative in her day and had been able to turn her hand to anything, sewing needles and crochet hooks the instruments of her craft. She created beautiful baby blankets, bonnets and cardigans. Delicate little things with lace trims and perfect rows of pearl buttons. And pretty hand-stitched patchwork quilts, one for every bed in the house. Christina still had a few of the quilts, rescued just in time during one of Ursula's big clear-outs.

The unordinary sound of raised voices from the lounge broke into Del Boy's rant at Grandad for unscrewing the wrong chandelier. She thought at first it was coming from the TV in the other room, the volume turned up excessively loud as if somebody had sat on the remote control by mistake. Her father turned Del Boy down.

'What's that racket?' he asked.

The volume of the voices increased. There was no doubt now. It was her brother they could hear. They sat still, staring at each other in bewilderment at the sound of Rob's voice raised in anger.

At his mother.

At the language he was using.

Then Ursula was shrieking back at him.

Totally losing her cool.

Screeching at Rob to get out of her house, threatening to call the guards on him.

It all happened so quickly.

The world slowed down outside Christina; her heart sped up inside her. She sat upright on the sofa.

Her father got to his feet. 'What in the name of …?'

He left the room, disappeared down the hall. She heard his voice from the kitchen, low and conciliatory, trying to calm Rob, who didn't sound like Rob at all.

'What the hell is wrong with you? Letting her walk all over you like a fuckin' doormat. She's like a bloody dictator, controlling us all, and we've let her away with it for years.' Her brother's voice crackled with anger.

Her father responded, a low murmur.

'Well, I'm done. I'm not letting her destroy my marriage. It's time somebody in this family stood up to her,' Rob shouted.

The French door slammed.

Silence.

She sat still, barely breathing as the seconds ticked by.

Her father came back down the hall, opened the door to the living room.

The rumble of low conversation.

Then her mother's voice rising again. 'If you were any kind of a man, you wouldn't allow your son to talk to me like that. The cheek of him. Not a scrap of appreciation for everything I do for any of you.'

The familiar *Corrie* tune floated into the hall before the door closed.

Her father trudged back into the room. Sank into his armchair. Stared at the frozen TV screen. Inhaled deeply. 'Don't you be worrying your head about that now, Chrissie – it'll all be sorted in the morning. Once they've both had a good night's sleep.'

'Dad?'

He kept staring at the TV.

'Daddy?' A little louder.

'Yes, pet.'

'I don't think you should sign those documents.'

He turned his head to look at her. 'Ara, don't be worrying yourself about those now, pet. That's just legal stuff that needs to be sorted out at some stage.'

'I know what it is, Daddy ...' She hesitated. 'There's something I have to tell you, before you sign anything. Something I should have told you a long time ago.'

9

The day after the event – Wednesday, 10 January
Kate

Kate had finally dozed off sometime around 4 a.m. and was woken less than two hours later by the cock crowing. Too early as usual. Gregory Peck was so ancient that his internal clock was crocked. She could kind of empathise with that man in France who shot his neighbour's cock after being driven insane by his constant crowing.

Jimmy had tried to convince them that Gregory's early starts were a sign of his social ranking. He had read about some study in *National Geographic* that suggested the head rooster had priority in breaking the dawn and his lower-ranking compatriots had to wait. He loved sharing these little pearls with the kids.

Jimmy! Jesus Christ. How on God's earth had she fallen asleep with everything that was going on? The false adrenaline-fuelled energy that had been keeping her going must be burning itself out. She had nodded off sitting upright on one of the lumpy armchairs in the cottage sitting room. Her neck was stiff and sore, and there was a disgusting taste in her mouth.

Rob was on the other armchair, and Christina was asleep on the sofa, her knees curled into her chest. Kate remembered tucking a soft fleece over her. The dog was sprawled on the rug in front of the fire. There was no sign of the cat, but she was well able to look after herself. Kate missed the children, wished she could go into their room and watch them sleeping peacefully in their own beds. It felt like she hadn't seen them in days, but it was better that they stay in Jenny's for now.

She hoped Rob and Christina stayed asleep for another while. She needed time to get her head together before they started over again with the same interminable questions about what the hell Jimmy and Ursula had been doing in that shed in the first place. She had warned Rob last night not to mention anything to the gardaí about the row with his mother the previous week. No point in putting any ideas in their heads.

Things had seemed to move very quickly once the bodies were found. You could almost hear the machinery of the garda investigation cranking up a few gears. Detective Inspector McGuire was all business all of a sudden. Issuing orders left, right and centre. This was no longer a potential missing person situation. There was no way Jimmy and Ursula were going to walk back onto the farm hand in hand having been out for a connubial stroll and apologising profusely to everybody for causing such unnecessary alarm. As unlikely as that would have been.

The farmhouse had been cordoned off and Christina, having just been informed that she had basically been orphaned – although formal identification still awaited – was told she would also have to leave her home, which was now a potential crime scene. All 'standard procedure', of course. Rita had been allowed to help her pack a bag of clothes and personal belongings before they were all, including the dog, ushered out of the farmhouse.

The examination of 'the scene' had been suspended until daybreak and all but one of the harsh artificial lights turned off. Rob had been appalled at the idea that his parents were going to be left lying in the tank all night, and he and Kieran had appealed to the detective inspector to let them sit vigil over Jimmy and Ursula.

'I'm very sorry, lads. I understand how difficult this situation is for you but we will have a guard on the door of that shed all night keeping a watch over your parents,' he said.

'We don't want some stranger watching them – that's our job, for Christ's sake. We're their family. As if it wasn't bad enough ... what's happened to them ... this is just cruel. All we want to do is sit with them. Can you not show a bit of respect?' Rob pleaded.

He could have got onto his hands and knees and begged all night and it wouldn't have made any difference. As the detective inspector explained – very patiently, it had to be said – any sudden, unnatural, violent or unexplained death had to be reported to the coroner. It was clear, he said, that Jimmy and Ursula's deaths were sudden, unnatural and currently unexplained, whatever about anything else. The scene had to be preserved to allow the guards to carry out a detailed forensic examination, and post-mortems would be necessary to find out exactly what had happened to Rob's parents. As it was after midnight at this stage, it was too late to get the pathologist on-call out to the scene so the scenes-of-crime team were leaving for the night. As well as the officer guarding the shed, he assured them that the cordon outside the farmhouse and the main gate would be manned all through the night.

Kate was amazed any of them had managed to sleep, wished there was something she could do to hold back the pain that would hit Rob, like an intruder with a club, as soon as he awoke. And Christina too. How she wished with all her might that she could have saved them from this shit-show in which unwittingly they had all been cast in lead roles.

How the hell were they going to explain this to the kids? What had happened to Grandad Jimmy and Ursula. They both adored Jimmy, especially Luke, who had always had a special connection with him, despite his lack of interest in anything farm related. And Lily had been fond of Ursula, even more so after the iPads.

After Rob had woken and emerged from the shower still looking half-dazed, he and Brendan had headed out to start the milking after getting permission to do so from Detective Inspector McGuire. Kate had tried to talk her husband into letting Brendan do it on his own, but Rob was adamant he wanted to go.

'I'll go insane just sitting here looking out the window. I'm better off keeping busy.'

Kate thought she might go insane herself listening to his Aunty Rita give her running commentary of the activity passing by the kitchen window, which looked out onto the yard. She had arrived before nine, along with Julie and Kieran. Nellie had arrived shortly after with Brendan. They were all sitting at Kate's battered kitchen table drinking tea, apart from Rita, who had been glued to the window since the garda cars had started pulling in. She was standing on her tippy-toes bent over the sink to try and get as good a view as possible.

'There's four or five cars up there now, and the van. The lads in the white suits are in and out of the shed like yo-yos again. That poor young lad from yesterday is back with his little notebook, the stout boy, God help him, and he here half the night.'

Kate wished the woman would shut up.

'Would you give it a break, Mammy, for five minutes?' Julie spoke Kate's thoughts. 'Come away from the window and sit down, for Christ's sake.' She nodded towards Christina, sitting like a waxen doll, her hands wrapped around an untouched mug of tea. 'You're really not helping.'

'God, I'm sorry, love.' Rita squashed herself into a chair beside her niece and gave her a hug. 'I don't know what to do with meself – this waiting is desperate altogether.'

Kate wasn't sure exactly what had happened between Jimmy's sister and his wife, but she knew Rita wouldn't be Ursula's chief mourner. She had always been close to her older brother, though, and his children.

'Is there anything I can do, Kate?' she asked now. 'Do you want me to ring anybody? All our lot have been told, apart from the crowd in England. I'll do them later. And I'd say there's not a soul in town that doesn't know at this stage. But what about Ursula's family? Has anybody spoken to Peter yet? And the uncle and aunt in Dublin?'

Kate had been in constant contact with her father and her friend Ruth the day before and had spoken briefly to them both first thing this morning while Rob was in the shower. Her phone was hopping with calls and texts from concerned friends and relatives and some numbers she didn't recognise; she had put it on silent for now. She had also been on to Jenny, who reported that the kids were fine. Kate told her to keep them home from school. She needed time to think about how to break the news without completely freaking them out.

'Rob was on to Ursula's aunt Catherine this morning, and I tried Peter's phone a few times last night, but couldn't get through. We'll keep trying him, though.'

Kate had never met Ursula's brother, whom she had apparently been very close to before he moved away. She had never met any of her family, in fact. Ursula and Peter had been reared by their aunt Catherine and her husband in Dublin after the death of their own parents. Ursula never mentioned them. It was as if she had snipped off her old life like the frayed ends of a ribbon. Kate would love to know what the story was. Was Ursula ashamed of her background for some reason? Of her family? Her mother-in-law had been a shocking snob, very quick to judge a person by where they came from or the cut of their attire.

A firm rap at the back door broke through her musing.

A woman stood outside. Early thirties maybe. Reddish-brown hair tied back in a tight ponytail off a pleasant face. She wore black skinny jeans and a grey puffa jacket.

'Hi, are you Kate?' she asked.

Kate nodded, then wondered if the woman was a reporter who had come across the fields to outfox the gardaí.

'I'm sorry to be meeting you under such difficult circumstances, and I'm so sorry for your loss. I'm Garda Niamh Harris, but please, just call me Niamh. I'm your FLO, your family liaison officer. I'll be responsible for liaising with you and the rest of Ursula and Jimmy's family throughout the investigation into their deaths.'

Rob arrived back as Kate stood at the door with her mouth open. He looked from one to the other as he shucked off his dirty wellies outside.

'Em, this is Rob, my husband.' Kate finally found speech. 'Rob, this is Niamh, she's an, em ...'

'Family liaison officer,' Niamh repeated.

'Oh right – hello, Niamh. Sorry, I'm not sure what ...' Rob lifted his hands in confusion.

'Please don't worry. It's normal in situations like this where there's been a sudden unexpected death to appoint an FLO. It's just easier for families to have one point of contact to keep them in the loop.'

'Can I ask you a question, Niamh?' Rob said. Then, without waiting for an answer, 'Is it normal when there's an accident on a farm to have an *FLO* appointed or to have a person's home cordoned off like a crime scene? Because none of this feels normal to us, none of it.'

'Of course there's nothing normal about this situation, Rob. You and your family have suffered a massive shock, a terrible bereavement, and I can't even begin to imagine how you must be feeling right now. Could I come inside and we could sit down while I fill you in on what's happening this morning?'

Rob shrugged helplessly and gestured with his hands for her to enter the house. After introducing herself to the family assembled in the kitchen, Niamh politely asked if it would be possible for her to have a few words in private with Rob and Kate. Once the others had made themselves scarce, Julie dragging her mother by the arm, Niamh began.

'Here's my mobile number and my direct line at the station.' She handed Rob a business card. 'You can call me any time. If I don't answer right away, I'll get back to you as soon as I can. If there's anything I can do ...'

Rob put the card on the table without looking at it. 'I just want to know when I can see my parents. They've been lying in that ...' He shook his head. 'It's fuckin' inhuman.'

'I understand, Rob. It must be so tough on you all. Detective Inspector McGuire, who is the senior investigating officer on this case, has asked me to fill you in on what's happening this morning. An incident room has been set up in Glenbeg garda station and the pathologist, Dr Deirdre Matheson, is en route from Dublin. She's only about fifteen minutes away now. She'll want to examine the scene before the bodies are removed to the morgue at Galway University Hospital for post-mortem. Normally we would ask a family member to go there to identify the remains, but in a situation like this where they've been submerged overnight in ... Well, it might be too distressing, so we can do the ID through dental records.'

'No, I'll do it,' Rob said. 'I want to do it.'

'I honestly think you'd be better off waiting to see them after the undertaker has finished, when they look more themselves again,' Niamh said gently.

'No, I need to do it myself. Uncle Kieran can come with me.'

Realising he wasn't going to take no for an answer, Niamh explained that, as there were two post-mortems taking place one after the other, it would be late that evening before the pathologist was finished and probably the morning before Rob would be called for the identification.

'That's fine once they're taken out of that filth they're lying in.' Kate realised it clearly hadn't occurred to Rob that his parents' bodies were in for a day of even worse indignity on a pathologist's slab. 'What time can my sister get back into her house?'

'Well, I'm afraid that won't be happening today. Once the undertakers leave, the crime scene team will continue their work in the shed before moving on to the farmhouse. They won't be out of there today and probably not tomorrow either, but I'll let you know as soon as I have any further information for you. Now, there's a fairly big media contingent down at the main gate, but rest assured, we'll have a car down there at all times to stop them from getting through.'

It was after noon by the time the two loaded-up hearses began to inch their way out of the yard, that iconic image the news cameras always zoned in on. They had all watched in silence from the kitchen window as the undertakers drove past on their way up to collect Jimmy and Ursula. Kate felt her breathing grow dangerously shallow as the bodies were carried from the shed in black body bags and lifted one by one into the back of the special removal vehicles fitted with dark privacy glass. Rob stood beside her, stoic as a tree, eyes glued to the bags containing his parents' remains. Christina sank onto one of the scuffed kitchen chairs, while Rita blessed herself and muttered holy words.

Then the remnants of the Kennedy family, along with Nellie and Brendan, made their way out of the cottage, where the gardaí joined them in an impromptu guard of honour either side of the long driveway leading down to the road. Rob stood between Kate and Christina, a strong arm wrapped around each of them.

A large group had gathered outside the main gate: some neighbours banding together in a horrified huddle, others armed with cameras and notebooks, all staring up the road, waiting. An RTÉ van was parked on the verge on the far side of the road, behind a *Connacht Tribune* van, a Galway Bay FM jeep and a number of random cars.

The clouds had come in low, as if the sky was crouching over the land. Then the first hearse came into view as it left the yard, and silence descended over the farmyard. There wasn't a moo or a cluck or a woof to be heard. It was eerie, the absence of sound in a place normally full of noise.

As the cars passed achingly slowly, Kate's breath caught in her chest and Rob's arm tightened around her. She could sense Detective Inspector McGuire watching them from the far side of the driveway, where he stood in line with his colleagues. She kept her eyes firmly fixed on the approaching cars. The first hearse inched past, a gleaming black Merc. She wondered if

Jimmy was in that one. Or Ursula. The blacked-out windows protected their occupants from lurking camera lenses. There were no flowers to soften the bleakness of death. No teardrop sprays. No floral arrangements spelling out Mum and Dad.

As the first hearse rattled over the cattle grid at the bottom of the drive, breaking the silent spell, Samson, roused by the sound, came tearing out the kitchen door like a bat out of hell and chased the second car all the way to the road, barking his furious disapproval until the lights faded into the distance.

10

Kate

When the cars carrying the bodies of Jimmy and Ursula disappeared in the direction of the motorway to Galway, Kate felt the last few drops of adrenaline drain from her body, giving way to a heavy lethargy that lay on top of her like a weighted blanket. She was going to have to get a few hours' sleep before the kids came back. She was about to suggest that Rob and Christina do the same thing when Detective Inspector McGuire caught up with them as they headed back to the cottage.

'We're going to need to get the three of you to answer a few more questions for us if that's OK.'

'I'm not sure what else we can add, really, to what we've already told you,' Rob said wearily.

'Can it not wait a while? We're all exhausted, as you can imagine, we need rest,' Kate said. It was vital that she get her head clear, and at the moment, she was too tired to think straight.

'I'm sure you must be falling on your feet at this stage. We won't keep you long, I promise.' The little bone of empathy he flung them followed by a firm no.

'Right so, I'll make some coffee to try and wake us all up a bit,' Kate said, heading straight for the kitchen. The last thing she wanted was for any of them to appear reluctant to cooperate with the investigation.

Detective Inspector McGuire led Rob into the sitting room, and Christina was brought into the kids' bedroom by one of the other detectives; it wasn't easy to get a bit of privacy in the cottage. The others had all gone home, having been told they could expect calls from the investigation team later. As Kate rinsed out the cafetière at the sink under her kitchen window, she took the opportunity to discreetly spy on proceedings across the yard. She had a clear view of the French doors to the farmhouse kitchen and could see the crime scene people moving around inside. A man, or maybe a large woman – it was hard to tell in those plastic suits – emerged with a handful of transparent plastic bags. It looked like there was paperwork of some kind in one of them. She couldn't make out what was in the others, though. *What the hell could they be taking from the farmhouse?*

The kettle came to the boil and she poured the water in on top of the ground coffee, leaving it to brew while she prepared a tray with mugs, milk and sugar, teaspoons and plates of biscuits. As she pressed the plunger on the cafetière, a dark shadow hit the window and she jumped back in shock, splashing roasting hot coffee all over the counter. 'Jesus Christ almighty!'

Cleo, Ursula's cat, sat on the window sill, staring haughtily in at her like the queen come for tea.

Kate couldn't stand the animal, especially since that time she'd scrawled Lily's little hand when she tried to pet her, but she couldn't let her starve either. The cat food was under garda surveillance up in the farmhouse so she'd have to make do with a couple of slices of ham and whatever other scraps Kate could find in the fridge. She opened the window. The cat just sat there, gazing at her from those extraordinary blue eyes.

'Are you coming in or not?' The cat didn't move. 'Come on, make up your mind. You're letting all the heat out.'

The cat still didn't move.

'Fine, so, you can stay there,' she said, slamming the window shut. She'd leave food and water outside for her later. If she was hungry enough, she'd have come in. *Hunger's a good sauce, Kate – she'll eat when her belly's empty*, as Jimmy used to say when she was battling with Lily over eating her dinner.

As she wiped up the spilt coffee, she felt Cleo's gaze burn through the window. She rapped sharply on the glass. 'Shoo.' The cat sat still as an ornament. 'Feck off!' As Kate stared back at her, the cat's eyes seemed to darken until they were nearly navy. Dark and knowing, accusing.

Jesus, she was losing it. *Hold it together*. She pulled the blind down, blocking out the cat and her freaky stare.

It was Kate's turn in the hot seat. She felt like a contestant on *Mastermind*. All she wanted was to collect her children, bring them home and snuggle up with them. Light a fire and put the TV on. Inject a bit of normality into all this awfulness. She felt jittery despite her weariness, as though she was after one too many espressos. And as if the cat hadn't discombobulated her enough, she now found herself at the end of another set of searing blue eyes. It didn't help that she was sitting on the saggiest end of the sofa while Detective Inspector McGuire was perched higher than her on the armchair.

He had already explained that they needed to account for everybody's movements the day before. That they would be talking to all members of the family and staff, to anybody who had set foot on the property the previous day – the milkman, the postman, any visitors at all. It was important they gather as much information as they could while it was 'fresh in people's minds'. There would have to be an inquest, he explained, to establish the causes of Jimmy's and Ursula's deaths. His words were going in through her ears, but she feared they might lose their way in the fog of fatigue that had descended over her brain.

The detective inspector stared straight at her as if scanning her irises for signs of guilt. She tried to hold his gaze, but her eyes kept darting around: at the manky carpet, into the empty fireplace, at the wall.

She reiterated everything she had told him the day before.

No, she had seen neither her mother-in-law nor her father-in-law the previous day.

It was sometime around 2 p.m. when her husband rang her in a state and they raised the alarm.

As she had already explained to the other detective yesterday, she immediately began looking for Ursula to tell her Jimmy might be in trouble, but was unable to find her or contact her by phone.

No, she had no idea who had been agitating the tank.

Yes, it was unusual at this time of year. There were strict restrictions around spreading, and Jimmy was a great man for sticking to the rules.

There was no reason for Jimmy or Ursula to go near the tank. Ursula rarely went near the farm – she had nothing to do with that side of the business, apart from managing the accounts.

Yes, he had dementia. She knew Rob was saying he wasn't that bad, but to be honest, she thought Rob and Christina might have been in a bit of denial about how bad Jimmy was. He was going downhill fast. The poor man couldn't even remember how to make a cup of tea any more.

Could he have got mixed up about the dates for spreading? Yes, it was a possibility, of course. He might have just woken up yesterday and got it into his head to go mixing slurry. It was an awful disease, the way it crept up on people and stole who they were.

She and Rob were in bed by about half ten on Monday night; she read for a while, and they were both asleep by eleven.

As far as she knew, the farm and business were to be left to Rob and herself, and the farmhouse and other properties to be left to Christina, but in fairness, Jimmy and Ursula were barely cold. The last thing on their minds was who was going to inherit what.

Feeling a little more alive after a couple of hours of deep sleep and a long, hot shower, Kate was getting dressed in her bedroom and wondering where they were going to put Christina for the night once the kids came home, when she heard raised voices and the dog barking from the front of the house. It was close to five now and the sky had turned purple; more rain on the way.

'You've got to be kidding me.' Rob was staring at Niamh in outraged disbelief. They were standing in the tiny hall, Rita behind them, holding onto Samson's collar as he growled menacingly.

'What's going on?' Kate asked. 'Rita, can you put the dog in the sitting room?' *And yourself while you're at it.*

'If they thought we had something to do with this, why did they let us stay here in the first place?' Rob demanded.

Kate felt sick. *No, please no. This can't be happening!*

'What's going on, Rob?' she repeated.

He threw his hands up. 'I don't fucking know, Kate. It's like a nightmare that keeps getting worse. They want us out of the cottage now. To leave our home and everything we own behind us, including our phones, so they can search them just in case one of us might have murdered my mother and father.'

'What? But why ...?' Kate looked at Niamh in confusion. 'I don't understand. Why now when we were allowed stay here last night?' What the hell was going on?

'Look, I know you're all upset, of course you are. Could we talk about this inside?'

Rob grudgingly stood back to let the guard in for the second time that day. Samson was hurling himself against the sitting-room door and barking frantically so Kate led Niamh into the kitchen. She didn't invite her to sit this time. Rob stood with his arms folded and a sour scowl on his face. Kate leaned against a cupboard for support. The volume of barking increased for a few seconds as Rita opened and closed the sitting-room door before joining them in the kitchen.

'As I was telling Rob, we have to keep an open mind in these kinds of scenarios, and this afternoon it was brought to the attention of the investigation team that there has been a bit of tension on the farm recently. In light of this new information, the cottage will have to be sealed off for examination, as well as the farmhouse, and the entire site will have to be searched,' Niamh explained.

Brought to the attention?

Tension? How the hell?

'So we're *suspects* now, are we? Do you seriously think one of us pushed my parents into the slurry pit? This is madness. I've never in my life heard the like of it. Putting a family out of their home because of *a bit of tension*. Christ almighty!' Rob shook his head in bewilderment.

The colour had drained from Rita's face, and for once, she was dumbstruck.

'But where are we supposed to go?' Kate asked. 'The kids. What about the kids? They're being dropped back here in about half an hour – they don't even know about Jimmy and Ursula yet.'

'I'm sorry,' Niamh said, making an apologetic grimace. 'I can assure you the scenes-of-crime lads will be in and out as fast as they can. They'll hopefully be finished in the farmhouse by tomorrow or the next day. In the meantime, we'd be more than happy to put you up in a hotel for the next couple of nights, unless there's somewhere else you'd prefer to stay yourselves. Is there any way the childminder could hold onto the kids for the night? It might be easier for you all.'

Yes, of course. She would ring Jenny and ask her to keep the kids for another night. She had already offered, but Kate had wanted them home.

'You're all very welcome to come and stay with us,' Rita

said. 'The kids too, of course. We've plenty of space.' Rita and her husband, Jarlath, had been given an adjoining site on the family land on which they built their bungalow, a modest affair compared to her older brother's residence, but a warm, noisy home. Filled with laughter and clutter.

It was very kind of her to offer, but Kate couldn't think of anything worse right now. She wouldn't have a second to think in Rita's house. There was so much to do. Rob had arranged for Brendan to come in to look after the animals while he was away, and Nellie had offered to ring people and cancel all bookings for the coming week.

'Thanks, Rita, you're very good, but it might make sense for us to stay with my father in Galway tonight.' She was thinking out loud. 'We have to go up to the morgue in the morning anyway, and we'll probably leave Lily and Luke with Jenny.' She was insisting on going with Rob to identify his parents instead of his uncle: he would need her by his side. She had tried to gently dissuade him from putting himself through this, to allow them to be identified through their dental records, but he was determined to do it himself.

'You'll be lost without your phones, though.' Rita addressed the FLO. 'How are they supposed to manage without their phones? There'll be people trying to get in touch with them and they'll want to check up on the kids.'

'I understand this is a major inconvenience,' Niamh said. 'We're all so attached to our phones – but they have to be taken away for X-raying. I promise I'll do my utmost to get them and your other electronic devices back to you as soon as possible.'

11

Kate

As Kate and Rob drove towards Galway, she tried to remember the last time they had been away together for a night. It had been Fitzie's wedding, one of Rob's friends, the last straggler in the group. The wedding had been in Killarney so it had been a long drive home the next day. Rob had suggested staying a second night to make it worth their while, but she hadn't wanted to leave the kids with Jenny all weekend. She felt guilty enough leaving them during the week.

It had pissed Kate off so much that Ursula had never, not once, offered to have the kids stay overnight, despite all her talk about how much she adored them. On the rare occasion that she had ever taken them overnight, or even minded them for a few hours, Rob had had to ask her, and Kate was too stubborn to ask more often.

She looked over at Rob. She had offered to drive, to let him get some sleep, but he had insisted. He had been so quiet the entire journey up; Kate could only imagine what was going through his mind. What had happened to his parents was just too big and too awful for words.

They had been allowed to pack overnight bags with clothes and toiletries and some extra bits and pieces for the kids, which they had dropped off on the way. Lily and Luke, thrilled to have another day off school, had happily waved them off. Kate dreaded the thought of the difficult conversation they were going to have to have with them; she couldn't give that headspace right now.

Niamh had offered to drive them to Galway right after she informed them that their cars were also being seized for examination. It was a firm thanks, but no thanks. Instead, Rita drove them to her house, where Christina and the dog were to stay for the night, and gave them the keys to Jarlath's ancient Corolla, which they were now travelling in. The radio was broken and their choice of listening material was Daniel O'Donnell or Big Tom, so they sat in silence. She had flung the empty Lucozade bottles and Supermac's wrappers from the footwell on the passenger side into the back. She felt intensely fidgety without her phone, kept reaching for it out of habit. She'd have to borrow her father's phone to say goodnight to the kids. She noticed Rob patting down his pockets and rooting around aimlessly too.

'You'd be lost without it, wouldn't you?' she said.

'You would.'

Her father had the heat on and the fire lit when they arrived at his snug mid-terrace house in the Claddagh. The place was baking. As if he was trying to heat the shock out of them. The house in the heart of the city, with its spectacular view over the River Corrib and across to Long Walk, had been where he was reared. Her father had bought his sister out after Kate left home, when he decided to downsize and move in from the suburbs.

She had such wonderful memories of this little house. It made her sad to think her children would never experience the magic of a loving relationship with Jimmy and Ursula that she had enjoyed with her grandparents. She couldn't remember much about her mother's parents, but she had been very close to her paternal grandparents; simple, good people.

She had spent many nights under this roof curled up beside Granny McCarthy in her bumpy bed after being allowed to stay up late watching TV. Granny had a special press in the front room from which she seemed to conjure all kinds of goodies: Iced Caramels, After Eights, even unopened boxes of Dairy Milk that Kate was allowed to take her pick from. All gifts to Granny in return for her many little acts of kindness.

Kate had laughed the first time she heard Rob call his mother 'Mother', but when she met Ursula she saw instantly that she was most definitely a Mother. Not Mum or Mam, and especially not Mammy. She wasn't a Granny either, apparently. Or a Nana.

On hearing that she was to become a grandmother, Ursula had announced that while she was, of course, thrilled at the good news, she didn't want to be addressed by anything other than her given name by her grandchildren.

As she whisked eggs in her father's kitchen and popped bread into the toaster, Kate tried to touch base with her own scrambled brain. She realised she was probably still in shock, her brain unable to process the fact that it had actually happened. Her heart broke for Rob and Christina, for the pain they were suffering, but while the thought of never seeing Jimmy again was incomprehensible, her feelings about Ursula were far more complicated.

She wasn't the slightest bit hungry, but they had to eat and eggs were light. They had another long day ahead of them tomorrow. She brought the food into the sitting room for them to eat on their laps in front of the TV.

Being in this house was like stepping back across two generations in time. Her granny's knick-knacks jostled for space in the cabinet and on the mantelpiece with her mother's collection of beloved figurines. They could all do with a good dusting. She was glad they were staying here tonight and not in some anonymous hotel room. Driving away from Glenbeg today, away from her children and their home and their normal life, she had felt as if her mooring rope had been cut and she was drifting in unknown waters. Being here was like being tied up to a buoy for the night. The hands of her mother's carriage clock still turned on the mantelpiece, and her family of Belleek china pigs beamed at her from the mahogany cabinet. She loved those pigs – they were always happy.

Rob and her father seemed to be engrossed in some action

movie on TV. She knew they were probably engrossed in their own thoughts too, just watching for the sake of having something to stare at besides the walls and each other. She closed her eyes and rested her head against the back of the sofa.

Being here always brought memories of her own early childhood flooding back. Memories of the lovely mother she had been so blessed with. The last morning she had with that version of her mother was still so clear. She was seven years old and was looking forward to making her communion that spring. Her mother was making her dress for her, a maxi with lace trim at the neck and bodice. She had already cut out the pieces and was planning to start sewing it up after the new baby came.

Mammy had kissed and cuddled her, and Kate had given the huge bump that swelled from beneath her flowing dress one last kiss.

'Bye, my little Katie-cat, be a good girl now,' Mammy had called back as she left the house.

Her father's car had pulled out onto the road, her mother blowing kisses from the window, smiling. As Kate stood at the front door hand in hand with Aunty Caroline, who had come to mind her while her mother was in hospital, she felt a huge wave of sadness well up inside her. As if she had known somehow that she would never see that mammy again.

Kate rang Jenny from her father's phone to say goodnight to the kids. The slight quaver in Luke's voice that he tried to disguise as a cough tugged at her heartstrings far harder than Lily's dramatic sobs. The novelty of staying over in their childminder's was wearing off, as she had known it would. She promised she would collect them when she got back tomorrow, although she had no idea where she would be bringing them.

She gave Ruth a quick call after that, conscious that her friend would be worried sick about her. Close pals since they met while studying law at University College Galway, it was through Ruth, who was from Glenbeg, that Kate had met Rob. She didn't get to see much of Ruth these days, between work and family commitments, but they were always on the phone to each other.

She trusted Ruth as much as she trusted Rob and her father, maybe even more. There was very little her friend didn't know about her. She knew about her mother and her mother-in-law, about her tight financial situation (she had been apoplectic about that) and her marriage problems.

'I can't believe they made you all leave your home, Kate – what are they playing at?' Ruth asked now. 'They hardly think ye had anything to do with Jimmy and Ursula's deaths?'

'I honestly don't know. They keep telling us this is all normal in this kind of situation, but it's hard not to feel like a suspect when your house has been cordoned off as a crime scene.'

'Who the hell told them about the row on the farm, do you think? I didn't say a word to anybody anyway, you know that.'

'God, of course I do, Ruth.' Kate had been so upset last week after her argument with Rob and then his with Ursula that she had called her friend after work the next day for a shoulder-crying session. She had needed somebody to tell her that she had done the right thing in bringing the situation to a head. 'I know you wouldn't say a word. The only thing I can think of is that maybe Christina said something to Julie, who told—'

'Rita! Fuck, it'll be all over east Galway so if that's the case. That woman has a mouth the size of the Shannon.'

'I know. Christ.' Kate groaned.

'Well, look, they're probably just grasping at straws. Accidents happen on farms every day of the week – they're dangerous bloody places. I should know, having grown up on one. Feck it, if I told you half the stuff we used to get up to … Dad was on earlier, by the way, wondering how you're all doing. He reckons Jimmy got confused with the timing of the slurry – the restrictions are being lifted next week, an easy mistake to make. Maybe one of them fell in and the other one tried to help, like that poor family in the North.'

'Yeah, that's what we think ourselves. Hopefully the results of the post-mortem might clear things up a bit and we can bring them home and organise the funeral.'

Kate felt like she was on the strangest sleepover ever, but she had never been so glad to sink into a mattress and pull a quilt over her. She was just drifting off to sleep when she felt the mattress sink beside her.

'Rob?' She reached out for him.

'There's only two of us left now. Out of five of us. I feel so fucking guilty.' He spoke so quietly she could barely hear him.

'Why, love? Sure, none of this is your fault.'

He had got out of bed, was sitting on the side with his back to her. 'I could have stopped it,' he whispered.

A swell of uneasiness rose inside her.

She sat up in the bed. What the fuck was he talking about?

'I never told you ...' He stopped.

Every nerve in her body was buzzing.

'He needed me and I wasn't there for him.'

What the hell was he on about?

'Mark. I let him down so badly.'

Mark, not Jimmy. She started to breathe again, scooched over to the other side of the bed beside him, pulled her legs onto the floor. Slid an arm around him.

'You were only young yourself, love. You can't blame yourself for what Mark did. He was obviously battling demons that nobody knew about, not even your parents.'

'That's the thing, you see. He tried to tell me. He tried to tell me and I didn't listen.'

'What do you mean? I thought he never talked to any of you about it.' Kate had given up trying to get Rob to open up to her about Mark; it was a closed subject as far as her husband was concerned. It was Christina who had told her how Mark had gone off the rails in the year or so before he put the rope around his neck.

'He didn't, because he never got the chance,' he said. 'That last weekend I was home, the weekend before he ... He knocked on my bedroom door. I was studying for my end-of-year exams, stressed out because I'd left it so late to start. I was pissed off with him too, for all the hassle he was causing at home. The drinking ... the drugs ... bringing the guards to the door while Mother was working every hour to try and get the business off the ground.' He took a deep swallow. 'He stuck his head around the door, asked me if he could talk to me for a minute. I said I didn't have a minute, was up the walls trying to study. I didn't even turn round from my desk to look at him. I never saw him after that – he was out working when I left to get the bus back to college the next morning.'

'Oh, Rob ...' *What an awful thing to have to carry around all these years, the thought that maybe if he had listened Mark could still be here today. And they could be living their own lives, instead of his.*

'If I had only listened to him, he might have told me what was going on with him. Why he just changed almost overnight. We were so close as kids, two peas in a pod. He used to be so chilled out, cool as a breeze, always in good form. Sure, you saw it yourself when you met him. But then he changed. Became this angry, aggressive person. Started hanging around with scumbags. And the way he spoke to Mother ...' He sighed. 'I told him to go away, and he did. And not a day has gone by since that I haven't blamed myself.'

'Oh, Rob, love, you weren't to know what was going to happen. Sure, siblings are horrible to each other all the time, a lot worse than that even.' She was aware her words were empty even as she spoke them; she would have been crippled with guilt too if she was in his shoes. Anybody would.

She felt bad for all the times she had cursed Mark in her own head for doing what he had done; for changing the course of her and Rob's lives by the choice he took to take his own. It would have been easier if he had left a note, some kind of explanation for what he had done, instead of leaving his tormented family forever trying to figure out why and whether it could have been prevented.

12

Christina

Christina felt wretched. What did she have to go and open her big mouth for? She had been rattled after the row in the house last week, and Julie had picked up on it straight away when she called the next day. Christina had never been able to hide her feelings; when she was upset, she lost control of her voice and it went all high pitched and quivery. Once she felt that horrible burning sensation at the back of her nostrils, no amount of blinking could dam the hot salty flood. Lily was the same, victim of an overactive tear fountain.

Her niece had a book all about the body and how it worked. She was fascinated with that kind of stuff. It was she who had explained all about tears to Christina. How your eye has special glands that make tears all day but normally they only produce a tiny amount, less than half a teaspoon. And how when your brain receives the signal that you're sad, it switches on the largest tear gland, which can produce a lot of tears at once, just like a little fountain. And how when this happens, the eye can produce more than half a cup of tears in a minute, which is, of course, way too much for the eye to hold, so they start running down your nose first and falling out of your eyes. Christina and Lily both agreed they could produce way more than half a cup of tears once they started.

She hadn't told Julie everything, of course not. Just that there had been a bit of a blow-up between Rob and Mother. And if Julie had confided in her mother, as Christina suspected, she wouldn't have done it out of any kind of badness, only concern for her cousin. There wasn't an ounce of badness in Aunty Rita either, but she seemed to have no control over that blabbermouth of hers. Christina didn't blame Julie or Aunty Rita: she blamed herself. It was her fault Rob and Kate had been forced to leave their home and the guards were so suspicious about the cause of her parents' deaths.

Deaths. It still hadn't hit her that her parents were dead. That they wouldn't be coming back. Ever. It felt like they had gone away for a few days, off to Adare Manor for a spa break or up to the Shelbourne in Dublin for a shopping weekend. One of those weekends where Ursula would indulge herself in luxury facials and relaxation treatments or 'shop till she dropped' in her favourite designer boutiques, while Jimmy sat at the bar sipping slow pints and counting down the seconds until he was back on the farm.

The realisation that she would never see him again, never see her mother again, was simmering away inside her, but she pushed it down. It was too big, too much. It would surely drown her if she let it up.

She had taken a Xanax to help her get to sleep the night before. She had considered taking another one this morning, but figured she was still numb enough from shock. She kept a pack in her bathroom cabinet, but tried to keep them for emergencies. Sedating her feelings had the unfortunate side effect of slowing down her body too, everything from her eyelids to her bowel becoming heavy and sluggish. And as she knew only too well from experience, all those feelings kept on ice by the chemicals would be waiting to hit her like an Arctic deluge as soon as she stopped taking the tablets.

The guards had already asked them all so many questions. The same ones over and over in different words. She had already told them everything – as much as she was prepared to tell them, anyway.

She was lying in bed in Julie's old room now with a book that she wasn't reading, Samson in a foetal curl at her side. She had pleaded tiredness, but had really just needed to escape the hubbub downstairs where Julie and her parents were welcoming a seemingly endless stream of people calling to pay their condolences. They obviously couldn't call to the farm, and while Christina understood how important it was for their neighbours and friends to try and offer comfort through their presence and home-cooked dishes, eating and talking to people about 'how desperate sad it was' and how sorry they were was the last thing she felt like doing. Nellie was keeping things going in Rita's kitchen, churning out pots of tea and sandwiches and slices of tart while Rita did what she did best: talked. Uncle Kieran was there too; he had closed the pub again tonight.

Snippets of conversation drifted down the hall.

'Julie, could you make me up a plate of ham sandwiches? On white. Just butter and ham for the plain eaters. Thanks, you're a star.' Nellie.

'Aren't some people awful fussy all the same? Sure, my Jarlath has me feckin' heart broke – he won't eat rice or pasta, only spuds, spuds, spuds ...' Rita.

'I was only talking to Ursula on Sunday. I met her for coffee in the clubhouse. We were due to go out and play nine holes, but it was rained off. She was in great form.' She didn't recognise that voice.

'Does anybody need a top-up? I've a fresh pot here.' Nellie.

Christina felt a gush of love for her former childminder. She had never seen the woman ruffled: she was so steady. A steaming mug of hot chocolate in human form. She had first arrived at the farm when Mark was a baby. Nellie had practically reared the three of them after that, had been utterly devastated when Mark died. Grieved him as if he were her own.

It was Nellie who brought Christina to her first day of school, who insisted on staying in the classroom until her sobs had eased off and she was finally able to catch her breath, in defiance of the unimpressed junior infants teacher. Christina could remember it as if it were yesterday. A much younger Nellie, her hair in a tight perm, kneeling on the ground beside the little wooden chair, holding both her hands and whispering in her ear that she would sit outside in her car until school finished. It had been enough to ease Christina's terror, the thought that Nellie was close. She had asked her years later if she really had waited outside, assuming that she had probably just gone about her morning and come back at pick-up time, but Nellie told her she had sat there with a flask of tea and a stack of old *Woman's Way* magazines for the first few days. Just in case.

Samson let out a long shuddering sigh. She rubbed his head. 'It's OK, Sammy, it's OK.'

It wasn't, though. The light he had shadowed his whole life had disappeared. He had never spent a night off the farm. The poor dog had been sleeping almost constantly since Tuesday and had lost all interest in food. When he was awake, he moped around the place, his mournful brown eyes filled with confusion.

Samson curled closer into her, his head on her thigh. He shouldn't be on the bed, it was a bad habit to get him into, but she hadn't the heart to move him, and Aunty Rita was pretty relaxed about things like that. Sam was suffering too. She had lost a mother and a father. He had lost his person, his everything.

Her father had said nothing for a long time after she told him.

Just sat there. Staring at nothing. Visibly trying to compute what he had just heard. She had wondered was he even capable of taking it in, of understanding what it meant.

When he spoke again, he seemed calm. No trace of the confusion or vagueness that came down over him like mist at times. He was the old Daddy. Solid and sound. A rock of reassurance.

'You get yourself off to bed now, Chrissie, pet. You won't

be able to get up in the morning. You're not to worry yourself about this any more now – I'll sort everything out.'

'Thanks, Daddy.'

'Goodnight, pretty face. I'll be up after you in a short while.'

'Night, Daddy.'

She leaned over to give him a hug, and he grabbed her tight and held on. It startled her slightly – it wasn't like him. Then he let her go.

As she left the room, he called after her. 'Chrissie. You did the right thing in telling me, pet.'

Now she wondered whether it had been the right thing at all.

13

Ursula

From a young age, Ursula had known she had to get out of St Joseph's Park. She watched the older girls, all glammed up in their thigh-high miniskirts and white go-go boots. Cheap Carnaby Street knock-offs. Lashings of mascara and pale-pink lips. Pouffed-up bouffants and beehives. The odd one brave enough to sport a Twiggy pixie crop.

She took it all in. The fluttering lashes and too loud giddy laughter. The games they played. The way the boys play-fought and jeered loudly at each other and pretended to ignore the girls and the way the girls giggled and whispered among themselves and pretended to ignore the boys while, all the time, they were stealing sneaky glances at each other and being drawn together by the magnetic field of teenage hormones.

She watched too as the group gradually began to split up, the boys and girls pairing off and disappearing in twos down the fields or down the back of one of the boarded-up houses. And she watched how some of the girls changed over time, how they wore longer tops to cover the swell of their bellies. She watched them push screaming babies in prams, dragging snotty-nosed toddlers beside them and wondered where the boys had gone. She watched the light in their eyes dim and fade. Not for her, no not for her.

Ursula's mother, Vivien (named, perhaps fittingly, after her own mother's actress idol, who also had a penchant for nervous breakdowns), had tried her best. She had taught her kids how to pronounce their words properly and use their manners, even while knowing they would be taunted for doing so by the other kids on the estate. She kept them inside as much as possible and away from the ruffians who roamed wild while their parents drank and dozed. She always kept them clean and well-presented despite the severe limitations of her household budget. This made them no friends among their neighbours; they were regarded as odd and *having notions about themselves*, which never went down well in a place like St Joseph's Park, especially in the terraces.

She managed to enrol Ursula and Peter in her old primary school in a slightly more salubrious part of Dublin's northside, a fifteen-minute walk to the bus stop in all weathers, followed by a twenty-minute bus journey every morning and afternoon. She knew her children were looked down on at Scoil Fhursa for living where they did, but in her eyes it was still better than putting them into the local community school where the teachers spent more of their time trying to tame their half-feral pupils than engaged in anything resembling formal education. Ursula knew she didn't fit in there any more than she fit in down the terraces.

Her mother took on a cleaning job close to the school and, through word of mouth, got another job and then another until pretty soon she was working every morning while the kids were in school. She saved every spare penny to buy fabric in town and made pretty dresses for herself and Ursula, using the remnants to fashion miniature replicas of the same garments for Ursula's dolls, as well as curtains and cushion covers, the dainty floral patterns and pretty pastels a rare splash of beauty amid the ugliness around them.

On the days that it all got too much for her, of which there were many, Vivien took to her bed as soon as the schoolwork was done and the children fed. She drew the curtains, climbed onto the sagging mattress propped up with concrete blocks, pulled the blankets over her head and fell into a deep, exhausted sleep. She would rise again after a few hours to make supper for Ursula and Peter and put them to bed, before getting back into bed herself to read one of her library books until she slipped again into the asylum of sleep.

Vivien's beauty was so faded by then it was barely visible to the human eye; Ursula wouldn't have recognised her as the radiant young bride in the sole wedding photo that hung in the hall. Not much more than a child, painfully naive and optimistic. Not built for the hard road ahead.

Ursula often wondered why her mother had stayed with her father. Was it because deep down she was still in love with the handsome young musician she had fallen for so many years before, or was it that she simply didn't have the strength to try to go it alone with two kids in tow? Things were different back then; women like Vivien had no option but to serve out the sentence they had submitted to when they said 'I do'. Ursula's father had proved himself an utterly useless husband and provider. There was no doubt he loved his wife and children dearly – he told them often enough in his maudlin way – but his words and songs and tears were not enough. He did nothing to prove his love; he had given up on them and himself at some point along the way.

Her mother was always sad around Christmas. Ursula couldn't understand why. She loved that time of year with all the twinkling lights and carol singing in school and the Christmas stockings her mother had handmade for herself and Peter hanging either side of the mantelpiece. She had overheard her crying one night when she snuck out of bed and was listening from the stairs.

'It's not fair on them, Sean.' She could hear her mother's gentle sobbing over the rustle of paper. 'It breaks my heart having to tell them they can't ask Santa for what they want when the other kids in school will be going in bragging about all the stuff they got. They'll think it's their fault, that they deserve to be on the naughty list, when they're so good, the two of them.'

'I know, Vivien, love, I know. The New Year will be different. Vinnie down the Oak has a cousin who might be able to get me work on a site, a new housing estate. They'll be able to ask Santa for what they want next Christmas.'

Her mother kept sobbing. That was when Ursula realised

that Santa wasn't real. And it made her feel a little bit better about the fact that she only got a satsuma and a skipping rope in her stocking the year before, and some new dresses for her doll that her mother had obviously made. It wasn't that Santa didn't think she and Peter deserved nicer presents, it was that he didn't exist at all.

It was many years later, when she had her own children and understood for the first time how utterly dependent they were on her, that Ursula realised just how much of a sacrifice their mother had made for her and Peter. She had known she was different to the other girls in her class, that there was a shame attached to the place she came from that latched itself to her very being. How could she not when Annette Quinn and her little band of bitches held their noses every time she passed. She often came in after lunch to find their little gifts on her desk: stinking banana peels, browning apple butts and soggy crusts that she had to clean up before the teacher saw. One day they left a broken mop head on her chair, its ragged dreadlocks dripping into a filthy puddle on the floor and across the classroom as she carried it to the bin. Mrs Aherne had shouted at her to 'clean up that mess at once' as Annette Quinn sniggered behind her hand across the table.

She didn't fully understand how huge a chasm there was between the terraces and the world outside, however, until the morning on a day off school when she accompanied her mother to one of the houses she cleaned. Until the moment she stepped over the threshold of that house, Ursula had had no idea that such luxury existed in real life. The Supreme Court judge and his wife who owned Hazeldene, a leafy period Georgian property, were out, so she followed her mother from room to room silently breathing it in. The air was perfumed with furniture polish and real flowers and something else crisp and clean and fruity that she couldn't put her finger on. Wealth, maybe. She wondered if rich people had their own special smell.

Ursula ran her hand along the dark rosewood furniture that her mother polished to a high shine and sank her stockinged feet (her mother had made her leave her shoes inside the front door) into the deep, soft carpet that her mother dragged a fancy vacuum cleaner across, sucking up every little speck of dirt. She wandered around the master bedroom with its four-poster bed and heavy velvet curtains, astounded that such opulence existed outside the cinema screen.

She followed her mother into the bathroom with its claw-footed bath, gleaming ceramic sinks – two of them, imagine – and black and white chequerboard tiles. As she peered into the spotless mirror above the wide washstand, she caught sight of her mother behind her, on her knees in front of the toilet, scrubbing ferociously. A sadness such as Ursula had never felt before came down over her. Her kind, lovely mother deserved to live in a house like this one surrounded by beautiful things, but instead she was forced to scrub poo from the toilets of rich people and live in what Ursula now saw very plainly was a hopeless dump.

It was no wonder her mother carried such a heaviness around with her. Oh, she tried her best to conceal it under her bright smiles, but there was no hiding the red eyes sunken into her head after she woke from one of her long, exhausted sleeps in the evening, or the purplish half-circles underneath. Ursula was ten years old when she came to the realisation that life was not fair, not fair at all, and she began to dream about rescuing her mother from her life of drudgery and dropping her into a new life in a fairy-tale home like Hazeldene.

Her dream wasn't to be, sadly, as Vivien hadn't been built for a life of such hardship, had neither the mental nor physical disposition to sustain it long-term. The long hours of scrubbing toilets, pulling scummy hair from plug holes, scouring greasy ovens and pressing hot irons back and forth, back and forth and back and forth over other people's shirts and sheets and undergarments had taken their toll.

As a child, Ursula had never stopped to wonder why her daddy didn't go out to work to support his family, even as her mother became more stooped and gaunt and weary. Few of the other daddies around them in the terraces worked either. Some whiled their days away tinkering with broken-down cars or go-carts for the kids, but there were plenty more like her daddy who watched TV and drank bottles of beer all day. It was the way it was at that time in that place. And she had loved her daddy with his big sad eyes and his warm hugs and the lovely songs he wrote for her. Not as much as she had loved her mother, though.

Vivien was gone before Ursula had even graduated childhood. Cancer of the womb. She was diagnosed on an unseasonably warm October day and buried less than four months later on a bitterly cold February morning. Thirty-two years of age. Ursula's father fell apart totally after that, and if Aunt Catherine hadn't stepped in, herself and Peter would have ended up in a children's home.

14

Two days after the event – Thursday, 11 January
Kate

'I'm going to make a coffee, would you like something, love?'
The unexpected normality of the kitchenette with its kettle and mini-fridge was a rope for Kate to reach for in the midst of such an abnormal situation.

The place wasn't at all what she had been expecting. It was more like a consultant's private rooms than a morgue.

Niamh had collected them from her father's house in an unmarked car. She had driven around the back of the University Hospital Galway complex, a sprawling mismatch of modern glass-fronted buildings, depressing 1950s blocks and ugly prefabs, following the signs for the Mortuary Department. There were cars parked all over the place, and Kate was glad they had taken up the guard's offer of a lift. The city was covered with a lid of heavy grey cloud as far as the eye could see and it was lashing down rain, as if the weather had matched itself to the task that awaited them.

The FLO had ushered them inside a flat-roofed, single-storey building where she introduced them to a short stocky man called Aidan with a round, friendly face – not at all how Kate would have pictured a mortuary assistant, or to give him his proper title, an anatomical pathology technician – before she excused herself to make a quick call. He shook their hands and expressed his sympathy for their loss, before leading them along a corridor into an ante room in the newer part of the building that he called the 'family room'.

It couldn't have been any further from the image Kate's mind had conjured up of a cold, clinical theatre of strange smells and stainless steel, dead toes bearing name tags poking from white sheets. Instead they were brought into a light-filled space furnished with comfy sofas and flocked wallpaper. A stunning mural of the sun going down on Galway Bay spread across the back wall. Narrow floor-to-ceiling windows opened out onto a small paved area with a bench carved from bog oak and a neat patch of landscaping.

'There's tea-bags and coffee and stuff there, just help yourselves,' Aidan said, waving towards a small alcove in the corner of the room. 'The cups are in the press above the sink and there's milk in the fridge. There's a toilet just down the corridor on your right.'

He noticed Kate and Rob both glancing at the heavy walnut doors at the far end of the room and explained that Rob's 'mam and dad' would be brought into the viewing room at the far side of the sliding door for the identification. Then he left them to settle themselves after their journey, saying he'd be back in about twenty minutes.

Kate switched the kettle on after he left and poured a sachet of coffee into a cup to distract herself from thinking about what awaited them behind that door.

'Did you manage to get any sleep at all last night?' She jumped, spilling sugar all over the counter. Christ, her nerves were in tatters. She hadn't heard Niamh coming into the kitchenette behind her.

'God, sorry. Here, let me get that.' The garda grabbed some napkins and efficiently swept the sugar into her cupped hand before throwing it into the bin.

'It was my own fault. I'm all over the place. We got a few hours on and off, it's all just been so ...'

'I know, it's a very tough situation. Very hard on you both,' Niamh said, her green eyes diffusing warmth. She nodded towards Rob, perched on the edge of the sofa, staring at the ground. 'How's he holding up?'

'I don't know, to be honest. I think he's still in shock, we both are, and the lack of sleep on top of everything isn't helping, being out of our own beds. I keep wondering when I'm going to wake up ...'

'I can only imagine, Kate. This,' she gestured towards the sliding door, 'isn't something any of us ever imagine we'll have to go through. I just want you both to know that I'm here if there's anything at all I can do to make things easier for you. Why don't you sit down there and I'll make the coffee?'

As Kate sank onto the sofa beside Rob, a weariness draped itself over her, like the bone-deep exhaustion of early pregnancy. She rested her head against the back of the seat and closed her eyes. Teaspoons clinked against ceramic and outside an ambulance went whoop-whooping past, some other poor family in trouble. A light sleeper, she could never drift off just anywhere like Rob; she usually had to be in her own bed to relax enough to fall asleep. But the sofa was so comfortable and her eyes so heavy ...

She came to with a jolt. Niamh was setting a plate of individually wrapped biscuits on the table in front of her, between the coffee cups.

'Oh God, I'm so sorry, I must have nodded off.' What must Niamh think of her? Falling asleep while waiting to identify the bodies of her husband's parents. Rob put a comforting hand on her leg, unable to summon the energy for speech.

'Not at all – sure, you must be exhausted, the two of you. It's only instant but it might give you a bit of a boost all the same.'

They sat in silence for a while, lost in their own thoughts with no phones to distract them, until the door opened and Aidan came back into the room.

'We're ready for you now, if you're OK to get started,' he said, looking from Rob to Kate.

Rob got to his feet. 'Yes, we're ready,' he said.

'I'm afraid you won't be able to touch them today,' Aidan said, stretching his lips into a sympathetic line, 'not until they've been released back to you. And bear in mind that, although your parents have been washed, they'll look ... em ... more like themselves once the undertaker has finished.'

Kate took a deep breath in as the doors slid back into the wall and prayed her knees would hold her up. She hadn't allowed her mind to go here, to think about this moment. She felt overheated and a bit weak; she forced another deep breath down. Rob needed her now: she had to stay strong. It was going to be hard enough on him, having to see his parents like this, without the added agony of having to fight the natural instinct to touch them.

Aidan led them into the dimly lit room, Niamh bringing up the rear. The smell hit her straight away, cutting through the clean cotton fragrance of the flickering scented candles. A sickly sweet blend of chemicals, shampoo and death. And it may have been her imagination, but she was sure she could get a faint reek of slurry. A puddle of warm saliva gathered on the floor of her mouth.

They were standing in what could have been a bedroom in a private nursing home, albeit a very chilly one. Two single beds stood side by side, two mounds covered with crisp white sheets and blankets in an ecclesiastical purple.

Aidan moved to the bed on the right first, closest to the door.

'Ready?' he asked Rob again. Rob dipped his head. Kate reached her arm around his back and held him tight.

Aidan lifted the sheet. She felt Rob inhale deeply. It was Jimmy, but not Jimmy. More like a slightly bloated relative who bore a vague resemblance to her father-in-law. Kate felt a lightning strike of horror zip through her spinal cord. This was really happening. Up until now, until the moment she saw the shell that had housed Jimmy lying pale and stiff and stone dead like a wax effigy of himself, she had been able to keep reality at bay. His eyes were sunken into his head, the undertaker not yet having had the chance to perform his blend of magic on the corpse, to plump out his cheeks and his eyelids, to coax the curl of a smile at the corners of his lips, hinting at a peaceful exit from this world. They must have removed his false teeth, the ones Ursula had insisted he replace with implants. He had been putting it off for years, pleading a dentist phobia, but she had finally worn him down and he was due to have his first implants fitted next month. He didn't have to worry about that any more anyway.

Ah, Jimmy, poor lovely Jimmy who had never been anything but kind to her and Rob and the kids. To everybody. A good man, a generous soul. His only failing, and a bloody big one, was his inexplicable inability to stand up to his wife.

Kate felt Rob's weight shift beside her. He made a strange sound, as if there was something stuck in his throat. She tightened her hold around his broad back, terrified the two legs would go from under him and he would bring her down with him. She was sweating despite the chill of the room.

'I have to ask you, Robert, is this your father, James Kennedy?' Niamh asked.

'Yes,' he said. 'Yes, it is.'

He released the sob that had been trapped in his throat. His eyes fixed on his father's face. Tears ran down his cheeks. Kate had never seen her husband's tears flow so freely before. Not even at his own brother's funeral.

The technician lifted the sheet back over Jimmy's face and moved around to the other bed.

Again he looked to Rob for his assent, which was granted in the form of a nod.

Aidan lowered the sheet.

'Oh Jesus.' Rob swayed on his feet.

Kate covered her mouth with her hand as her stomach turned.

The body lying in the bed looked nothing like Ursula. Instead of her usual sleek bob of creamy vanilla and butterscotch highlights, her hair had been roughly dried off and hung in dull, flat curtains either side of her face. There was a greenish tinge to her skin, like the faint, lingering remnants of Halloween face paint, and her lips were cracked and swollen. Her eyelids weren't fully closed; it looked like she was trying to peek out from under them. The undertaker would have his work cut out with her.

'No, *no*, nnnnnnn ...' Rob staggered back a few steps, banged his shoulder hard off the door frame as he rushed from the room.

Kate was frozen at the side of the bed. She wanted to turn off the grotesque scene that was playing out in front of her. For somebody to call 'cut' and for her husband's parents to pull back their sheets and get out of bed and for them all to leave this strange little death chamber masquerading as a bedroom.

'Kate, it's OK. We can use her dental records.' Niamh touched her arm lightly.

'You don't need to do that. It's her. It's Ursula.'

'So you can confirm that this is the body of your mother-in-law, Ursula Kennedy?'

'Yes, it's her.'

Aidan was pulling the sheet back over her mother-in-law's face as she turned on her heel.

The family room was empty so she went out onto the corridor, where she followed the sound of retching to the door of the disabled toilet.

She gave a quiet knock. 'Are you all right, love?' she asked, fighting a hot rush of queasiness herself.

More wretched retching from behind the door. Poor Rob. How the hell was she going to get him through this?

'Are you OK in there?'

'Yeah,' he said croakily. 'Just give me a few minutes.'

She went back to the family room where, thankfully, the sliding doors had been closed. Rob came back in after a few minutes and sat heavily on the sofa beside her. She felt the weight of the grief that she imagined had soaked into the cushions like tears, the anguish of other families pulling them down. She wanted to get out of this place, get back to Glenbeg. She had no idea where they were going to sleep that night; they would have to sort it out later.

The sound of purposeful footsteps on the corridor signalled Niamh's return.

Rob stood up. 'We need to get out of here,' he said.

'Of course. I'll drop you back to the Claddagh now. I was just on to Detective Inspector McGuire on the phone. He said the scenes-of-crime guys will be finished in the farmhouse by this evening. And he also hopes to have your phones back to you by then – the tech guys should be finished with them.'

'Oh, thank God. That's great, we can all stay there tonight.'

'Look,' Niamh said, 'I know you're exhausted, but he wants you both to pop into the station at Glenbeg at three today to give formal statements. Christina too.'

The room tilted. Kate's heart skidded in her chest. *Formal statements. At the station.*

'Sure, we already gave him our statements last night at the house,' Rob said. He looked fit to erupt.

'Surely this can wait until tomorrow?' Kate asked. 'We've already told them everything we know and we're both dead on our feet at this stage.' She winced internally at her unfortunate choice of words given their location. 'We just want to get back to our kids, to get some sleep.'

'I totally understand where you're coming from, Kate, but the DI needs to get your statements as soon as possible, while your memories are fresh. We need to build up as clear a picture as we can of the circumstances surrounding Jimmy's and Ursula's deaths. It's often the smallest, most unimportant-seeming details that can make all the difference in a situation like this.'

Kate got to her feet. Underneath the FLO's nicey-nice exterior was a guard, at the end of the day. Easy to forget that with her coffee and biscuits and her kind eyes.

'I need to go to the loo before we leave,' she said.

In the bathroom, Kate splashed cold water onto her face and the back of her wrists. She stared into the mirror. Guilt stared back at her.

15

Christina

'Jesus, Mammy, you're un-feckin'-believable! I told you that in confidence – I knew that mouth of yours would get you into trouble someday ... Now look at all the trouble you're after causing.' The sound of Julie's raised voice halted Christina in her tracks halfway down the stairs, the dog at her heel.

'All I said to her was that Ursula was up to ninety and I was worried about Jimmy and the kids. She walked all over him – sure, everyone knew that.'

Christina was frozen in place, one foot on one step, the other on the one below. It was nearly midday. She had been awake most of the night, finally falling into a deep sleep sometime around seven. She had practically jumped out of bed when she saw the time and thrown the voluminous dressing-gown Rita had left out for her on over her navy silk pyjamas.

'Well, you must have said more than that because it's all over town that there was some big family row over inheritance. And Nuala Hehir, Mammy, of all people. Christ almighty! That one has a gob the size of the Grand Canyon on her.'

'I didn't tell her it was a big row and I said nothing about inheritance. I don't know where that came from, but it didn't come from me, and I'd be shocked if Nuala said anything anyway. I told her to keep it to herself.'

'Well, you might as well tell Gregory Peck to stop crowing as tell Nuala Hehir to keep a secret,' said Nellie. 'She was telling anybody who cared to listen to her at bridge last night, apparently, that there were ructions on the farm last week. Betty Quinn had the cheek to ask me if it was true when I popped into the post office on my way here. I felt like slapping her through her little hatch. She's in her element with all the drama.'

Christina could only imagine the talk going on around town about them. Her mother had not been particularly well-liked locally, despite being highly respected in business circles. Not that she had cared much about the opinions of others. The opposite of her daughter, who cared far too much about what people thought of her.

'God, I hope it's not my fault they're being brought in for questioning. Rob sounded dreadful on the phone.' Aunty Rita sounded on the verge of tears.

'I'm sure it's not just that, Rita,' Nellie said. 'The guards have to be seen to investigate thoroughly in these situations, especially when two relatively healthy people have died suddenly. They probably need to rule out anything more sinister, like with that man up the country a couple of years back.'

'God, that was desperate altogether. That poor woman and her children, why did he have to take them with him? Let him take his own life if that's what he wanted. It doesn't bear thinking about, does it?' Julie said.

'Jimmy would be the last man in the world to do anything like that anyway. Such a gentle soul, probably too gentle for his own good, really,' said Nellie.

'No, there'd be more chance of Ursula doing it to him than the other way round, but there's no way she'd kill herself and definitely not in a slurry pit,' Aunty Rita said. 'This was an accident, plain and simple. Jimmy obviously got confused with his dates. Wasn't Kate only saying he'd got a lot worse lately. I didn't notice it myself, but then we didn't see as much of him as she did.'

Definitely an accident, both Julie and Nellie concurred. And the guards would have to reach that conclusion too eventually.

Christina hoped they were right. And that this wasn't somehow all her fault. Because there was no way Rob could have had anything to do with it. An image flashed into her head of her older brother carrying his daughter in his arms after she came off her new scooter in the yard on Christmas Day. How he gently dabbed at her grazed knee with an antiseptic pad and wiped her tears away with his big thumb. The Rob she knew didn't have a violent bone in his body. But then again, the Rob she knew wouldn't have roared at their mother the way he had. Or shouted at their father and told him he was a doormat. Or slammed the door of the farmhouse so hard it shook in its frame.

She cleared her throat loudly and the kitchen fell silent.

Nellie started chattering inanely about the weather as she reached the hall. 'Bleddy drizzle, wouldn't it put years on you?'

Aunty Rita made her sit at the table while she bustled around making tea and toast she really didn't want. Samson settled his heavy warmth on her feet, as if he was afraid she would disappear if he didn't physically pin her down.

'Rob was on to Mammy a few minutes ago, Christina. He said—' Julie started before her mother interrupted her.

'Would you let the girl get a bit of breakfast into her first, for God's sake?'

'It's fine, Aunty Rita, I can't stomach anything yet.'

'They're on their way back from Galway. He said to tell you that ye can move back into the farmhouse this evening, although you're very welcome to stay on here, of course – whatever you prefer. Himself and Kate are going to stay there tonight with the kids either way,' Julie said.

An immense surge of relief that she could go home to her own bedroom was instantly followed by a surge of desolation at the thought of how empty the huge house would be without her parents.

'And also that ye – yourself, Rob and Kate – have to go into the garda station in town this afternoon to answer a few more questions.'

Another surge of fear rose. *Oh no!*

The back door opened and Uncle Kieran stepped inside, tall and broad like her father.

'Wellies,' Aunty Rita warned.

He went back out and returned in his socks. 'Happy now? Is there tay in the pot?'

Uncle Kieran had just come from the farm, where he had been

giving Brendan a hand. He told them that Daniel O'Sullivan, the vet, had offered to help them out until Rob got back to work.

Christina felt herself float for a long moment in a swirl of déjà vu. Triggered by the image of the last time Mark's best friend had helped them out on the farm.

'Well, you know Niall is very happy to help out too if you're stuck,' Aunty Rita said. 'He's between jobs at the moment.' Christina's cousin Niall had spent more time between jobs than he ever had in gainful employment, but his mother never lost hope that, one of these days, her youngest son was going to make something of himself.

The bad blood between her mother and Aunty Rita dated back to the months after Christina's grandfather's death, when Ursula had instructed her husband to kindly ask his sister to refrain from dropping into Hazeldene without invitation whenever the notion took her. Christina could only imagine how awkward that conversation must have been for her poor father, who shied away from confrontation at the best of times.

She had some idea of how well it had gone down with her aunt, though. As a young girl, Julie had told a young Christina: 'My mammy says your mammy is an uppity jackeen with a bear-faced cheek and she can stick her invitations up her arse.' Christina had inspected her mother closely that evening, but couldn't see any bear hair on either of her cheeks. She assumed her aunt had been raving; whenever her mother got odd with her sister-in-law, she told them: 'Your Aunty Rita is raving again.'

As a child, Christina had always been a bit wary of Aunty Rita as a result. The woman had never been anything but kind and generous to her, but Christina had feared she could start frothing at the mouth at any moment. Looking back as an adult, she understood how much it must have hurt her aunt to be made feel unwelcome on the farm where she had been born and reared. And by a city dweller, no less, who clearly had no idea how life worked in the rural west of the country, where doors were left on the latch and people *just dropped in, as we were passing*.

The invite-only insult had been further compounded some years later when Rita asked her brother to give Niall a summer job on the open farm, a request which was swiftly vetoed by Ursula. *Not a good idea to mix business and family* was her reasoning. A hard one to justify, really, when her own kids all worked there. Rita had maintained a very cool relationship with her sister-in-law after that. She had never held it against Christina, though, or any of her brother's kids, had always been very good to them all. It was clear that she was genuinely heartbroken over the loss of her brother and devastated for her niece and nephew.

Julie, a midwife in Our Lady's, had the patience of a saint with her mother, was inured to her chronic tone-deafness. There was a steel girder of love underpinning their relationship, Christina realised, that would support it through anything.

She looked at her cousin now as she reached for a biscuit from the plate Rita had set in the middle of the table and dunked it into her mug. The two of them couldn't have been more different but were closer than sisters. Julie as crude as Christina was refined. As fat as Christina was thin. As content as Christina was discontented. If they were weather systems, Julie would have been sunny with the odd scattered shower;

Christina cloudy and overcast with the risk of torrential downpours.

'Christina?'

Everyone was staring at her.

'Sorry, I was miles away.'

'Mammy was just wondering if ye managed to get through to Peter in England,' Julie said.

'Kate left another message yesterday, but we don't know if he's been trying to contact us because the guards have all our phones. I don't know when we're going to get them back.'

'Oh, I forgot to tell you, ye'll be getting your phones and all your other devices and stuff back this evening as well. Rob said they're finished with them. So that's good news anyway,' Julie said.

Truth be told, Christina hadn't really missed her phone at all.

Kate had tried calling Uncle Peter a number of times on Tuesday night once her parents were confirmed dead by Dr Kenny, but got straight through to his voicemail. She left a number of messages for him to call her urgently. When they had heard nothing back before they had headed for Galway the previous evening, Kate had been left with no choice but to break the sad news via voice message; better that, she said, than hearing the news of his sister's death on the expat grapevine in London. Kate didn't go into detail in her message, just explained that Ursula and Jimmy had died in a tragic accident the previous day and asked him to ring either herself or Rob urgently. Even as Christina had listened to Kate leaving the message, it hadn't seemed real to her that her parents were dead.

'Well, I think it's very odd that Peter hasn't contacted any of us at this stage,' said Rita. 'I always wondered what—'

'Mam!' Julie growled and, for once in her life, her mother gauged the mood in the room and stopped herself.

'Maybe he didn't get the message. I never listen to my voicemail,' Kieran said.

'Sure, he'd have seen all the missed calls,' Rita said. 'Ye'll have to try him again later.'

16

Kate

Kate sat staring at a wall while she waited. There was nothing else to look at. Sergeant Tuohy had left her in the interview room, assuring her he'd be back in a few minutes. A blinking red light in the corner alerted her to the presence of a camera mounted high on the wall, above a shelf bearing a big black machine that looked like an oversized DVD player. The eye of the camera seemed to be aimed directly at her, as if her every movement was being analysed for signs of her guilt; little tells glowing like luminol at a crime scene.

The room had obviously undergone a recent facelift, with its smartly painted grey and white contrasting walls and contemporary office furniture; but the old building sagged beneath its new skin. The room's only window, an old-fashioned sash, which looked out over the car park at the rear of the garda station, was shut. The room was stuffy and stale, the revamp clearly not having extended to air conditioning, and the strong smell of synthetic carpet was turning Kate's stomach. None of this felt real. She had never been in the business end of the station before, had never been beyond the front desk when she came in to get a passport application form signed.

Today, after presenting themselves at the front desk of Glenbeg garda station shortly before 3 p.m., Snitcheen Tuohy had come down to meet them. He tapped a code into a pad on the wall and led them through a door and up a stairs and along a corridor of closed doors. She and Rob were taken straight into separate interview rooms while Christina was left waiting on a chair at the end of the corridor.

The door opened and Snitcheen came in, Detective Inspector McGuire on his heels. With his roundy face and berry-red cheeks, all the sergeant was missing was a set of twinkling eyes and a white beard and he would have made a great Santa for the farm's Winter Wonderland. And a personality, of course. The last thing you'd describe her husband's distant cousin as would be *a bit of craic*. The proud teetotaller had always been a dry shite, apparently, even going back to his school snitching days.

Detective Inspector McGuire didn't exactly look like a bundle of laughs either, but Kate knew only too well that you should never judge a man by his scowl. For all she knew, Noel McGuire could be a mad party animal who could skin up the neatest little spliff you ever saw in under a minute. Or the star stud of his local S&M community. An image of him clad in leathers spanking the stout bottom of his junior officer with a tasselled whip developed in her mind. What the hell was wrong with her brain, coming up with this kind of shit? It must be the stress. *Keep it together, for fuck's sake!* It was bad enough that she already felt he could see inside her head.

Looking at him now, the vibe he gave off was definitely more M&S than S&M. He had given up trying to wedge his lanky legs under the table that sat between them and had settled sideways in his seat instead, like a woman riding side saddle, his gangly limbs crossed at the knee. After fiddling around with the black machine in the corner, Snitcheen took the second chair on the opposite side of the table to Kate. There was only one chair on her side. No need for a solicitor, they had been assured. Although, of course, it was totally up to them if they wanted one.

As the sergeant ran through the formalities about recording the interview in writing and reading it back to her at the end, Kate wondered when *popping in to give a statement* had turned into an interview.

'Are you OK to begin, Kate?' Detective Inspector McGuire was looking directly at her. He had all the makings of handsome – the bone structure, eyes an unusually striking shade of blue – and the height, but he was short about two stone of meat to pad out his scrawny frame. And those eyebrows needed a serious grooming.

'Yes.'

'All right, so we just want to run back over a few things again. From what you and other people we've spoken to so far have told us, Jimmy was pretty security conscious.' She was surprised that Snitcheen was asking the questions while his senior officer began to take notes.

'Yeah, he was. There was a spate of break-ins around the area last year and he'd become a bit paranoid about it, had the place locked up like Fort Knox. He was always going on about that poor man in Mayo, the one who was jailed for shooting a burglar.'

'I believe your husband, Robert, had a CCTV system put in around that time.'

'That's right. A wireless system. He had cameras installed around the houses and the farm buildings, and calving cameras in the sheds. Jimmy was able to watch everything – it gave him great peace of mind.' *Peace of mind was the last thing the poor man had.*

'Would the cameras have been on all the time?' Snitcheen asked.

'As far as I know, they would. Some of those burglaries had taken place during the day, as I'm sure you're aware yourselves. A gang down from Dublin. They just waltz in in the middle of the afternoon bold as brass and help themselves to whatever they want: cattle, sheep, machinery, power tools. Jimmy used to kill Rob for leaving the key in the tractor, making it easy for them. You just can't do things like that any more, unfortunately.' *Stop bloody babbling.*

'Would you have any idea, given Jimmy's normal pattern of having the CCTV on around the clock, as to why it was switched off on Tuesday morning?'

She could feel the blood wash up her neck, stamping her cheeks with guilt. She had to stop herself from scraping her nails across the initials *JP* that were scratched into the desk in biro; she didn't want to look fidgety.

'No, I wouldn't, to be honest. There was no reason for him to turn it off. But as I mentioned already, Jimmy's condition had been deteriorating, particularly in the past few months. His memory was getting worse and the confusion ...'

'So you think he might have turned the CCTV off by mistake, that he was confused?'

'Well, it's possible, I suppose. I mean, obviously I don't know for certain, but it didn't make any sense for him to have deliberately turned it off and, sadly, more and more lately Jimmy wasn't ... well ... making a lot of sense.'

Her nose started running. She fumbled in her bag for a clean tissue.

The sergeant continued: 'We've spoken to the security company and they were able to tell us that the system was turned off via Jimmy's phone shortly before midnight on Monday.'

'He must have turned it off himself, so. Unless Ursula did, but there'd have been no reason for either of them to.'

'Can you run through your movements over the course of the morning again for us?'

Kate sighed wearily.

'I'm sorry, Kate,' Snitcheen said, looking not one bit sorry. 'I know you're probably sick of answering questions at this stage, but we just need you to go through it again for us if you could.'

She reiterated the events of the morning of her in-laws' deaths from the minute she rose at 7.05 a.m., after pressing the snooze button on her alarm once, to the time that Rob rang her in a panic about his father.

She hoped they'd let her go after this, but suspected Detective Inspector McGuire was biding his time.

She was right; it was a tag team.

When she stopped talking, the detective inspector sat forward, elbows on the table, and Snitcheen took over the written record.

'Thanks, Kate. Tell me, how did you get on with your mother-in-law?'

His curveball hit her square in the chest.

A memory flashed into her head. Ruth laughing so hard she nearly pissed herself on a night out as they swapped mother-in-law jokes. 'No, seriously, Kate,' she had said. 'I really do have a soft spot for my mother-in-law. It's just been freshly dug in the garden behind the garage.' They had howled with laughter. There was an ongoing competition between them as to who could lay claim to the title of worst mother-in-law. It was a tightly run race. Ruth's husband's mother was mean, the worst of all traits, in Kate's opinion. Once meanness got into a person's bones, there was no getting rid of it.

Her mouth opened before she had time to think about what she was going to say. 'Em ... good. Yeah. I got on fine with her. We both worked for her, as you know, myself and Rob, and we lived close by so we saw a lot of her. And Jimmy. I got on great with Jimmy. He's ... was ... it's so hard to take it in ... that he's gone ...' Her voice stumbled; she coughed to clear the phlegm that had gathered in her throat. 'He was a lovely man, a pure gent.'

'It can't have been easy working for your mother-in-law, though, Kate. It's hard mixing business and family, as I know only too well myself. I grew up in a family business and got out as soon as I could, left the rest of them to fight among themselves.'

Ah, so that's what he was up to. The old 'butter her up by pretending to identify with her' trick. Family business, her arse. He probably came from a long line of guards.

'No, it wasn't always easy, we all work hard, but, sure, that's par for the course in a family business. We were all invested in growing it.'

'Your mother-in-law had a reputation as quite a formidable business woman. And it's become clear from our interviews over the past couple of days that she ... shall we say ... liked to wear the trousers in the marriage too.' Detective Inspector McGuire leaned back in his chair, recrossed his legs. Snitcheen sniffed loudly.

'Well—' She was a bit taken aback by his directness. The woman was lying in the morgue as they spoke, after all. She had often wondered herself how the hell Jimmy and Ursula had ever got together. Two more different people you couldn't meet. It wasn't just the trousers she wore in that relationship, it was everything else too! 'I suppose you could say that. Jimmy was a quiet man, very soft, really. Ursula was the boss – she was the one with the business head. Jimmy and Rob worked the farm, but she did the books, kept on top of things that way. She set up the farm park herself from scratch and was in charge of that. Jimmy had nothing really to do with the management side of things.'

'So there was no tension between yourself and Ursula at all over the business? Or between Ursula and your husband?'

She felt like a specimen spreadeagled on a pinning block. She wriggled around to try to give her sit bones a break from the rock-hard moulded plastic chair that wouldn't allow her to sit back properly. She wondered if there was a little workshop in Templemore where they produced a special line of chairs guaranteed to make suspects so physically uncomfortable they'd crack faster.

'Nothing major, no. Just the normal day-to-day niggles you'd have in any employer–employee relationship,' she said.

'And tell me about Jimmy. You say you had a good relationship with him. How did Rob get on with him?' the detective inspector asked.

'They had a great relationship – you couldn't not get on with Jimmy. He's a dote, was a dote, he'd do anything for you. Himself and Rob were very close.' She was on solid ground here.

'And how about Ursula? What kind of a relationship did they have?'

'With Jimmy or Rob?'

'Jimmy.'

A Heil Hitler kind of relationship. 'They had a good relationship. They were very different but opposites attract, I guess. Jimmy just wanted a quiet life. He was happy in his own company, a real homebird. Ursula was the total opposite – she loved being out and about – but it worked for them.'

The detective inspector sat back in his seat and recrossed his legs, which must have been a pre-agreed signal for the sergeant to take over. *How long can they keep going with these questions?*

Snitcheen's tongue flicked out and licked his top lip. 'Just one final question before we finish up here. Have you ever heard of estoppel?'

'Estoppel.' Her brain flicked back through its archive to her dusty university years file. 'I have heard of it. It's a legal term, if I'm not mistaken, but I can't remember what it means,' she said uncertainly.

'Didn't you study law in college? Like your husband?' the sergeant asked.

'Yes, but that was years ago and neither of us ever actually practised. We came down to Glenbeg to help his parents out straight out of college. After Mark ... Rob's brother ... died and, well, we're still here.'

'Can you tell me what the reason was for Rob's consultation with his solicitor on Tuesday morning?' Snitcheen asked.

She felt the detective inspector's gaze burn through her skin. 'I can't, because I don't know. I assume it was something to do with the business,' she lied.

'So you're telling me your husband made an appointment to see his solicitor and didn't mention to you what it was about. Would that not be a bit unusual?'

'To be honest, inspector, he might have said it to me and it could have gone in one ear and out the other. We're both so busy, like ships passing in the night a lot of the time. And since then, well, we've been a bit distracted as you can imagine.'

'Right. And the substantial estate the Kennedys left behind – the land, properties and business – are to be shared between you and your husband and his sister, isn't that correct?'

'Yes, I assume so.'

'You assume so?'

'I believe that to be the case, yes. It's not exactly high on our priority list at the moment.'

'Thanks, Kate, that'll be all for now.'

17

Christina

Christina looked at her watch: 3.03 p.m. She was sitting at the end of a long corridor upstairs in the garda station, waiting for her turn to be interviewed. She hoped they wouldn't be there too long; she badly wanted to go home. She didn't know how Rob and Kate were still standing after what they had been through already today. They looked as if they had just come off a rough long-haul ferry crossing, not a relatively short drive on the motorway from Galway. It must have been horrific for them. Seeing her parents in that place.

She distracted herself by looking out the window beside her onto Main Street. An elderly woman in a navy coat stood outside Deacy's Fruit and Veg picking through a display of tomatoes, weighing each one carefully in her hand, putting one back, placing another in a plastic bag. She moved along to the cabbages, pulling her tartan trolley on wheels behind her. She meticulously picked through the box until she found one that pleased her, toting it under her arm like an ugly green head while she moved on to the carrots. All the time in the world.

Darkness was hinting at falling outside, the January sky slung low and heavy over the street. Two women stood chatting outside Keane's newsagent's, clogging the entrance with their buggies and babies. One mother took a break from jiggling her buggy back and forth to root around underneath it before triumphantly producing a dummy that she plugged her toddler's mouth with. She turned her attention back to the other mother, who was pushing a double buggy occupied by two young children who were either twins or very close together in age. *How do they do it? Day in, day out. Year in, year out.* Christina loved children, adored her niece and nephew, but the thought of being a mother herself utterly terrified her. She could barely care for herself, never mind having a whole other human totally reliant on her.

She shifted her attention to the hotel next door to the newsagent's, directly across from the garda station: Glenbeg House Hotel, known to locals as Lydon's after the family who had run it for years. The place was badly in need of a facelift. It was such a shame to see the town's former grand old dame let herself go like that, paint peeling from her once handsome exterior, her slovenly windows badly in need of a scrub. Christina had spent many an hour in the foyer with Granny Kennedy as a child, contentedly ensconced in their usual vantage-point by the fireplace, which offered the best view of the wedding parties passing by on the way into the function room. A fizzy orange and a pink Cadbury's Snack for her. A pot of tea and coffee cake for Granny or, on special occasions, a glass of sherry. She had been happy then.

There had been talk of the hotel being turned into a hostel for asylum seekers. Mother had been appalled at the idea; so horrified, in fact, that she had approached the eccentric Lydon son who now owned the hotel and put in an offer for the building, which he had turned down flat. Christina had rarely seen her mother as furious as she had been that day after coming away from the meeting with Marcus Lydon.

'That ignorant pig,' she had fumed. 'I've warned him what'll happen if he tries to turn that place into a hostel. It would destroy this town bringing that lot in on top of us. I'll have protestors outside that place day and night, I told him. The cheek of him, telling me I'm only a blow-in. He won't be able to show his face in this town ever again if he goes ahead with this.'

That had been over a year ago and nothing had happened since. The hotel had continued to flake and peel and there was no sign of any asylum seekers. Three men came out of its main door now onto the street. They stood outside for a few minutes talking animatedly, as if discussing matters of great import. One man with grey hair and a beard looked vaguely familiar. An acquaintance of her father's maybe. Jimmy had a smile for everybody, an easy, open way about him that made people comfortable. The men all turned to look towards the garda station. She pulled back from the window as it hit her what they were probably talking about.

The realisation of what had happened came rushing towards her like an express train. *Daddy. Gone. And Mother. Gone. For good.*

She couldn't catch her breath.

She got to her feet.

No air.

Somebody threw a black shawl over her head. Fuzzy grey carpet tiles came up off the floor to meet her. And she was gone.

'... tina ... Christina ... can you hear me?' A woman's voice. Where did she know it from?

She felt something hard beneath her. Something soft under her head. *Cold, so cold.* She smelt Fuzzy Felt and coconut and stale coffee breath. Her eyelids popped open. The FLO was down on her hunkers beside her, green eyes brimming with concern.

'You're OK, Christina, it's Niamh here. You just got a bit weak. Stay where you are for a few minutes ...'

She was lying on the floor in the corridor. She shivered. She hadn't felt herself fall. Or hit the floor.

'I'm fine.' She got to her knees hastily, pushed herself off the floor. Scarlet.

'Take your time, you're all right. Sit down there now.' Niamh guided her back to the chair, hunkered down in front of her again. There was a lovely shine off her hair – coconut oil, maybe. 'Put your head between your legs for a few minutes.'

'No, I'm fine now, honestly. I just ... found it hard to catch my breath ...'

It wasn't the first time she had fainted. She had been a fainter as a child. Whenever she was in a stuffy room. Or a church.

Once in the queue for Santa Claus at Moon's in Galway. She had woken on a sofa in the furniture department. Rob had been mortified, but somewhat mollified when they were brought straight to the top of the line.

'Do you want me to get Robert or Kate out for you?' Niamh asked.

'Are they not finished yet? They've been in there for ages.' The poor dog would be pining for her.

'They'll be a while longer, they've only been in there about ten minutes, but I can get one of them out to you if you need them.'

'Ten minutes! That can't be right.' She looked at her watch: 3.14 p.m. Time had warped along with reality.

'Would you like me to take you home, Christina? We can do this in the morning if you're not feeling up to it now. You're under enough pressure at the moment.'

'No, no thanks.' She couldn't face the thought of having to go home only to spend the night worrying about coming back again. Better to get it out of the way. 'I'm OK, really.'

'Grand so, but if you change your mind, just let me know and I'll drop you out. It's no problem at all. How about we go out for a bit of fresh air while you're waiting?'

'No. Thank you. I'm fine here.' There was no way she was going out there. A static target for the gossips.

'It's all in the statement I gave you yesterday. Nothing has changed since then,' she explained.

'OK, well, the last time I saw ...' Her throat was so dry.

'Thank you.' She took a sip of water, tepid with a tang.

'The last time I saw Daddy was on Monday night. We were watching TV together all evening in the den. He was still up when I went to bed.'

'Around 11, maybe a few minutes past.'

'I said goodnight, he said he would see me ...' She swallowed hard, had to stop for a second to compose herself. 'He said he would see me in the morning.'

'I don't know what time he went, I didn't hear him coming up to bed, but he usually went up around half ten or eleven.'

She peeled back the sliver of loose skin at the side of her thumbnail, worked it back and forth with her index nail.

'I heard Mother going to bed at about 11.30. I was still awake reading. Her room is right opposite mine, and I could hear her pottering around in there, taking her make-up off and brushing her teeth in the en suite.'

'No, they slept in separate rooms some nights.' *Every night.* 'Daddy's snoring kept Mother awake so he sometimes slept in the guest room over the far side of the house.'

'A row? No, I wouldn't call it a row, more of a heated discussion, really. Probably just business. We couldn't really hear what they were talking about.'

She forced another sip of water down her throat.

'Not at all, no. Daddy spoke to Robert before he left and to Mother after that and everything seemed fine.'

'No, I slept like a log. Like I mentioned to the other garda at the house on Tuesday evening, I take medication that helps me to sleep. Not sleeping tablets, just ... something to help take the edge off.' She cringed at having to share such private information with strangers.

'I didn't hear Daddy in the morning at all, but that wouldn't be unusual. He's always the first one up and out of the house, but he makes sure to keep quiet so he doesn't wake the rest of us. He's like a little mouse – you'd never hear him in the mornings.'

She wriggled in the plastic chair, her bottom was starting to ache.

'I didn't hear her leaving, I might have been in the shower, but she was gone when I went down to the kitchen to make coffee around half nine.'

'No, thank you, I'm fine with water.'

'I didn't leave the house at all on Tuesday morning. I was working from the desk in my room. I did hear the dog barking at some stage, but I didn't really think anything of it. Maybe if I had gone out to see what was wrong with him ...' Her voice caught.

'No, it's OK, I'd prefer to keep going.'

'I heard one of the girls from the restaurant come in to the kitchen around lunchtime, dropping off Daddy's dinner. Then Rob came in a little while later, maybe an hour or so, and left again.' She dug her nail into the exposed flesh of her thumb under the loose flap of skin; the familiar sharp shot of pain so exquisitely calming.

'It was unusual. Daddy is such a creature of habit. Was, I mean,' she stumbled. 'He always ate his dinner at lunchtime, like clockwork. No matter what else was going on. Mother was rarely at home during the day – she was always on the go between work and golf and stuff. But she never went anywhere without her phone. When I saw her handbag and phone on the table with no sign of her anywhere, I did think it was strange.'

Her thumb was bleeding now; she could feel it congealing under her nail. She brought it to her mouth, sucked it. A ribbon of blood sailed down her throat on a stream of saliva. She savoured the taste, like salty pennies diluted with spit. She had heard somewhere that mosquitoes preferred people with type O blood over those of other blood groups, could pick up a chemical signal secreted through the skin that indicated which blood type you were. She was O positive, the most common group in Ireland, and had to douse herself with mosquito repellent on holidays abroad when she was younger to avoid being eaten alive.

'Sorry?' *Stay focused*.

'No, I didn't see or speak to Kate at all that morning. Or Rob. I didn't leave the house.'

'The farm? Well, the farm will be left to Rob.'

'God, no. I have no problem with that. He's worked it for years with Daddy, and I'm no farmer.'

'We have a very good relationship – we've always been close. I'm mad about Kate too. The two of them have always been good to me, especially when I'm ... not well. And I adore their kids, Lily and Luke. I'm Luke's godmother.'

'No, my parents always assured me I'd be looked after too. It wasn't something I ever worried about, to tell you the truth.' That was true. 'I thought they'd be around for a good few years yet, though, and so did they.' She slumped back in her seat as much as it was possible to. 'I'm sorry, I'm too tired to even think any more.'

'Pardon?' *Think, think*.

'When was the last time I saw them?' *Delay, delay*. 'Em ... the last time I saw them both was when I said goodnight to them on Monday night. If I had only known ...' She gargled a sob. She couldn't allow herself to break down here, in front of these strangers.

She wondered if they could tell she was lying.

18

Rob drove straight from the garda station to the farmhouse. Kate wanted to clean up before Jenny dropped the kids back. She had visions of the place being ransacked: clothes spilling out of drawers, the contents of Ursula's kitchen cupboards pulled around the place and everything covered in fingerprint powder, like on the TV.

It wasn't that bad at all, though. The place wasn't up to Ursula's usual anal standard of tidiness, but everything had been shoved back inside drawers and behind doors, so on the surface it looked pretty normal. Rob went out to check the cattle while Christina went straight to her room to have a shower and *freshen up a bit*. Kate wished she had that luxury. Her sister-in-law had no idea, really. How people lived in the real world. Her parents had done her no favour allowing her to moulder away at home after Mark instead of coaxing her back out into the world. Rob said she had always been sensitive, even as a child, but it was as if the trauma of Mark's death had emotionally skinned her. God only knew how she was going to keep going now.

Kate was beyond exhausted at this stage. She would have loved nothing more than to fall into bed after a hot bath. Lily and Luke had been fizzing with excitement when they heard they were going for a sleepover to Ursula and Grandad's house. Even though it was less than a one-minute walk away, an overnight stay in the farmhouse was a real novelty for them.

She half-expected Ursula to come bustling into the kitchen now, giving out about the state of the place. Kate felt she had come to know her mother-in-law as well as anybody could over the years. It had astounded her how Ursula was never in the wrong even when she so often was. The finger of blame for her actions was always pointed firmly outwards, away from her. She would genuinely have not been able to comprehend why Rob and Kate were so upset over her turning their dream home into a cookery school. She seemed to be utterly devoid of any scrap of empathy at all. Incapable of putting herself in somebody else's shoes when the designer ones she was wearing were perfectly comfortable.

Her sense of entitlement was off the scale, wherever it had come from. Kate had never come across anything like it. The woman used to park in disabled parking bays, for crying out loud, oblivious to the dirty looks she got. The one time she was confronted by the irate husband of a wheelchair user, she came home fuming about his aggressive attack when she had only run into the pharmacy for five minutes *(it wasn't her fault the queue was so long, they should have had more staff on)* and Jimmy had to talk her out of reporting the man to the guards.

Kate would never forget the day of Luke's communion when Ursula told Julie she should stay away from horizontal stripes as they made her look 'even heavier than you already are'. Of course, Ursula 'hadn't meant to cause offence' and was flabbergasted when Rita went through her for a shortcut for being 'such a thunderin' bitch'. As if she was the one who had been wronged when she was 'only trying to give her a bit of fashion advice'.

More and more recently, though, as Kate had begun to stand up to her husband's mother, and her mask had dropped exposing the real Ursula, her intense dislike for the woman had begun to fester into something darker.

Jimmy had let his wife away with murder for a quiet life. And while there were times, plenty of them, when Kate had felt like grabbing him by the shoulders and shaking him hard, he was just too soft. Too soft for his own good. And sadly, for the good of his family. Rob and Christina didn't seem to see what Kate saw. They'd been exposed to Ursula's behaviour their whole life; it was the only normal they knew. Kate could see, though, even if they couldn't see it themselves, that Ursula's children had never really had a mother. Not in the true sense of the word.

Despite this, Rob had turned out a good man, decent and loving, his main failing his inability to see his mother for what she was and stand up for his own wife and kids. It was clear that Christina had really suffered, though; the little girl inside her crying out for a mother would probably never grow up. And Mark. How much had the lack of maternal love and warmth steered him towards the terrible choice he'd made? she wondered. Not that Jimmy was blameless in all of it either, of course.

Kate had forgotten how utterly draining her youngest child could be; her incessant '*MOM*'s, the constant vomit of thoughts, the endless questions. Lily wasn't home ten minutes when Kate had begun to regret not taking Jenny up on her offer to keep the kids another night. It was so conflicting: the overwhelming need to have her children close at this time, butting heads with the desire to pull out all the leads that were sucking energy from her.

Niamh had dropped off their phones sealed in transparent plastic bags bearing the blue Garda Síochána logo, saying they would get the rest of their electronic devices back over the next couple of days. Kate was itching to get her hands on her phone, but she needed to get the kids to bed first.

She had been dreading the conversation with Lily and Luke. How do you even begin to tell an eight- and eleven-year-old that both of their grandparents had drowned in gallons of fermented cow shite? Kate could only imagine what her daughter's vivid imagination would do with that scenario.

Herself and Rob had sat them both down at the kitchen table and broken the news as gently and simply as they could. Kate did most of the talking. The children had said very little so she wasn't sure how much they had taken in. She had expected tears and endless questions, especially from Lily, but there had been none of either. Ruth had emailed her an article from Google last night on the dos and don'ts of talking with a child about death.

She was relieved to read that it was common for kids to seem unaffected by loss, that Lily and Luke's seemingly indifferent reaction wasn't an indicator of sociopathic tendencies. It was just their way of trying to process trauma.

Rob put the telly on for the kids afterwards while Kate heated up milk for Rice Krispies. Nellie, thoughtful as ever, had dropped in a bag of groceries – fresh milk, bread, eggs and bacon – along with a batch of casseroles that people had left at Rita's house for the family, and Samson the dog, who made a beeline for Christina as soon as he arrived. Again, Kate wondered how she would ever manage without that woman.

Lily was ready for her when Kate went to tuck her into bed, fired one question after another at her from her ammo belt. Having had time to percolate, her daughter's queries were brewed from a blend of morbid curiosity and childish reasoning rather than any kind of grief or sorrow.

She was sleeping in Mark's old room, the uncle she had never got to meet. Luke was next door in his father's childhood bedroom, reading the latest *Diary of a Wimpy Kid*.

'How did the slurry tank kill them?' Lily demanded loudly.

Kate grimaced, glad Christina was downstairs out of earshot. 'Well, you know how we always warn you about how dangerous the tank is and how you should never go near it ...'

'Yes, and we never do because that would be really, really bold,' said Lily. 'Why were Grandad and Ursula being bold? Is it their own fault they're dead?'

'Lily, God, make sure you don't say anything like that in front of Aunty Christina,' Kate warned. 'That would make her very sad. They weren't being bold, pet. Grandad must have ...' Christ, she wasn't about to get into the ins and outs of the slurry-making process with an inquisitive eight-year-old at this hour of the day. 'Look, nobody was being naughty – it was a very sad accident that was nobody's fault.'

Then it was Luke's turn. Her beautiful boy. Skin so soft and silky still. He had her fair hair, his father's sallow colouring and big brown eyes. Eyes that were now filled with worry. She had known his thoughts would lead him here; he had been anxious about something happening to her or Rob ever since a boy in his class lost his mother – far too young – to cancer the previous year.

'Are Dad and Aunty Christina very sad?'

'Yes, they are, pet. They've had a terrible shock – we all have. It's normal to feel sad at a time like this.'

'If anything ever happened to you and Dad, who would mind us?'

Kate took a deep breath. She didn't have the wherewithal for this tonight. 'That's not going to happen, Luke,' she said.

'But what if it did? Grandad and Ursula weren't even sick and they're dead now.' His bottom lip stuck out. 'I don't want you and Dad to die.'

'We're not going anywhere, pet, don't you be worrying your little head,' she said. 'Now shove over there and make some room for me.'

As she held her child in her arms, rubbing his warm back to comfort him as she had so often when he was a baby, Kate remembered feeling the same fear that her son now felt. As a child, her worst nightmare was that something bad would happen to her mother; looking back now, she had been overly attached to her. Her fear had grown and grown until one day it came to fruition.

Her own early years had been the best years of her mother that she got. A mammy through and through, her mother had so much love to give back then, it literally spilled out of her. Kate had been hit with the sheer force of that kind of love herself when she held Luke in her arms for the first time.

She sat on the bed in Ursula's restful guest room – tastefully decorated in crisp white and pale lemon – where she and Rob were to sleep tonight, with her phone in her hand. She ignored all her text and voice messages; she would deal with those tomorrow. She rang her father and Ruth and quickly filled them both in on everything that had happened since she had last spoken to them, promising to let them know if she needed anything.

'Kate, are you coming down?' Rob called from the bottom of the stairs. 'You need to eat something.'

'I'll be down in a minute, go ahead without me,' she shouted back.

She would have given anything for a night on her own, some time to get the jumbled filing cabinet in her brain back into some kind of order. The pressure of having to support everybody else seemed to expand inside her skull, where the first tendrils of a headache had taken root. Gravity was pulling her lethargic bones down towards the soft mattress; sleep wasn't an option, though, not yet.

She brought up the browser on her phone and typed *estoppel* into the search bar. Scrolling down the page, she found a link to a legal website. Her eyes scanned the text. *Proprietary estoppel: Where an assurance is given in relation to property or property rights … The assurance may be stated or implied … not necessary to show there has been an irrevocable legally binding promise. Many cases of estoppel involve a gift which is not completed.*

It was a strange term – *estoppel* – but then, legal terminology was full of strange terms. She sped quickly through the document. The way she understood it, a donor was likely to be 'estopped' from reneging on their promise to gift a property or piece of land or whatever it happened to be where the donee had 'relied to his detriment' on the apparent gift or apparent promise to give the gift. 'The classic situation is where a parent promised particular land or buildings … If, for some reason, the property is not legally transferable due to a change of mind or debt or other circumstances, proprietary estoppel may require that the gift is made effective.' Why had the guards asked her about estoppel? Did they know about the barn? Surely if they did they would have mentioned it. Unless. Maybe they were keeping their cards close to their chest.

She could hear the murmuring of Rob and Christina's voices downstairs, the fridge door closing, the clink of cutlery. She clicked on another link. An *Irish Independent* article about a man who left school at the age of fifteen to work on the family farm and who, despite having been promised a ninety-acre plot by both his father and mother before their deaths, was left just three acres in his mother's will after a family rift. He had been bullied out of the family business and resorted to operating a hackney business to try and support his own young family. The man had successfully challenged his mother's will and the High Court judge found he was entitled to the ninety-acre plot based on his claims of proprietary estoppel, testamentary contract and moral duty to make proper provision.

Kate whistled through her teeth. It had always astounded her how families could tear each other apart, usually over money or land or property. How sometimes even a small amount left or not left in a will could cause such bitter enmity that it ate through generations of the same family. As a mother, it would be anathema to her every instinct to even contemplate doing or saying something that would pit her children against each other.

She closed the link and googled 'Galway slurry deaths'. There were over 353,000 results. Most after the first page were unrelated.

The *Irish Independent* had a big piece under the heading 'Gardaí Investigate East Galway Slurry Pit Tragedy'. Apart from the first few lines about gardaí setting up an incident room in Glenbeg and a separate investigation being launched by the Health and Safety Authority, the article focused mainly on quotes from suitably shocked members of the community about the respected Kennedy family and, in particular, on Ursula's entrepreneurial achievements. There were quotes from a previous interview Ursula had done with the paper when she won a national Business Woman Award. The article mentioned that the family had been hit by tragedy in 2002 when 'the eldest Kennedy son, Mark, took his own life at the age of twenty-one'. Kate was relieved to see that the comments section underneath was closed.

It was strange to see Christina taking on the role of hostess in her mother's kitchen. Kate had expected her to be in bed under the covers long ago, hiding from everything that was happening around her. She was grateful, though; she hadn't a drop left in the tank herself and it felt nice to be looked after for a change.

Rob sat at the worktop, pushing chunks of juicy beef around his bowl. He pushed his fingers deep into his hair, expelled a long sigh. 'I need a drink.'

'The kettle is on,' Christina said, reaching for the tin of tea-bags.

'I think I need something a bit stronger than that tonight,' he said. 'We all do.'

He went into the lounge where Jimmy and Ursula's expansive drinks cabinet was permanently stocked with the finest of spirits, port and cream liquors; her art deco gin trolley looked as if it had been arranged by a food stylist. Rob emerged with a bottle of Grey Goose vodka and a Glendalough gin. Cubes from the ice dispenser on the big American fridge tinkled into glasses, the alcohol glug-glugged from the bottle, cans popped. He poured a can of fizzing 7up into Christina's vodka and artisan tonic water into the gins, no Schweppes in this house. It almost felt normal, the three of them sitting down together having a relaxing drink.

Kate took a deep slug of her gin, shuddered at the strong taste. Rob had been heavy-handed with his measures, and the alcohol traced a warm path down to her empty stomach, sending an instant message through her nervous system to her brain. *Relax*, it whispered seductively. *Relax*. It was a dangerous source of solace, as Kate was only too well aware, but she could understand how it had lured her mother in, promising her respite from the pain. It wasn't until she had been tightly enmeshed in its sticky web that she realised she had been tricked. The pain always came back, even worse than before.

The slap of the cat flap signalled the grand entrance of Queen Cleo. She sniffed at her food bowl, before stalking away in disgust, and ascended her velvet throne, the one Ursula had paid a small fortune to have delivered from Harrods. From there she stalked Kate with her eyes.

Kate turned her back to the cat and tried to force herself to eat, but even the mere act of breaking down the meat between her teeth felt like too much effort. She had to take a deep drink to wash the bolus of semi-masticated beef down her windpipe. She had lost weight she couldn't afford to lose over the past few days; it was as if the guilt was stuck in her throat, preventing her from swallowing properly. There was a brief moment of panic when her airwaves became partially blocked by the meat and she couldn't catch her breath. It made her think about what Ursula and Jimmy must have gone through in their final moments. She hoped they had been overcome by the fumes quickly, that they hadn't suffered. The alternative was too horrific to imagine.

After an hour of trying and failing to get to sleep, Kate gave up. She blamed the alcohol: three gins and not enough food. Even though she knew it was a really bad idea, especially at this hour of the night, she reached for her phone, which was charging on the bedside locker, trying not to wake Rob who was breathing deeply beside her. Some masochistic impulse she was powerless to resist urged her to google *Ursula Jimmy Kennedy Glenbeg Slurry Deaths*.

The other national papers had run with their own versions of the *Independent* story, with the headlines ranging from 'Slurry Pit of Horror' in *The Sun* to the more refined *Irish Times* version: 'East Galway Town Hit by Double Farm Tragedy'. She read every one she could find. All different versions of the same bare facts, filled out with background about Ursula's business accolades and quotes from local politicians and business people. All the comment sections were closed. Her eyelids were beginning to droop and she was about to turn her phone off and make another attempt at sleep when a link to a website called therealsceal.ie caught her eye. The real story. A popular site for those who weren't too bothered about the veracity of their news content. She decided to have a quick look and then call it a night.

The article about the slurry-pit deaths was short and not as well written as the mainstream media pieces. She was shocked to see a long list of comments underneath. How was this allowed? Surely it couldn't be legal to have people commenting on a public online forum when a garda investigation was ongoing. All hiding behind ridiculous fake names.

She knew she shouldn't read on, but ...

ProZack 9865: *What a shitty way to go.* 💩

Anonymous Smith: *Bet it was the son.*

Carrie_eatingcake: *That place must be cursed, heard another son hung himself years ago.*

Numpty Dumpty: *It could have been an accident, that slurry is lethal shit.* 💩💩💩

Kuhkimonster: *Sounds like he's up shit creek without a paddle.* 😄

Yabbadabbadoobydoo: *My sister's going out with a lad from Glenbeg, says the shades down there are convinced this was no accident.*

Czarcasm99: *Who inherits the land and the business? That's your answer right there!*

Kate threw her phone down, and lay staring into the darkness.

19

Three days after the event – Friday, 12 January
Christina

Christina was roused from a deep Xanax-induced sleep by the grinding of her mother's Gaggia and the booming of Rita's voice from the kitchen. A delectable blend of the aromas of freshly ground coffee and burning turf drifted down the hall to draw her from her bed.

She stood in the shower for what felt like ages, letting the hot water, as hot as she could bear it, stream over her head, over her face, down her body. She tried to block out thought by focusing on the sounds and sensations around her. The squelching of the shampoo as she lathered it into her scalp, the tang of the lime body scrub, the exfoliating granules rough against her skin. Mindful awareness. Something she normally found almost impossible to do, the thoughts sneaking up on her like stealth bombs, exploding in her head. This morning, though, it seemed to work. Maybe because the thoughts she was trying to avoid were just too awful for her mind to cope with.

After dressing and smoothing her hair into a ponytail, she was surprised to feel hunger. Standing at the kitchen door, the heat and chatter coming out to greet her, Christina was brought back in time to all those childhood mornings when Nellie had the range lit for her and the boys. She felt a wave of gratitude that they still had her in their lives, still looking out for them after all these years. The little woman bustled around now in an apron she had brought from her own house, lifting a loaf of brown bread from the oven. Mark had loved that bread, used to put away half a loaf at a time, sliced thickly and lathered in butter. The real stuff, 'none of that low-fat crap'.

Rita and Julie were sitting at the breakfast bar drinking tea. Kate was on her feet, pouring milk into a mug of coffee. She looked dreadful. As if she hadn't slept a wink.

Nellie immediately started fussing over Christina. Did she sleep? Would she have a bit of breakfast? A drink to warm her belly? She would have preferred a glass of water, but agreed to tea to keep Nellie happy.

'What's the story with the funeral?' Rita was asking Kate. 'Do ye know yet when they'll be releasing the ... em, Jimmy and Ursula?'

'We don't know anything for definite yet,' Kate said, 'but Niamh said they could be held for five days. I'm going to give her a buzz this morning to find out if there's any update. We can't make any arrangements until we know for definite.'

'That's a bleddy disgrace, keeping them up in that place when there's a grieving family waiting to organise a funeral,' Aunty Rita said.

There was a bang and a smash and a shriek of pain.

The mug Nellie had been filling from the kettle for Christina lay in smithereens on the floor and she was clutching her hand to her chest. Before the others had time to even react, Kate had turned the cold tap on and plunged Nellie's hand under it.

'God almighty, I'm so stupid. I left it slip right out of my hand.'

'You gave yourself a right scalding. Christina, is there a first aid kit here anywhere?' Kate asked. 'And can one of you pull over a stool? She needs to sit down.'

Christina grabbed the first aid kit from the cupboard beside the fridge and rooted in it for a burn gel. Rita had brought one of the high stools over to the sink for Nellie to sit on. She was shaking like someone in shock and her face had turned a peculiar colour. Christina hoped she hadn't done herself any serious damage. It was disquieting to see Nellie, the one who always minded everybody else, in such a state. Dependent on others for once.

It didn't last long, though. Within about five minutes, she had composed herself and was chiding Kate for fussing over her. As Kate applied the cooling gel to her swollen red hand, Nellie was ordering Julie to clear up the broken crockery. 'You missed a bit there, and look, there's another bit over there under the stool.'

She pooh-poohed Kate's suggestion of going to the doctor with a dismissive wave of her hand, seemingly back to her old self again. It was worrying, though, maybe a sign that Nellie was doing too much. That they expected too much of her. She was getting older, easy to forget that when she ran around the place like a Duracell bunny. There was definitely something going on with her. She had always been thin, but these days, she looked positively gaunt.

There was still no word from Uncle Peter. Kate had called Mother's aunt in Dublin last night to see if she had any other contact details for him. She reported that Catherine, who was now well into her eighties, sounded shaky and frail. She had no other number and had trouble even remembering the last time she had spoken to Peter. She assured Kate that she and her husband, Arthur, would be down for the funeral.

Kate had wondered aloud whether Peter was sick himself, in hospital with cancer or something serious like that, which would explain why he wasn't answering his phone, why he hadn't responded to dozens of missed calls. He was younger than his sister by about five years, and as Rob had pointed out, Mother hadn't mentioned anything about him being unwell. But then, she had never mentioned Peter at all any more. His Christmas card came like clockwork every year in mid-December; Christina assumed her mother sent one back. It wasn't the kind of thing you could ask her, though, unless you wanted your nose bitten off.

She hadn't seen her mother's brother since she was a teenager. He hadn't even come home for his nephew's funeral. It had all been so odd. He and Mother had been so close; no other siblings. He had been a regular visitor to the farm, zipping into the yard in his open-top sports car with his cool floppy hair, like a vitamin shot of urban sophistication. Uncle Peter had been the coolest old person she knew, the coolest person full stop. He was in his forties then, which had seemed positively ancient to the teenage Christina, but he wasn't like other people his age. He looked and acted much younger. He wasn't married and had no kids, so as her mother said, 'he only has himself to worry about'. She had asked one day how he made enough from his job as a piano teacher to own a sports car, and Rob had said, 'It's a second-hand Mazda MX-5, a Japanese import, hardly a Porsche 911, so he's not exactly rolling in it.'

He used to come down to Glenbeg at least two weekends every month and stay for a week every Christmas. The house was always full of laughter and noise when he was there: Christmas songs blaring from the stereo as he bellowed along, his endless stream of hilarious anecdotes, the big laugh that came from deep inside his belly and boomed around the house. Her mother had christened one of the guest rooms 'Peter's room' and Daddy didn't seem to mind his brother-in-law's frequent stays; whatever kept Mother happy. She was always in such great form when Peter was around. It had made Christina sad as a child to think of Mother and Peter losing their parents at such a young age. To think of them clinging together in their grief. Losing their mother first and then their father. They must have been devastated. They were lucky their Aunt Catherine was there to take them in.

It had come out of the blue when, one day, Mother told them that Peter had moved away. Christina could remember the conversation clearly. Herself and Mark were in the den watching telly. She wasn't sure where Rob was or when he heard the news.

'I have some news. Uncle Peter's moved to England – he got a new job over there.' Her mother's eyes looked as though they were rimmed with red pencil.

'Will he still be able to visit at the weekends?' Christina had asked. She loved Uncle Peter, loved the lightness and gaiety he brought to the farm. Hated change.

'No, he's going to be working at weekends so he won't be able to visit for a while,' her mother said abruptly.

'When is he going? Is he coming to say goodbye?'

'He's already gone.' Her mother left the room.

Christina felt like a tyre that had been punctured with a nail, the air slowly hissing out of her. She looked at Mark. He looked as shocked and upset as she was. She knew now, though, it was for a different reason to her.

The French door opened, drawing her back into the present, and in stepped Daniel O'Sullivan in his socks. The farm vet and Mark's childhood friend. Samson leapt at him, tail going like the clappers.

'Any chance of a hot drop, ladies?' A cheeky smile split his face.

Daniel had the build of a rugby player, but was GAA through and through: a strong back and thighs that looked like they were hewn from rock. The five-year age gap between Christina and her older brother's friend that had seemed so vast when she was still in school had shrivelled over the years. Daniel had always made time for her. He had a lovely way about him of putting people at ease.

'That sky is ready to open – it's just starting to spit ...' He stopped when he noticed Christina sitting at the table. 'Christina. I'm so sorry for your loss.' He reached out his hand to shake hers, before changing his mind and pulling her into a bear hug. He smelt like the sea, fresh and salty. She wondered what deodorant he used.

'I'm so sorry,' he whispered again before he let her go.

'Thanks, Daniel.'

Kate put a steaming mug in front of him, having had to shoo Nellie away from the kettle, and a plate of biscuits. 'Help yourself to milk and sugar.'

'Tell me, how's this little man doing?' he asked, rubbing Samson behind the ears.

'He's still not really eating,' Christina said. 'And he's sleeping a lot. He won't let me out of his sight. He goes out to do his business and is straight back in again. No interest in roaming around the farm any more.'

'Poor little guy. Dogs grieve too, just like us. It's perfectly normal for him to mope around the place for a while and lose interest in his food. You'll be OK, though, Sammy,' he said, looking into the dog's mournful brown eyes and patting his scruffy head.

'Did you get a chance to check the rabbits, Daniel? Brendan was saying one of them was a bit under the weather,' Kate said.

'That's next on my list. I'll have a quick look at them all while I'm here.'

'You're very good, Daniel. You were always good to Jimmy and Mark. Lord, it brings it all back, doesn't it?' Rita sighed.

Every time she saw Daniel, which hadn't been very often over the years, Christina was yanked back in time.

Mark and Daniel had been so close, joined at the hurley since junior infants. They were always up to something, those two. Always laughing and messing. And always hungry, Nellie complaining that she couldn't keep them fed. They got great mileage out of Mark's green plastic tractor and trailer, the two of them squashed onto the seat, transferring muck from the front loader to the trailer and dumping it in a big pile before starting all over again. One blond head (Mark had been white-blond as a young child), one dark. Two mops of curls. They eventually moved on to shiny BMXs and then sturdier mountain bikes, cycling everywhere, hurleys sticking out of their rucksacks. And the curls gave way to gelled spikes and undercuts. It was around then, too, that Mark started to change, to get spikier himself. And when Daniel went off to Dublin to study veterinary after the Leaving, Mark stayed at home and went off the rails.

The day of the funeral was a typical pre-Leaving Cert scorcher. Teenagers around the country sweltered in the sun streaming through their windows, as it did the first week of June every year before disappearing again for the rest of the summer. That's what Christina should have been doing too. Studying. Instead of burying her brother.

She would never forget the look of utter desolation on Daniel's face as he hefted the heavy wooden box onto his broad shoulder along with her father, brother and uncles – bearing his best friend aloft for the final time. He must have thought in that moment of all those times he had carried Mark on his shoulder in celebration of yet another hurling victory. Mark had been a gifted hurler. There would be no more victories for him now, no more celebrations.

Daniel had always maintained that Mark was smart enough to study medicine if he set his mind to it, smart enough to study anything he wanted, but her brother had shown little interest in books. Not even in agricultural science. Like his father, the love of the land was scored into the marrow of his bones. All he had ever wanted to do was work the farm with Jimmy; another reason it had come as such a shock when he pulled the emergency stop cord on his life.

Daniel was barely out the door after his cup of tea when Rita started.

'D'ya know, it's beyond me how a fine young man like that is still single, how he hasn't been snapped up a long time ago. I wonder is he batting for the other—'

'Mam ...' Julie warned.

'Shure, wasn't he going out with one of the Hegarty girls for years,' Nellie said. 'Apparently, she told him to either put a ring on it or take a hike so he took the hike. She was gutted. Lovely girl she is too, married now with two kids. He could have done a lot worse for himself.'

'There's some lads that never settle down,' Rita said, casting a meaningful look at her daughter, who had been engaged to her fiancé Sean for going on a decade now. 'Shame, though, a handsome-looking lad like that.'

'Himself and Mark were a right pair, weren't they? Always

up to some divilment, the two of them. I'll never forget the state of him at the wake, he was in bits,' Julie said.

Christina would never forget either. The anguished sobs coming from deep in his belly, his face puce with the effort of trying to muffle his pain. He had managed to pull himself together for the funeral, though.

She sat on her bed later that afternoon staring at the wall. This waiting in limbo was torture. She wished they could just move on, that Mother and Daddy could be *released* (as if they were in prison) so they could get the next awful bit out of the way. That the gardaí would stop with their endless worrying questions. She wished she could talk to somebody about what she had done, but there was nobody. She couldn't tell Julie in case she ever let it slip to Aunty Rita. And she couldn't tell Rob or Kate. She wondered if they knew anything, and if they did, how much they knew. About Mark. And now her parents.

She shifted her focus to the painting that hung on the back wall of her bedroom, a scene that she often sought solace in. Her parents had presented her with it, an original, from her favourite artist, for her thirtieth birthday. Mother hadn't had a clue what to get her, had allocated her a generous budget and told her to pick something out herself. She didn't have to ask twice. Christina had long coveted one of Jimmy Lawlor's unique su-ruralist (as he described it himself) depictions of everyday Irish life.

The painting, *A Delicate Touch*, greeted her when she opened her eyes every morning. A girl dainty as a doll hovered in the air, wearing a skirt that looked like it was made of dancing fireflies. A delicate finger reached out to touch one of the tiny pieces of glowing light that had broken away from her gown and floated around her. It was the kind of art Christina would have liked to create herself, otherworldly and innocent, if things had turned out differently. Lawlor had won a Texaco Art competition as a teenager, just like she had.

Her fantasy of being an artist, of going to the National College of Art and Design to study painting, had been just that. A fantasy. A pipe dream. Especially after Mark.

She didn't blame him. He would never have expected her to be the one to find him; it would have been the last thing he wanted. Her teenage self rarely ever paid a visit to the working end of the farm. Like her mother, Christina had always kept well away from that end of the family business. Back then, she was most likely to be found curled up inside reading a book, sketching in her pad, or studying for her exams. She could never understand or explain why she had gone to look for him that day, what sense had niggled and nagged at her until she went.

He had timed it badly, the week before her Leaving Cert. She had still managed to scrape together the points for arts in the university in Galway, her year of solid study paying off. It hadn't been her first choice, but that hadn't mattered. Nothing had mattered.

She had lasted until about halfway through the second term of first year. Then she was transferred from her student accommodation via A&E to a private room in a Dublin psychiatric unit. Nobody believed her when she tried to tell them she had no intention of taking her own life. All she had been trying to do was stop the dreams, to get a few hours of uninterrupted sleep.

Yes, she had to admit, she had become overly interested in the act of suicide. Obsessed, possibly. And, yes, with hanging in particular. Her mind kept dragging her to places she didn't want to go. Forcing her to fixate on stuff that had no place inside her head. Like whether Mark had considered his options and what made him go for hanging in the end? Had he mulled over the type of knot? A fixed knot was the most common (according to a study of autopsy findings she had googled) in cases of 'self-suspension'. Self-suspension, how harmless it sounded. Like a child hanging from the branch of a tree by their arms to see how long they could last before tumbling playfully to the ground. Had he deliberated for long over the position of the knot? Had he gone for the back, the side or the occipital protuberance at the base of the skull?

These morbid details had engrossed her. The how stopped her from thinking about the why. Why Mark hadn't talked to Daddy when they had once been so close. Why he had felt he couldn't talk to her or Rob. Why he couldn't tell them how he was feeling.

She had tried to live out in the world again after the hospital, but look how that had turned out. There was no escaping the fear. It followed her everywhere she went, folding itself up and packing itself into her head. A permanent stowaway. It was pointless even trying. Like when Helen, her therapist, tried to get her to remember a time when she felt happy and to feel those feelings. She couldn't remember, couldn't feel, every last scrap of happy buried deep under the heavy grey weight of her depression, unreachable.

She had been so confused. After Mark. Confused about what she had seen that day in the milking shed, what her mother had almost convinced her she couldn't have seen. The piece of white paper on the ground, the faint Belvedere Bond watermark, ripped at the top where it had been torn from her mother's writing pad. 'Dear Mother', it said. The words below a blur.

20

Kate

There was a message on her phone from Niamh to say the search of the cottage was complete and they were free to move back in. Although she would be glad to see the back of the scene-of-crime team, and a return to some kind of normality on the farm, the thought of returning to those gloomy rooms after the light-filled luxury of the farmhouse depressed her. And they couldn't leave Christina on her own, rattling around this great big house. It made sense for them to stay here for the time being.

It was a good distraction for the kids too. Kate suspected they still didn't realise that Ursula and Jimmy's absence from their lives was a permanent one. It was their first experience of loss – how could they be expected to understand the perpetuity of death? That this time Ursula and Grandad wouldn't be coming back with a bulging duty-free bag stuffed with last-minute gifts. Her own first real experience of loss had been her mother; but she had lost her years before she went into the ground.

The broken creature her father had helped from the car into the house ten never-ending days after she went in to have the baby didn't even look like her mother, looked more like Granny after the arthritis sank its teeth into her. Bent and shuffling and whitewashed. Her empty stomach hung off her, a limp, useless pouch. Every day while she was gone, Kate had asked Aunty Caroline when Mammy was coming home. Every evening, she greeted her father at the door with the same question.

'Soon, Katie love, soon', he had promised.

She had known something bad was happening. It was as if the house itself was on tenterhooks. She heard the adults speak in loud whispers, heard her father tell Sandra from next door that he was coming 'bottom first', which by the sound of the neighbour's gasped reaction was not a good thing. It had been a he. A baby boy.

The day before the wraith imitating her mother came home, her father sat Kate down.

'I need to talk to you, Katie love. It's about the baby. Baby Kevin.' His voice had broken. 'He was a very sick little baby so Holy God had to take him back to heaven. Mammy will be coming home tomorrow, but she won't be bringing the baby with her.'

She had been sad about the baby but happy that her mother would be home soon. She missed her so badly it hurt.

'That's OK, Daddy. Don't worry. We can get another baby. When Mammy comes home.'

He had nestled her into his chest, her head under his chin, and she felt the moist heat of his tears tickle her scalp.

Her mother had spent the best part of three months in bed after that, crippled with pain. Aunty Caroline had to go back to her job in Dublin, so Sandra next door and a couple of other neighbours kept an eye on Kate while her father was at work. She spent many hours lying on the bed in the darkened room beside Mammy, afraid to get too close in case she hurt her, but craving to be closer at the same time.

It had been years later before she found out what had happened. Before her father even fully understood the horror of it. Symphysiotomy: a brutal word for a barbaric procedure seldom carried out in Europe after the 1950s. Apart from in Ireland. Her mother had been one of hundreds of Irish women who were sliced like animals, through the cartilage and ligaments of their pelvic joints, without their consent or even knowledge of what was happening to them. It was a major scandal when it all came out, of course, but that was cold comfort to the hundreds of surviving women with lifelong pain, disability and emotional trauma, while their babies, in some cases, died or were left brain damaged or injured.

Her mother had been left with permanent lower back pain that no medication seemed to be able to touch. She walked with a limp and was condemned to flat shoes for the rest of her life, a woman who had loved her high heels. The baby had stopped breathing while he was being suctioned out of her. Despite this, her mother had insisted on trying for another baby, and when she lost that baby, another one and another one, until she gave up trying for babies and took up drinking instead.

Her father had only told her the full extent of what her mother had endured after Kate became a mother herself.

'She never wanted you to know this, but she was left incontinent after that operation. That's why she stopped going out. She had a few accidents outside the house and she just ...' He broke off, shaking his head. 'She felt so ashamed. The day of your communion was the final straw for her. For a woman who had always loved her style so much, it was just too much for her to cope with, on top of the pain. God help her, forced into wearing those big thick pads like an old woman and she only twenty-six.'

The day of her communion.

They had gone to The Galleon in Salthill where they always went for special occasions because she loved the gravy there.

The rapidly spreading stain on the back of the pleated floral skirt Aunty Caroline had brought for her mother to wear.

The matching stain that crept up her mother's neck and flooded her face.

'She told us she was after spilling a glass of water on herself. I remember our main courses had just arrived and she tied her cardigan around her waist and we all carried on with our meal,' Kate said.

'She didn't want to spoil your special day, love, after you'd looked forward to it for so long,' her father said sadly.

She was sitting in the den with Christina and the children watching *The Boss Baby*. The temperature had dropped overnight and a cold spell had been forecast for the next few days. It was her favourite kind of weather: crisp and bright and dry. Rob had been up and out early that morning, no shortage of work on the farm to keep him busy. The kids would normally be in school at this time of day, and she would usually be running around like a blue-arsed fly during the lunchtime rush. She couldn't remember when she last had the time to sit down and watch a movie with them. They had lit the fire earlier than usual and its warm glow enveloped the room. The dog was stretched out on the rug in front of the hearth, snoring gently, having apparently taken early retirement. For a few moments, she felt content. Despite everything that was going on.

It's going to be OK. It will all work out.

Lily was curled up beside her, a box of Cadbury's Heroes open in front of them. Luke was thrown across Jimmy's armchair, his long legs dangling over the side. Christina in the other armchair on the far side of the fire, her feet on a tartan pouffe in front on her. Kate felt almost relaxed, as if they were protected inside this cosy room from the craziness going on outside. From dead bodies and guards and trying to stay one step ahead of their endless questions. She reached for a Wispa from the box, let the velvety chocolate melt against the roof of her mouth before licking it off with her tongue. She had her hand out to reach for another one when the door opened.

It was Rob. Still wearing his filthy wellies. Ursula would have had a stroke if she saw him. What was he thinking? And why was he acting so strangely? He was standing in the doorway making weird eyes at her.

What the hell is he at?

An icy breeze slid into the room, burgling the warmth and crawling up her back. Rob must have left the French door open.

The dog lifted his head. Luke paused the movie. Kate sat up. Christina dropped her feet to the floor, shoving the pouffe to one side, staring at her brother.

'Can you come out for a minute, Kate?' he asked.

'Sure.' She got to her feet. 'Don't pause the movie for me, guys, I've seen it before,' she said. 'Be back in a few minutes.'

She closed the door to the den behind her. Followed Rob to the kitchen. Through the open door, she saw the squad car. Niamh standing beside it, a uniformed garda behind the wheel.

'What's happening?' Fear grabbed her by the throat, making it hard to speak, to breathe. *They've come for me. Sweet Jesus, how have they found out? What have they found out? The poor kids. And Rob.* She clutched the back of a chair.

'I'm being arrested,' Rob said.

Oh fuck!

21

Four days after the event – Saturday, 13 January
Kate

Kate was clearing up after breakfast with Newstalk on in the background when she heard it. On the ten o'clock news.

A man in his thirties has been arrested by gardaí as part of their investigation into the circumstances surrounding the tragic deaths of a prominent County Galway businesswoman and her husband on their family farm on Tuesday. Ursula and Jimmy Kennedy, both in their mid-sixties, died in an incident at the slurry pit on their eighty-hectare farm in Glenbeg, east Galway.

The half-eaten bowl of Ready Brek slipped out of her fingers, splattering glutinous oats and shards of porcelain across the floor and up the front of the solid wood cupboards. She stood rooted to the spot as the newsreader droned on in her flat Midlands accent.

The bodies of Mrs Kennedy, owner of the award-winning Glenbeg Farm Park, and her husband, Jimmy, a well-known local dairy farmer, were recovered from the farm's slurry pit on Wednesday. It is understood that the couple had not been seen by anybody on Tuesday.

An incident room has been set up at Glenbeg garda station where the man is being questioned today in relation to the deaths.

Glenbeg gardaí are appealing for anybody who may have information in relation to the final movements of the Kennedys or to the circumstances surrounding their deaths to contact them at Glenbeg garda station ...

'Mom, what happened? Are you OK?'

The sound of her daughter's voice jolted Kate into motion. She walked across the kitchen and snapped the radio off at the wall, as if she could somehow stop what was happening by cutting off power to the airwaves.

How long had Lily been standing there? How much had she heard?

'I heard something smashing.' Lily gestured at the floor. 'There's cereal everywhere.'

She mustn't have heard. Thank God. For now anyway.

There was only so long they could keep the kids out of school, though, protect them from the gossip. She could just imagine the conversations going on over breakfast in the homes of their school pals these mornings. She had told the kids their dad had stayed the night with his Uncle Kieran because he was lonely after Jimmy, and they hadn't questioned it.

'Em, hello. Earth to Mom.' Lily was staring at her, holding a pretend phone to her ear.

'Oh, sorry, pet. My hands were wet and the bowl just slipped. I'm an awful eegit, amn't I?' She tried to make her voice sound normal, but it came out squeaky.

'Silly goose, Mom.' Lily wrapped herself around Kate's waist, snuggled her head into her belly. Kate held her close for a few moments before gently pushing her away, afraid the stress would seep through her skin into her child. 'You go back inside now, Lils, and I'll be in to you in a little while. I just need to make an important phone call.'

'OK. Can I have some more toast, please? Soldiers. With the crusts off.'

'You'll have to wait a few minutes, Lily. I have to make my phone call and then I have to clean up this mess. I'll bring it in to you when I'm ready.'

'Thanks, Mom, lots of butter, don't forget.' Lily skipped back into the sitting room, her ponytail swinging behind her. Kate shut the door firmly behind her.

Jesus fucking Christ. Did she not have enough on her plate without having to fill the kids' bottomless bloody bellies as well?

She grabbed her phone, dialled the number she had saved.

'Kate, hello, is everything OK?'

'No, Niamh, everything is not OK,' she said, panicked. 'Did you hear the radio? It's on the news about Rob, that he's been arrested.'

Silence for a beat. 'Are you sure?'

The TV blared from the den. 'Sorry a second.' She rapped on the door, shouting at the kids to turn the volume down. She put the phone back to her mouth. 'Yes, I'm sure. It was just on the national bloody news. He wasn't named but it's pretty obvious who they're talking about. A man in his thirties? I mean, come on!'

'I didn't hear that, Kate. It definitely didn't come from us, though, not officially anyway. I'd have told you if the press office was releasing anything to the media.'

'Well, it must have bloody well come from somebody in there because it sure as hell didn't come from any of us. How can they do this? Surely it can't be legal? As if the gossips around here don't have enough to be talking about already.'

'He wasn't named. A man in his thirties could be anybody, sure—'

'Oh, come off it, Niamh, you know as well as I do that everybody will assume it's Rob. Is it not bad enough that he had to spend the night in a cell? How the hell is he even supposed to be able to grieve his parents properly with all of this going on?'

She hung up. *What's the point? There's no way of shoving this genie back into the radio.*

People would automatically assume that if Rob had been arrested, he must have had something to do with the deaths of his parents.

Bet it was the son. Who inherits the land and the business? That's your answer right there!

She could only imagine the comments section on therealsceal.ie after this, the poison seeping from fingertips.

Michelle McDonagh

All out there floating around in cyberspace for Lily and Luke to find some day in the future.

If there was one thing Glenbeg had galore – no different to any other small Irish town or village – it was begrudgers. As if Schadenfreude was sewn into the fabric of the place, the malicious glee that small minds took in the misfortunes of those deemed to have, God forbid, gotten *above themselves*. Kate had read an interesting article about it once in the *Irish Times*, quoting a psychiatrist who explained that behind the resentment and envy of the begrudger lay the assumption that there was only so much happiness to go around. That the begrudged had too big a share of the pot and the begrudger too little. What a sad way to go through life, she had thought, believing that happiness was a finite commodity and you had been cheated out of your fair share.

She could only imagine the conversation going on at the post office on Main Street today, Schadenfreude Central. Betty Quinn must be doing a roaring trade in single stamps. Kate could just picture it. Customers lining up like finches at a feeder while Betty dropped delectable little titbits of tittle tattle into their gawping beaks. Enough scandal to fill their bellies for months on end. Mrs Keane in the newsagent's was another reliable source, a quarter pound of gossip with every paper. While children made crucial decisions in the penny sweet corner (it would always be called that no matter how many times the currency changed), Mrs Keane leaned over the counter to share her latest *Did you hear about* or *You'll never guess who*. As for the mothers at the school gate, there would be a feeding frenzy over the news of Rob's arrest there, like

194

throwing the carcass of a freshly slaughtered cow in among a shoal of starving piranhas.

Even Mrs O'Flynn, the principal of Scoil an Croí Naofa, had clearly been dying to ask Kate more questions when she rang yesterday to explain that she would be keeping the kids at home for a few more days. Beneath her earnest display of support for the family – *if there's anything we can do, anything at all, just pick up the phone* – Kate could sense her hunger to get closer to the drama. Ruth, whose motto in life (one of many) was 'fuck the begrudgers', always told her she shouldn't worry so much about what people outside her family and close friends thought of her, pointing out in her inimitable way that 'it really doesn't matter a shite at the end of the day', and Kate did find that as she got older she was learning to care less about the opinions of others. But this was different. Her husband had been arrested in connection with the deaths of his parents, for Christ's sake; it was impossible not to care what people were saying about it.

As the gloopy mess stiffened around her, cementing itself onto the floor and up the cupboards, Kate sank onto the stool beside her, elbows on the breakfast bar, face cradled in her hands. She felt like bawling, but her tears had frozen into a hard ball that was wedged in her windpipe. It even hurt to swallow. *When is this fucking nightmare going to end?* If she knew it would end in a couple of weeks or even a month, she could handle that. Take one day at a time. But it was the not knowing. The investigation could drag on for months and months. Why were the gardaí so reluctant to entertain the entirely plausible notion that this had been a tragic farming accident? Accidents happened on farms all the time and everybody knew slurry pits were lethal. There was no going back, though, she had to stick to the plan. For now anyway.

Her phone rang. Niamh. She could piss right off. Probably feeling guilty that some big mouth in the station had leaked the news of Rob's arrest. Well, she could stew in it. It would be very easy to fall for the FLO's 'we're all in this together' bullshit, but Kate couldn't afford to let her guard down for a second. Niamh was not their friend. *Liaison between us and the gardaí, my arse. That one is a spy in plain clothes.*

She picked up her phone again. She was waiting for a call from Rob's solicitor. Their usual solicitor, Paul, didn't do criminal law work himself, but he had arranged for a criminal defence lawyer he knew, 'a good guy, one of the best around', to represent Rob. She willed the phone to ring. She needed to clean the mess up but a deep inertia kept her glued to her stool.

The door to the den opened. 'Are my soldiers ready yet?'

God give me patience!

22

Kate

If somebody had told Kate and Rob that first night they met that one day they would find themselves married with two kids, and with Rob after spending the night in a garda station under arrest for the murder of his parents, they'd probably have scoffed and said, 'What are you on and have you any going spare?' Maybe made a joke about getting the Innocence Project onto the case. And yet, here they were.

That night was a propitious one for Kate. Not only was it the first time she met Rob, it was also the night she figured out what she really wanted to do with her life. She had arranged to meet a group of her fellow third-year law students at an Amnesty International talk at the King's Head in the city centre.

Having missed her bus into town, she had arrived late into

the heaving bar. She squeezed through the throng of students and tourists and spotted her friends seated at a table in front of the stage. As the main speaker was already being introduced by the event organiser, she didn't even have time to get a drink at the crowded bar.

Ruth, her closest friend in college, waved her over, pointing at an empty stool beside her that she had kept. She had only got to know Ruth properly at the start of the year when they had sat beside each other at a tutorial, but they had clicked instantly and she felt like she'd known her for years. Ruth had brought laughter and fun into her life, something that had been missing for a long time.

'Thanks, Ruth, you're a star,' Kate said.

'No prob, thought you weren't going to make it. This is Rob, by the way,' she said, nodding towards the brown-eyed boy sitting the other side of her. 'Another blow-in from Glenbeg like meself. Rob, meet Kate.'

'How're you doing, Kate? I know you to see from around campus.' He knew her to see! Christ, he had a smile that could melt icebergs.

'Nice to meet you.' *Cringe!* Why couldn't she have casually said, 'Good, thanks, yeah, I've seen you around too.' She just hadn't been expecting to find the seriously cute guy she had spotted around the law department sitting next to her.

Luckily, she was saved from making even more of a eegit of herself as the main speaker took to the mic. For over an hour, the packed pub was unnaturally still and hushed as the speaker, a petite black American woman with silver-grey hair and thin-rimmed glasses, told her story. A tale of unimaginable horror.

It all started when her nineteen-year-old son Andre was wrongly convicted of murdering a young white woman, whose badly beaten body was found in woodland close to their home. Despite his mother providing a genuine alibi, Andre was charged, convicted and sentenced to death.

He spent fifteen years on death row before he was put to death in the electric chair, affectionately known as Old Sparky, in Florida in 1989. Kate felt sick to her stomach as the dignified, quiet-spoken woman before her outlined how the execution had to be interrupted twice as flames and smoke shot out of her son's head. Of how he continued to move and breathe during the first interruption. Of how it took the poor man fifteen minutes and twenty-two seconds to die a slow, torturous death. Of how the odour and sizzling sound of her son's burning flesh filled the viewing room where she and other family members watched the barbaric spectacle in horror.

It was found afterwards that the sponge, which was designed to conduct electricity to her son's head, had been improperly used. Not the first time this had happened. The Department of Corrections admitted that the execution 'did not go according to plan'.

Shockingly, despite this botched execution, and several similarly barbaric ones, it was another eleven years before Florida signed a law allowing inmates to choose between electrocution or lethal injection.

Five years after her son's death, the woman finally managed to have him exonerated of all charges.

The hush hung heavy in the smoke-filled air for long seconds after she stopped speaking. Then somebody at the back of the room started clapping and somebody else joined in and there was an almighty racket as stools were shoved back and people got to their feet and the whole room erupted into applause.

A break was announced before the next speaker.

'Fuckin' hell,' Ruth said. 'That's nuts. Imagine spending fifteen years behind bars for a crime you didn't commit. And then to be tortured to death. How the hell did they get away with that?'

'Insane, but not uncommon, unfortunately,' said Rob. 'There are innocent people locked up a lot longer than that, many of them on death row in the States. A lot more black than white too. We just don't hear about them.'

'That poor woman,' said Kate. 'Knowing her son was innocent and being totally powerless to help him. And then to have to watch him die like that. How did she survive it?' What a harsh place the world could be, what cruelties some humans had to endure. At the hands of their fellow humans. And how cosseted she and her fellow students were in their safe middle-class lives, she had thought.

'Well, I for one need a drink after that,' Ruth announced. 'Anybody else coming to the bar?'

'God, yes,' Kate said.

'Stay where you are, girls, and mind the seats. I'll get them – it's manic up there.' Rob gestured towards the bar which was mobbed with thirsty students.

'Thanks, Rob, you're an aul' dote. I'll have a vodka and Coke. Same for you, Kate?'

'Ah, OK, yes, please. I'll get the next one,' she said.

'No bother at all,' he called over his shoulder as he headed for the bar.

'What are you like, Ruth? You cheeky cow. That poor guy doesn't even know me – he probably felt he had to offer.' Kate hit her friend lightly on the arm. As Ruth was the first to admit herself, she had 'a neck like a jockey's bollocks'.

'Ah, would you stop, those Kennedys are loaded. He's certainly not short a few bob. He's actually a really nice guy, considering. Very down-to-earth.'

'Considering what?' Kate was intrigued.

'Well, considering how much of a ride he is. He could get away with being an arsehole. And considering his mother. Although Mr Kennedy is a lovely man, very well-liked.'

'What's the story with his mother then?' Kate kept one eye on the bar to make sure he didn't come back and catch them gossiping about him.

'Ah, she's just a bit up her own arse,' Ruth said. 'Thinks she's a cut above everybody else. Which doesn't go down well in a small town like Glenbeg, as you can imagine. Anyway, what do you think of him?'

'He seems nice.'

'Nice, me hole, what do you really think of him?'

'I think he seems nice.' She paused. 'Does he have a girlfriend?'

'Hah, I knew it ...' Ruth said, smirking gleefully.

Rob returned from the bar just as the event organiser was introducing the next speaker, one of the directors of the Innocence Project at Cardozo School of Law in New York.

Kate would have to play it cool in front of Ruth – she didn't trust the notorious matchmaker to keep her gob shut – but the truth was she felt drawn towards Rob in a deeply physical way. Lust at first smile. It was probably due to the heady atmosphere in the room, everybody's emotions running high. Christ, she needed a drink to calm herself down.

'Move in one there, Kate, and let Rob sit on the outside, nearest to the bar,' Ruth said, with a roguish wink, as she shifted onto the stool Rob had vacated. Kate aimed a bullet of a glare straight between her friend's eyes.

'So how can an innocent person end up behind bars, sometimes for years?' asked the Innocence Project speaker, a tall dapper man with a moustache and a waistcoat. 'The truth is it can happen very easily. Lives are upended and destroyed all the time on the basis of false convictions.'

They turned their attention back to the stage. Kate was appalled yet inspired by what she heard that night. The international statistics that suggested between 4 and 10 per cent of prisoners were innocent of the crimes for which they were convicted. The fact that one-quarter of cases of exoneration on the basis of DNA in the US also included a false confession. That there was a much higher rate of death sentences where the victim was black compared to white.

Up until that night, she had been aimlessly meandering through her law degree, without any sense of passion or ambition, and had begun to question whether she had picked the right course. There was no question of her switching programmes; she wouldn't dream of putting that financial burden on her father. She was stuck with her choice. Lost and hollow after her mother's death, she had only gone into law in the first place because her career guidance assessment suggested her talents might lie in that direction. She hadn't any notion of what she really wanted to do; all she did know was she couldn't move away from home and leave her dad on his own.

Now, for the first time since leaving school and starting college, she felt alive. For the first time, she could see a potential career path stretch out ahead of her that she felt excited and enthusiastic about. The Innocence Project had been founded to exonerate the wrongly convicted through DNA testing and to reform the criminal justice system to prevent future injustices around the world. Here now was a way for her to make a real difference.

Even as she listened to the man from Cardozo Law speak and as she planned a different future inside her head, Kate was conscious of the heat of Rob's body beside her, the contact his arm made with hers every time he lifted and replaced his pint on the table.

By the end of that incredible night, Kate had found her calling in life and lost her heart.

23

Kate

Rob's new solicitor, Simon Sheridan, finally rang just after midday. Kate was feeling a bit less frazzled by then. Rita and Julie had arrived to find her in a heap in the kitchen and immediately took control, sticking the kettle on, getting the mop out and making Kate sit at the table. Nellie had arrived hot on their heels, followed shortly after by Kieran and Brendan. She was glad of the company, felt a need for people around her, people she could trust even if she could never tell them the truth.

She looked around the table now. Rita and Julie good-naturedly picking at each other as always, Kieran and Brendan divvying up farm jobs for the afternoon, Nellie chatting away to Christina, helping to keep her mind off things. This would never have happened if Ursula was around.

There was a burst of laughter from the den where the kids were still watching the TV, taking full advantage of the lack of normal screen-time rules, the lack of normal anything. She'd have to send them out for some fresh air soon.

She went into the lounge to take the call, mouthing to the others 'It's the solicitor'. Simon Sheridan clearly wasn't a man for niceties; he got straight to the point.

'So this is the situation, Kate. Rob has been arrested under Section 4 of the Criminal Justice Act, 1984.' He clearly wasn't a local either, not with the stretch on those vowels. 'He was questioned for six hours up until midnight last night, and this was extended by the super for another six hours this morning, starting at 8 a.m. So they have up until 2 p.m. today to decide whether they're going to look for another extension or let him go. If they do extend his period of detention, they can hold him for a further twelve hours.'

She sat on the arm of the sofa. Ursula and Jimmy's expensively framed faces smiled down on her from the opposite wall. The photos that had been taken a few Christmases back. Ursula had booked a photographer to come to Hazeldene to take some 'festive holidays snaps', had her hair and make-up professionally done and bought a new red dress for the occasion. Rob and Kate had been requested to attend the photo shoot with the kids. It made the happy family scene look more authentic with a couple of kids thrown in. 'Make sure you put something nice on them for the photos, Kate,' Ursula had said, as if she was planning on bringing them over in rags. Christina was there too, smiling beatifically as if she hadn't a care in the world.

There were photographs everywhere in this room. On the walls, the mantelpiece and the sideboard. Photos of Ursula on her own. Ursula with the cat, Ursula with her golfing buddies, Ursula drinking wine at an outdoor table at Lake Garda. Kate could never understand it, why anybody would want to live surrounded by photos of themselves. She hated herself in photos. And it wasn't as if her mother-in-law was particularly photogenic, despite being an attractive woman – the opposite, in fact, apart from the professionally altered images. That wasn't the real her, though. Most people never got to see the real her, only the filtered version.

'What? So they could keep him in there tonight again? Is there nothing you can do to get him out? Rob had nothing to do with any of this. His parents' death was an accident, but the guards seem to be hellbent on proving it wasn't. His father had dementia, it was bad. I'm sure he's told you this ...'

'Yes, he filled me in yesterday. The gardaí have to have grounds on which to arrest somebody and they have outlined a number of grounds here, none of which worry me unduly, really, apart from the fact that he has no alibi for a couple of hours around the time that it looks like Ursula and Jimmy may have entered the pit.'

No alibi! With everything that had gone on from the moment that Rob rang her to say he couldn't find his father, she hadn't thought to ask him where he had gone after his appointment with Paul Sheehan – the appointment Kate had set up for him. After he had gone to the supermarket, the butcher's and the chemist and got everything on the list she had given him to keep him busy away from the farm. She had assumed he must have gone for lunch with Paul, a friend since their school days, when he hadn't arrived back straight after. *Where the hell had he gone? How had he no alibi?*

The solicitor continued: 'The fact that the CCTV was turned off has raised a major red flag, but there's no evidence that Rob had anything to do with that. It could have been anyone, including Jimmy himself. The main reason they brought him in yesterday seems to be down to the witness statement of a woman by the name of Nuala Hehir.'

Bloody Rita and her big bloody mouth.

'She said she heard there was a massive blow-up between Rob and Ursula. That Ursula had gone back on a promise she had made to Rob to do with a property and he was planning to get legal advice about it. Look, I'm not overly worried about this. It's all hearsay. This Hehir woman heard it from Rita who heard it from Julie who heard it from somebody else. It does, however, make Rob a suspect in the eyes of the gardaí, and was enough to give them grounds for his arrest when taken along with the CCTV and lack of alibi.'

'Do you think they're going to charge him with something?'

'I don't think they have enough to charge him at the moment, but that's why they're holding him. They're hoping they'll get more.'

'Is he allowed to call me?'

'Hold tough until we see what happens when his period of detention is up. If they extend it again, I'll arrange for him to give you a call.'

He rang back just after two to say Rob's period of detention was being extended for another twelve hours. Nuala Hehir's statement had made sure of that.

'Her statement gave them the grounds to arrest him in the

first place, and now to keep him in there for another night,' Kate reported back to Christina and the others. Her voice was tight with barely restrained fury. She couldn't even look at Rita.

'Sweet Jesus, Mary and Joseph. What have I done? Oh God, poor Rob. This is all my fault.' Rita's cheeks had turned a worrying shade of purple and she was breathing funny.

'Breathe, Mam, you'll bring on your angina,' said Julie, standing behind her mother and rubbing her back.

Rita left soon after that, wearing her shame like blusher, swearing she would never speak to 'that treacherous cow Nuala Hehir' ever again. Julie had gone into work and the two men were back out on the farm. Nellie had brought Lily out to visit the llamas. Luke had refused to go because the new challenges he had been waiting for on *Fortnite* had just come out, and he was going to try to 'grind to a new level'. She had no idea what that meant and didn't have the energy to argue with him. Too much screen time was the least of her worries right now.

The minutes crawled by as she waited for Rob to call from the garda station. She wondered how he was coping, what he was thinking. He must be so angry, so confused, so utterly exhausted at this stage. Like a stunned boxer in the ring with no referee to stop the fight. She could stop it. She could stop it right away by telling the truth. But no. She needed to keep her nerve. They'd have to let him go – he hadn't done anything wrong. She had to hold it together, for all their sakes.

She went upstairs to call Ruth in private and had just come off the phone when Luke appeared at the door to the guest room where she and Rob were sleeping.

His eyes were watery and red. Maybe it had finally hit him that Jimmy and Ursula were gone.

'Are you all right, pet?'

'Where's Dad?' He was on the verge of tears.

'Dad, em ... he didn't come back yet from Uncle Kieran's. He might need to stay another night.'

'What happened to Grandad and Ursula?'

'What happened to them? Well, like we told you, Luke, we think they were probably overcome by the fumes and they fell into the pit and ... they died. Come here, pet, sit down beside me and we can talk about it.' She patted the bed.

'Is that what really happened?' He stayed standing.

'Well, we don't know exactly what happened yet because none of us were there but—'

'Did they get' – he stumbled over the word – 'murdered?'

'My God, no, Luke. It was an accident, a terrible tragic accident, but these things happen on farms. That's why we're always warning you and Lily to be so careful out there.'

He looked strangely at her.

'What is it, Luke?' Had somebody said something to him? But he hadn't been out of the house, and she hadn't given him his phone back yet just in case. She had told him she couldn't find the charger in the cottage and he hadn't pushed it.

'I was playing *Fortnite* with Jamie Kenny and he asked me if it was true that my dad had been arrested for murder. He heard his parents talking about it this morning, and they said Jimmy and Ursula were murdered and the guards think Dad did it and they have him locked up in jail.'

Fuck. The Xbox. She'd totally forgotten that he could chat to the lads through his headset. What the hell should she say?

'Look, we didn't tell you because we didn't want to worry you, and there is nothing to worry about really, you see.' Her son looked even more horrified. 'It's all a misunderstanding and Dad's solicitor is sorting it out as we speak. Your dad didn't murder anybody. You know Dad, for God's sake, he wouldn't hurt a fly. It was an accident. Jimmy and Ursula fell in. We don't know exactly how, but we do know that nobody pushed them.'

'But why would they arrest Dad if it was an accident?'

'The guards get it wrong all the time, pet. Somebody gave them wrong information and they brought Dad in to ask him some more questions, but his solicitor is in there with him right now sorting the whole thing out. He'll be home soon, I promise you.' She hoped to God he would.

Kate had almost missed Rob's call, but Lily spotted the phone flashing.

She opened the French doors and went outside, away from little ears.

'Hi, love, are you OK?' Rob asked. He spoke in a low voice, flat and lethargic.

'Never mind me, are you OK? Do you know when they're going to let you out?'

'Not yet, it'll probably be tomorrow by the look of things, though.'

'You must be exhausted, love.'

'They're giving me plenty of breaks and I had a rest period from midnight till eight this morning, but they're just asking the same questions over and over and getting the same answers. It's draining.'

'Will they let me in to see you this evening? Christina can stay with the kids.'

'No, Kate, I don't want you to come in. You wait there and look after everybody.'

'Just for half an hour. I'll bring you in something to eat—'

'No, love, please. Paul dropped me in some stuff earlier – I don't need a thing. I want you to stay with Christina and the kids, mind them all until I get back.'

She wanted to ask him about the break in his alibi, where he went after he left Paul's office on Tuesday, but somebody might be listening in; she'd have to wait until she got him home.

'Look, love, there's somebody coming. I'll talk to you properly tomorrow.'

'But—'

'I have to go. Tell the kids I love them and I said goodnight. Love you.'

He was gone.

24

Five days after the event – Sunday, 14 January
Christina

It was the sight of her nephew's anxious little face going off to bed the night before that made Christina's mind up for her. She couldn't let this go on any longer. Rob had just spent two nights in a cell in a garda station, and the way things were going, he could end up being charged with the murder of their parents. Something she knew he could have had no involvement with, could never have even contemplated. *Surely not?*

Rob had always looked out for her, ever since they were children. In so many ways. Bringing her back souvenirs from his school tours, pushing her patiently on the swing in the back garden while she shouted, 'Again, again,' teaching her how to cycle. Mark had been the fun brother, the one who always came up with the best ideas for games and adventures. Rob was the more sensible one. Amiable and even-tempered. He had tried so hard to reach her after Mark. To find a way in to the place deep inside where she had curled up and hidden. Sitting on the end of her bed night after night trying to coax her back out with mugs of hot chocolate, the latest issues of *Smash Hits* and *Kiss*, and her favourite Perri onion rings. None of it worked; she had gone in too far and got stuck.

He had always been the most stable one of the three of them. He hadn't sounded stable the night of the row, though; he had sounded crazed. The way he had spoken to Mother. Such fury and disgust. *Had he cracked? Good people did bad things sometimes. If they were pushed far enough.* She had been shocked herself when she heard her mother had changed her mind about the barn conversion. She knew how much they had all been looking forward to moving into their new home. *How could Mother do such a thing? It was incomprehensible.*

But still there was no way Rob would have had anything to do with ...? Surely? It made no sense.

Which was why she had to do this. Why she had picked up the phone and called Niamh. Why she was waiting now for the FLO to come and collect her.

She hadn't said anything to Kate. She would leave a note on the table, telling her she'd be back in an hour. They had just waved Lily off for the day. Ruth was bringing her over to her house to play with her son, Oscar, who was one of Lily's many 'besties'. Kate had brought Luke over to the cottage to pick up some more of their stuff. It was the first time the house had been empty since Tuesday.

It felt as though her father's family, despite being kept at arm's length by her mother for so many years, had wrapped their arms around them now and were holding them tight. They had been in and out of the farmhouse all week, bearing thoughtful little offerings. Bags of Haribo for the kids, a packet of unicorn hair-clips for Lily and a giant bunch of sunflowers which Rita had bought to 'brighten up the place'. No more ringing in advance to arrange a visit, it was back to the *just dropping in* of Christina's grandparents' day.

It warmed her insides. The knowledge that she, Rob, Kate and the children weren't alone in their grief and pain, that they had a wider family, people – including dear Nellie, of course – who loved and cared for them. It made it even harder for her to try and fathom why her mother had pushed the Kennedys away over the years, especially when she had no close family herself. She had often talked about blood being thicker than water, but she seemed to want to dilute her own blood. Like a homeopathic tincture. Ursula had no contact at all with her father's family, the Nolans. Never spoke about them, as if that branch of the family tree had been snapped clean off.

Even her mother's relationship with Uncle Peter, which had always been so close, had shrunk to an annual exchange of Christmas cards. It was as if her work was the only relationship she seemed to want or need outside her immediate family, and even then work came first. It always had. Uncle Peter had never married or had children, not that they knew of, anyway. After his visits to the farm stopped, her mother used to fly over to see him once a year in England. She went the weekend before Christmas every year and came home like a briar, her low mood persisting into January and lifting only when the business reopened and she could refocus all her energies on work. Even those trips had stopped about five years ago, with

Ursula claiming she was too busy to go because of the Winter Wonderland. Christina had often wondered why she couldn't go a different weekend instead but knew better than to ask. She had overheard a phone conversation one evening as she was passing the living-room door, which was slightly ajar, and had paused outside.

'I'm sorry, I can't do this any more. You need to get help, Peter.'

She heard sniffling and then the sound of her mother blowing her nose loudly. That was around the time the December trips had ended.

Christina had wondered if Peter had developed an addiction of some sort, drink or drugs or maybe gambling, and if her mother had been left with no choice but to cut him off unless he got help. He certainly wouldn't have been the first Paddy to have found himself in such straits. It had only been more recently that she had come to suspect that it may have been far worse than that.

'May I ask why you're only coming forward with this information now, Christina?'

She stared at the table that sat between her and the detective inspector. She was glad it was him and not Snitcheen; she had the sense that Sergeant Tuohy was enjoying the drama engulfing his distant family.

'I was hoping I wouldn't have to tell anybody, that it could stay our secret. Myself and Dad and Mother.'

'So you're telling us that your father had been suicidal in the weeks before his death?'

She looked up at him. He had lovely eyes, but those eyebrows were insane. 'Yes.'

'And he told you that he was planning to take his own life?'

'Yes.'

'And you were so concerned about this you told your mother?'

'Yes.'

'Tell us, Christina, did your father have a plan for how he was going to do this?' The other guard, with the heavy thighs and a trendy undercut, had been introduced as Detective Garda Emma Malone.

'I don't know. He didn't tell me if he did. He just said he'd had enough and he didn't want to end his life the same way his father had.'

'Why did you not tell anybody else? Bring him to his GP?'

'My mother said she'd deal with it herself. She was a very private person – she'd have hated it to get out. For people to hear that my father had … mental issues. Especially after Mark. She warned me not to tell anybody, even Rob.'

'So your brother was completely unaware of your father's state of mind?'

'Yes.'

'And tell us, how did your mother *deal* with the situation?'

'She started keeping a very close eye on Daddy. Popping back from work regularly to see where he was, checking up on him on the CCTV.'

'What I don't understand about all this, Christina,' Detective Inspector McGuire leaned forward over the table, shrinking the space between them, 'is why you continued to keep this information to yourself even after your brother was arrested and taken in for questioning. Why you didn't immediately contact us to tell us what you knew.'

'I told you, I was hoping it wouldn't get out. Dad never had a day of mental illness in his life – I didn't want people talking. Like son, like father ... the stigma. I know there's all this talk now about being open about mental health and there's more and more people going public about depression and stuff, but the reality is that people look at you differently, treat you differently, like they're afraid they'll catch it off you if they hang around you too long.'

'So what made you decide to change your mind?'

'I had no choice. You have it all wrong. Arresting Rob? My God. Rob wouldn't have harmed a hair on the head of either of our parents. He came back here to the farm after Mark died to help my parents out. He and Kate were planning to work in humanitarian law. They had big dreams. But he gave that all up, they both did, because my parents needed him. He would do anything for any of us, me, Kate, the kids. My parents. He had nothing to do with their deaths – you have to believe me.'

There was a whirring sound from the electronic box in the corner, reminding her that she was being recorded. The blast of a car horn outside, a shout of greeting, laughter.

Detective Inspector McGuire shifted in his seat. 'Can you outline again for us what you think happened on Tuesday morning?'

'I think my father must have decided to take his own life that morning.' Her voice trembled. 'I think he had it all planned out. He had sold off the last of the beef cattle the previous week. So the shed was empty, but the slurry tank was full. He knew the dangers full well. I think his plan may have been to mix the slurry and be overcome by the fumes. But he wouldn't have expected my mother to follow him.'

'A pretty novel way to commit suicide, I would have thought,' the detective garda observed wryly.

Christina really didn't like her. She felt like telling her that she shouldn't say 'commit suicide' as if the act of taking one's own life was a crime. As, incredibly, it had been in this country until the early 1990s. The term was still common parlance and it made Christina cringe to hear seasoned broadcasters still regularly using it. Was there not some kind of media training in this area? It may have been decriminalised, but suicide was still a sin in the eyes of the Church and, for some of a certain generation, that was worse than any crime punishable by law. The stigma was still alive and kicking, especially in a rural community like theirs.

'And how do you think they both ended up in the tank?' the detective inspector asked.

'I don't know. Maybe she tried to argue with him, to pull him away. They must have both been overcome by the fumes and toppled in.'

'Is there any possibility, do you think, that your mother might have pushed your father in and somehow been overcome or fallen in herself?' he asked. 'His sister, Rita, has made us aware that your mother was putting pressure on him to give her power of attorney over his affairs. Is there any way she could have taken matters into her own hands to speed things up a bit?'

'I don't think so but ...' She sighed deeply. 'I guess anything's possible.'

25

Kate

Kate was reading Lily her bedtime story when the call came. Rob was being released without charge.

As her daughter ran squealing delightedly down the stairs to tell Luke that he was on the way home, Rob filled Kate briefly in on what had happened. It turned out that his release had been hastened by the guilty conscience of one of Uncle Kieran's regulars, a man called Bernard Flood, who had been illegally fly-fishing at the river on Tuesday morning. He had noticed Rob in the distance sitting on a bench around noonish.

When news spread on Tuesday evening of the double tragedy on the farm, he mentioned to his wife that only that morning he had seen Jimmy Kennedy's son sitting alone at the river just staring into the water. His wife caught wind of the rumours about Rob's arrest swirling around the bookie's where she worked part-time and rang her husband. Bernard had hummed and hawed for a couple of hours, trying to think of a good excuse for why he was at the river for such a long time without landing himself in it, but then his wife pointed out that the gardaí had more to be worried about than a few illegally fished trout. He had called into the station that afternoon and given a statement that provided Rob with an alibi for the missing hours.

'Simon said that Bernard's statement, on top of Christina's, meant they hadn't enough to charge me with anything so they had to let me go. They may still send a file to the Director of Public Prosecutions but he doesn't seem too worried about that.'

'That's great news, thank God. What do you mean Christina's statement? Why does that make any difference? Sure, they arrested you after she made it.'

'No, her new statement, the one she made today. Did she not tell you she was doing it?'

What the hell?

Christina had gone out for a short while earlier, but Kate assumed she went over to see Rita or Julie. She had gone straight up to her room when she got back.

Kate had to talk to her before Rob returned. To find out what was going on. She went up the impressive curved staircase, with its luxurious carpet the colour of an expensive claret that had been Ursula's pride and joy. She remembered the first time she had seen the house; the carpet was one of the only things that hadn't been replaced or changed since then. It was hard to believe it was over twenty-five years old: it still looked brand new.

Ursula had still been in full disguise at that stage, full of convivial welcome for her son's new girlfriend.

'It's a V'Soske Joyce, made in Oughterard, would you believe? Pure new wool. Hand-tufted. They make carpets for practically all the royal families, Harrods, the Dorchester in London, the Ritz in Paris. The Arabs love them, all those sultans and sheiks, they all have them in their yachts. That carpet will be there till the day I die.' *She had been right there, anyway.*

Kate continued to the end of the hallway, past doors closed on uninhabited rooms and around the corner to the back of the sprawling house, the size of a large B&B.

She tapped lightly on Christina's door.

Her sister-in-law was lying on her bed under a soft throw, a book in her hand. A clock ticked gently; the flame of a candle swayed on her bedside table. A hint of seaside in the air, comforting. It was a peaceful room, even if the same couldn't be said for its occupant.

'Rob's been released – he's on the way now.'

'Oh, Kate, that's amazing. I knew they'd have to let him go.'

'I wasn't so sure, to be honest. You just never know … but a man came forward to say he saw him during the period he had no alibi.'

'Rob did nothing wrong. They were always going to have to accept that.'

'It's not always that simple, though, is it?' Kate sat on the side of the bed. 'He told me you went into the station today to give another statement. You never said anything …'

'Sorry, Kate, it took me so long to psych myself up to do it that I was afraid I'd change my mind if I let myself stop and think about it. Niamh arranged it for me.' Christina looked down at her hands.

'I don't understand. What did you have to say that you hadn't already said in your original statement?'

Christina glanced up at her. Glanced quickly away again. Why couldn't she look Kate in the eye?

'I told them my father was suicidal before he died and that I thought he might have killed himself and my mother tried to stop him but somehow ended up ...'

Kate was aware her bottom lip had dropped. She stared at Christina. *What the actual fuck?*

'Why did you tell them that?'

'Because it was true.'

'But it wasn't true, was it?'

'I'm sorry I didn't tell you and Rob before now, but Mother warned me not to tell anybody. She wanted to deal with it herself. You know what she was like, how private she was.' She still wouldn't look at Kate.

'What made you think he was suicidal?' *He may have been low at times with the dementia, but suicidal? And why would he tell Christina of all people? She was about as stable as a wobbly baby tooth.*

'He told me he was going to kill himself, Kate.'

Kate sat frozen. 'When did he say that?'

'A number of times. In the months before he died.'

'Did he say he was going to ... do it in the slurry pit?'

'No, he didn't say anything about how he was planning to do it. And I never actually thought he would go ahead with it.'

What had Jimmy been up to? How long had he been thinking this way? And how much of it had been his illness talking? What the hell had she got herself involved in? Jesus Christ, her head was fried.

She heard the thud of the French doors downstairs heralding Rob's arrival home, followed closely by Lily's hysterical shrieking. Kate stood in the hall outside Christina's door and took a few deep breaths. She needed to gather herself before facing her husband and keeping up the pretence that she believed his parents' deaths had been accidental.

Rob was flopped on the sofa in the den, Lily clinging to him on one side like a baby monkey, gibbering away at a speed of knots, and Luke cuddled into him on the other. He smiled weakly at her, putting on a front for the kids.

'Oh, here comes Mom, we're in trouble now.'

His skin looked grey, as if he hadn't seen sunlight in months, and the shadows under his eyes were like bruises. There were new hollows in his cheeks. He looked like he had lost half a stone in weight since she saw him last. She realised she couldn't remember the last time he had eaten anything; he hadn't been able to stomach any more than a cup of tea before he left the house on Friday. And it was unlikely he had eaten much, if anything, since then.

Christina didn't have to ask twice when she offered to put the kids to bed. Kate whipped up a ham and mushroom omelette while Rob showered and changed. He returned looking almost jolly, wearing the Santa pyjamas she had bought them all for Christmas. She served him his food on a tray on his lap in front of the fire, a bottle of ice cold beer on the side, condensation bubbles clinging on for dear life. She threw a couple of logs onto the fire, before she sat down beside Rob with a glass of Sauvignon Blanc she had found in the fridge.

It felt strange helping herself; she kept expecting Ursula to walk up behind her and ask her what she thought she was doing. She took a deep sip: delicious. Not that she'd expect anything else; her mother-in-law had always had exceptional taste, she had to give the woman that much. She had got it right with the room they were sitting in too, with its soft, comfy sofas, dark-blue walls and plush curtains. It was like a cosy cave, especially tonight with the fire lighting and the candles Christina had lit scenting the air with cinnamon and spices.

'You're looking a bit better now, love, how are you feeling?' she asked. His colour looked slightly more normal, as if some of the grey had washed off him in the shower. He had knocked his beer back and was making short work of the omelette, his appetite obviously having made a comeback.

'How am I feeling?' he asked, fork in mid-air. 'Fucked if I know. I think I'm just numb at this stage, to be honest. Just waiting for the next dip of the rollercoaster. It's all so unreal, everything that's happened over the last few days.'

'I know.' *If only he knew the half of it.*

'They did the whole "you are not obliged to say anything unless you wish to do so". I was almost waiting for Jeremy Beadle to step out from behind the door to tell me I'd been framed, but then I remembered that lad's been dead for years.'

'It's desperate what they put you through. Locking you up in a cell when you should be at home with your family grieving your parents,' she said, her anger at the injustice of it all spilling over.

He chuckled bleakly. 'I wasn't exactly on death row, Katie.'

'Christ, Rob, it's hardly a laughing matter ...'

'No, I know it's not.' He reached for her hand. 'It's just ... you reminded me there of what you were like back in college. How passionate you were about the project. You wanted to save the world and you would have done it too ... if it wasn't for me.'

He looked at her from pained eyes.

'Oh, love.' She put her hand on his warm face. 'I do regret that neither of us got to follow the careers we planned, but I never regretted giving it up to be with you. That was simply never an option for me.' She rubbed his cheek with her thumb. 'I just wish things had been a bit easier for us, you know.'

'Me too, love. Me too.' He nodded, covering her hand with his.

'You said you'd tell me later. About Tuesday morning. What you were doing at the river?'

He sighed heavily, raised his empty bottle. 'I'll go and get us both a refill first.'

When he returned with a fresh beer for himself and a full glass for her, he explained that he had gone to the river to think.

'To think?'

'Yeah. I just needed some time to get my thoughts together before I came home. I might have had my head in the sand over Mother and the business and everything, but I still knew it wasn't right. What we were being paid for all the hours we were working. I just kept thinking ... she's been through so much, losing a son in that way and ... I let it go on too long. I let you down, and I let the kids down. The thought of losing you all ... I couldn't bear it.'

He perched on the edge of the sofa with his head hanging, reminding her of Lily when she did something naughty.

'None of us are perfect, love, and that's for sure, but we all love you so much, and we'd be lost without you. All of us, Christina too. We're just so relieved to have you home again.' She squeezed his hand.

'Well, hopefully I'll be staying here,' he said, taking a hefty slug of his beer. 'If they do send a file to the DPP, which Simon thinks is unlikely given the lack of evidence, he says it's even more unlikely that the DPP will decide to prosecute. He seems fairly confident – hopefully he knows what he's talking about.'

'Well, let's pray they just drop all this nonsense now and leave us alone. Leave us to grieve your parents in peace. Any word on when we can bring them home?' The spectre of the funeral still hung over them, but at least when that was over with, they could try and get back to some sort of normality.

'Oh yeah, I meant to tell you. Christ, I totally forgot with everything else that's going on. They're releasing them tomorrow. Tommy Kirwan is going up with the hearse to collect them. We're to get onto him tomorrow about the arrangements. I know Mother and Daddy are never coming back, but it's a comfort to know they'll be home in Glenbeg, at least, out of that awful place.'

'It will indeed. Did your mother ever mention any kind of funeral plan or anything?' Kate would be astonished if Ursula hadn't; surely her need for control would extend to stage-managing every last detail of her exit from this world.

'She never said anything to me anyway. I'd say she thought she had a long time left before she needed to start worrying about that kind of thing. It's shocking, isn't it? To think she's gone, they're both gone. I can't get my head around it.'

'It's going to take a long time to sink in, love. It was so sudden and things have been so crazy since. Once the funeral is over, you'll have time to try and start to process it all.'

It had been months after her mother's death before Kate stopped hearing her voice calling up the stairs to her, and years before she stopped looking at clothes in shops and thinking how much a certain coat or top would suit her. Walnut Whips still brought a lump to her throat, her mother's favourite.

'Speaking of crazy, did Christina tell you what she said in her statement? I had a quick chat with her upstairs.'

'Yes, I was talking to her when you arrived back.'

'What do you think?'

'I was shocked, to be honest. I certainly never saw signs of anything like that with your father.'

'I didn't either, but given the events of the last few days, nothing would surprise me any more, nothing at all.'

A thought popped into her head. 'Did the guards say anything to you about estoppel?'

'Yes, I was doing a bit of digging on my phone. After the row with Mother. To get an idea of our rights, you know, if she reneged on her promise to give us the barn. If it had gone down the legal route, we might have had to try to estop her from going back on her word. Myself and Paul discussed that possibility on Tuesday when I was in with him. Anyway, the guards must have found it in my search history and that's why they were asking about it. They asked me too.'

So that's where that had come from. It must have raised a blazing red flag for the gardaí. Another one.

26

Six days after the event – Monday, 15 January
Christina

Christina stood in her parents' walk-in wardrobe waiting for Kate to help her pick out the outfits her parents would be buried in. Samson sniffed around her father's shoes and let out a little whimper. Mother would have been livid if she'd caught him in here, shedding mongrel hair all over her expensive carpet. Her presence felt so strong in the confined space of her wardrobe, the scent of Chanel No 5 as potent as if she had just walked out of the room.

Daddy had been easy. She had bypassed the smart Louis Copeland suit he had only worn once, to his nephew's wedding in May. A navy herringbone wool and silk blend. It was a handsome suit but he had been clearly uncomfortable all day in the slim-cut tailoring. Christina had chosen an older suit to bury him in, one he had bought in Malone's on Main Street and worn for funerals. It would see him through one last funeral.

She studied the rails of her mother's clothing, which took up at least three-quarters of the wardrobe space. All colour coordinated and neatly folded or hung. Her mother's signature style had been timeless classic. Serried ranks of crisp white shirts, classic blazers in navy and black and well-cut designer jeans and trousers. Soft cashmere knits. Splashes of colour and some Breton stripes sprinkled in for the summer months.

There was her mother's well-worn Burberry trench, her beloved camel MaxMara coat. And her shoes. Her mother had loved shoes. Boots, pumps and runners. Stilettos and strappy sandals that were pulled out for the annual chamber ball or the Oyster Festival in Galway. And bags, so many bags in soft supple leathers, not a garish logo in sight.

She wondered about underwear. Did she need to choose underwear? It wasn't as if anybody was going to see what was under her parents' clothes, apart from the undertaker. Yet somehow it felt unseemly not to. She took out boxers and socks for her father, stuck them into the pockets of his suit. She opened her mother's knicker drawer, picked a pretty floral pair from the immaculately folded rows. Opened her bra drawer for the matching bra. It wasn't at the front so she rooted around at the back until she found it. She felt something underneath it, pushed to the back of the drawer. A Christmas gift bag with ribbon ties. She lifted it out.

She sat down on the upholstered bedroom chair, the shiny green bag in her hand. She wanted to see what was inside, but it felt like such an invasion of her mother's privacy. She would never have dreamt of opening it if her mother had been alive.

But she wasn't alive. And Christina had questions that needed answers.

She pulled the ribbon, opened the bag. Slid the contents out onto her lap. A stack of Christmas cards. Neatly secured with a thick elastic band. She started leafing through them. They were all from Uncle Peter, every single one. All saying pretty much the same thing.

I'm sorry, Ursula.
I miss you so much.
Love always,
Your brother,

Peter

One of the cards had a picture of adorable kittens playing with tinsel in front of a blazing fire – her mother would have loved that one. In aid of the RSPCA. As Christina opened it, a sheet of notepaper fluttered to the ground.

I'm going to stop. I'll get help, proper help this time, Ursula.
I swear to you. Please give me one more chance, I'm begging
you.

It was dated 2013. Five years earlier. Her mother's trips to England had stopped after that year. Pennies began to drop into slots all over her brain.

Christina had known for some time that one day she would have to stop or at least reduce the meds, to rip off the dressing and confront the wound beneath, an ulcer that had gone gangrenous over the years since Mark's death and was burrowing deeper and deeper into her soul. Her GP argued that if she was a diabetic, she wouldn't dream of coming off her insulin, trying to make out it was the same thing. But it wasn't, it was a very different thing. It wasn't as if the meds even took away her depression, far from it – they merely filed its sharp claws a little. She lived with a chronic low-level sense of discontent punctuated by dips into the black pit of depression. If you could call that living.

God knows she had tried to fight it. Years of talk therapy and crying her way through boxes of tissues hadn't worked and cognitive behavioural therapy was about as effective as a dam made from toothpicks against the tidal force of her emotions. She had done her research into EMDR before she started. Extensive as always. She had been here so many times before. Scrolling for hours at night in bed in search of a 'cure'. Reiki, reflexology, acupuncture. Chinese medicine, energy healing, neurofeedback. The list went on and on. There was a pattern to her mission. So full of hope each time she started something new, so certain this would be the one. She wasn't searching for the utopia of happiness – she wasn't that deluded. She would be quite content to feel content. To find some bit of peace in her head. Sometimes, the placebo effect kicked in, mocking her, fooling her into thinking she had finally found it, the magic bullet. But each time without fail, usually after the second or third treatment, that voice inside her that she hated so much came back and told her, *This won't work either. You're always going to be this way so you might as well just give up trying.*

Eye movement desensitisation and reprocessing. The name alone was nearly enough to put her off. It was a fairly new type of psychotherapy that was supposed to work for people who had trouble talking about the traumatic events they had been through. Despite all the years of therapy, Christina had never been able to talk about that day in the milking parlour. She could talk about the before and after until the cows came home, but not the event itself. As if that particular chunk of memory had locked itself into a panic room in her brain for which she had no code. Which was why her therapist, Helen, had suggested she try EMDR and recommended a colleague who did it.

She told nobody she was going, apart from Helen. It sounded completely bonkers. Using your own rapid eye movements to dampen the power of emotionally charged memories of past traumatic events. And indeed, Christina had felt ridiculous as she flicked her eyes back and forth as quickly as she could during that first session. And not a little sceptical. She had been stunned when it worked.

It turned out that the images of the day she found Mark were tattooed onto her brain, buried beneath layers of fear and confusion. They weren't false creations of her 'vivid imagination', as her mother had convinced her. Any doubt Christina had about the existence of the note had been eradicated during her first EMDR sessions, when her memory of the day of Mark's suicide was disinterred. His last words exhumed.

She had been guided back in time to the milking parlour that bright May morning. Saw the long shadow on the ground. Saw her seventeen-year-old self look up. Felt the horror. Saw herself freeze and then reach her hand out to touch her brother's runners to check if they were real. Felt the tremor that ran through her from her teeth to her knees, a bodyquake.

Heard her teenage screams. She had clearly seen her younger self bending down, scrabbling to pick the note up with her crazily shaking fingers. And the words she had managed to take in that day, written in Mark's sloppy scrawl, had jumped off the page at her all these years later.

> *Dear Mother,*
> *Can't do this anymore. Keeping quiet. Uncle Peter tearing me apart. So messed up. Best for everybody. No other way. Sorry.*
> *Mark*

Over the course of only a handful of sessions, Angela, the psychotherapist, had helped Christina turn down the intensity of her anguish to the point where she was able to simply let the memories be. To a level where she could live alongside them. She still had bad days, had been having a bad week when her parents died, but something had changed inside her.

During one of her sessions, another long-buried memory had slipped back into her consciousness. Like an old VHS tape that had emerged from the back of a drawer during a clear-out. It was a night about a month before Mark's death, when he had fallen in the door of the farmhouse in the early hours in an awful state. Drunk (and God knew what else) out of his mind. Roaring and shouting. As she moved her eyes rapidly back and forth, she saw her father in the kitchen trying to calm her distraught brother. Saw Ursula coming up the hall, tying the belt of her dressing-gown, her features twisted in anger, demanding to know 'What the hell is going on here?' And heard Mark's voice clear as day screaming at their mother: 'I HATE YOU, FUCKIN' HATE YOU, HATE YOU!'

When she had told her mother about the sessions and the memories they were bringing up, Ursula had angrily dismissed them as quackery: 'There's plenty of scam artists out there happy to take money from vulnerable people, Christina, telling cancer patients they'll cure them on a juice diet and the like. Don't start that nonsense again unless you want to end up back in hospital.'

'Well, how are you getting on in here?' Kate stood at the door.

Christina started. Knocked the bundle of cards to the ground.

'Oh God, I'm such a klutz.' She started picking them up, shoving them back into the bag and into the drawer where she had found them. Until she decided what she was going to do about it all. 'I got distracted going through some old stuff.'

She turned to Kate. 'I've Dad sorted but ... well, I don't know about Mother. I don't know if she'd like black for a funeral or something brighter ... I know the coffin isn't even going to be open but ... well, you know how particular she was.'

It felt really important that Christina get this right. Appearances had mattered to her mother. A lot.

'What about that beautiful cashmere jumper she got in London? The white one with the pearls. Here it is,' Kate said, pulling a garment that looked as if it had been spun from candy floss from a shelf. 'With a nice pair of black pants, maybe?' She flicked through the rails. 'Something like this?' She held up a pair of tailored black trousers.

'Oh, that's perfect. She loved that jumper.' And it was cosy, even though it wasn't as if her mother could ever be warmed up again. 'I would have been here all day trying to make a decision if it wasn't for you.'

'I'm only glad to be able to help, Christina. You're being so strong through all of this … And you've been amazing with the kids the last few days, helping to take their minds off everything and making us all feel so at home.' Kate gently squeezed her arm.

'It's so strange, isn't it? It's like we're living in some kind of weird bubble. I haven't even cried – I don't think I'm able to, which is so not like me. It kind of feels like this is all happening to somebody else. Some other family.'

'I know what you mean. It's not something anybody could ever be prepared for. Rob's the same, he's just numb at this stage after everything he's been through. Thank God he's home, though, I was so worried …'

'Me too.'

There was something about the cloistered space of the wardrobe, almost like a confession box, that invited the sharing of confidences. She was tempted to tell Kate what she had found out about Mark. But she couldn't expect her to keep it to herself. Kate would have to tell Rob and then others would have to be told. She wasn't ready yet.

27

Unlike her parents, it hadn't been love at first sight for Ursula and James, not on her part at least. That first encounter took place in a dingy pub a stone's throw from St Stephen's Green. Ursula was nineteen and with a rather stuffy group of work colleagues from the solicitor's office where she worked as a secretary. James had been in the company of a rowdy gang of Trinity students; it wasn't until later in the night that she discovered he wasn't a student himself, but a farmer from a big farm in a small town in County Galway up in the Big Smoke for the night.

It was his cousin who introduced them. Desmond, a med student at Trinity with a Paul McCartney haircut and lazy blue eyes that seemed to gobble her whole when he looked at her. He started chatting her up at the bar and insisted on paying for her drink before a sharp-featured fiancée called Juliette (whose father she later learned was a big-deal property developer) arrived and staked her claim by literally elbowing Ursula to one side. She could feel those sensuous eyes track her back to her seat in the corner, though, and again as she made her way to the ladies a short while later, not looking his way for one second but intensely conscious of his gaze. It was on her way back from the toilets that he grabbed her arm and dragged her over to meet his cousin James.

'Here's the right man for you, Ursula. He's not short a few pound, but unlike the rest of these wankers,' he drunkenly indicated his group of friends, 'he's not a ... wanker.'

'How're you, Ursula? Don't mind that clown. Des, would you leave the poor girl alone?'

'He's fine. I'm happy enough to escape that crowd for a while,' Ursula said, nodding towards the corner where her colleagues were carefully sipping their drinks and looking like they were having as much fun as swine in an abattoir. 'They're not really friends of mine – I just work with them.'

'Well, in that case, sit in here, make yourself comfortable and tell me what you're having to drink.'

James had a broad smile that came easy to him and a nice way about him. He seemed wholly unconscious of the clash of his culchie accent with the elongated vowels all around him and was well able to hold his own among the group of cocky, entitled young men – unlike her, he didn't feel the need to fake it. He was comfortable just being himself.

The fact that James (or Jimmy as his friends insisted on calling him) was a bit of a hunk himself, with his deep tan and tall, strong build, didn't hurt either. She didn't feel that heavy pull of lust that she felt for Desmond, but she understood how it worked. Desmond and his friends had all gone to boarding school together; they had that reek of privilege and affluence. She knew their type well. These rich south Dublin boys with mothers whose sense of smell was sharp as a cadaver dog when it came to sniffing out the pedigree of the girls their darlings brought home to them for approval, like spoils of the hunt. Ursula may have had the looks (which she was learning to use to her advantage), but no amount of elocution lessons or elegant tailoring could hide the tracks of her St Joseph's Park roots from those mothers. Looks and sex appeal didn't stand a squirt of a chance against a property developer's fortune.

James started travelling to Dublin most weekends after that to see her, bringing her out for a meal or to the cinema in town before they joined his friends later in some watering hole or another. He rang her twice a week without fail and she grew to look forward to his calls, skipping down the stairs from the flat in Rathmines she shared with two other girls to the communal payphone in the hall. Although James talked about Glenbeg and the farm all the time, he was never one to blow his own trumpet. It was from Desmond that she learned of the extent of the Kennedy family's wealth, the valuable land they owned, the properties in the town. On the nights her boyfriend came to Dublin, she stayed with him in Desmond's flat on Pembroke Road, sleeping on the sofa together. He never pushed her too hard, seemed content to kiss and fool around a little before falling into a deep inebriated sleep. As if he knew she wasn't that type of girl.

The first time Ursula slept with Desmond, she had known it was going to happen that night. She was wearing a silver minidress that clung in all the right places and knee-high white leather boots. As she'd got ready earlier, it was Desmond's reaction she'd been thinking of, not James's. Desmond's eyes on her body. She knew how badly he wanted her – he had sent enough signals her way since she had started going out with James. The night it happened, he had been devouring her so blatantly with his eyes in the pub, she was surprised nobody else seemed to notice. Juliette was away at some fancy hotel for the weekend, the first time she had let him out of her sight since Ursula had started dating James.

Emboldened by alcohol, she stared back at him, returning his signals. Each surreptitious touch inflaming her own desire to feel his hands on her, all over her. She thought James would never fall asleep when they got back to the flat, and as soon as his breathing turned heavy, she slid out from beside him on the sofa and went to the bathroom. She had no intention of being the one to make the first move. She took her time using the toilet and washing her hands, and when she opened the door, her boyfriend's cousin was waiting for her as she had known he would be. He pushed her back into the bathroom and took her there first, bent over the sink. That first time together was fast and furious, but she was well lubricated with lust and alcohol. Then he pulled her into his bedroom where he played with her with all the techniques and expertise of the playboy he was, making her beg him to take her again as James snored gently in the room next door.

The first time Ursula visited Glenbeg, she had been going out with James for three months. As soon as she set eyes on the modest cottage his parents lived in, despite the acres of land they owned, she decided they would be building their own house. She waited until they were going out for nine months and newly engaged before informing James of this in no uncertain terms. His parents had readily agreed to sell off a parcel of land to pay for the construction of the new house, although they had balked a little when they saw the plans for Hazeldene. Ursula and James were married in the Glenbeg House Hotel, the only hotel in the town at the time. The sight of her fluttering around all day in her virginal white turned Desmond on so much he coaxed her into a hot risky shag in an unlit function room while the wedding band entertained their guests down the corridor.

She organised a massive housewarming party when they moved into Hazeldene. She and Desmond christened her new en suite bathroom while her new husband and his fiancée danced on the floor below. She was meticulous about using protection; it was one thing making a cuckold of your husband, another thing entirely having to pass another man's child off as his. She loved Jimmy – how could she not when he was so good to her. So generous and caring. Offering her the security and protection she had craved her whole life. But security and protection weren't exciting or sexy. She often cursed the day she had set eyes on Desmond. She would have been perfectly happy with Jimmy if his cousin hadn't awakened a latent passion in her that only he could satisfy. And she wouldn't have fallen deeply in love with a man who would never love her back in the same way. She knew exactly what she was to him: a plaything. One of many. It was actually a relief when it finally ended, but all the king's horses and all the king's men couldn't put the shattered pieces of her heart back together. She knew she was wrong to take her pain out on Jimmy, that most men would have thrown her out. But she had to take it out on somebody and he was the closest to her.

Two decades later, herself and James were in an enviable position and she had buried her heartache over Desmond with all the rest of her pain. They had three smart, handsome children, a beautiful home and a successful new business on top of their lucrative property portfolio. It hadn't all been plain sailing, not by any stretch of the imagination. Building the business to such a level in such a short space of time had been a hard slog. And of course, there had been a price to pay. There had been times over the years when she had felt guilty at seeing so little of her children, especially as her mother-in-law, Nancy, when she was alive, had liked to constantly remind Ursula that 'they don't stay young for long'. Each time, she reminded herself that her children had every material benefit they could ever want, had never once experienced lack in their lives.

As soon as she was old enough to start earning her own living, Ursula had been determined that she would never worry about money again. That she would have not just 'enough', but plenty. Her children would never be kept awake at night by the draught coming in through rotting window frames or sent to school in shabby cast-offs. They would have all the privileges that she never had. Her children had a housekeeper to pick up after them, to keep their home immaculate and cook them warm, wholesome meals. Nancy had had the cheek to hint on more than one occasion that Ursula should be spending more time at home rather than having strangers raise her children.

The usual guilt crap that working mothers had thrown at them. Ursula just shrugged it off. Her mother-in-law was from a generation where it was traditional for women to stay at home up to their elbows in Fairy bubbles, while the men went out to work. So there were some who might accuse Ursula of being a workaholic, but there were far worse vices, as she was only too aware, and her children were much better off with a mother who worked too hard than one who drank too hard or stayed in bed all day.

She could never have stuck staying at home all day, the hours measured out in bottle feeds and nappy changes and, later on, in times tables and swimming lessons. She would have lost the plot, her brain cells dissolving to mush as one groundhog day followed another. Her role as head of the family business fulfilled her. She thrived on the new challenges that each day brought and enjoyed the respect it earned her in the community. As the newly elected chairperson of Glenbeg Chamber of Commerce, she felt she was only starting to get the recognition that she deserved.

And now Mark was threatening to take it all away. When he told her what had happened, Ursula wanted to block his mouth, to block her ears, to make him *shut up, just shut up!*

28

Eight days after the event – Wednesday, 17 January
Kate

The solid oak coffins sat side by side at the top of the church. Kate had gently steered Rob away from the intricately carved crown of thorns coffins in Kirwan's, picturing Ursula's horror at its vulgarity, and towards the simple, elegant Italian ones. A graceful spray of white *Dendrobium* orchids and calla lilies lay on top of each.

The smell of the lilies was overpowering. A smell Kate hated.

They had deliberately kept the funeral service as simple as the coffins. No tear-jerker eulogies or personalised offertory gifts. Kate felt Ursula would have approved of the dignity of her send-off, the simplicity of the mass. And Jimmy. Poor lovely Jimmy would have said, 'Ara, sure, I'm easy, love.'

Kate didn't go to mass any more, only funerals and weddings that she couldn't get out of, but its signature scent hadn't changed since the days of her interminable holy communion practices. Stale incense, melting wax, wood polish and ancient limestone. Overlaid with the whiff of damp coats drying in centrally heated air.

Rain pattered against the windows, a weak January sun bleeding through the elaborately stained glass. A smoker hacked at the back of the church, kickstarting a symphony of throat clearing and sniffling along the pews.

She was sitting with Rob, Christina, the kids and her father in the front row to the left of the central nave. Rob was doing the first reading, Julie the second. He had practised it out loud before they left the house. It was the one about a time for everything. It always reminded Kate of Kevin Bacon in *Footloose*. God, she had loved that movie, had been able to recite the lines almost word for word.

She leaned in to Rob, his bulk solid as the trunk of the horse chestnut tree that shaded the cottage garden. How had she ever considered leaving this man? He pulled her closer, placed a featherlight kiss on top of her head.

There was a loud porcine snort from the pew behind them, the sound magnified in the high-ceilinged building. Rita's allergies were playing up again. Her siblings sat stiff-backed beside her, doing their best to pretend they didn't know her as she snuffled and grunted and foosthered around in her gargantuan handbag. Julie and the rest of the family sat in the rows behind with a pick 'n' mix of Kennedy relations and friends.

Niamh was back there too somewhere. The FLO had gone

over and above since Rob's release, making sure they were kept in the loop about the investigation at all times, anxious to help out in any way she could. She was clearly trying to compensate for the leak about his arrest, the source of which was still unknown and likely always would be. They were still waiting on toxicology reports from samples taken from the bodies, which could take weeks due to a backlog in the state lab, but in the absence of anything being found that shouldn't have been there, Rob's solicitor seemed optimistic that the gardaí would not be sending a file to the DPP in relation to the deaths of his parents.

A delicate sniff from across the centre aisle caught her attention. She stole a sideways peek at the front pew opposite. A petite elderly woman wiped tears away from her eyes before accepting a white hankie from the tall, thin man beside her. He was wearing a beige Crombie so old it was back in fashion and was so pale that, as her father would say, 'he looked like he died years ago and somebody forgot to tell him'.

'Who are they?' she whispered into Rob's ear, discreetly rolling her eyes in their direction.

'That's Mother's Aunt Catherine and her husband Arthur,' he whispered back. She had thought as much.

Kate made a mental note to seek the elderly couple out at the reception in the hotel afterwards. Never once in all the years since she had moved to Glenbeg had the couple who reared Ursula and her brother visited the farm. They lived in Donnybrook and had no children themselves. Rob had no idea why they never visited Glenbeg and had never seemed bothered about finding out, but Kate had always been intrigued.

She glanced back across the aisle. Ursula's aunt appeared

genuinely upset, her eyes rimmed in red as if she had been crying for some time. She dabbed at her cheeks with the hankie. Maybe Ursula had been the daughter she never had, was unable to have. Poor woman if that was the case. Kate couldn't imagine Ursula had been an affectionate child, couldn't picture her as a child at all. She wondered if it was losing her own mother so young that had made her the way she was. Had her need to be in complete control of the people around her, the world around her, been the result of having the ground pulled from under her feet when she was only ten years old? And her brother only five, still not much more than a baby. Kate felt empathy tug at her heart. They had been so young. How would her own kids cope if anything happened to her? It was all the little things they'd miss, the way Lily liked her butter spread thickly on her bread and Luke hated his vegetables touching his meat. Who would put Lily's hair in French plaits for her? And gel Luke's to one side the exact way he liked it? She had been sixteen when her own mother died – although she had lost her years before that – so she knew that pain. It was almost unbearable, but unbearing it was not an option.

Not surprisingly, it had been standing-room-only in the church last night for Ursula and Jimmy's removal mass, every pew squashed to capacity. Kate was so sick of shaking hands with people. 'Sorry for your loss', 'Sorry for your loss', 'Sorry for your loss'. Like a needle stuck in a groove. They had stood for hours in the funeral home first, people coming from near and wide to pay their respects. The long snake of mourners had wound in the front door of Kirwan's funeral parlour and been spat back out the side to congregate in small nodding groups outside. This was not one of those 'celebration of a life well lived' types of funerals. This was the final goodbye to a couple whose lives had been shockingly and suddenly ended before their time. In about as horrible a way as it was possible to imagine.

Kate and Rob had gone in earlier with Jimmy's siblings to say a final goodbye to his parents before the coffins were closed, Christina having chosen not to. Kate had been worried about how they might look having spent five days in the morgue, but the undertaker had worked a veritable miracle. They both looked a damn sight better than the last time she had seen them. As if they had simply slipped away peacefully in their sleep. Kate was thankful that Rob's final memory of his parents wouldn't be those awful images from the morgue. Ursula's hair was frizz-free and smooth, if a little flat and dull compared to her usual glossy bob, and her make-up looked very natural. Her cheeks had been plumped out from inside; Kate could just imagine Ruth joking that they were the cheapest fillers she ever got. Jimmy had looked a lot more like his old self too. And to her relief there wasn't a hint of the stench of slurry.

Kate had stood in line with Rob, Christina and the rest of Jimmy's close family, her good winter coat no match for the bitter breeze sidling in with the mourners, trying to keep a half-eye on the kids, who were sitting with some older, more rickety relatives at the back of the room. Lily had been in a moochy mood, wriggling in her seat, far too close to the flickering candles for Kate's liking.

The inevitable questions had come last night as she was putting Lily to bed.

'I wonder how long it takes to get to heaven. Do you think

Ursula and Grandad are there by now?' Lily asked, as if her grandparents had taken a scheduled Aer Lingus flight.

'I think they're probably there by now, pet,' she said, stroking her daughter's cheek. *Grandad anyway.* She had an image of Ursula arguing with St Peter at the pearly gates as Jimmy waited patiently on the other side for her.

'How do they get up there? Do the angels have to come and collect them?'

'I'm not exactly sure, pet, but—'

'Oscar said it's just their ghosts that go up to heaven and the rest of them gets buried down in a big hole in the ground and gobbled up by worms. Is that true, Mom?'

'Em ...' Christ, she was too tired for this. Bloody Oscar. Why did Rob never get these questions? 'When somebody dies, their soul leaves their body and goes up to heaven and they don't need their body any more.'

'So they do get eaten by worms,' Lily said matter-of-factly.

'No, no, that's not what I'm saying.' She could picture her daughter enthusiastically regaling her classmates with this gruesome detail. 'But you're gone out of your body so it doesn't matter anyway. Now, stop trying to drag out bedtime, Lily. Lie down and go to sleep.'

There was a kerfuffle as people got to their feet and began to shuffle out of their pews to queue in the aisles. *It's communion time already. How could that be?* A voice rang out from the choir gallery at the back of the church. A mezzo-soprano. Glorious Gloria (so called because of her brazen, unashamed vanity), one of Ursula's cronies from the golf club, with her daughter on violin. And just like that, Kate was pulled back in time. To another pew, in another place. The sweet high notes filled the church, soaring up to the vaulted ceiling and flying playfully around up there before swooping back down to flutter around her. She felt her father's eyes on her and she smiled sadly over at him. His eyes were wet. 'Pie Jesu'. Her mother had loved that song. They had played it at her funeral. Kate and her father had never mourned her properly, had never known how to, their grief mired so deep in the dense sludge of guilt. Because they had failed her, hadn't been able to save her.

Kate let her sorrow wash over her in waves, resurrected by the soprano's divine voice, the exquisite vibration of the violin. The tears came then, streaming down her face. And this time she let them, let the pain and guilt flow, carried away on the sublime notes. The music giving expression to her feelings far more than any words ever could. She allowed her whole body to shake as she cried for her mother and for her father and for herself. She cried for Jimmy, she even cried for Ursula. Her husband reached out for her right hand, held it gently between his. A smaller hand curled itself into her left one, her son offering comfort.

A canopy of umbrellas formed a colourful roof among the grey headstones in the older section of the cemetery where the Kennedy plot was located. Ursula and Jimmy were going down into the double plot on top of Jimmy's parents. The two wooden boxes sat side by side on timber planks above the gaping brown hole. The grass squelched muckily underfoot, it had been raining all night and was refusing to let up.

Kate stood at the side of the grave under the striped golf umbrella. It seemed like a lifetime ago, not a mere week, since she and Rob had stood in the yard under the same umbrella waiting to find out if his mother was in the tank. She felt a deep weariness, but also strangely calm, after her letting of tears. She had always thought it curious how people were admired and described as 'dignified' if they didn't cry or get too upset at the funeral of a loved one. Numb the pain with medication by all means if you had to, but keep all that messiness inside.

'Lily, come back.' Kate pulled her daughter back as she edged closer to the open grave. She knew well what the monkey was up to. Had heard and ignored her whispered conversation to Luke in the back of the car about trying to see if she could 'spot any bones in the hole'. That would have been quite the tale to report back to Oscar.

The priest was finishing up his final blessing. 'Lift us from the darkness of this grief to the peace and light of your presence ...'

'When can we throw our flowers in?' Lily asked loudly, oblivious to the solemnity of the occasion.

'Shhh, Lily, quiet.' Kate pressed her finger to her lips.

Rita had given the children a cellophane-wrapped red rose each, and Lily was dying to throw hers in on top of her grandparents' coffins.

They were walking away from the grave back towards the car, gravel crunching underfoot, the kids running ahead of them, when she saw Niamh coming towards her. The officer's green eyes met hers. Behind her, pulled up outside the gate, was a dark-blue saloon, Snitcheen in the front passenger seat.

Her heart clenched.

'I'm sorry, Kate, we're going to have to bring you back in.'

29

Christina

Rob and Christina had no choice but to act as normal as possible, and carry on hosting the funeral lunch, to ensure their parents got the send-off they deserved. People had travelled from all over the country, north and south, from across the Irish Sea, and even the Atlantic in the case of one of her father's brothers and his wife, to pay their respects. The three-course meal, which Kieran had insisted on footing the bill for, was taking place at Glenbeg House, right across the road from the stuffy interview room where Kate was probably being grilled as they tucked into their cream of tomato soup.

Christina couldn't think straight, her thoughts tangled up like Christmas lights. Why had they arrested Kate? Could she have had something to do with her parents' deaths? Had they completely disregarded Christina's statement? Did they know she had been lying?

Hopefully they would release Kate without charge too. Please God, let them not hold her overnight. The kids were upset enough as it was, Lily clinging pettishly to her father and Luke silent and glum-faced, as Rob tried to play the role of congenial host to a roomful of people who must all be wondering why the hell his wife had just been carted off in the back of a squad car.

Rob had explained to those closest to them, those who were genuinely concerned, that the gardaí just needed Kate to help them with something that had come up in the course of their investigation. To others not so close but with enough neck to ask, he assured them there was nothing to worry about, that Kate would join them soon.

Christina could only imagine the conversations people were having behind their starched napkins, eyes widening and heads nodding as the speculation spread around the room like head lice in junior infants. Her eyes roved the tables. The place was in dire need of refurbishment, with its dated dado rails and salmon-pink walls. A coat of fresh paint and some tasteful wallpaper would make a huge difference. If her mother had been involved in the planning of her own funeral, she would have gone for the Kingfisher, the new modern four-star hotel owned by a consortium on the outskirts of the town; Glenbeg didn't stretch to a five-star. Her father would have approved of their choice, though, keeping the business local.

Someone, probably Nellie, had set up a little table of framed photos of her parents at the back of the room. There was the photo that Kate had placed on top of the coffin in the church earlier. Her mother looked so glamorous. And her father, with his big beaming grin, his twinkly eyes. He looked so happy. They both did. But then it was easy to look happy in a photo. As Robin Williams had put it so well, 'All it takes is a beautiful fake smile to hide an injured soul'.

Seated just in front of the photo table was Great-Aunt Catherine. So tiny and frail. And Arthur. The last time she had seen them was at Mark's funeral. She remembered Catherine putting her arms out to her mother, their awkward embrace. And Arthur standing behind his wife, looking as upset as she was. Her mother had ignored him completely. Christina had thought at the time that he seemed like a nice man, an old-school gentleman, linking arms with his little wisp of a wife.

Bingo! Her eyes landed on their target. Her father's cousin Bríd, home from London for the funeral, was sitting at a table near the door with her husband, Noel. Reaching for the bottle of white wine in front of her on the table, refilling her empty glass. Good.

The conversation she had had with Bríd last night had been playing on repeat in her head ever since.

Christina had been coaxed by Rob and Kate to join everybody in Uncle Kieran's pub, where they had gathered after the removal. Bríd had cornered her as Christina was on her way to the toilet. The older woman was drinking brandy and was clearly after a few.

'I can't believe it, Christina. I was only talking to your father in November when I was home for Aunty Nora's funeral and he was in great form.'

'I know, it's hard to believe he's gone. And Mother.'

'And no sign of Peter at his own sister's funeral. Wonder if he's up to his old tricks again?'

'What do you mean? We haven't been able to get in touch with him. Is he sick, do you know?'

'Oh, he's sick all right. Sick in the—'

'That's enough now, Bríd,' said Noel, sporting a set of dentures bright enough to blind a man, as he caught her by the elbow and deftly steered her away. 'Apologies, Christina, it's been a long day. Time to call it a night, I think.'

She would have to try and corner Bríd later on today and get her to elaborate on what she meant without her husband around to muzzle her tongue.

The meal seemed to go on forever. Rob was crackling with nervous energy beside her. A fractious Lily had been whining for her mother since they sat down; Luke was still monosyllabic and morose.

The worst part of Mark's funeral had been the closing of the coffin; she would never forget it. Everybody apart from close family had been asked to leave while the family said their final farewells. Christina had become hysterical when the undertaker closed the lid on his face. She cringed now at the thought of it; she had made a complete show of herself, unable even to stand, her legs going from under her like a new-born calf trying to get on its feet.

Even though she knew Mark was dead, she had panicked. He had been terrified of the dark as a child, always had to sleep with a bedside lamp on, which her mother had always turned off when she went to bed herself. On the nights when Mark would wake screaming in the blackness, her father would go in to him, turn the light back on and lie on the bed beside him until he fell off to sleep again. As the heavy lid had gone down over his face, she had visualised him waking up and realising he was buried in the dark. With no light and no Daddy to go to him. The fear, which seemed so ludicrous now, looking back, had seemed so real in that moment as the undertaker walked around her brother's coffin tightening the screws on either side.

She had been spared that awful experience this time round. It meant she hadn't got to say goodbye to her parents, but she knew it was better that she remember them as they were. This time the part she had been dreading most was when they put their coffins into the ground.

It was as her father's coffin was being lowered into the dark hole that she had seen him. The little robin. Perched on a neighbouring headstone, a lopsided slab of limestone, the names of those who lay there long since buried beneath lichen and moss. She was sure it was the same bird. Plump of body, a bright orange-red breast, tiny black pebbles for eyes. He had turned up last Wednesday morning, standing on the patio table at the back of the house, looking in the window at her. It wasn't unusual to see a robin in the garden, but it was unusual for him to maintain eye contact with her for so long. He seemed to be staring right at her now. She had always felt comforted by the idea of a robin appearing after the death of a loved one to let you know they were still near, but it had never happened after Mark. There had been plenty of robins around the place, but they never looked at her in this way. This fellow was different; she could feel her father's presence in his gaze. While the idea of her father appearing to her in the form of a robin wasn't something she intended on sharing with anybody else – they'd think she'd really lost it – the thought that he was close by was like a hot-water bottle beneath frozen feet.

It was after five and the crowd was beginning to thin out when Christina spotted Bríd weaving her way across the room, heading in the direction of the bar. Her eyes sought out and pinpointed Noel, dentures flashing, deep in conversation with her father's cousin Desmond at the other side of the room. She intercepted Bríd before she reached the bar.

'Bríd, let me get you a drink. What are you having?'

'Thank you, 'Stina – I'll have a white wine, please, a large one.' Christina didn't bother to explain that the wine in Irish bars was one size fits all.

The barman handed Christina a miniature bottle of Chardonnay and a glass. Her father's cousin didn't seem the type to be too fussed about the variety of grape.

Christina guided her into an alcove from where she could keep an eye on Bríd's husband. She didn't waste any time pussyfooting around.

'So, Bríd, you were talking about Uncle Peter last night and, em … you mentioned his old tricks … I was just wondering what you meant. It's very odd that we haven't been able to contact him to let him know about Mother when they used to be so close.'

'Well, ye know he had to leave Coventry that time and move to London.'

'No, we didn't know that.'

'Are you joking me?' Bríd looked incredulous. 'Well, there was talk of some funny business with one of the youngsters he taught piano to. We don't know what happened exactly, but anyway he left Coventry under a bit of a cloud and came to London, and then he got himself into trouble there, but much more serious.' She raised her glass to her lips and swallowed thirstily, wiping her mouth with her hand.

'He was caught with dirty pictures of children on his computer, got a s'pended sentence cos it was his first offence. Bloody disgrace, some of those poor kiddies were as young as four. Got put on the sex offenders register, he did. There was a little piece about it in the *Metro* at the time, four or five years ago now. They were all talking about it down the pub, we heard he was 'posed to be part of a ring ... other s'gusting pervs like himself.' Her slurring was becoming more pronounced.

Out of the side of her eye, Christina saw Desmond stand up and move away, saw Noel scan the room. Her heart was pounding. She needed to get as much out of Bríd as she could before he noticed them.

'Do you know if my mother knew?'

'Ara, she must have, my love. She'd have to be blind not to. Sure usen't she visit him in London? He was living in a luxury pad in Canary Wharf, a river view, no less. He wasn't paying for that with piano lessons, I can tell you. Sheila Dillon's eldest lad – you know Sheila who works in the deli in Centra? Well, her son, I can't think of his name, he has a big job in computers in London, and he works with a lad who was at a party in Peter's place one night. Out of this world, he said it was, chandeliers and a hot tub and all. I don't know is he still living there.' She took another deep slug from her glass. 'Oh, here's my Noelie now.'

30

Kate

Kate had been left in the interview room for nearly half an hour to stew in the humiliation of being taken away from the cemetery by the guards in front of everybody. Mixed into the stew were dread, fear and paranoia. Why had they arrested her? There was no evidence that she had any involvement in putting Jimmy and Ursula into that pit. Not a pick.

Her pot had finally bubbled over as Detective Inspector McGuire finally sauntered in with his slíbhín of a sidekick, Snitcheen. She didn't even give him time to finish folding his gawky limbs onto the chair.

'You'd better have a very good reason for dragging me in here today,' she said, her voice tight, 'mortifying me like that in front of all our family and friends. And Rob's parents only just gone into the ground. It's an absolute disgrace.'

'I'm sorry if you were embarrassed, Kate,' the detective inspector said, 'but you were fortunate to get to the funeral at all, to be honest. Yesterday evening, one of the officers tasked with going through the items taken during the search of your cottage made us aware of a finding that's of great concern to us. It was out of respect to the deceased and yourselves that we held off until after the burial.'

'Finding? What are you talking about?' *What the hell could they have found?*

'You're aware that your laptop was taken during the course of the search of your home? I believe it's your work laptop, but that you also use it as a personal laptop,' said Detective Inspector McGuire.

'Yes, I'm well aware of that. I meant to tell Niamh that I need it back, but it went out of my head with everything else that's going on.'

'Right, well, let's back up a bit first, Kate.' The detective inspector shuffled through some sheets of paper until he found what he was looking for and pulled them out. 'In your previous statements, you said that you had a good relationship with your late mother-in-law, Ursula Kennedy.' He looked up at her for confirmation.

'Yes, that's right,' she said. Her armpits were damp.

'No run-ins over the business or anything? It can't have been easy working for your mother-in-law.'

'As I already told you, no. Nothing major anyway. Just the usual differences of opinion you would get in any business.'

'We found a letter on your laptop.'

She stared at him, unblinking. 'A letter?' What was he on about? She couldn't remember the last time she had written a letter to anybody. She looked blankly at Snitcheen. He stared back at her.

'Yes, a letter. To somebody called Ciara.'

'Ciara?' She didn't know any Ciara, apart from one of the part-timers in The Creamery and she certainly wouldn't be writing to her.

'I'll read it out to you. Maybe this will help jog your memory.'

And he had started reading. Another McGuire curveball. So totally out of left field, it nearly floored her. Her face was burning. It sounded so much worse when somebody else read it aloud, her most private thoughts. In a flat, emotionless monotone. While Snitcheen sat watching her like a cat waiting to pounce on a cornered shrew.

Dear Ciara,

I'm at my wits' end and I don't know where to turn. My mother-in-law is ruining my life and my family's life. She basically has full control over all aspects of our lives, which is exactly how she wants it. Not only do we live beside her on family land in a house owned by her, unfortunately we also work for her.

Although the land has been in my father-in-law's family for generations, she is very much the boss of the family business. She controls the purse strings, which she keeps a very tight hold over. In fact, I'd go so far as to say she's a control freak.

My husband and I have worked ourselves to the bone for her for years for not much above minimum wage on the basis that 'it will all be ours some day'. We are both constantly exhausted and stressed to the limit, and don't have the time or energy to enjoy our two beautiful children.

I have had a number of heated conversations with my husband over the past couple of years about our situation and he has tried to talk to her, but the truth is that he is afraid to stand up to her. As are his father and sister.

We live in a grotty, run-down cottage while she lives in the lap of luxury next door. When myself and my husband moved down to help his parents out after their eldest son took his own life at the age of twenty-one, she promised to do up the cottage for us but this never happened. Now she is saying she will convert an old barn on the property for us to live in, but there's no sign of that happening and I don't believe a word that comes out of her mouth any more.

She seems to genuinely believe she's an amazing mother and grandmother but she has no real bond with my children, her only grandchildren, and doesn't even seem to have any bond with her own children.

I have tried to stand up to her myself a few times, but she is so skilled at twisting things to make it look like I'm the one in the wrong or I'm being really ungrateful and unappreciative. Last week, I confronted her over her harassment of a member of our staff, and this time, I refused to back down and apologise. Since then, she has been extremely cool towards me.

I think there is something mentally wrong with my mother-in-law. She lies compulsively and, most worryingly, seems to genuinely believe her own lies. The worst part of all is that my husband, his father and sister just can't seem to see it. My father-in-law is a placid, gentle (weak) man who allows her to walk all over him despite the fact that the family wealth is from his side.

I don't think I can take much more of this. There are days I feel like my head is going to explode with the stress of it all. I am losing respect for my husband due to his inability to stand up to his mother, and I am seriously contemplating giving him an ultimatum – either he stands up to her, or I am leaving him and taking the kids with me. I love my husband dearly and I really don't want to have to do this. The tears are falling as I write, but I can't go on like this for much longer. Somebody needs to stand up to this woman before she destroys us all. I could murder her for doing this to us.

Please help, Ciara,

From a hopeless mother in County Galway

The detective inspector finally finished reading after what felt like an hour. He pinned her to her seat with his eyes. 'Do you have anything to say now, Kate, that might help us further our investigation?'

FUCK!

Kate had completely forgotten about the letter. She had written it one night the previous year when the kids were in bed, after a particularly crap day at work. She had no intention of ever sending it – certainly not the way it was, anyway. She would have had to heavily disguise it first as she knew that Ursula, like herself, was a regular listener to Ciara Kelly on Newstalk. A GP-turned radio presenter, Ciara had a way about her that listeners really seemed to resonate with. People opened up to her, shared the most personal of stories frankly and honestly. She often read out emails from people stuck in bad situations, with advice and support pouring in from listeners all over the country. It was one such email that had spurred Kate to write her own letter. A woman who had written in about her difficult sister-in-law. The Queen of Sheba, she called her. She could have been describing Ursula.

Kate remembered feeling calmer after writing the letter, pouring her frustration and anger onto the page, and having a good sleep that night. The following morning, though, when Ursula came down to the kitchen in The Creamery ranting about costs and forced her to cut the hours of one of the kitchen girls to the point where Kate knew she would just leave, her calmness evaporated. And now her purgative words had come back to bite her in the arse.

'I know that sounds really bad, but it was just me venting. I was never going to send that letter. I was just feeling really stressed around that time. And I remembered after my mother died years ago, the grief counsellor told me to write a letter to her, to put my feelings onto paper. I felt a bit better after that so I decided to write a letter to this agony aunt on the radio but, like I said, I never had any intention of sending it. To be honest, I had forgotten all about it.'

The two gardaí stared at her. Neither spoke. She had watched enough police procedurals to cop what they were at. The old 'silence the suspect into talking' ruse. She clenched her jaw to stop herself from babbling on. Her top was stuck to her armpits now; the acrid odour reached her nostrils. She wondered if they could smell her fear from the far side of the table. They were in a different interview room to the last time, at the front of the building. The blinds had been pulled down blocking out the street outside, where people were going about their normal routines and where, across the road in the hotel, her husband was hosting his parents' funeral meal without her by his side.

The detective inspector cleared his throat. 'It's clear from this letter, Kate, that your relationship with your mother-in-law wasn't quite as cosy as you made out in your previous statements. Which leads us to wonder why you lied to us about this and what else you might be lying about.'

That stupid letter. Why had she not deleted it? Although they probably would have found it anyway. Nothing's ever really deleted these days.

She took a deep breath. 'I didn't want to wash my family's dirty laundry in public. It's mortifying. I mean, look what happened with Rob – he was the talk of the town after his arrest was leaked to the media.'

'So you do admit now that your relationship with Mrs Kennedy was … strained, to say the least, and not …' he read from the page in front of him, '*fine* as you stated previously, and that there were far more than the … where is it?' He ran his finger down the page. '*Normal day-to-day niggles you'd have in any employer–employee relationship.*'

'Well, I may have exaggerated a bit in my letter – I just kind of puked my stress onto the page – but, yes, Ursula could be … difficult sometimes. She liked to be in full control. And that wasn't easy to live with, as you can imagine.'

'I can imagine it very well, Kate. It can't have been easy at all. Working for the woman, living beside her, you and Rob being financially dependent on her. That would put a strain on any relationship.'

He was playing the empathy card again, but there was no way he was going to lull her into a false sense of security.

'We just got on with it, really. There's always more expected of you in a family business, that's just the way it is. There were times when it got on top of us, of course there were, but we always knew … well, we just got on with it.'

'You always knew that Rob would inherit the business one day, or at least half of it. Isn't that right?' the detective inspector asked. Snitcheen was obviously sitting this one out.

Her top was soaked under her arms, and her palms were soggy. She wiped them on the rough plastic chair under her thighs. Another of the Templemore torture chairs. Her arse had gone numb. 'Yes, that's right.'

'And was there some arrangement between Ursula and yourselves about moving into a new house on the property? A converted barn, I believe.'

'Yes, that was the plan.'

'But that plan changed, did it not?'

'Em … not really, no …'

'Surely you were aware that your husband and his mother had a very heated row over her apparent decision to change her mind about this arrangement on the Wednesday before her death, and that he had made an appointment with his solicitor on the morning of his parents' deaths *coincidentally* to discuss this?'

Rita and Nuala Hehir had a lot to answer for, stupid cows.

'I knew Rob and Ursula had had words, but I don't think it was "heated". He didn't seem upset when he came back that night.' If you counted downing half a bottle of whiskey and passing out on the sofa not upset, that is. 'And I don't think that's right about her changing her mind. I think she might have been thinking of delaying things for a while, and Rob felt a bit left out of her plans. That's all it was, really. I'm sure the story grew arms and legs by the time his Aunty Rita got hold of it and passed it on to her bridge buddy.'

'Did you give Rob an ultimatum?' *Shit. How did they know that? Who could have told them?*

'An ultimatum? No, of course not. Why would you ask me a question like that?' Her cheeks were burning.

'You said in your letter you were seriously contemplating giving him an ultimatum. I was wondering if you had gone ahead with it.'

That stupid fucking letter. 'No, I didn't. I was just letting off steam, as I said before.'

Detective Inspector McGuire wasn't giving up that easily, though. He kept going for another hour and a half, digging away about the row in the farmhouse, Ursula's reneging on her promise, the difficulties in her relationship with her mother-in-law, with her husband. She tried to focus on his crazy-professor eyebrows, imagining the difference some hot wax and a tweezers would make. She wondered if he was married or had a partner and, if so, how the hell they could let him out of the house like that.

'Tell me, Kate, what do you think brought Ursula, who by all accounts rarely set foot in the farmyard, out to that shed at the back of the yard on the day of her death?'

Think, think. Don't rush into it.

'What brought her there? That's a question we've obviously

all been asking since last Tuesday. Like, she did go out to the yard from time to time if she was looking for Jimmy and he wasn't answering his phone, but she'd usually send somebody else. She was particular about her shoes. I don't know what she was doing out there that day, but all I can think, and Rob and Christina agree, is that Jimmy got into trouble and she heard him calling and went out to see what was wrong. Or that maybe, given what we now know, he went into that pit willingly and she tried to stop him. I wasn't aware of Jimmy's state of mind – I mean, I knew he got confused with the dementia and it was getting worse, but I had no idea he was feeling so low, and neither did Rob until Christina told us on Sunday.'

'You say you don't spend much time around the farm yourself?'

'I don't, no. I work in the main building and in the farm park.' *That much is true.*

'How much do you know about the working of the slatted tanks?'

'Enough to know they're bloody dangerous and to keep my kids well away from them. But not enough to open one up, start the agitator and kill my mother- and father-in-law if that's what you're trying to get at.'

She was released without charge, but Detective Inspector McGuire warned her 'not to leave the jurisdiction' in case they needed to bring her in again. Simon, who was now her solicitor as well as Rob's, hadn't been at all happy that she hadn't contacted him when she was arrested. It had occurred to her, of course it had, as she sat in the back of the garda car en route to the station, but she was so sure they had nothing on her – *How could they?* – and she felt asking for a solicitor would make it look like she had something to hide. She probably should have asked for him to be called when they produced the email in which she tore strips off Ursula, but she had been too shocked to think properly at that stage.

The gardaí had officially informed Simon that they would be preparing a file for the DPP in relation to the deaths of Jimmy and Ursula, on the basis of their interviews with Rob and Kate. The solicitor hadn't seemed quite so nonchalant when she spoke to him on the phone after Rob collected her from the station.

'Is this all because of that stupid email?' she asked.

'It obviously hasn't helped our situation, taken alongside everything else. Nor has the fact that you allowed yourself to be interviewed under arrest without legal representation,' he added snippily, 'but we are where we are. They'll send their investigation file to the office of the DPP and it will be up to them to decide whether or not to take a prosecution against one or both of you. They need to have enough evidence to convince a judge and jury beyond a reasonable doubt that you're guilty which, right now, I don't think they have.'

He doesn't think. Jesus Christ almighty!

Sitting on Ursula's sofa now, in Ursula's house, in front of Ursula's smouldering fire, Kate recalled the incident last year when she had confronted her mother-in-law about her treatment of Maura Lally, the staff member she had alluded to in the letter. Kate had found Maura in tears in her car during her lunch break and asked her if everything was all right. Was one of her kids sick? Did she need to go home? She knew Maura was devoted to her children, had worked a string of menial jobs to support them for years. As well as her waitressing job in The Creamery, Maura cleaned houses and worked late shifts in The Happy Chip in town to make ends meet. Ursula was well aware of this, yet for some reason, she was always picking on her.

Clearly embarrassed at being caught crying, Maura had tried to brush it off, to pretend it was nothing, but Kate had pressed her.

'Maura, you're one of our most dedicated staff members.' It was true, she was always so reliable and willing to help. 'If there's something bothering you at work, please let me know.'

It all came out then. Ursula had called her up to the office the previous day to say the black trousers Maura was wearing were too shabby and didn't meet the standard she expected from her staff. She had insisted she have a decent pair for her next shift, which was the following day so Maura had borrowed a pair of trousers from her sister.

She had only been in work ten minutes the next morning when Ursula rang down to the restaurant and summoned her back up to the office.

'She said the trousers were too tight for me,' Maura said, pulling at her bulging waistband, 'and could I not get a pair that fit me properly. I'm a bit heavier than my sister, you see. I'll tell you straight, Kate, I just can't afford a new pair right now. Me eldest lad needs a new tracksuit, the proper school one with the logo, and I'm tryin' to put a bit aside to pay for that. The one he's wearin' is a show, the knees are gone in it and he's bein' slagged in school, and I can't borrow any more. I'm so sorry about this.' She gestured towards her swollen eyes. 'Things are just gettin' a bit on top of me at the moment.'

Kate had to hold herself back from saying what she really thought. She never used the C word, thought it crude and unnecessary, but by God, it could have been invented for her mother-in-law in this moment. Did she not possess a single scrap of compassion for Maura, a single mother who was clearly struggling just to survive? Kate knew what financial stress felt like only too well, but she had the support of a husband and a fairly solid roof over her head. She couldn't even imagine the kind of pressure poor Maura was under, bearing sole responsibility for five children. Their fathers – two in total, one of whom she had been married to, and not five as Ursula liked to insinuate – were both wastes of space.

Kate felt like marching into Ursula's office, dragging her out by her expensively highlighted hair and forcing her to apologise to her victim in front of everyone. For there was no doubt in her eyes that Maura was a victim.

Kate had taken €50 from the till in the restaurant and forced Maura to take it; she would deal with the discrepancy in the till receipts later – she couldn't care less about it at that moment. She assured Maura she would talk to Ursula about the way she had been treated and reiterated how much she valued her as a member of her team. She probably should have left it until she calmed down a bit to confront Ursula, but she was propelled along on a riptide of outrage.

She had knocked on the door of Ursula's office and walked straight in.

Ursula had turned from her screen, surprised at the interruption. 'Kate, can this wait? I'm up the walls here.'

'No, I'm sorry, it can't,' Kate had said, the fury in her voice barely restrained.

Ursula's eyes widened.

'I need to talk to you about Maura Lally.'

'Oh, for God's sake. What now?' Ursula muttered.

Anger forced the words up Kate's throat and out her mouth. 'I'm not sure what your issue is with her, Ursula, but things can't go on as they are. The poor woman can do no right in your eyes. She's one of my strongest team members, and if things continue like this, she's going to walk. Her morale is already at rock bottom. I found her crying in her car earlier,' Kate said, hot with indignation.

'For heaven's sake! I am perfectly entitled to reprimand *my* staff when they are out of line, so please do not storm into my office all over-emotional just because Maura Lally turned on the waterworks. You can't say boo to some of them—'

'What you're doing to Maura is more than just reprimanding somebody who's out of line and well you know it. That poor girl is under serious stress and what you're doing is ... well, it's verging on ...'

The B word teetered on the tip of her tongue, but she knew if she let it out, it would be like detonating a bomb on the floor between the two of them – there would be no going back. On her own, she was powerless against Ursula. That realisation flung a bucket of freezing water on her anger.

'I am not responsible for the poor life decisions Maura Lally has made. If she chooses to have a load of kids she can't afford to keep, that's not my problem. I was good enough to give the woman a job and, to be honest, it's a decision I regret, as she's proved nothing but trouble. I've told you before, Kate, you need to learn to separate your personal emotions from work, especially in a family business.'

Ursula had turned her back then, facing her computer screen again. Kate was dismissed like an insignificant midge she had flicked away. Trying to make Ursula see her point of view was like trying to juggle jelly. She was a genius at twisting scenarios to make it look like you were wrong and she was right.

Their relationship had shifted after that, though, after Kate had had the cheek to confront her. An invisible forcefield of icy energy had settled between them.

Less than a month later, Kate had taken a phone call from a brittle-voiced Maura Lally.

'This is just a courtesy call, Kate, as you've always been good to me. I wanted to let you know that my doctor has signed me out on stress leave. I don't know when, or if, I'll be back.'

'Oh, Maura, I'm so sorry. I tried talking to her but ...' Kate felt like crying herself.

'You don't need to apologise, I know what she's like. I was married to a man like her – he nearly put me in my grave, but I got away from him and I'm not goin' to let it happen again. My kids need me,' Maura said, her voice breaking.

'This is so unfair, Maura, you shouldn't have to leave your job. If there's anything I can do to help, a reference or anything, please just give me a shout. I really mean that.'

'I know you do, love, and I appreciate it. You look after yourself now. Sooner or later, karma will catch up with that woman – she'll get what's due to her. I'm sure of it.'

31

2002

Ursula

S he had been sitting at the patio table in the garden, enjoying a glass of chilled white wine and the soporific heat of the evening sun on her face while fat fuzzy bees droned in the rose bushes, when Mark came out and sat down across from her.

'Mother. There's something I have to tell you.'

'What is it, Mark?' Why was it so bloody hard to get a few minutes' peace and quiet when she was going all day?

'It's a ... well, it's ... em, kind of embarrassing.'

She groaned internally. Embarrassing had the potential to cover a wide spectrum, anything from crabs to pregnancy. He'd better not be about to tell her he was gay. She wouldn't be long putting a halt to his gallop. 'OK.'

'Well, it's to do with Uncle Peter.'

'Peter?'

'Yes'

'Well, what about him?'

His mouth twisted funny, making him look unnaturally ugly. 'Look, Mother. This isn't easy for me to say and it's not going to be easy for you to hear, but I can't keep it inside any more, it's killing me.'

He was shaking. What the hell was wrong with him? His face had drained to the colour of milk.

'Mark. You're starting to frighten me now. What on earth is going on?'

'He ... Uncle Peter ... He messed around with me when I was younger. It started when I was about nine or ten, and now my head is all fucked up.'

'What do you mean he messed around with you?' There was a loud, hot buzzing in her ears as if one of the bumblebees had crawled inside. The blood throbbed in her earlobes. Time stood still around them.

He kept opening his mouth to speak, but was choking so hard on his sobs that he couldn't get anything out.

'Shh, Mark, calm yourself now.' She glanced in through the patio doors at the back of the house to make sure there was no sign of Jimmy or Christina. Rob was gone back to college. She moved her chair to try and block him from the view of anybody who might look out. She had to get in control of this situation; she needed to think fast.

'It sounds to me that you may have taken things up wrong. You know what Uncle Peter's like, always acting the fool. He's like a big child himself.'

Feelings that had lain dormant for years, molten orange rock and hot gases, had begun to expand and rise as her son's words caused a massive increase in pressure in her core, overheating her body. She could not allow this lethal lava to force its way through any fissures in the thick crust she had developed. She put her hands on her stomach and pushed down hard to try and physically stop it. She poured the contents of her almost full wine glass down her throat.

'This wasn't that kind of fooling, Mother. For fuck's sake! I know the difference. He swore me to secrecy – why would he do that if it was innocent?'

'Mark, this is a very serious accusation.' Her voice sounded sharper than she meant it to, but she needed to shut this conversation down quickly. 'You can't just come out with something like this.'

'Please, Mother. I know this is serious. That's why it's taken me so long to tell anybody. It went on for nearly four years, until I threatened to tell you and Dad.'

'Look, Mark, it sounds to me like there has just been a bit of a misunderstanding here. You haven't mentioned this to anybody else, have you?' The most important thing right now was to contain this.

'No, I haven't, it's been so hard for me to even tell you. I've wanted to for years but ... You need to understand, Mother. I'm not talking about just a bit of messing around here – it was a lot worse than that. He ... he went all the way.' He raised his voice.

'Shush.' She glanced back at the farmhouse again.

'No, I won't fucking shush. Can you not hear me? YOUR BROTHER RAPED ME.' He was on his feet now, shouting into her face. It was only a matter of time before somebody heard him, came out to see what was going on. 'He fucking raped me! In our guest room. While he was supposed to be minding us. I was eleven, for fuck's sake, only a child.' He was like a gushing tap that she desperately wanted to turn off. 'The pain was so fucking bad, I thought I was going to die. I wanted to die. He made me touch him and do the most dirty, disgusting things. He made me a dirty, disgusting thing.'

She blocked her mind to the reality of the words coming out of his mouth. 'I hear you, Mark dear, I hear you. Sit down now, sit down and take a deep breath. It's OK, you've told me now. You've done the right thing. There now, deep breaths, good lad.'

He sat down heavily, his head in his hands. She patted him on the back. She was trying to think on her feet, but she needed to be very careful in how she handled him.

'He's fucked me up so bad I don't even know if I like girls or ... what. I'm so fucking confused. You have to help me, please.' He sat there, sobbing and shaking. A mess.

She had to make sure this never got out. It would destroy them, destroy their reputation and the business she had worked so hard to create. Destroy Peter. They would be the talk of the town, the whole country, if it got out.

'Listen to me, Mark. I'm going to sort this all out – you can stop worrying yourself sick about it now. This kind of thing happens in families more often than you might think, it's just not talked about. I want you to push those memories out of your head, just don't allow them any space in there, and I want you to get on with your life. Of course you like girls, you're just a bit confused at the moment with everything and the best thing you could probably do is to find yourself a nice girl. I need you to promise that you will leave this matter in my hands now. I'll make it go away, make Peter go away. Away from here. Tough things happen in life sometimes, but we just have to push through them and move on.'

He pulled away from her, horror scrawled across his face, as if she was the one who had abused him. 'Push them out of my head? Are you for actual real? It's all I think about. How the fuck do you expect me to just forget about four years of hell? As if I'm some sort of fucking robot or something?'

'You can and you will, Mark. Going back over it again and again in your head is the worst thing you could do – why would you want to torture yourself like that? Do you want to end up in a mental unit drugged up to your eyeballs? The whole place talking about you? Now, go on off up to your room and we'll hear no more about this business. You're clearly exhausted. Everything will seem better after a good night's sleep.'

'I think I need to get help, proper help, like. To talk to somebody, like a professional or something ...'

Over my dead body. 'Mark, you're not listening to me. This is not something we want to get out – this kind of thing could haunt you for the rest of your life. It could stop you from getting married and having a family of your own some day, and while I know that's not high on your priority list at the moment, one day it will be. I'm not even going to tell your father what you've told me. This stays between the two of us. Trust me, I'm going to take care of it from here.'

32

Nine days after the event – Thursday, 18 January
Christina

The house was quieter. The kids had been sent back to school and the stream of visitors had dwindled to a dribble. Now that the funeral was over, the official business of death done and dusted, she was going to have to reattach herself to reality. It felt bizarre that the world was still turning despite the fact that her parents' lives had come to a halt. She had too much time to think again. To face living in a world without her mother and father in it. They were all restless and edgy about the file going to the DPP. No end in sight to the nightmare their lives had become.

Kate had been in no fit state to talk when she got home from the garda station last night, apart from saying it had all been a misunderstanding and she would explain everything in the morning.

'They're hellbent on finding somebody to blame for what happened to your parents,' she had said wearily. 'I'm really frightened now. People are falsely accused all the time and end up spending years in prison. Mothers separated from their children. I don't think I could cope.' She put her face in her hands.

Rob had pulled her into his arms. 'That's not going to happen, love. You're just exhausted now, imagining the worst-case scenario.'

After she'd returned from dropping the kids to school this morning, Kate had sat down with Christina and Rob and explained about the unsent letter. She apologised for the things she had written about their mother, especially now after what had happened, but said it was an honest outpouring of her emotions at that time. A personal account that, like a diary, was never meant for any eyes but her own. Christina had wondered how on earth her sister-in-law had stuck things out as long as she had – she hadn't realised quite how bad things were for her. Too busy feeling sorry for herself all the time.

Uncle Kieran had arrived then for the 'reading of the will' which, contrary to TV and the movies where the bereaved family sit formally around a solicitor in a panelled office, turned out to be a far more casual event. He, as executor, brought over two copies of the joint will he had collected from her parents' solicitor, one each for her and Rob.

The only surprise had been the codicil her mother had added to the will in 2013, leaving a penthouse apartment in London and £1.5 million sterling to Peter. Rob and Kate had looked as gobsmacked as Christina felt at the size of the bequest. The farm and cottage were left in full to Rob and his family, as expected. The farmhouse had been left to Christina to live in for the rest of her life, and everything else, including the farm park, properties, monies and assets, were to be divided equally between herself and Rob. The extent of their parents' estate was far bigger than Christina or Rob had ever imagined; it was going to take the probate solicitor Uncle Kieran had hired months to calculate the value of each of their parents' assets and debts so that estate taxes could be paid. On top of that, there was a long backlog in the probate office in Dublin.

Christina was happy for the land to stay in the Kennedy name, passed down to the next generation in time-honoured tradition. It hadn't always been the plan, of course. The plan had been for the farm to go to Mark, the eldest son, who, as his father used to joke, 'came out of the womb in his welly boots'. There would have been no dispute on the parts of Rob and Christina. It would have been a natural progression for the land to stay with the only natural farmer among the three of them. But it had not come to pass.

Luke had about as much interest in farming as he had in ballet; he aspired to be a video-game developer when he grew up. Of course, a lot could change between now and then – look how Rob had been won over by the land – but Rob and Kate were adamant that their son would never feel obliged to take over the farm. In fact, it was Lily who was showing the most potential as the one to follow in the footsteps of her grandad and Uncle Mark. And her father. Things were changing and the next generation of dynamic young farmers were putting their predecessors to shame. The new breed was diversifying into all kinds of things, from organic farms and rural tourism projects to artisan foods and renewable energy. More and more women were opting for careers in agriculture too and emerging as leaders in their fields. There had even been a feature on it in *Image* lately, an interview with a young dairy farmer in Limerick who was an 'influencer with a difference', posting photos of tractors and cattle. Christina could just picture Lily in years to come sitting in Ursula's office, ruling the roost and coming up with all kinds of ambitious ideas for the business.

Before he left, Uncle Kieran awkwardly mentioned that the solicitor had asked him to 'flag one last thing'.

'It's just with the guards and the investigation and what have you. If it was the case, and this isn't going to happen of course, but ... em ...'

'Just come out with it, Kieran, and put us out of our misery,' Rob said, laughing nervously.

'Well, if it was a case that anybody was to be convicted of the murder or manslaughter of Jimmy and Ursula, they'd be barred from inheriting any share of the estate. But that's not going to happen, so you don't need to worry about it.'

Christina watched the colour literally drain from her sister-in-law's face at his words.

The farm was reopening tomorrow and they were all going back to work. They had made the decision between them – Rob, Kate and herself. It was a quiet time for school tours, but they still had a number of bookings for birthday parties over the weekend (there had been surprisingly few cancellations under the circumstances), and they needed to start bringing in money again. They had been closed for over a week now, and they had staff to pay. They couldn't stay shut forever. It would be strange without her mother sitting in her office, running the ship, and no doubt there would be no shortage of speculation among their visitors about how her parents had ended up in the tank, but she found herself looking forward to getting back to the structure of a daily routine and having less time to think.

It would also be strange being back without Nellie there. They hadn't seen her since the funeral, which she had left early pleading exhaustion and not looking at all well. In all the years she had known Nellie, Christina had never once heard her complain about being tired. The woman seemed to have boundless energy, was built of hardy stuff. It was a source of immense pride to her that in all her time working for the Kennedys she had only ever called in sick once, and that was when she was struck down with food poisoning after a dodgy prawn chow mein from the Golden Sun. Kate had tried calling her yesterday morning about the reopening, but there was no answer. Brendan had popped into the farmhouse a short while later to explain that Nellie had been struck down with some kind of bug and would be out of action for a few days. Christina had offered to pick up some bits and pieces for her – 7up, paracetamol, Lemsip, a bunch of grapes – as Nellie did so often for everybody else, but Brendan said she was in bed trying to sleep it off and she had everything she needed. Christina hoped she was OK. That it was just a bug.

She sat at the desk in her room now checking her emails. Nothing urgent. She needed to post details of the reopening on their social media accounts – that would keep her busy for a while. She had opened her curtains and pulled up the blinds. A watery sun was playing peekaboo with fast-moving grey clouds. Another shower on the way. The fragile bubble that had separated her from the world around her since the discovery of her parents' bodies felt stretched so thin that too heavy a breath could burst it.

Their deaths seemed to have awakened something in her, a heightened awareness of the fragility of life. She had lost so much time already. She had another EMDR session booked for next week and had been planning to cancel, with everything going on. She knew she needed to do it, though, go back there again. To dig into the beating, pus-filled core of her pain and feel it. She had never really understood what people meant when they said *go with your gut*, but for the first time she was able to hear what her gut was trying to tell her. It was as if the shock of her parents' deaths had forced her to look at her own pathetic excuse for a life. To wonder at the possibility of a different life, a different future.

'Howdy, anybody home?' A cheery voice came from the kitchen. Daniel.

She jumped to her feet, glad of the distraction. But more than that. Her heart heated up at the sound of his voice. She had begun to look forward to his regular visits to the farmhouse.

When she entered the kitchen, she found him standing beside an empty pet carrier, a strong stench of ammonia in the air.

'I'm just here to return this little miss,' he said, indicating the rabbit peeking out from the front of his jacket where she was snugly tucked. 'I had to take her into the clinic for a couple of nights to keep an eye on her. She was a bit wheezy but she's grand again, and I'm sure poor old Flopsy is pining away for her below.' He grinned. He had such a lovely smile.

'Oh, Lily will be thrilled. She was all worried about Mopsy. I'll bring her down later to see her.'

'Why don't you walk away down with me now? Get a bit of fresh air before it starts bucketing down again?'

She hesitated.

'Go on. Grab your coat. You might need a hat too – it's Baltic out there.'

So she did.

They chatted away as they walked. There were very few people she felt she could be herself with, but there had always been something about Daniel. And he had been so kind since her parents' deaths, so genuine in his desire to help.

'So how are you feeling about going back to work?' He asked like he really wanted to know.

'Grand, but it still all feels a bit ... I don't know ...'

'Surreal?'

'Yeah. Weird.'

'It is weird. I remember feeling like that after Mark, too, for a long time. I'd be out with the lads laughing and having the craic and then it would hit me and I'd feel so shit and so guilty ... you know, that I was carrying on as normal with my life and he couldn't.'

They reached the petting hut. It was dark and smelly inside. Daniel opened one of the cages, removed the rabbit from inside his coat and gently put her back in beside Flopsy. The other rabbit welcomed his companion home with a lick and she snuggled back into the straw beside him and closed her eyes.

Daniel closed the cage and turned to Christina. 'I always felt there was something, you know.' She couldn't see the expression on his face in the dark, but his voice sounded sober, unsmiling.

'What do you mean?'

'Something that was troubling Mark, that he wanted to tell me but couldn't, for some reason. That year before he … you know … the way he was behaving. The drinking, the drugs, the mood swings. I couldn't understand it at the time – sure, we were only kids. I thought he was just being a dick, but looking back now, I can see that he was angry, really angry. There was one night where we had this big row; he had gone for Fitzie, floored him with a punch for no reason really. Fitzie was just being his usual arsehole self, talking shite. Anyway Mark was thrown out of the pub and I went out after him. I was roaring at him, asking him what the hell was wrong with him. And … I think he came close to telling me … but then he closed up again and he said he couldn't. He was rambling on about telling your mother, but that it only made things worse.'

Her heart skipped a couple of beats. 'I wish he had told you. The two of you were so close. Or Daddy, he was so close to Daddy too.' Her voice wobbled. 'Or me, he could have told me. I loved him, I would have listened … I would have.'

She felt Daniel reach for her in the dark. She wiped the tears from her cheeks with the back of her hand, not caring if he saw her crying.

'Shh, it's OK, you're all right, let it out.' She nestled in against his chest and he rubbed her back in soothing circles.

She wished she could curl herself up inside his jacket and stay there, safe and cosy against his warm beating heart like Mopsy had been.

She was exhausted, but her mind wouldn't switch off. Outside she heard a cat yowling; it sounded disturbingly like a baby being tortured.

She felt physically attracted to Daniel, there was no denying that. And she thought he might have feelings for her too. But what was the point in even thinking that way when she couldn't perform a very basic, vital function of a normal woman. Daniel would probably want kids some day, and even if he didn't, surely there wasn't a man in the world who'd be happy in a sexless relationship.

Christina had known having sex would be painful the first time – she had picked that much up from the girls in school. The general advice was that it was better to be drunk the first time, or at least merry, so you wouldn't feel too much. She had really wanted it to be with Kevin. She had been understandably nervous but ready at the same time, or so she thought. Because he was the one. Her one.

She had been out of hospital a few months, back in college, tentatively picking her way along, when she met him. At the Novena of all places. An annual event at Galway Cathedral. The highlight of the city's religious social calendar, drawing thousands of pilgrims from near and far. Stalls were set up outside hawking all manner of holy stuff. Rosary beads, votive candles and miraculous medals. Babies and young children were brought along to be blessed.

Two of the girls Christina was sharing a house with had written petitions to pray for their special intentions. The petitions were placed in a wooden box in the cathedral, and some were read out at each Novena mass. Christina wrote a petition for Mark, praying for him to be at peace and for those he had left behind to also find some peace. Her petition wasn't read out, but she had met Kevin on the way out of the cathedral. He was a barman in McSwiggan's, a popular student haunt, and she knew him to say hello to. He was linking arms with a stout elderly woman who turned out to be his grandmother.

'Christina, I haven't seen you in ages. I thought you'd done a runner on us.' He had seemed genuinely pleased to see her.

She was flattered that he had noticed her absence, even more so that he had remembered her name. He had always been friendly to her, but that was his job. The girls all agreed that he was seriously cute, 'small but perfectly formed' as her housemate Elaine put it. Dark-haired and green-eyed.

'No, I've ah … been keeping my head down,' she muttered.

'Well, make sure you pop in to see us soon. We've missed you.'

She had gone into McSwiggan's the following Thursday night with her housemates hoping to see him. She didn't have a huge amount in common with the girls she lived with, was shocked by the string of one-night stands that they boldly paraded in and out of the house, but she hadn't made any other friends since she had started at UCG.

Kevin gave her a big smile and a wink from behind the bar when he spotted her, but he was run off his feet all night so she didn't get to talk to him properly. She was leaving for the night club, feeling a bit deflated, when she heard her name being called.

'Hey, Christina? Are you heading to CPs?' he called from behind the bar.

'No, we're going out to the Warwick tonight.' She felt a thrill at the realisation that he must have been keeping an eye on her.

'Grand, I'll see you there after my shift.' She felt an even greater thrill that he was prepared to follow them out to Salthill instead of his usual haunt in town.

True to his word, he was there. She fell for him, fell hard. She had known her mother would never approve of a barman from the wrong side of town, but she pushed that reality to the back of her mind, her feelings for Kevin even stronger than her fear of her mother's reaction. She had wanted him to be the first so badly, had wanted him so badly. Had never experienced desire like that before. That giddy tingling when he looked at her with those eyes. He didn't push it; she was the one who instigated it, a few weeks into their relationship.

She had expected pain, but nothing like the stabbing agony of their first attempt. As if he was trying to shove a dagger inside her. They had tried again another night. And once more after a lot of drink. But it was no good: there was something wrong with her. Vaginismus, the college doctor had diagnosed, a not uncommon condition.

'Could there be something wrong with me physically?' she had asked, hopeful that this was a problem that a minor surgical procedure could solve. 'It feels like I'm just too small down there.' The doctor, a man who looked close to retirement age, had assured her that there was nothing physically wrong with her. That it was more likely there was a psychological cause for her condition. That they didn't know exactly why vaginismus happened. But that for some women it might be caused by a traumatic past experience such as sexual abuse or painful intercourse.

She stopped taking Kevin's calls, stopped going to the pub. Dropped out of college again. For good this time. Moved back to Glenbeg. What was the point in trying to be normal when she was nowhere near it?

33

Six weeks later – early March

Kate

She had been woken in the middle of the night by a nightmare. She usually didn't remember her dreams, but this one had been so clear. So vivid. The cottage had been turned on its roof. It didn't even look like their house, but somehow she knew it was. Just like she knew she was responsible for Ursula ending up trapped beneath it, only the bottom of her legs and her feet visible, her new Marco Moreo patent leather lace-ups sticking out. Kate was holding hands with four or five other women who were dancing in a wide circle around the cottage, their faces contorted in maniacal glee. She was holding Maura Lally's hand. Ruth was there too, and some other shadowy shapes she couldn't make out. They were chanting 'Ding dong, the witch is dead', emitting shrill witchy cackles. Then somebody had pointed a long crooked finger and she turned and saw Rob and Jimmy standing there, staring at her in revulsion.

She had lain awake for hours after that, battling panic.

What if she told the truth and nobody believed her? She had no proof, after all, no evidence.

What if herself and Rob were both charged and found guilty, their children left not only parentless, but penniless too?

Yes, it was the worst-case scenario, but worst-case scenarios happened. All the time.

Why the hell hadn't I just said no? Figured out some other way.

She had eventually given up trying to get back to sleep, got up and made a pot of tea. She couldn't remember the last time she had slept through the night. Not in the past two months anyway. Rob told her she was moaning in her sleep a lot. There was still no word from the DPP, and Simon had given a vague and unreassuring 'No news is good news, I guess' when they had asked him whether this was good or bad.

She was wrecked now, and her night panic had stalked her into day.

She had no choice but to try and hold her nerve for another while. Until the DPP decided to put them out of their misery. Or not. She had no idea what the repercussions of telling the truth would be for her at this stage, but the fear churned away in her stomach. Day and night. She thought constantly about her babies. Lily with her tantrums and her endless questions. *Do birds have tongues? How do dogs make their tails wag? How does the sky stay up? What colour do you think a fart is?* And Luke, hurtling headlong towards his teens, with his big smile and his soft heart. If the worst happened, Christina would do her best, would try to mother them, but how could she possibly be expected to cope? A girl-woman who spent her whole life frantically doggy-paddling just to keep her own head above water. *What would happen to them all?*

The first day she had taken over Ursula's role, only days after the funeral, she had sat at her late mother-in-law's desk wondering where to begin. This wasn't your typical promotion. There would be no handover of tasks. No week of induction training. Stepping into her mother-in-law's shoes was a formidable undertaking. For all her failings, Ursula had been a bloody good businesswoman, able to spot an income-generating opportunity a mile away and always thinking ahead. Kate's unused law degree was going to be feck-all use to her when it came to running Glenbeg Farm Park. The only area in which Kate was confident of doing a better job than her mother-in-law was HR.

It was far too soon to make any major decisions on the future of the business, of the farm. They just had to keep things ticking over until probate came through; they had staff depending on them for their livelihood, suppliers who needed to be paid. Rob had agreed with her decision to out-source accounts, wages and outgoing payments to an accountant, so that was one worry off her plate at least. And the plan was that Nellie would eventually take over the restaurant, starting on a part-time basis next week, when she returned to work, taking another huge burden off Kate's shoulders.

It had been such a shock when Brendan finally admitted that there was a bit more wrong with Nellie than food poisoning. But so typical of Nellie. Not wanting to make a fuss or worry anybody, she wouldn't let him tell them until she was over the worst of it. She'd had a lump removed from her breast in early January, when she was off work for 'a minor gynae procedure', and lymph nodes taken from under her arm. Fortunately, the cancer hadn't spread and she had tolerated the treatment very well, although she had lost more weight she couldn't afford to lose. Kate and Christina had tried to convince her to take more time off, that there was no rush back (even though she was badly missed), but she was having none of it. She was 'raring to go' as Jimmy would have put it.

She had popped into The Creamery last week to meet Kate and Christina for lunch and hadn't been one bit impressed with the standard of the food that was being 'thrown up to people', as she described it, in her absence.

'Lord almighty, I could sole me shoes with that beef it's so tough. I'll be back to work next Monday before the place falls apart altogether.'

When Christina tried to protest that it was far too soon, Nellie admitted that she was going insane stuck at home staring at the walls.

'Lookit, they caught it early, thanks be to God, and I'm grand again. I need to get back to work for me own head. I'm coming back next week and let that be the end of it.'

It had been hectic since they'd reopened, but hopefully things would calm down a bit once their new general manager took up her role at the end of the month. Kate had spent the weeks trying to familiarise herself with Ursula's wide-ranging job spec and interviewing for a new farm park manager to replace herself. The successful applicant was an enthusiastic young woman with a strong background in retail management who was keen to move back to Glenbeg from Dublin and was lured by the attractive package on offer.

Kate hadn't a notion of allowing work to take over her life again; she wanted to reduce her stress levels and see more of her kids, not less. She had agreed with Rob and Christina that, for the time being at least, she would be finishing up at 2 p.m. three days a week so she could do the school pick-up herself. Christina had offered to take on more responsibilities, and if necessary, they would take somebody else on to help out part-time in the office. Kate fully intended to go back to work full-time in the future, but for now, when they had just suffered a major double bereavement, it was important to her and Rob that she was there for the children as much as possible.

She was fastidiously working her way through all the folders on Ursula's desktop, trying to learn as much as she could about how her mother-in-law had run the farm and the family's wider business interests. Ursula had been a compulsive micromanager, and there was no aspect of the business that she hadn't had her nose stuck in, which had driven the rest of them mad but was proving beneficial now that she was no longer around. She had separate folders for everything from animal feeding and vaccination schedules on the open farm to CVs of prospective employees. Kate found a five-year corporate plan, an annual business plan and comprehensive budgets and revenue flows.

Her eyes had been out on stalks as she went through the property and investment folders. She had no idea the

Kennedys had owned so many properties – as well as the houses and commercial premises in Glenbeg, they owned rental houses in Galway and Athlone and had an interest in three hotels. Neither did Rob, nor Christina.

Of course, she had known her parents-in-law were wealthy, but was stunned to discover that they had been multi-millionaires. The income from the open farm was only petty cash compared to everything else. Play money for Ursula. *With so much cash sitting in their bank accounts, why the hell had she been so reluctant to share it?* She could have quadrupled their wages and it would barely have put a dent in her pile. Power and control. That's what it had all been about for Ursula. Yet no matter how much she had, she had never seemed content. Her hunger insatiable. Kate wondered what had caused the hole inside her mother-in-law that she had never seemed able to fill.

She looked out the window now, over the empty car park. It was a pleasant day, bright and clear and full of the promise of spring. There were two people walking from the direction of the farm trail. She smiled to herself. She had long suspected that Daniel held a bit of a flame for Christina, either that or he was the most dedicated vet in Ireland. Any excuse and he was over at the farm. She turned back to the laptop. Continued working her way through folders, printing out information as she needed it.

It was hidden in a folder marked Hazeldene Investments Ltd. A folder within a folder titled C.C.S. Ltd. True to Ursula's form, everything was meticulously recorded. Statements dating back to 2002. The payments to Canary Consulting Solutions Ltd had started at £4,000 sterling per month, rising gradually over the years to their current £12,000 per month. Over £144,000 in the last year alone. *Who the hell was she forking out these huge consultancy fees to every year?*

She opened the Company Registration Office website, did a search under C.C.S. Ltd. No results. Tried Canary Consulting Services Ltd. Nothing. She googled the UK equivalent of the CRO and clicked onto a gov.uk link. Typed Canary Consulting Services Ltd into the search box. Bingo.

> *Registered address: Belgrave Court, 36 Westferry Circus,*
> *Canary Riverside, London E14*
> *Company status: Active*
> *Company type: Private limited*
> *Incorporated on: 14/10/2002*
> *People: One officer: Peter Nolan. Address as above.*
> *Role: Director*
> *Nationality: Irish*
> *Country of residence: UK*
> *Occupation: Director*
> *Appointed on: 16/12/2002*
> *Nature of business: Business development consultancy*
> *services*

Holy shit! That was some jump. Piano teacher straight to director of his own business development consultancy.

Jimmy mustn't have been aware of these payments – he would have mentioned it. It was as if every time she thought the woman couldn't possibly have sunk any lower, she did. It baffled her that Peter still hadn't been in contact, as if somehow he knew it wouldn't be a good idea for him to show his face at the funeral.

Kate closed the laptop, sat back in her seat. What she had just discovered had further cemented it for her. Whatever the outcome, she had made the right decision for her family. She might sleep a bit easier tonight.

34

Friday – 30 March
Kate

It was Good Friday. A very good one as it turned out. The kids were on their Easter holidays and Kate had taken a few days off to spend with them. She was doing her best to function normally, but she was only human and the waiting, the not knowing what was going to happen, was cruel.

It was a rare day in the west of Ireland. Blue sky as far as the eye could see, marred only by the odd flimsy wisp of cloud. The sun had even graced them with her presence, provided enough heat for them to discard their jackets. Kate and Ruth had packed a picnic and brought the kids on a busman's holiday. They had worked their way through the indoor play zone, the outdoor playground and the furry corner, and a pile of ham and Tayto sandwiches. Lily and Oscar had raced off to see the alpacas while Luke and Ruth's daughter, Ava, were like two junkies chasing the digital dragon, unblinking eyes fixed on screens.

Kate began clearing the table. She threw the crusts in the grass for the birds and started to gather up the rest of the picnic detritus: empty Fruit Shoot bottles and crisp packets, sandwich bags and KitKat wrappers.

'Sit down and relax, Kate, leave that a while,' Ruth said.

Ruth had brought a couple of mini bottles of Prosecco and two plastic champagne flutes, and the bubbles had brought a flush to her cheeks. Kate was trying to enjoy the day, to be in the moment with her closest friend and their children, but relaxing was not an option for her any more. She forced down a sip of the sparkling wine, smiled weakly at Ruth. She could see Lily in the distance, giggling and playacting with Oscar. And at the next table, Luke, head down, thoroughly engrossed in his screen. All she wanted was to protect her children, keep them safe. It was all she had ever wanted.

'Are you getting any sleep at all?' Ruth asked. She didn't need to say more. Kate knew she looked like crap.

'Some nights are better than others. When I wake up, it's hard to get off again, you know? I start imagining the worst.'

'God, it must be torture. I don't know how you do it – keep everything going with that hanging over you.'

'What choice do I have, sure?'

'It's not just that, though. You're strong, Kate, stronger than most. I'd have cracked under the pressure by now. You don't give yourself half enough credit. Rob and the kids don't know how lucky they are to have you.'

'Ah, would you go away out of that,' Kate said, smiling. She knew her friend meant every word, though. Knew she could rely on her to be there for her no matter what way things went. Even if the truth came out. She took a long slug of Prosecco, handed the glass to Ruth. 'Top us up there, will you.'

She didn't know what made her reach for her phone. It was in the pocket of her jacket slung over the bench beside her.

Eleven missed calls.

'Jesus Christ.'

'What's wrong, Kate?'

'My phone was on silent – I didn't realise. Oh God.'

She scrolled down. Two missed calls from Niamh. She hadn't heard from her in a couple of weeks, since the FLO had last touched base to see how they were doing. And nine from Rob. One after the other. She tried to call him back, but her fingers kept hitting the wrong buttons.

'Kate, it's Rob.'

'I know, I'm trying to call him back. I can't work this stupid bloody thing. Can you—?'

'No, I mean he's coming. There.' She pointed down towards the entrance to the picnic area and animal enclosures, behind Kate's head. 'Who's that with him?'

Kate turned and saw him at the same time he spotted her. Who was that with him? Niamh. *Oh God oh God oh God!*

Now her legs weren't working properly either, too weak to stand her up. She stayed sitting on the bench, her body facing Ruth and her children, her head twisted in the opposite direction facing her husband and the guard. Rob was running now, shouting and gesticulating frantically. Panic ran havoc through her bloodstream, racing hysterically all around her body. She would surely have a heart attack, drop dead in front of them all.

It was only as Rob came closer that she was able to make out his features. He was smiling, laughing and crying. Holding his thumbs up in the air.

And closer still when she could make out what he was saying. 'IT'S OVER, KATE.'

And then he was beside her and his arms were around her and he was murmuring into her hair, 'It's over, love, it's all over.'

35

One year later – March 2019

Christina

Christina and Kate stood outside the barn looking up at the new sign: Solas Artists' Retreat. The logo was a beaming yellow sun with rays around it, *solas* meaning light in Irish. She had been so thrilled that Rob and Kate had loved her idea of a space for artists of all kinds to hire out for retreats. It had come together so perfectly. When Kate had discovered that not only had Ursula applied for and been granted a further change of use for the barn and the surrounding acre of land from residential to commercial, but also had an order in with a company in the North for eight luxury glamping pods, herself and Rob had initially been furious.

However, once Christina had eventually managed to convince her brother and his wife that it made much more sense for them to move permanently into the farmhouse, which was far too big for her to rattle around on her own, they began to talk about what they should do with the barn. The idea for the retreat had come to Christina during one of her woodland walks, as many of her best ideas did these days. She had her first booking already and they weren't even officially up and running yet; a group of MA creative writing students from a university in Dublin were coming down for a poetry workshop with their tutor next weekend.

The glamping pods had arrived last month and had already been well road-tested by Rob and the kids. Shaped like beehives, each wooden pod slept four to six people and had a shower room and tiny kitchenette. They had small patio areas at the front and outdoor campfire pits. Christina thought the pods were adorable, like a little housing estate for elves.

Someday in the future, she hoped to attend a retreat here herself. She had a long way to go before that, though, before she had the confidence to show her work to anybody, apart from those closest to her.

Daniel had presented her with a set of Rembrandt oil paints for Christmas, but she hadn't been ready then. They had walked a lot together, herself and Daniel, in those early days of their relationship. Hand in hand through the forest, a short drive from the farm. Hard to believe this beautiful place was on her doorstep and she hadn't visited it in years. There was an enchanted forest there now, deep in the woods in a hidden grove of native trees by a flowing stream, where the fairies and gnomes and trolls were said to live together with the animals of the forest. She felt as if she was walking through an Enid Blyton story come to life.

Cheerfully painted miniature doors were built into trees and stone walls and banks with wooden signs proclaiming the names of their fairy inhabitants. Names like Fentwick Fizzlebank and Filius Fillydook and Sissy Stitch. The wishes of visiting children hung from brown-paper luggage labels on a wishing tree like a fairy washing line. As she stood in the dim light surrounded by deep-rooted trees snug in their blankets of moss, Christina felt that the place was truly enchanted.

She had needed more time to absorb the magic of the forest. For the creative part of her to unfurl from its long hibernation. The images in her head had a childlike quality to them, the natural beauty of the woods and the water forming a backdrop to a world of mystical creatures and animals. Tiny doorways to another world created pops of colour amid the greens and browns and dark yellows of her setting.

She spent most of her free time these days trudging through the woods, sometimes with Daniel but more often contentedly alone, making pencil sketches and taking mental snapshots. Autumn was her favourite time, with the trees dressed in their best gowns of russet and yellow, their fallen leaves lining the paths like crunchy petticoats.

She had been rambling through the grounds of the Slieve Aughty Centre – set on thirty acres and surrounded by more than two thousand acres of forest – one day when she happened upon a wedding ceremony taking place in the garden. A green wedding. It was like stepping inside a children's storybook illustration. A lavender-lined walkway led to a wooden pergola covered by a living roof of grass and wildflowers. A glass chandelier hung from the ceiling of the pergola and diaphanous white curtains were tied back with fresh flower corsages. In the midst of this scene, a bride and groom were taking their vows. The bride like a wood nymph, a slip of a thing in a slip of a dress, lavender flowers winding through her white-blonde plait. The guests, who had been seated on rustic white folding chairs, got to their feet and their clapping echoed through the clearing.

Christina had peeked through the leaves like a peeping Tom, trying to take in every tiny detail to recreate later on canvas.

She had never been one of those girls who was obsessed with the Big Day, who had the hotel picked out before they even had the fiancé. For so long, she had never allowed herself to even imagine the possibility of a normal life with normal relationships and marriage and children. But who knew what the future held. Daniel seemed to be on the same wavelength as her, happy to take things slowly and ease their way into a relationship.

She had finished her EMDR sessions and begun her healing journey. Just like the body closing around a foreign object, her memory of the day she found Mark had become encapsulated by emotional scar tissue, festering away inside her mind until it had finally worked its way to the surface. By re-experiencing the events of that day in the safe environment of Angela's room, she had been able to treat the infection and allow healing to begin. She had also been able to reduce her meds to a level that kept her mood from dipping too low, but freed up her physical and creative energies for the first time in years.

With the healing came a flood of memories that had been hiding in the shadows of his death all this time. The way you always heard Mark before you saw him. The thwack of his sliotar off the side of the house. The crunch of gravel beneath the tyres of his go-cart as he skidded round the yard. That infectious laugh. And later, the hip-hop music that he loved so much (and their mother detested) blaring from his room. Tupac, Snoop and Dr Dre. The go-cart traded in for a ten-year-old VW Golf GTI, his beloved first car that bellowed up and down the driveway like a metal bull, alloys flashing. And still, the thwack of the sliotar between ash and concrete.

She had somehow found the confidence to mention her vaginismus to Angela, who on hearing that she had never had a smear test due to her condition, advised her to see a GP she knew who specialised in women's health. The GP had referred her to a gynaecologist, who had diagnosed a partially imperforate hymen, and she was due to go in for minor surgery to release that extra hymenal tissue and create a normal-sized vagina. After all those years of thinking her sexual issues were psychological, they had turned out to be physical. The college doctor had been wrong, both in his diagnosis and his cognitive bias. There simply wasn't room for a penis, or as Julie would call it 'a mickey' to fit in there.

It was Angela also who had introduced her to mindfulness initially, and out of that, very gradually, she had developed a daily meditation practice. It hadn't 'cured' her anxiety, nothing could do that, but it had turned it into something she could live with and manage, rather than live in constant fear of. It had helped her cope with her shock and worry about Nellie's cancer, and also taught her to be grateful for what she had. She had always known Nellie was important to her, but the realisation that things could have been so much worse made her appreciate how fortunate she was to have had the love of this extraordinary woman her whole life. And that to some women, mothering came naturally whether they gave birth or not. She thanked the universe every day for putting Nellie in her life and for her speedy recovery from her illness. The woman seemed to have more energy than ever these days and was thriving in her new management role in the café.

The work on the cottage had started three months ago and it was almost ready for her to move into. The renovation of her grandparents' home had truly been a labour of love, one she had put her heart and soul into. Under her direction, the builders had delicately exposed the potential that she knew had always been there – buried beneath layers of thick paint and plasterboard – to create a quaint, cosy home, with plenty of room for expansion if she ever needed more space.

Christina had enjoyed living with Rob's family over the past months, had been amazed at how much it had helped to deepen her bond with her niece and nephew. She couldn't imagine loving a child of her own more than she loved her brother's kids. She watched how Kate was with them. How she was constantly attuned to the needs of her children, no matter how tired or stressed she was herself. And how when she did lose her cool with them from time to time, she always told them she was sorry and that she loved them. She couldn't remember her mother ever saying the word sorry.

Christina mentioned it to Rob one night when they sat in the den watching telly and sharing a bottle of wine and a takeaway. Kate had gone to the cinema with some friends.

'Kate's a great mother – it comes so naturally to her. Your kids are so lucky, Rob, lucky to have you both,' she said, the alcohol giving voice to thoughts that would normally have stayed in her head. 'Mother just didn't seem to have it in her, did she? That maternal instinct.'

'No, I don't think she did,' he agreed.

She looked over at him. 'Did she ever tell you she loved you?'

'No. You?'

'No. Dad did, all the time, but he didn't need to. I knew anyway. I never felt that way about Mother, though, never felt as sure.'

He nodded. 'Dad loved us all, there was no doubt about that. And Mother? I'm sure she did in her own way, I just don't think she knew how to show it. I don't think she was able.'

The light-bulb moment for Christina had come not as a result of her years of counselling, but from a discussion that Julie heard on the radio a few weeks after the inquest and insisted Christina listen to, sending her a link to the podcast with the message 'YOU NEED TO LISTEN TO THIS'.

She had listened to it as she drove to Galway one evening for a meditation course she had signed up for. It hadn't so much been a case of the penny dropping as a cascade of coppers clattering over the edge of a coin-pusher machine into the tray below, like the one at Claude's Casino that herself and Julie had loved to play as kids on their Sunday drives to Salthill with Aunty Rita and Uncle Jarlath.

A psychologist, who was being interviewed on the topic of narcissistic mothers, spoke of how children being raised by mothers like this suffered continual psychological whiplash. How the mothers were unable to give their children even the most basic emotional support and were almost impossible to please.

The presenter read out a text from a woman in her fifties: 'All my life my mother told me I was oversensitive, I was unstable. That I was overreacting like I always did. It took me years to realise that she was the one with the problem, not me.'

Christina felt as if somebody had turned her upside down and shook her. She had to pull in to the hard shoulder.

That was her mother they were describing. So many little cruelties wrapped in loving terms. 'I only want the best for you.' 'I'm sorry your feelings were hurt, but it's for your own good.' 'I'm only trying to help.'

And she wasn't the only one who felt that way, judging by the number of texts and emails to the show from listeners saying the same thing. It seemed insane that she hadn't seen what was staring her in the face. But she genuinely hadn't.

As she sat in her car on the roadside between Glenbeg and Galway city, it struck her that maybe she hadn't been as mentally ill as her mother had told her she was. That just maybe it was normal for a sensitive seventeen-year-old to feel intense psychological distress after finding the brother she loved and had been so close to all her life hanging by his neck from a beam. And that if she had been allowed to express how she felt back then, instead of being silenced and convinced that she couldn't trust her own mind, the past sixteen years might have been less hellish.

Narcissistic personality disorder. NPD. Her mother's personality perfectly encapsulated in three letters. Possibly the same thing that was wrong with Donald Trump – one of them, anyway. She had stopped going to Helen after that; she couldn't fathom how in all the years she had been pouring her heart out to the therapist, she had never really delved into Christina's relationship with her mother. Helen had put Christina's many *issues* down to the trauma of finding Mark that day. But her problems had started long before that, and if Helen had been any good as a therapist, she would have seen that.

With Angela's support, Christina had come to accept that, no matter how hard she tried, she could never have changed her mother. She could only change her own reactions to her mother's behaviour. She had struggled with this idea for a long time. It had uncorked a lot of stuff that had not aged well, turned sour and acidic. The memories and feelings of a child who had ached for a bit of warmth and affection from her mother. A child who was constantly told she was 'far too sensitive' and accused of having 'a vivid imagination' – as if it was a bad thing – had grown into a woman who was told and believed the same thing. And now her mother was gone. She had no choice but to give up trying. To accept that the love she had hungered for had never been there to give. And to try to give it to herself instead, to see if she could love and nurture that little girl who still ached inside her.

In her new habit of practising gratitude, she came to see that it hadn't been all bad. She had wonderful memories of birthdays and Christmases that she needed to take out and polish every now and then like good crystal. It was as though her mother had needed to create these picture-perfect family scenes which she captured on celluloid and hung in frames around the house. Maybe to convince herself that she had created the picture-perfect family. Or was she trying to freeze those happy moments in time? Mother had thrown big parties in the farmhouse for each of their birthdays every year, festooning the place with balloons and banners and burying the long kitchen table under a blizzard of sweets and crisps and fizzy drinks. The pièce de résistance in the centre was always the huge chocolate cake, baked by Nellie.

At Christmas the farmhouse was lit up like the North Pole of Christina's imagination. White lights twinkled across the roof and twined around the trees all along the driveway. Ursula put up three Christmas trees. Real ones. Two enormous ones in the lounge and entrance hall, and a smaller one in the den. Each beautifully decorated in a different colour scheme by her mother. To a small Christina, looking at these majestic spruce trees, it seemed as if a forest was growing inside the house. The air was filled with an exquisite blend of cinnamon, roasting turkey, burning turf and Christmas tree. In the hall, there was a miniature wooden sleigh painted a cheerful red and stuffed with gaily wrapped presents, Santa in his splendid velvet costume holding Rudolph's reins. She wondered where that was now. Probably landfill. Her mother had seemed to sparkle during the festive season, along with the house. She took great pleasure from wrapping their presents, garnishing them with ribbons and bows and placing them under the tree in the lounge. She took even more pleasure from watching them open the gifts on Christmas morning, the shrieks of excitement as they ripped the beautiful paper off. And she had loved having Uncle Peter there with them. It was the one time of year that Mother seemed to really relax.

In her early teens, Christina had once asked her father why Ursula never talked about her family, her own parents.

He had stroked her cheek with his big gentle thumb. 'I don't know, peteen, but I suspect your mother and Uncle Peter might not have had the easiest time of it as children.'

She could see now as clear as the nose in the middle of her face that her father had enabled Ursula to behave the way she did. For the quiet life. But even when Angela pointed out that her father had let her down, let the boys down too, she found it hard to summon anger towards him. Dad had hated conflict – it was just the way he was. He couldn't help it. He was built weak. It would take her a lot longer to forgive her mother, if she ever could.

Christina would never know if she had done the right thing in telling her father the truth about Mark's suicide note, about her mother trying to convince her it was all in her head, some kind of trauma-induced hallucination, but she did what she thought was right at the time. Even as she had heaved it off her chest that night in the farmhouse, she had questioned the veracity of her own memory, but it was as if her gut had discovered its voice and was screaming at her, 'It's true, you saw it. You know you saw it!'

That was why she had lied to the gardaí, made up the stuff about Daddy being suicidal, about her and Mother being on suicide watch.

36

June 2019

Kate

Kate wasn't exactly sure when it had dawned on her and Rob that the fields around them were the perfect shade of green after all. Probate had still not come through, but Kieran had been able to arrange it so that they were able to pay themselves a decent salary through the business – for the first time. They would soon be coming into a level of wealth that would allow them to never work a day in their lives again if they so chose. Or to live the dream they had thought was lost. They could sell up or let the land, go back to college and do their master's.

After the DPP had directed there was to be no prosecution in relation to the deaths of Jimmy and Ursula, there had been a brief statement given to the media. And that had been the end of it as far as the garda investigation was concerned. The retraction of the official finger of accusation hadn't stopped the whispers, of course. That was something they were always going to have to live with.

Rob had been incensed that that was it. Not a word of apology for the way the family had been treated in the wake of his parents' deaths. He had muttered something about bringing a complaint to the garda commissioner about it, but Kate had convinced him that they needed to leave it behind them and get on with grieving and living. His anger had dampened and cooled over the weeks. And now months on, with the perspective of hindsight, he could see that the gardaí had only been doing their job. That it was nothing personal. Yes, there had been a couple of fuck-ups along the way, and maybe they could have shown a bit more sensitivity, but their suspicions had been raised, and given that the vast majority of people, especially women, murdered in this country were killed by somebody they knew, it made sense that the guards had focused their lens directly on the close family of the deceased.

It was a relief to have the inquest over as well; it meant they could look forward now, get on with living. The pathologist had reported the cause of death as inhalation of the liquid in the slurry tank. She had said the levels of hydrogen sulphide and other toxic gases in the blood samples taken from the deceased were high enough to render the victims unconscious pretty quickly, and assured the family that both deaths would have been swift. Kate hoped she was right, that they were unconscious before they went under the slurry, because the alternative didn't bear thinking about.

It had been a unanimous verdict: accidental death.

The coroner had used the occasion to highlight once again the serious dangers associated with slurry tanks, and to urge farmers to be vigilant at all times in making safe slurry practice top of their farm-safety agenda, pointing out that 'the consequences of not doing so can be utterly devastating'.

With the weight of too much work and too little money lifted off them, Kate and Rob were able to see the wood for the trees for the first time in a long time, and nobody was more surprised than Kate to discover that the youthful dreams she had clung to for so long had changed behind her back.

She was thriving in her role as MD of the business, her confidence and experience having leapt and bounded over the past year, while Sarah, her new general manager, was doing a great job keeping the farm park on an even keel. Christina had never been so busy, between doing the social media for the farm, running the artists' retreat and her painting, but she seemed to be handling it all well. Kate was keeping a close eye on her, just in case; if things got on top of her, they could hire somebody else to do the social media stuff. They were hectic this month with school tours, but it was an enjoyable busyness, not the overwhelming stressfest it used to be.

She looked down at the restaurant through the side window of her office. She kept the blinds permanently raised, a visual signal of the open-door policy she operated with her staff. It was just gone half twelve and the place was buzzing, most of the tables occupied. There was a party in full flow, a princess cake with flickering candles being carried by a young woman with a face full of freckles and a shiny copper ponytail to the table where the birthday girl sat on her pink throne, her little pals lined up either side. The table erupted into a rambunctious rendition of 'Happy Birthday', which everyone in the room sang along to – the mother and baby group who filled the tables at the window with their noise and mess sang and clapped along; Jimmy's old gang in for their dinner raised glasses of milk and mugs of tea; and Nellie and Maura and the rest of the staff came out from the kitchen to join in.

The young cake-bearer glanced upwards as she bellowed out 'For She's a Jolly Good Fellow' and threw Kate a wide smile. Kate smiled back at her. Chloe had been a godsend, and not the only one. It was a completely different workplace now, somewhere she and her staff looked forward to coming every day. Her first major decision as boss had been to take on more staff in the café – just three, one full-time and two part-time, nothing crazy. It had made a big difference, though. Her first hire had been Maura Lally, who agreed to return to the farm on better pay and terms as Nellie's deputy (allowing her to give up her shifts in The Happy Chip). Her second had been Maura's eldest daughter, Chloe, who had started working as a guide at weekends, but proved herself such an invaluable asset that Kate had offered her a full-time job after three months. The business was paying for Chloe to study hospitality and tourism at Athlone Institute of Technology part-time. Staff morale was consistently high.

There had been changes on the farm too. Rob had taken his cousin Niall on for a few hours here and there to get Rita off his back, but to all of their surprise (except his mother's, who always said he just needed to be given a chance) he turned out to be a natural farmer. He was now a full-time employee and, again, to all of their surprise (except his mother's, who always said he just needed to meet the right girl), he had his first steady girlfriend, Carol Broderick, the girl from The Creamery who had brought Jimmy's dinner over to the farmhouse the day he died.

Never in many months of Sundays could Kate have seen herself and her family settled happily in the farmhouse. That was another thing that had happened very gradually. Over the weeks and months, as more and more of their own belongings were transplanted from the cottage, the farmhouse began to feel like home. There was no arguing with Christina – she was adamant about the house swap – and Kate and Rob had to admit, when they had the time and headspace to sit down and discuss it properly, that it did make sense. The thought of moving back into the cramped cottage after living among all this space and light did not appeal to any of them, including the kids. And Christina had been positively giddy at the idea of getting her hands on the cottage.

Kate's first project had been to transform Mark's and Rob's old rooms into bedrooms for the kids – blush pink walls and llama bedding and curtains for Lily (unicorns were for babies now, apparently, and they couldn't find alpacas), white walls and a grey and red colour scheme for Luke. The kids were thrilled to have their own rooms at last. Herself and Rob were still sleeping in the guest room, a palatial suite compared to their dark cramped bedroom in the cottage. Maybe at some stage in the future they would do up his parents' room and move in there, but it wouldn't be any time soon. Jimmy's and Ursula's clothing still hung in their wardrobes, and Kate had subtly moved the rest of their personal belongings in there from around the house. She would help Christina and Rob sort through it all when they were ready, whether that was in months or years. There was no rush.

Having seen the effect it was having on Christina and being swayed by her sister-in-law's new-found evangelism, Kate had allowed herself to be talked into going along to a drop-in meditation one night. She had been bored stupid. It reminded her how much she had hated yoga; maybe she just didn't have the patience to be zen. So she had taken up running instead, and her only regret was that she hadn't discovered this release years ago. She might not have as much steam inside her to vent these days, but she had finally discovered the right valve.

Rob had broached the subject of their future hesitantly one night as they lay in bed.

'Katie, I've been thinking.'

She put down her book. 'That sounds dangerous,' she said.

'It's about us and what we're going to do, you know ... after ... when probate comes through. I've been thinking about it a lot lately and ... like, I know we always said we'd go back and do our master's some day, but, well ...'

'You've changed your mind.'

'No, well, yeah. It's just ... living here, rearing the kids here. The thought of leaving, of moving away ... it feels so wrong. I was wondering how you'd feel about us maybe staying here while you go back and do your master's in Galway. You'd fly up and down on the motorway now.'

'And what about you? Your master's?'

'I've lost interest in the idea, to be honest. I'm happy as I am, farming the land, working with the animals. The thought of selling it or even handing it to somebody else to work ...' He shook his head. 'My father and grandfather and his father, they started out with a few acres and put their heart and soul into this place. Christ, they'd be spinning in their graves. I mightn't have been born with the love of the land as strong in me as in Mark and Daddy, but it's caught a hold of me all the same. The thought of leaving here and moving to a city, sitting in traffic every day, taking the kids away from all of this ...' He gestured towards the window. 'The wide open spaces, the fresh air, their lovely school, all their little friends.' His voice wavered.

'Stop, love,' she said softly.

'No, I just need to—'

'You don't, it's OK. I agree with you. It's a wonderful life here for the kids, for us all. Sure, we'd be mad to leave this behind.'

His jaw slouched in relief, his eyes glistening. 'I know I let you down before, Katie. I promise that'll never happen again.'

'That's all in the past now, love. We've been through so much, more than would break many couples, but we've come through it even stronger. And we're building our own legacy now, for the children.'

'You should email NUIG, ask them to send you out some information on the master's.'

'Hmm, yeah. I might think about going back and doing it down the line. Or maybe I won't. There was an article in the *Sunday Independent* about an online diploma UCD are running in leadership and management that I was thinking of looking into. For starters.'

Rob had been stunned when Christina had told them about the note Mark had left, and Kate had to pretend she felt the same. Christina had spewed the whole story out, barely pausing for breath, one evening a few weeks after the inquest, when the kids were in bed.

She had turned to Rob afterwards, dry-eyed and calm. 'I'm so sorry I had to tell you all this, Rob, but you need to know the truth. We both do. To understand why Mark did what he did. He had no choice, you see. I can't imagine what he must have gone through, but it all makes sense now. The drinking, the aggression, all of it ... it was his way of trying to cope with the hell he was living in.'

Rob sat there, dumb and motionless. Trying to take it in. The expression of confusion on his face gradually melting into an awful understanding. Kate sat with him in silence, sensing that he didn't want to be touched. Knew he was probably thinking about how he could have tried to get that poor, poor boy the help he so badly needed if only they had known the truth back then.

'And there's more,' Christina said.

Kate had been almost as shocked as Rob when her sister-in-law told them what she had found out since about their Uncle Peter, about the horrifying pictures of defenceless children found on his computer and his possible association with a paedophile ring. Even Jimmy hadn't known the full extent of how bad it was.

Rob had finally agreed to go for counselling himself after Christina's revelations. He had managed to cope without grief counselling after the deaths of his brother and his parents, had found solace in work and family. But he had been so lost after what he had learned about Mark and what his mother had done that he admitted to Kate that he needed professional help.

Christina had been incredible. She was like a different woman these days. Kate had been astounded by the strength she seemed to have dug up from nowhere. The eye-flicking stuff might sound bonkers, but it seemed to be working for her sister-in-law. Along with the meditation. And the work she was doing on her mother issues. She would always be sensitive, but she was a long way from the neurotic shell of a woman she had been for nearly as long as Kate had known her.

Kate had been revolted by what Ursula had done to her own son, the extent that she had been prepared to go to protect her reputation and power. Kate had genuinely thought that she was beyond being shocked by her mother-in-law's behaviour by then, but when Jimmy had told her about Christina's revelation and Mark's note, it had rocked her to her core.

It was Kate who raised the matter of Uncle Peter with her husband and his sister in the weeks after Christina's revelation about his conviction and possible links with a paedophile ring. It had been keeping her awake at night.

'As a mother myself, it makes me shudder to think that man has got away scot-free with what he did to Mark and God only knows how many other poor children. He could still be at it for all we know. We have to go to the guards about this.'

'You're right.' Rob agreed straight away. 'I've been thinking about it too. We'll never know what the hell was going through Mother's mind, why she didn't go to the guards straight away when Mark told her what he did to him. I can only assume it was some kind of misguided loyalty to that disgusting prick …'

'I'd say that was only part of it, Rob,' Christina said. 'I think a bigger concern for Mother would have been the scandal it would have caused.'

Rob and Christina had met with Superintendent Mick Power in Glenbeg, and told him about how their Uncle Peter's abuse of Mark had ultimately led to their brother's death. Even though Peter would never face charges over his nephew's abuse, as the victim was dead and there was no evidence that it had ever happened – apart from words on a note destroyed long ago that had been seared into Christina's brain which was basically hearsay – the super had promised them he would make a call to a detective he knew working in the Met's Child Sexual Abuse and Exploitation Unit in the UK. There would be no formal record of this call, but the super assured them his colleague across the water would continue to keep Peter firmly on his radar.

Christina had thrown herself wholeheartedly into the cottage renovation, a true labour of love. The little house was blossoming with the attention being lavished on it, as if it was delighted to be getting the chance to show itself off at last. It was virtually unrecognisable from the kip it had been, with its bumpy whitewashed walls, retro kitchen units, which Kate and Christina were at that moment hand-painting the perfect shade of powder blue that she had spent months searching for, and colourful patchwork curtains and cushions made from her Granny Kennedy's old quilts.

Christina had furnished the walls first, after painting them stark white, like her own personal art gallery. Some of her own renderings of the Enchanted Wood hung in the sitting room: dreamlike, ethereal scenes of dark, earthy woods shot through with shafts of dazzling sunlight, the swirling skirts and vivid coats of her phantasmagorical creatures, the little wooden doors in bright primary colours set into tree trunks and stone or suspended mid-air. Her paintings, so full of charm and magic, could have been used to illustrate a fairy-tale book from olden days. Lily was fascinated by them, spent long moments of rare silence just staring at them, drinking them in. Kate too felt herself drawn to the paintings, to their calming, tranquil energy. It was as if Christina had somehow managed to capture some of the magic of the woods in her hands and transfer it through her paintings into her home.

Samson stretched his paws out as far as they would go and gave a long sigh of contentment as he supervised the painting of the cupboards from his new bed in the corner of the kitchen. He was happy wherever Christina was. Kate was hoping the cat, who was spending more and more time curled up on her sister-in-law's vintage Chesterfield sofa, would eventually move in permanently too. So she would stop feeling stalked in her own kitchen.

'I'm so jealous, Christina – it's so cosy here now and peaceful. It's hard to believe it's the same house,' she said, as she guided her brush carefully around the glass door of the unit. Kate found she was enjoying the painting. It was quite therapeutic brushing the smooth, viscous liquid over the freshly sanded wood.

'Well, you're welcome to sneak over whenever you like to get a break from the madhouse,' Christina said. 'I had no idea just how much work would be involved, but it's been worth every second of it.' A smile of contentment spread across her features as she stood back and surveyed her new home. 'And speaking of a break, I'm gasping for a cuppa.' Christina put her brush down on the newspaper covering the counter, pulled a candy-pink kettle out of a cardboard box on the ground and dug around for two mugs and a plate. She plugged the kettle in and switched it on.

'You know, I've been thinking a lot about my own mother lately with everything you told us about Ursula ...' Kate began, and then stopped. *Where is this coming from?* She dipped her brush into the tin, shook the excess off.

'I've often thought about that too. You were so young – it must have been so hard for you growing up without her.'

'I don't know if Rob ever told you, but I was the one who found her.'

'Yes, he did but I never wanted to pry. That must have been awful, Kate, at such a young age.'

Kate got a carton of milk from the door of the squat fifties-style Smeg fridge that matched the kettle. She poured it into the mugs: a good dollop for her, just a dribble for Christina.

Christina brought the two steaming mugs to the table. She looked at Kate: 'If you feel you're ready to talk about it now, I'm here to listen.'

'Do you know, I think I might be,' Kate said. And she told Christina about the last night of her mother's life when, for once, Kate had gone straight to bed without checking on her, as she always did when her father was away on the road. Of how some time during that night, her mother had choked on her own vomit. Of how Kate had spent the years since wondering if she could have saved her if she had only gone in to check on her that night. And finally, only recently, coming to the realisation that maybe her mother hadn't wanted to be saved.

It had felt good to open up to Christina, but there was another secret she could never share with her. With anybody. A secret she would have to take with her to her grave.

37

Kate

When Jimmy had come to her with his plan, she thought he was losing his mind. On top of the dementia. Literally losing it.

He called into the cottage two nights after the row between Rob and Ursula. A Friday night. He'd waited until the kids were in bed and Rob had gone down to Kieran's for a few pints with the lads. She was surprised to see him: the *Late Late* had just started and that was as much part of her father-in-law's weekly routine as milking the cows. He was in funny form, twitchy and talkative. She poured him a can of draught Guinness and they settled on the sagging sofa in front of the open fire. She still had the Christmas tree up, the twinkling lights cheering up their drab surroundings.

Jimmy circled around for a while talking about the weather,

asking about the kids, before eventually coming to the shocking point of his visit. He outlined the plan he had worked out in minute detail, and the role he wanted her to play in it.

She laughed first, thought he was joking. Then she saw his poor tormented face. The anguish in his eyes.

'Jimmy, you can't be serious – this is insane! Why don't you and Rob go in to your solicitor and get some advice? Could you not just give Rob power of attorney instead of Ursula?'

'I've thought about it, of course I have, but she'll challenge any move like that to the highest court in the land and win too. I've been diagnosed with dementia, for Christ's sake, she'll use that against me. I don't know how long I've left, Kate – I'm losing bits of myself all the time. I need somebody to help me and you're the only one I can ask.' He paused. 'You're also one of the people with the most to lose if she's not stopped, along with Rob and the children.'

'But—'

'I'm deadly serious here, Kate. This is happening with or without your help. But if you help me, Rob and Christina and the kids will be spared having to live with the knowledge that their grandfather killed their grandmother and himself.'

He caught her hands, spoke more vehemently than she had ever heard the man speak in all the years she knew him. 'If you think things are bad now, Kate, just wait till she has full control. That woman will make your life an absolute hell, I can guarantee you that. She's furious with Rob, is threatening to teach him a lesson. Look what she did with the barn. She wouldn't think twice of feckin' ye out on the side of the road, kids and all, if you go up against her. You're not dealing with a rational mind here.'

He was so coherent, had it all worked out; it was hard to believe there was anything wrong with his brain.

'Is there no other way, Jimmy?' *Without you having to go too?*

'There's no other way to make it look like an accident, Kate, and I don't want to face what's ahead of me. I'm a weak man, always have been. I don't want to end up like my father.' He shook his head sadly. 'She's getting worse as she gets older – you can see that yourself. I wouldn't put it past her to move that disgusting sicko back here, on top of the children, and to leave it all to him.'

'She couldn't do that.' Horror flooded her veins.

'She can do what she wants! There's no proof Peter did anything to Mark – it's the word of a dead man. This is a mother who destroyed her own son, Kate, for Christ's sake! If he had got the help he was begging for, he would still be alive today. He died because we let him down. Me and his mother. You and Rob will never have a chance of a normal marriage with her around: she destroys everybody around her. She's sick, Kate. There's something wrong with her. I buried my head in the sand for too many years – I see her now, though.'

'But you're asking me to—'

'I'm asking you to turn off the CCTV, get Rob away from the farm on Monday morning and let the dog and the cat out afterwards ... that's all I'm asking you, Kate.'

'That's not all you're asking me, though, Jimmy, is it? You're basically asking me to aid and abet you in a murder. And a suicide. Jesus Christ, you couldn't make it up. And you're asking me to live with this for the rest of my life? It's insane!'

'I know and I'm sorry. I can't think of any other way, but it has to look like an accident.'

When he came back the next day and told her what he had learned about his wife's plans, it was clear he was hellbent on doing this with or without her help. It was the fear for her own kids that swung it for Kate in the end.

She would always wonder if she had made the right decision. Even as she had gone through the farce of running through the café that day searching for Ursula when she knew it was fruitless, she wondered, but it was too late by then. Should she have followed her initial impulse to call Rob and tell him what his father was planning? To stop this madness? Looking back now, she wondered how she hadn't cracked up in those interminable weeks and months after the deaths as faceless people in the DPP's office in Dublin had pondered her fate. And Rob's.

And she would always wonder how the dog got out of the shed before she arrived to release him, if Jimmy had forgotten to lock him in with everything else that was going on.

There were days where she was 100 per cent certain she had done the right thing in going along with her father-in-law's plan. Like the day she had found out that Ursula had financially supported her brother to live a five-star lifestyle after he destroyed her son. And definitely on the day that Christina told them what Peter had been getting up to in the UK. Kate had been right to protect her children from that monster. From them both.

There were plenty of other days, though, when she wondered if there could have been another way. A way where Jimmy stayed alive and Ursula was somehow banished from their lives. And if maybe she hadn't been at such a low point in her own life – so weighed down beneath years of stress and fatigue – when Jimmy approached her, that things could have turned out differently. That they could have figured out another way between them.

She may not have physically pushed her mother-in-law into that slurry, but she had to live with the knowledge that she could have stopped it from happening. The hardest part was never being able to talk to anybody about it. Not to Rob or Christina or her children when they were older, not to Ruth, who she had always been able to talk to about anything. She couldn't even share it with a counsellor. Her secret was wedged inside her. It had taken up residence in her gut where it gurgled and churned and clenched. IBS, her GP had diagnosed. Likely stress-related after all she had gone through. She knew what it really was, though. A pulsating guilt tumour that would never show up on any scan but had firmly tethered itself in her right bowel, dragging at her side like a permanent stitch. Her penance. She could live with that, though. Her kids were safe: that was all that mattered.

38

Ursula

I t was the little things over the years that would trigger the
horror of it. A waft of Old Spice, a whiff of Major. The sweet
minty smell of golf ball chewing gum. Her reward. One day
he brought her a little paper bag filled to the brim with those
bumpy white balls. Her mouth watered against her will. He
knew they were her favourite. Aunt Catherine gave out to him
that day. *Do you want to rot her teeth?* Blind to the fact that he
was rotting the whole of her, not just her teeth. That he was
rotten inside himself.

When Mark came to her that evening outside the house and
told her what Peter had done to him, she wanted to die. All
that stuff that she had managed to squash down, to sit on all
those years, was threatening to blow. She couldn't let it out.
Couldn't let Mark let it out. If it came out about Peter, then it

might come out about Uncle Arthur. What he had done to them. To her. The whole place would be talking about it. She could just imagine the whispers in the golf club, the sly looks outside the church after mass on Sunday. Everything would be ruined; she couldn't let that happen.

If she hadn't already known by the state he was in that Mark was telling the truth, she would have known straight away by the look on Peter's face. He had never been able to lie, even as a child. Had one of those too honest faces that would always sell him out. She was so angry at him for what he had done to her son, his own nephew, but she understood that her brother was deeply, deeply damaged. Like her, she supposed. And she should have protected him. But she hadn't.

She had been so relieved when it stopped. When she started to menstruate. So relieved her nightmare was finally over. She never ever thought he would go after Peter next. She hadn't even known it was possible for a man and a boy to be together in that way. And Peter had never told her, never said a word about it. Silenced by shame, just as she had been. Until she asked him straight out. After Mark.

It broke her heart to send him away. What he did was wrong, shockingly, horribly wrong. Of course she knew that, but it wasn't his fault how he'd turned out. It wasn't either of their faults.

39

The day of the event – Tuesday, 9 January 2018
Jimmy

He had sat up all night after Christina had told him. Trying to get his head around it. He had known there was something missing in Ursula, that she wasn't a normal wife, a normal mother. *How could I not, for crying out loud?* But he had chosen to bury his head and now, like a blind man gaining sight, he was bedazzled. *If only I had been a stronger man. A better man. If only I had stood up to her years ago. Been the father my children deserved. The type of father a son in utter desperation had been able to confide in.*

Too late now for *if only*s. He had to protect the two children he had left and his grandchildren. And Kate. When Christina told him about the note, Jimmy had known without a doubt that it was true, even though she had doubted her own memory for so long. Kieran had told him about the rumour he had heard from England about Peter some years back, but Jimmy had chosen to accept Ursula's version of the story without question. A misunderstanding involving a smitten student who believed himself in love with his music teacher that had been blown out of proportion. Far easier to believe that than even consider the alternative.

Jimmy patted the dog lying on his feet. He snuck him in at night now after Ursula went to bed. He couldn't allow himself to think about Samson, how confused and depressed the poor creature would be after he was gone. He had asked Kate to make sure they took good care of him. As well as Christina and Rob. And his grandchildren. He knew he was putting a lot on his daughter-in-law's shoulders, but he could see no other way. It was for her own good, for all their good.

His wife had taken him for a fool and rightly so. She thought he didn't know about Desmond, the way they had been carrying on behind his back for years. Of course, he had known. Sure, the whole place knew. He could never prove it, though. The one time he had confronted her about it, she had furiously denied it. She ignored him for weeks after that, as if she was punishing him for daring to accuse her of something they both knew she was guilty of. Ursula had never liked to be challenged. So he had rung Desmond and sorted it out himself.

He wondered where it had all gone wrong. Where the Ursula he married had gone. What had happened to her because there wasn't a trace of that lovely girl left.

He would never forget her face when she set eyes on the farm for the first time.

'All of this belongs to your family?' she had said, gazing out across the fields in awe. 'You can't be serious.'

He knew she had had a hard start in life, but he respected her wish not to go there. It must have been pretty bad, though, as she was so touchy about it.

That first night he met her in that pub in Dublin, she had stood out among all the pinch-faced posh girls that stuck to Desmond and his pals like cobwebs. It wasn't just that she was so much prettier than they were, with her long blonde hair and the petite features that Christina had inherited, she had a naivety about her that made him want to tuck her inside his arm and mind her. He had no shortage of female interest in Glenbeg back then, the size of the farm guaranteed his eligibility, and he had been doing a line with a nice girl from the square in town. He asked Ursula for her phone number that night, but didn't call her until he had let Anne Ryan down as gently as possible.

He rang her every Monday and Friday night after that and they talked for an hour. They never ran out of conversation. They would have kept going longer, but there was always somebody waiting for the phone in the house where Ursula lived in Rathmines. He travelled up to Dublin to see her as often as he could given his responsibilities on the farm. He had no idea when she started messing around with Desmond, but he didn't think it was back then. She had seemed as smitten with him as he was with her. He heard the pleasure in her voice when she picked up the phone to him, saw the shy excitement in her eyes when she met him off the train at Heuston Station on Friday nights.

She had never been what you'd call overly affectionate, but she hadn't been cold either. Somewhere in the middle. And that was grand with him. Especially after Anne Ryan, who used to make a right show of him in front of their friends.

His wife had probably been at her happiest when she moved to Glenbeg, in those early years before the children were born. When it was just the two of them. After they first moved in, she used to walk around the house touching things – the kitchen counter, the sofa, the mantelpiece, even the walls – as if she couldn't quite believe they were real. That they were hers. She put such energy and effort into decorating that house and she did an incredible job, as stylish when it came to interior design as she was in her own wardrobe. There wasn't a house that could touch it in the whole county by the time she was finished.

Back then, she never stopped telling him how grateful she was for this new life he had provided for her, how lucky she felt. And she showed it too, constantly. She cooked him his favourite meals and was always buying him little gifts. Socks and shaving gear, quarter-pounds of pear drops from Keane's, woolly hats to keep his head warm on the farm. She showed it in the bedroom too.

It was around that time, after her work on the house project was complete, that she started to get restless, a bit edgy. When he suggested that maybe it was time for them to start a family, she had other ideas. She brought him to see a boutique in town that was up for sale.

'I could make a real go of this, James, I know I could. The town is crying out for a good boutique – you have to go to Galway or Dublin to get a decent outfit for a wedding or an occasion. I've been doing a bit of research since this place went on the market, and I've found some fabulous stockists willing to supply me.'

She had been so enthusiastic, so impassioned about her plans for the shop. How could he say no to her? Coco Boutique, she had named it, after Coco Chanel. And she had made a real go of it, had worked around the clock to get it up and running. Soon word spread and women were coming from all over Galway and further afield to shop in the boutique. Ursula had a great eye, was able to look at a woman and know instantly what would suit her and what wouldn't. All her customers wanted Ursula's personal service so she had to be there all the time. She didn't mind, though; she thrived on being busy. On seeing happy customers leave with their CoCo's bags and the till filling with cash.

She seemed shocked when she fell pregnant with Mark just over a year after opening the shop. He wasn't sure why. They hadn't been using contraception and it was always their plan to have children. Once she got used to the idea, though, she seemed really happy about it. Was looking forward to this new chapter in their lives.

Looking back now, it was probably after the baby was born that she started to change. It was subtle at first. She struggled to bond with the baby and fretted about the boutique, despite or maybe because of the fact that it was being run in her absence by a very competent young woman who had been working there at weekends and was delighted to be offered the opportunity to cover Ursula's maternity leave. Mark was only weeks old when she started looking for a childminder. Jimmy presumed she was planning for the future, when the baby was older, and was shocked when she told him that the minder would be starting the following month.

'Ursula, you can't possibly go back to work and leave a three-month-old baby at home. It's unheard of. Especially when there's no need for you to be working at all. We can afford for you to stay at home with Mark and any other babies that come along. Rearing our kids is a much more important job than selling dresses.'

He had never seen her so angry. Like a spitting cat.

'How dare you! It may be unheard of here in the sticks for a woman to have a career of her own after giving birth, but I'll have you know I'm not like the women around here who are content to stay at home changing nappies and washing bottles all day and have to put their hands out to their husbands for grocery money at the end of the week. How would you feel if I asked you to give up your work to mind the baby?'

'That's just ridiculous, Ursula. I'm a man, and a farmer at that. It's my job to go out to work and provide for my family. And what's mine is yours. I'm just saying, you don't need to do that—'

'Well, I'm just saying I bloody well do need to do that. I need to do it for me, for my own ...' She struggled to find the word she wanted. 'I'm going back to work, and let that be the end of it.'

So Ursula went back to work when Mark was thirteen weeks old, and after a succession of disastrous childminders, Jimmy's farmhand Brendan mentioned that his wife, Nellie, was looking for a job. To say they had struck gold was the understatement of the century. Nellie adored Mark and he her. Jimmy had bumped into them in town one day, Nellie parading the baby down Main Street in his pram as if he were a little king, she beaming from ear to ear while he gurgled contently up at her.

Then Rob came along the following year and four years later Christina. And with each baby, Ursula returned to work earlier and became less like the woman he had married. Having Nellie there minding the kids, providing stability in their lives and loving them as if they were her own, helped ease the guilt Jimmy felt at the fact that their own mother seemed to have no interest in rearing them herself.

When she came up with the idea for the farm park, he thought it was crazy. Ireland was not the UK; the country wasn't ready for such a concept. But a determined Ursula was a formidable beast and when she convinced the bank manager her proposal had potential, Jimmy had no choice but to go along with it. He knew he'd never hear the end of it until he agreed so it was easier to just say yes. And true to form, she had made a huge success of it. She had a great business head on her shoulders, wherever she got it from.

As the years passed and Ursula became more and more immersed in the business, her gifts to him became more extravagant – expensive aftershaves, designer shirts and suits, cashmere scarves that would never be worn – and the intimate side of their relationship began to gradually fade away, until one day he realised it had been over a year since he had had sex with his wife. There were only so many knock-backs a man could take before he admitted defeat. She stayed up working later and later at night after he had gone to bed and fallen asleep. They had slept in separate rooms for years now, even though his clothes still hung in the master bedroom wardrobe – an Irish divorce. Marriage in name only for appearance's sake. He wished now he had had the courage to finish it years ago, but the idea of it was anathema to him. He was old-fashioned that way. Nobody in the Kennedy family had ever separated or divorced; not that he thought for a moment that they had all been happily married, but they lay in the beds they had made. Or separate ones. And so because of his lack of a set of *liathróidí*, his wife had all the rights as his next of kin. The rights to the land his family had tended for generations, the land that would pass on now to his children and their children.

It had been an effort to act normally around her since Christina told him on Wednesday, to speak civilly when he felt like slapping her and tearing at her skin. Screaming 'How could you?' and 'What the hell is wrong with you?' and 'How could any mother do that to her child?'

How had it come to this? That he, a man without a violent bone in his body, now found himself not only contemplating, but planning in detail, the ultimate violent act.

As he had tossed and turned through the nights in the silent house while his wife and daughter slept, the projector inside his head played scene after scene. Incidents he had ignored over the years, let her away with for a quiet life.

The way she had treated his parents, the way he had let her. She had been all about them in the beginning. It was after the children came along, and his mother began to gently voice her concerns about the way they were being reared, that the other Ursula started to emerge. He clearly remembered the first time it happened. They were sitting in the farmhouse garden on a summer's day, the children splashing around in a paddling pool his mother had brought over for them. He could still hear the sound of their laughter, Mark acting the maggot as always, cannonballing into the pool, spraying water everywhere.

His mother, enjoying the rare heat on her painful joints, had smiled lovingly at her grandchildren. 'They're young for such a short time – you wouldn't believe how fast it goes. It's like one day we were sending you off to school and the next you have your own beautiful babies. If there's one bit of advice I can give ye, it's to make the most of the time with them when they're young. They don't care about the labels on their clothes or fancy holidays, all they want is their mammy and daddy to spend time with them.'

'Well, things have changed since you had your kids, Nancy,' Ursula snapped. 'Women no longer have to give up their jobs just because they get married and rightly so. It's a disgrace that was allowed to go on for so long. We're perfectly entitled to have successful careers in our own right without feeling guilty about it. You don't see men feeling guilty about not being at home with the kids, do you?'

The look of shock on his gentle mother's face. 'Of course you are, Ursula, I didn't mean—'

Ursula cut her dead. 'I'm going in to get a cold drink. Would anybody like anything?'

And the evening not long after that when Mammy came over to babysit for them. She had offered to have the children sleep over in the cottage, but Ursula had turned her nose up at the idea.

'I want them to sleep in their own beds in their own house where it's warm and clean,' she said.

'My mother's house is warm and clean, and it would be nice for the kids,' he had replied. His mother had the range and the fire going all day – the cottage was always toasty.

'Your mother's idea of clean and mine are very different,'

she muttered under her breath. He heard though he pretended not to. He should have pulled her up on that, pointed out that his mother was half-crippled with arthritis at that stage but still kept a good house, while Ursula paid a housekeeper to keep hers.

His mother had been dead within a few years, and the kids never did get to stay overnight at the cottage. His father had gone downhill very quickly after that. Despite having a young family of her own, Rita had been his devoted carer; it was down to her that they had managed to keep him at home in the cottage until only a few months before his death when he didn't know where he was anyway. Rita worked out an overnight rota at one stage so their father would never be left alone in the cottage. She put Ursula's name on the rota, but Ursula had kicked up such a stink about being put on the list without being consulted in advance that she took her off again. Ursula never did one night for her.

Jimmy had an image clear as a Polaroid in his mind of the look of distaste on his wife's face when his father was ranting and raving about cattle running loose in the cottage and keeping him awake all night. As if the man had ground dog shit into her ludicrously expensive carpet. Exactly how she would look at Jimmy if he ever got to that stage.

Another scene played out across the screen of his mind. Another shocked face. Rita's this time. Not long after his father had died. When there was no longer anybody left to visit in the empty cottage that had been their childhood home, she started calling in to the farmhouse more often. Jimmy shook his head. How had he agreed to his wife's demands that he tell his sister – lonely and grieving the deaths of both parents within two years – that she wasn't welcome to just drop in whenever she felt like it, that she had to ring in advance and make sure it was convenient for her to visit. But he had, like the weak fool he was. Rita hadn't set foot in the farmhouse for years after that, beeping outside in the yard when she came to collect Christina to bring her over to her house or out on some excursion or other. A testament to the type of woman she was, she had never taken their shoddy treatment of her out on the child.

He had called to her on Saturday to apologise. She wasn't surprised to see him. He was always welcome at her house, despite everything, and often popped over for a chat and a slice of her homemade apple tart, their mother's recipe. It wasn't as good as Mammy's, but it wasn't half-bad either.

'I owe you an apology, Rita,' he had said, when she finally stopped bustling around the place and sat down at the table with him. 'It's long overdue.'

'What are you on about, Jimmy?' She looked puzzled.

'That time I told you to stop dropping by the farmhouse unannounced. That was a shocking thing to do. And I'm very sorry. I've felt bad about it ever since, and I just wanted you to know that.'

'Ah, Jimmy loveen. Sure, I knew that wasn't coming from you. I was hurt at the time, I can't lie, after losing Mammy and Daddy. It felt like I was losing home, you know? But then I realised my home was here with my own family.'

'It was still wrong, Rita, there was no need for it. You should have been made welcome in our home, on the land where you grew up. As welcome as you have always made us in your home.'

'It was you my heart went out to, Jimmy. And not just then.'

He had hugged her as he left, and if she was surprised by this unusual gesture, she didn't show it.

There were so many incidents over the years, and though he had ignored them at the time, he hadn't forgotten a single one. Filed them all away in a folder in his brain.

He was tired now. His own life was over; it was all downhill from here, a downward slide into demented misery. To a time when he would stare blankly at the faces of the children and grandchildren he loved more than life and see only strangers. Not an appealing vista. He couldn't live with himself, anyway, knowing just how much he had let his youngest son down.

It had to look like an accident, one of those sad farming tragedies all too common in Ireland. He had deliberated long and hard. The fog that shrouded his brain so often these days had lifted and his mind was clear despite the lack of sleep. He was himself again for a while, for however long it lasted. He had considered and discarded various options. Poison? There was plenty of rat poison in the shed. He knew an adult would have to consume a lot of rat poison to die, but had no idea how much it would take or how the hell he would get it into her in the first place while making it look like an accident.

He didn't want the kids to have to live with the reality that their father was a murderer on top of everything else, God help them. They would have enough to cope with in losing both parents suddenly. He thought about a tractor crush, but dismissed it straight away. Too hard to coordinate – she was hardly going to willingly stand there and allow herself to be run over. And that was another option that could go drastically wrong; it would be just his luck to end up having to suck his dinner from a straw on top of the dementia.

A fall down the stairs wouldn't work either. There was just no guarantee it would kill her and the last thing he wanted was for his kids to be burdened with looking after a disabled Ursula.

And then it came to him. In the small hours of Friday morning as darkness began to shrug off its heavy overcoat. Out of nowhere emerged the perfectly formed plan. Every little detail was there. A plan that would cause the least amount of pain possible to those left behind. You often heard of people killing a loved one during a psychotic break, where they had disconnected from reality for a short period – a son stabbing a father or brother, or a mother smothering her baby – only to realise the horror of what they had done when they were plugged back in. Jimmy felt the opposite to this; he was completely clear in his mind about what he had to do. He was afraid that if he didn't take his chance now, in this increasingly rare period of lucidity, it would be too late. The fog could swallow him up again at any moment. This was why it had to happen now.

Johnny Brennan had been only too happy to take the remaining dry cattle off his hands at a knockdown price, the only condition being that he collect them over the weekend. He didn't ask any questions about Jimmy's urgency in shifting the cows, nor did Rob when Jimmy told him Johnny had given him a great price for them. That left him with an empty shed and a full slurry tank.

They would wonder why in the name of God he had been

mixing slurry at this time of year, would probably put it down to his eroding brain, shake their heads and tell each other *he must have been worse than we thought.*

He ran through every detail of his plan in his head one last time as night shed the rest of its layers and dawn revealed herself. He had to get her down to the tank within the first thirty minutes to be on the safe side. It was all about timing. She wouldn't know what had hit her – he couldn't have gone through with it otherwise.

The only downfall of this plan, of course, was that he had needed help for it to work. Which was where Kate had come in.

40

Jimmy

Conditions were perfect that morning, as if the universe was on his side. The air was dry and still, so still. Not so much as a scrap of wind out. Jimmy left the house at dawn, hitched the agitator to the tractor with some difficulty, as he wasn't getting any younger (wouldn't be getting any older either) and it was really a job for two. A job Rob usually helped him with. One of many. This was one job he couldn't ask his son to help him with, though. This was something he had to do on his own.

He had planned to do it yesterday, but Kate couldn't get an appointment at the solicitor for Rob until this morning, and he needed Rob to be away from the yard. Kate had snuck out to meet him at midnight last night and turned the CCTV off from his phone. Skulking through the dark out of view of the cameras. That had been her idea. He had asked her to turn it off from Rob's phone, but as she pointed out, the security company would be able to trace it back and they didn't want any suspicion to fall on Rob. She was smart, that girl. Far smarter than Ursula had ever given her credit for.

The house had still been sleeping when he left this morning, Samson at his heels. By the time he got back, he was sweating and out of breath after getting the agitator in place and locking Samson and Cleo into their sheds, but still strangely calm. He had hugged the dog close to him and told him he was sorry and he loved him before he shut the door on him. The big bowl of scraps from the café that Kate had given him last night would keep the dog busy for a while.

His wife was in the kitchen eating her breakfast. Some class of rabbit food in a bowl with chopped fruit on top. There was a pot of tea on the table in front of her. A china cup and a jug of milk. Ursula was finicky like that, couldn't abide a vulgar carton on the table. Jimmy got a mug for himself. Popped two slices of wholemeal bread he had no intention of eating into the toaster. Went to the fridge and took out the butter. It felt like he was operating in slow motion but his watch, which he was keeping a close eye on, told him otherwise. The seconds were ticking away. He poured tea from the pot into his mug. He was thirsty. Ursula always used tea-bags instead of making it the proper way, but it would have to do; he didn't have time to make a fresh pot.

'Top-up?' he asked her, holding the pot up.

She pushed her cup towards him, not lifting her eyes from her phone.

'Toast?'

'Just one slice, please.' She kept reading whatever was so interesting on her screen.

He buttered and cut the toast, his hand shaking slightly, put one slice on a plate, which he placed on the table in front of her, took one bite out of the other one and threw the rest of it in the bin. He sloshed a couple of mouthfuls of tea down his arid gullet and poured the rest down the sink. Then he quickly washed his plate and cup and cutlery and placed them on the draining board. She had finished her breakfast so he took her dishes to the sink and gave them a quick rinse too. Everything had to look as normal as possible.

Then he turned towards her. 'I'm off so, I'll talk to you later.'

She lifted her head for a second or two, looked vaguely in his direction and said, 'Bye,' before turning back to her screen.

He walked down to the cattle shed at the back of the yard, checked that everything was as it should be. He said a silent apology to Samson, who was yowling furiously from the feed shed, having obviously cleaned his bowl. Kate would let him out soon to raise the alarm.

Then before he had time to change his mind, he turned around and ran as if he was being chased back through the yard. He stuck his head in the kitchen door. 'Come quick, Ursula, it's the cat!'

She jumped to her feet, followed him as he had known she would. 'What is it? What's wrong with her?' There was an uncharacteristic note of panic in her voice.

He had shut the cat into an old shed behind the cottage, left a tin of John West sardines in oil on the ground to keep her quiet for a while, the lid peeled back like a miniature metal sleeping bag. Her favourite treat. It had always pissed him off how the cat had her own treat press, while treats were banned for the humans in the house. Kate would release her as well and dump the sardine tin.

Ursula followed him through the yard. 'James? Where is she? What's wrong with her, for heaven's sake?' Ursula's voice was shrill. 'Cleo ... Cleo.'

'Over here, in the shed.' He opened the door. She paid no heed to the tractor rumbling away outside, the agitator hitched up to it.

She rushed into the shed and he closed the door behind them.

'Will you open the door, for God's sake? I can't see a thing in here.'

'She's just over here ...' he said, catching her firmly by her upper arm. He couldn't remember the last time he had touched her. Sorrow lashed him like a whip. An image emerged in his mind clear as a Polaroid. It was early on in their relationship. His train had just pulled into Heuston and through the window he spotted her. She had taken his breath away that day. Standing there in her turquoise blue minidress with the little white buttons, a matching white hairband holding her blonde hair back from her lovely face. Her knee-high patent boots, a light tan on her skin. Beautiful. And then she spotted him and her eyes lit up.

He snapped himself out of it; there was no going back now. That Ursula was long gone. He led his wife towards the opening to the tank in the middle of the shed where he had lifted the slats earlier.

Then before he had time to think about the reality of what he was doing, to change his mind, to let the old Ursula into his head, he pushed her. Hard. Right in the base of her spine. She shrieked as she fell and he blocked his ears. Then he knelt down beside the opening and waited. To make sure. He kept his hands tight over his ears, muting the horrifying sucking sounds from the tank. It was mercifully short. His skin felt tight and strange, like somebody had sucked all the air out of his lungs and wrapped cling film around his face. He tipped over the edge. He didn't think about where he was going – that didn't matter once those he was leaving behind were OK. His last thought was of a beautiful girl standing on a platform in a blue dress smiling. And then somebody pulled a blackout blind down and the lights went out.

Epilogue

Christina

When Christina heard the racket the dog was creating the morning of her parents' deaths, she knew, just knew, something was up.

She had been watching her father like a hawk since she'd told him about the note. About Mark. Wondering what was going on inside his head. Waiting for the showdown with her mother. Surely he couldn't just do nothing, she had thought, with the truth that she had handed him, an unexploded grenade that had lived among them for so many years. Surely he couldn't just let Mother get away with what she had done.

On hearing Sam's furious barking and yelping, she'd rushed from her bedroom, through the empty kitchen where the breakfast dishes were drying on the draining board, to the feeding shed. Sam shot like a greyhound out of the traps when she opened the door.

He hared off towards the farmhouse, then stopped abruptly

and turned tail, heading towards the back of the farm. A dog on a mission. She followed him through the yard past the milking parlour and the hay barn and ancillary sheds, gathering pace as she went. She caught sight of her mother running ahead of the dog in the direction of the dry cattle shed, saw her disappear inside.

Christina started running too. She passed the tractor, hooked up to the agitator which was sunk deep into the tank churning up the slurry. It hadn't struck her as significant or unusual at that point, not compared to the sight of Mother running in the mud in her good shoes.

She saw the shed door slide shut behind her mother. She stood outside for a moment trying to think, ignoring the dog as he clawed at the door, incensed at having been refused entry. She snuck past the door and around the side of the barn where, if she remembered rightly from playing hide and seek there with Julie and her brothers as a child, there was a narrow opening in the side wall. The opening threw a shaft of light onto the floor on her side of the barn and it took a few seconds for her eyes to adjust to the gloom inside, to make out the two figures on the far side.

She heard Mother frantically call out what sounded like 'Leo, Leo' but later, when she put two and two together, realised must have been Cleo. She saw her move closer to the edge of the open pit. Saw her father move in close behind her. And she knew then. Knew what he was going to do.

That was the point when she could have stopped him. The point when she automatically opened her mouth to form the *s* and then the *t* ... but then she thought of the conversation she had overheard on Friday night, when she passed her mother's bedroom on her way to bed.

It was the tone of voice that had stopped her in her tracks. She had never heard her mother sound like that. Frightened and paranoid. Unhinged. Ranting about everybody turning on her, all waiting to stab her in the back. How nobody appreciated her and she couldn't trust any of them, how she needed somebody on her side.

Who was she talking to?

Christina leant closer to the door to listen. She heard her mother tell the uncle who had helped put the rope around her brother's neck how she would give him a job and a place to live. How this was his only chance and he couldn't mess it up. How he'd better have 'grown out of all that nonsense' because if she saw him so much as look sideways at one of her grandchildren, or any child for that matter, she would march him into the garda station in town herself.

Christina had gone back down to the den to her father.

'Daddy, there's something else I have to tell you ...'

Now, as she witnessed her father push her mother into the pit, she didn't shout stop.

She watched her mother fall.

Did she call out? Christina didn't know, couldn't hear anything above the thundering of blood in her ears.

She saw her father drop then.

Time lost all sense after that. Hours compressed into blurred fragments of memory.

She rang Uncle Peter that night to tell him about the tragic accident on the farm and warn him that if he dared show his face at the funeral, the gardaí would be waiting to question him in connection with his abuse of her brother. She told him she still had the note Mark had left. She had hoped he wouldn't take the chance that she was bluffing, and he didn't.

She had taken the truth of what she knew about the deaths of her parents and buried it deep down in the darkest recesses of her mind, never again to be exposed to the light of day.

And later, when it became clear that her father must have had help from somebody to carry out his plan, she buried that down with it.

There were some things you could never tell anybody.

Acknowledgements

Heartfelt thanks to everyone who has made this lifelong dream come true. I may never stop pinching myself.

To my agent Faith O'Grady of the Lisa Richards Agency who believed in my writing and this story from the very beginning, thank you so much.

To my talented editor at Hachette Ireland, Ciara Considine, for seeing the potential in the first book I ever actually finished (or even got beyond 30,000 words). Your incisive editorial eye and gentle suggestions for changes made the editing process so much easier than I had expected, and the finished product is so much better for your input. You have a way of making my brain sit up and pay attention, and it's been a privilege to work so closely with you.

To Elaine Egan, Hachette Ireland Publicity Director, the most enthusiastic cheerleader any author could wish for.

Thanks to Joanna Smyth, Marketing and Publishing Operations Director at Hachette Ireland for all of her fantastic work on the marketing end of things.

To all of the team at Hachette Ireland for your enthusiasm and support of my debut novel. You are all so good at what you do.

To eagle-eyed copy editor Emma Dunne, I was blown away by the skill of what you do.

A special thanks to Sue Booth-Forbes of Anam Cara Writer's and Artist's Retreat on the stunning Beara Peninsula. Sue describes Anam Cara as like a Brigadoon that rises out of the mist when you arrive only to disappear again when it's time to leave and return to the real world. It's the perfect description because there truly is something otherworldly about Anam Cara and Eyeries and its incredible surroundings and people, a creative energy I've never felt anywhere else. Sue gave me the best piece of writing advice I've ever had: 'get out of your own way and just write'. So I did. Thanks to the artist Derek Behan, whose stay at Anam Cara overlapped with mine; your kind words of encouragement and support made me believe that I could and should write this book.

To Vanessa Fox O'Loughlin, founder of writing.ie and journalist Maria McHale for helping to get my creative juices flowing through their Facebook Writers Ink online writing group. Irish writers, particularly those of us just starting out, are incredibly fortunate to have such invaluable resources available to us.

To my Faber Academy lockdown family, especially Michele Rashman, who has supported, encouraged and made me laugh along every step of this incredible rollercoaster of a journey to publication. I look forward to meeting you in person some day soon, and seeing your own brilliant debut on the bookshelves.

To Gillian McAllister and Holly Seddon of The Honest Authors podcast; thank you for motivating me to keep going with the book while on my daily dog walks, and for educating me in so many aspects of writing and the publishing industry that I knew nothing about. I highly recommend this podcast, particularly for authors starting out.

To Sally O-J, book doctor extraordinaire. You had the hardest job in helping me to knock an early draft of the book into shape. Thank you for pushing me to stretch myself further than I knew I could go.

To Sara O'Keeffe, thank you for taking the time to meet me in Dublin, and for your clear and concise advice on what I needed to do to fix my book.

To Assistant State Pathologist Margot Bolster who was so incredibly generous with her time and expertise and never baulked at any of the strange questions I asked her. Any errors are my own.

To Alan Crowley, crime scene examiner, who walked through my fictional crime scene with me, and advised me on what would happen in real life. Thanks so much for sharing your time and expertise. Again, any errors are mine.

To William J. Martin, agricultural consultant, who helped dig this city girl out of a major plot hole (involving a full slurry tank in an empty shed) and to map out Glenbeg Farm in precise detail.

To Brendan O'Connell who was kind enough to give me a tour of his slurry pit and an in-depth explanation of how it all works, not a request he gets every day of the week, I suspect.

To retired Detective Garda Jim Byrne, and his lovely artist wife Esther, for the books and the brainstorming session and all their support. To my unnamed undercover mole, thank you too, for all your help and advice.

To my own lovely mother Lucy, gone far too soon, but always with us. She touched everyone who knew her. Her family was her life. She would have loved this, especially the chance to get all dolled up for the book launch.

To my father Seamus who nurtured my love of reading from an early age, and helped me to craft my English essays to a standard high enough to scoop a plastic watch or a *Spraoi* annual in primary school. Daft as a brush, with a big soft heart. Gone from us too soon also.

To Aunty Ena (Cathy) for being the best aunty anybody could ever ask for. As daft as Dad (it's a McDonagh thing), with the biggest heart of anybody I know.

To my sister and best friend Cathy, by my side through every up and down. You must have mopped up gallons of tears over the years at this stage. Love you, sis, I'm so lucky to have you!

To my baby brother Shane and his family of waifs and strays, especially Sam, the adorable three-legged yorkie who lent his name to the dog in my book.

To all the wonderful friends I am so fortunate to have who encouraged me every step of the way and always believed that I could do it even when I didn't believe it myself, especially my oldest and dearest (not in age) Galway friends Fran, Tracy, Bernie and Judy. And to my lovely new friend Margaret Pinfield, who I met and got to know through a window during lockdown, one of the kindest people I know. Thanks to our former childminder and close family friend, Maria Cooney, for all her love and support over the years.

To my husband Greg who made such a show of me by announcing during his wedding speech that I was writing a novel that I was put under pressure to actually do it. It only took fifteen years after that! Thanks for all your love, support and encouragement, and for giving me the space to write. To our three beautiful children who bring me limitless joy and laughter every day and whom I am so incredibly grateful for.

And thanks to my own furry shadow, Brody who sits patiently beneath my desk every day as I write, and stalks me everywhere I go. Love you, my little pal.

And most importantly, to you, the reader, thank you so very much.